## PRAISE FOR ROISIN MEANEY

'A wonderfully woven, beautiful book full of hope, love and characters so fully formed I feel like I know them. I adored it'
**Emer McLysaght**

'A warm, insightful story about new beginnings and the power of kindness'
**Rachael English**

'A cracking yarn . . . Meaney can excavate the core of our human failings and present it to us, mirror-like on the page . . . Which makes her utterly credible, utterly authentic, utterly irresistible'
***Irish Independent***

'Roisin Meaney is a skilful storyteller'
**Sheila O'Flanagan**

'A real treat . . . Meaney wraps her readers in the company and comfort of ordinary strangers'
***Sunday Independent***

'Meaney weaves wonderful feel-good tales of a consistently high standard. And that standard rises with each book she writes'
***Irish Examiner***

'This book is like chatting with a friend over a cup of tea . . . full of all the things that make life interesting'
***Irish Mail on Sunday***

'Heartwarming and unputdownable'
**Carmel Harrington**

Roisin Meaney was born in Listowel, County Kerry. She has lived in the US, Canada, Africa and Europe but is now based in County Clare, Ireland.

She is the author of twenty-three novels and has also written books for children.

www.roisinmeaney.com

## ALSO BY ROISIN MEANEY

*Moving On*
*A Winter to Remember*
*Life Before Us*
*The Book Club*
*It's That Time of Year*
*The Restaurant*
*The Birthday Party (a Roone novel)*
*The Anniversary*
*The Street Where You Live*
*The Reunion*
*I'll Be Home for Christmas (a Roone novel)*
*Two Fridays in April*
*After the Wedding (a Roone novel)*
*Something in Common*
*One Summer (a Roone novel)*
*The Things We Do for Love*
*Love in the Making*
*Half Seven on a Thursday*
*The People Next Door*
*The Last Week of May*
*Putting Out the Stars*
*The Daisy Picker*

## CHILDREN'S BOOKS

*Puffin with Paulie* (with illustrator Louisa Condon)
*Don't Even Think About It* (co-written with Judi Curtin)
*See If I Care*

# Second Chances

## ROISIN MEANEY

SPHERE

SPHERE

First published in Ireland in 2026 by Hachette Books Ireland,
First published in Great Britain in 2026 by Sphere

1 3 5 7 9 10 8 6 4 2

Copyright © Roisin Meaney 2026

The moral right of the author has been asserted.
All characters and events in this publication, other than those
clearly in the public domain, are fictitious and any resemblance
to real persons, living or dead, is purely coincidental.

All rights reserved.

No part of this publication may be reproduced, stored in a retrieval
system, or transmitted, in any form, or by any means, without the prior
permission in writing of the publisher, nor be otherwise circulated in any
form of binding or cover other than that in which it is published and
without a similar condition including this condition being imposed
on the subsequent purchaser.

A CIP catalogue record for this book
is available from the British Library.

TRADE PAPERBACK ISBN 978-1-4087-3176-5
PAPERBACK ISBN 978-1-4087-3175-8

Typeset in Arno Pro by Palimpsest Book Production Limited, Falkirk, Stirlingshire

Printed and bound in Great Britain by Clays Ltd, Elcograf S.p.A

Papers used by Sphere are from well-managed forests and other responsible sources.

Sphere
An imprint of
Little, Brown Book Group
Carmelite House
50 Victoria Embankment
London EC4Y 0DZ

The authorised representative
in the EEA is
Hachette Ireland,
8 Castlecourt Centre,
Dublin 15, D15 XTP3, Ireland
(email: info@hbgi.ie)

An Hachette UK Company
www.hachette.co.uk
www.littlebrown.co.uk

*For Mary Moriarty*

# Prologue

'YOU MISSED YOUR TURN,' SHE SAID.

He kept going, along the village's single street and out the other side, taking the coast road at the fork. 'I've got something to show you.'

'What?'

'Wait and see.'

She sat back, smiling. She loved surprises, and he was good at them. Every time he left her Dublin apartment to take his long road home she found a treat hidden somewhere – her favourite chocolate, a framed photo he'd taken of the two of them, a bar of the seaweed and loofah soap she was addicted to. Once he'd replaced her bookmark with two tickets for an upcoming play he knew she wanted to see.

She planted her feet back on the dashboard and admired her blue toenails. They'd been on their way home from the beach: when she wriggled her toes she felt the not unpleasant graininess of sand between them. His car was always full of sand. She lifted a hand to lick her palm, and tasted salt.

In the hedgerows she saw dots of orange among banks of bright green spears. *Montbretia getting ready to bloom*, Damien had told her when she'd asked. *Few more weeks, it'll be like the hedges are on fire.* Beyond was the patchwork of fields, some with animals, others with crops, and past that the shimmering turquoise ribbon of ocean that travelled along with them, the black shapes of wheeling gulls in the blue sky above it all.

A week before Christmas, a month after they'd met, in bed with flu and unable to cross the country to see him as planned, she'd answered a persistent knock at her apartment door to find him standing there with a large Thermos. He'd made the green bean, miso and noodle soup she loved, and driven three hours to bring it to her. Was that the moment – aching and feverish and shivery, hair a mess, not a scrap of make-up, wearing old comfy PJs she'd never have dreamt of letting him see her in – she'd fallen in love with him? She thought it was.

And now it was the last week of May, their sixth month together, and the weather had been unseasonably warm for the past few days, and they'd been swimming – or rather he'd cut through the water like the half-fish he was while she'd bobbed about closer to shore. He kept threatening to teach her to swim; she kept promising to learn. *When we're living together*, she always added in her head.

Although nothing had been said, no promises given, no plans made beyond their next encounter, everything, it felt to her, was pointing towards a life together: the only unknowns were when and where. The when part would happen, but not just yet – six months of only seeing each other at weekends was probably not long enough for that particular conversation, impatient as she was for it.

The where part was a little more uncertain. Dublin was the only home she'd ever known, while he'd grown up in the little west coast village she travelled to every other Saturday to stay two precious nights and one full day with him. The village, with its single street, consisted of a church, a chemist, a primary school, two pubs, a chipper, a café that opened when its owner felt like it, a tiny hair salon, a butcher's, a small supermarket with a post office tucked away at the back, and a hardware shop that was bigger than all the other premises put together, selling everything from lawn mowers to kettles to table lamps to birthday cards.

Between the shops were houses, and beyond the street more houses, gradually petering out as the countryside took over. The population, according to Damien, was around seven hundred.

But despite its small size, or maybe because of it, the place was very friendly. Everyone smiled at her on the street, everyone said hello, even children, and she loved that the bigger town half an hour away – still tiny in Dublin terms – was known simply as 'the town', as if it was the only one in Ireland, or the only one that mattered.

If Damien asked her to move here, she would. She'd live anywhere with him. He'd move for her too, she was sure of it, but sometimes when he came to Dublin it felt like he was trying on clothes that didn't quite fit. He was a son of the village, known by all, perfectly content here. She couldn't uproot him, not when she was willing to relocate.

It would be a massive change, after having everything on her doorstep in Dublin, but doing it for him, and to be with him, would turn it into something great, the best kind of adventure. She'd never been afraid of taking chances, and she wasn't about to start now.

She'd have to travel for work if she lived here. Given its size, there wasn't the smallest chance she could make a living from teaching yoga in the village – but again she didn't care. She could look for work in the town; Marian said there was a community centre that might take her in – and maybe she'd organise a weekly class somewhere in the village, just to involve herself in local life. The school might let her use their hall.

She caught herself then, and smiled. Listen to her, planning their future. He probably wasn't giving it a thought, not yet. She reached across to lay a hand lightly on his thigh, and he threw her a glance.

'What are you smiling about?'

'Nothing.'

He started humming. He was a hummer, always something playing in his head that had to come out. He wasn't in perfect tune, but it didn't bother her. She loved the happiness in him, the way he grabbed each day with the enthusiasm of a small child, and made the most of it.

She studied his profile as he drove. His eyes were between blue and grey, depending on the light. His nose had been broken in childhood from the accidental whack of a hurley, so now it had a small bump in the bridge that she decided gave it character. His mouth was wide, his cheeks ruddy and burnished from year-round swimming. Little creases radiated from the outer corners of his eyes.

And when he smiled, which was often, she melted. It was a thing of glory, a crooked grin with a kind of bashful quality to it that sent happiness into all areas and transformed his face into an adorable thing that she wanted to press between her hands and kiss fervently – and she did, anytime they were alone.

His smile caused butterflies to rise inside her and flutter madly. His smile had been the reason, on the night they'd met in a busy Dublin pub, she'd accepted his offer to carry her tray of drinks back to her table. In the city for a friend's stag party, only his third time ever in the capital. 'Complete culchie,' he'd said, laughing, and something – the laugh, the merriment of him, the careful way he'd set down the tray and said a cheerful hello to her gang – something about him had found her tapping her number into his phone when he'd asked.

She'd been certain she wouldn't hear any more from him – stag parties tended to blot out memories – but she *had* heard, late the very next morning. *It's the culchie*, he'd said. *A bit worse for wear, and in dire need of food*, and their lunch date in the little Italian bistro she'd directed him to had lasted three hours.

In that time he'd told her he was a chef, still living in the seaside village where he'd grown up, and working in a busy restaurant in the nearby town. He had an older brother and no sister, and he was hopeless at DIY, and his favourite ice-cream was mint chocolate chip, and he loved music but couldn't sing, and he'd learnt to swim before he started school.

They clicked. He made her laugh. He seemed impressed that she was a yoga teacher, and asked lots of questions about it. Her vegetarianism amused him – he himself, he told her, was a proud omnivore, nothing he wouldn't try.

By the time he was leaving, she was smitten. When he leant in to kiss her goodbye her heart leapt, just the brush of his lips on her cheek leaving her wanting more, much more, and she couldn't wait to see him again.

*He's the other side of the country*, her friends had said, when she'd reported on the lunch. *Do you really want to do a long-distance thing, Lydia?* The answer to that, of course, was no. A long-distance relationship was definitely *not* what she wanted – she'd rather meet him every day, or at least every second one – but she'd take it over never seeing him again, and so it had begun.

Over the following weeks of long phone calls and snatched weekends – happily, both their work schedules gave them Sundays and Mondays off – they'd nurtured the precious thing they'd coaxed into being, and infatuation had quickly grown into love, and here they were.

'Now,' he said, turning down a lane on the coast side of the road. It was a mix of gravel and packed earth, barely wide enough for two cars to pass, a strip of grass running along its middle. Was he taking her to another beach, after just having left one?

He wasn't. They rounded a bend and the lane petered out beside a set of rusting metal gates on the left. Damien pulled up at the gates and switched off the engine, and Lydia looked out at a big old ivy-covered two-storey house set at an angle to the lane at the end of a short curved gravel driveway.

The gates were closed, briars and more ivy clambering along the dry-stone pillars that anchored them. She saw gaps in the roof tiles of the house, and greenery climbing from chimneys, and glass missing from several of its windows. The front door, black paint peeling, had a broken fanlight above it. Sad, she thought, to let such an impressive building go to rack and ruin like that.

'I need you to come with me,' Damien said.

She turned and saw the excitement in him, the shine in his eyes, the smile that was on the cusp of forming. 'What are you up to?'

In response he opened his door and went around to the boot.

She followed him in time to see him lifting out two pairs of green wellingtons. 'Put these on, Cinderella,' he said, offering her the smaller ones.

She looked at them. She'd never owned wellingtons, never worn a pair.

'Go on,' he said, shucking off his sandals, 'and bring your fleece too.'

'My fleece? I'll be too hot.'

'Trust me,' he said. 'You'll be glad of it.'

'Where are you taking me?'

'Surprise,' he said, and she knew she'd get no more, so she shook off her flip-flops and wriggled her bare feet into the wellingtons, which made her feel like she was dressing for a part in a play. They must look wonderful with her yellow sundress. She got her blue fleece and tied it loosely around her waist.

He took a walking stick from the boot before he closed it.

'What's that for?'

'Wait and see.'

He didn't bother locking the car. Nobody locked cars or houses around here. He pushed open one of the gates, making it screech, then took her hand and led her through.

'Damien, this is private property,' she said, but not with any real qualms. The house was clearly empty. 'Who owns it?'

'A family called Chance,' he told her. 'The last resident died about thirty years ago. Apparently he was a bit of a recluse.'

They stepped over creeping briars and around clumps of nettles in the driveway, and she understood the wellingtons. 'How old is it?'

'Nearly two hundred years. It's called Chance House.'

He looked as if he was about to add something else, but didn't. She was aware of a wonderful sense of peace, even as the air hummed with things that darted and fluttered and flew about them, and birds that chirped loudly in the trees flanking the building, and various rustlings from the undergrowth. No traffic: that was it. No sound of cars from the road. She could imagine the recluse sitting inside all on his own, savouring the uninterrupted sounds of nature.

They approached the house and he made to bring her around the side, but she eased her hand from his – 'Hang on' – and stepped up to a bay window. She cupped her hands the better to make out whatever was within, but saw only darkness. She tried the adjoining window, also a bay, and still saw nothing.

'The shutters might be closed,' he said.

Chance House. Nice name. She loved these big old houses, full of history. She wished she'd known it in its heyday. She imagined high ceilings, covings and architraves, a sweeping marble staircase, giant fireplaces, lots of heavy mahogany furniture that gleamed with beeswax.

Maybe there had been a butler. Maybe a maid or two, and a cook. Maybe the Chance family had dressed for dinner, the meal attended by a silent footman.

Maybe she'd seen too much *Downton Abbey*.

'You'll need to put on your fleece now,' he said as they rounded the corner of the house. On seeing the dense overgrowth, she pulled on her fleece and zipped it up. He went ahead of her, using his stick to beat at the vegetation and create a path through it, but every now and again a rogue bramble would pull at Lydia's sleeve.

'Hang on to me,' he said, 'and watch your footing.' She grabbed a handful of his shirt and stumbled along behind him over bumps and dips in the ground for what seemed like a long time. 'Do we know where we're going?'

'I do,' he answered. 'Trust me' – and all of a sudden, above the birdsong, she thought she heard the wash of the sea somewhere ahead. They must be close to it, walking in the direction they were going.

Damien gave a final whack – and she gasped as they emerged to a scene she hadn't imagined. Beyond a low rusted railing the land fell a few feet to a small sandy cove, and beyond the cove was the ocean, huge and breathtaking, its edge rushing onto the sand and running away again.

'A private beach,' he said. 'A few of us used to swim here as teenagers, until the garden got too overgrown. I thought you'd like it.'

She loved it. It was a little haven. She imagined a round table and two chairs on the sand. The perfect setting, on a summer's evening with a glass of wine, to watch the sun slip below the horizon.

At one end of the railing was a gap that allowed access to a set of ramshackle wooden steps that led down to the beach. They negotiated the steps carefully and stood together, the water lapping just metres away.

Something, a bolt of excitement, took hold of Lydia. They were trespassers on a private beach. Like all forbidden things, it was thrilling. She unzipped her fleece and pulled it off. She shook her feet out of the wellingtons and strode to the water, the cool touch of it refreshing after the confinement of the rubber. She gathered up the hem of her dress and took another step, and another. With the water at her knees she kicked out, and a spray leapt into the air and arced back to drench her. She laughed happily and turned to give him a drenching too, to find him on his knees on the damp sand.

No, not on both knees, just one.

What was—?

Her hands flew to her mouth as he reached into his shirt pocket and drew out a small box, a new, different smile spreading now across his face. A nervous smile.

'Oh,' she breathed, her heart hammering in her throat. Her eyes filled with hot, happy tears that spilt over to mix with the cool water of the sea on her face.

'Will you?' he asked, opening the box, holding it out to her. 'I know it's soon, maybe I should have waited longer, but I'm as certain as I need to be. Will you please marry me, Lydia Foley?'

'Yes!' she cried. 'Yes! Yes, I'll marry you, Damien Cotter!'

She splashed from the water and pulled him to his feet. Half laughing, half crying, she covered his face with kisses, and he put on the ring and they danced on the sand, and then he caught her up, still in his wellingtons, and waded into the sea and whirled her around, and nobody was as happy as they were.

When they ran out of breath she sat on the steps and he pushed her wellingtons on again, and they scrambled back up and returned through the jungle of overgrowth to the house, panting, wet dress clinging to her, hands intertwined.

Engaged. She was engaged. They were going to be married. Her insides kept giving happy little swoops. Back at his car they packed up the wellingtons and sat in, and only then did he tell her that the property was for sale.

'Really?'

She looked at it again. Once upon a time it had been beautiful. She imagined owning it, calling it home. She'd be the envy of everyone she knew. She wondered how much it would cost to buy it, and how much more it would take until it was beautiful again. Someone in the village might go for it, make it their project. The publicans might be well off, or the owner of the giant hardware store.

'We could put in a bid,' he said.

She turned. '*Us?*'

'Why not? We have assets. I have my house here. You have your apartment in Dublin.'

'Damien – are you serious?'

He laughed. 'I think I am.'

She felt a leap of excitement. Was it possible? Could they really consider this? 'What's the asking price?'

He told her. Lower than she'd expected – but of course they'd need far more to restore it. Then again, she'd get a lot more for her apartment than she'd paid for it seven years ago. Property prices in Dublin were climbing all the time.

God, could they do it?

She turned to look at the house again. It would have been a family home through the ages but everyone lived in more modest properties now, easier to heat and maintain. Still, she imagined it filled with children. She pictured a girl playing a piano, a boy reading in a big armchair by the fire. She saw herself and Damien hosting dinner parties around a long table. The thought was intoxicating: she literally felt her head spin.

'Listen,' he said, taking her hands. 'This house would make the perfect destination restaurant. Not just somewhere you'd go for a meal, but a place that offered a night away too, or maybe a weekend. And I'm talking quality: the best of ingredients for the food, the best bed linens, tasteful finishes and furnishings, the works. I could see families looking for it, or a group of friends, maybe to celebrate a big birthday or an anniversary. Some occasion they'd want to make a fuss of.'

A restaurant, not a family home. Of course it made more sense to run a business in it, but she was sorry to let go of the piano-playing girl and the reading boy. 'So where would we live?'

'We'd be in there, in our own private quarters. We could always extend the house down the line, if we needed to.'

He had it all worked out. 'How long have you been thinking about this?'

'Since I heard it was up for sale last week. I gave the estate agent a shout – she was at school with Tom.'

Tom, his brother. Everyone had some connection here. 'Has anyone bid on it?'

'No. She said my house should make enough to buy it.'

'Wow. So whatever I made on the apartment—'

'– would cover the renovations,' he finished. 'We could get my father to do the job – it's just the kind of project he'd love, and he'd give us a good price.'

His father Brendan owned a small building company, managing a team of local tradespeople. He'd built his own house, and one each for his sons. If he could handle a job on this scale, he would be the one to ask. She liked him, with his quiet, gentle ways.

'Does he know about this? Have you spoken to him?'

'Not yet. You had to be the first.'

It would be a huge undertaking. They'd be selling their properties and sinking the proceeds into what amounted to a dream – but dreams came true, didn't they, if you worked on them? Look at herself and Damien, overcoming the long-distance challenge.

'And Marian would help us kit it out,' he said.

Marian was his sister-in-law. Infant teacher in the local school, jangle of bracelets, blue streaks in her hair. She always looked good, hunting down designer labels in charity shops, putting items of clothing together with style, wearing colours that should clash but didn't, and knowing exactly how to use accessories. And yes, her house was very nicely put together too.

'And we could find room for a yoga studio in there,' he added. 'Just if you wanted it.'

She stared at him. 'What?'

'Why not?'

'Would there be enough demand around here for that?'

'Course there would. You'd be a real novelty – first yoga teacher in the area.' He started the car. 'We'd put it on the sea side of the house, so you'd have that view once the garden was cleared. In the summer you could teach out of doors, put mats on the lawn.'

All the way back to his house, she saw nothing of the scenery beyond the windscreen. She was seeing the overgrown weeds and brambles gone, the garden returned to the thing of glory it must once have been, the sea spread out at the bottom of it.

She was seeing yoga students unrolling their mats, filling their lungs with the clean ocean air as they went through their sun salutations and warriors and cobras and downward dogs. And in the winter a heated studio, with big windows to hold on to the sea view.

Was he right, saying she'd get enough takers? She liked the idea of being the first to bring yoga here. A novelty. A pioneer. She'd surely find her students among the seven hundred.

He pulled into his driveway and turned to face her. 'It has to be an omen,' he said. 'The name, I mean.'

'Chance House,' she said.

'It's our chance to make something wonderful there.'

She nodded, her eyes brimming again. This day had too much in it.

He thumbed away the tears as they fell. 'You're with me, sweetheart?'

'All the way.'

'You don't mind the thought of moving from Dublin?'

'Not in the least.'

'Brilliant. I'll arrange a viewing for when you're down again.'

'Do.'

Chance House. She hardly dared to hope.

Later, showered and changed and on the train back to Dublin, she phoned Brona to tell her of the engagement.

'About time,' Brona said. 'I can't believe he took six whole months to propose.'

A year ago, Brona had married her childhood sweetheart at the age of thirty. They'd been together since she was fifteen.

'I can smell your sarcasm from here,' Lydia told her. 'Six months isn't a long time, but we're both sure.'

'I know you are, Liddy. I don't think I've ever met a more perfectly suited couple – apart from me and Shaun, obviously – and I'm thrilled for you.'

'And there's more.'

'Tell me absolutely everything.'

Lydia told her.

'Let me get this straight,' Brona said. 'You're planning to buy a tumbledown house and do it up. You'll be moving three hours away from me to live in the middle of nowhere.'

'It's very near the village, only about half a mile outside it. And my own yoga studio, don't forget.'

'Yes, your own studio is wonderful. So you'll be moving three hours away from me to live near a village that's in the middle of nowhere. Am I right so far?'

Lydia laughed. 'Oh come on, don't be negative. You and Shaun can come and stay once it's done up. And I won't be going anywhere until that happens, so I'll be around for ages. And that's all assuming we get the house – we might be put off it when we see the inside, or someone with more money might come along and outbid us.'

'But if you get it, you'll definitely be leaving. What will I do without my Liddy?'

'Don't,' Lydia said. They'd known each other for as long as she could remember, grown up two streets apart, started school on the same day. 'We'll still see lots of each other. Dublin isn't a million miles away.'

'Have you told all this to his parents – and yours?'

'Only his so far, and only the engagement part. We won't mention the house to anyone unless it happens.'

'And how did they react?'

'His father's happy. I've told you what Kathleen's like.'

'You have.'

His mother hadn't taken to Lydia. Nothing had been said, but it was clear in the way she never called her by name, never spoke to her unless she had to, never made proper eye contact. At the start, Lydia had wondered if she'd inadvertently said the wrong thing, but Marian had put her right.

*It's nothing you've said or done – Kathleen would rather a local girl for Damien, that's all.*

*What does it matter where I'm from?*

*Maybe she's afraid you'll whisk him away to Dublin.*

*I'd never do that.*

*Well then, you have nothing to worry about* – but Lydia still had to endure the aloofness, the feeling that she was not appreciated by the woman who was now destined to be her mother-in-law. It was all Kathleen could do to congratulate her when they'd broken the news of their engagement. Anyone could see it wasn't what she'd wanted to hear.

No matter: all the Kathleens in the world couldn't spoil this wonderful day. 'Wait till you see the ring,' she told Brona. 'It's gorgeous.'

She tilted her left hand to watch it sparkle. Damien had said they could do a swap if she didn't like it – the jeweller was a neighbour of his father's cousin – but she liked it a lot. A simple, sweet solitaire, the band white gold because Damien knew she preferred it to yellow. Exactly what she would have picked herself.

Brona was right: they were perfectly suited. It had taken a long time for their paths to cross – they'd met a week after her thirtieth birthday – but he was worth the wait. She conjured his smiling face in her mind's eye and felt the happy little inner flip it always caused.

On the way to the station they'd decided to put marriage plans on hold to focus on Chance House. Their engagement might be a long one, but now that they'd committed to one another, now that their future together was assured, she could handle a long engagement.

What a life they were going to have.

# EIGHTEEN MONTHS LATER

# 1

'YOU CAN COME BACK ANYTIME,' HER MOTHER SAID at the station. 'Your old room will always be there.'

Lydia gave an inner sigh. 'Mum, I'm moving to make a life in the west, remember? In a few months I'll be getting married. It's not a trial run.'

Patience, she told herself. They meant well. She was their only child: of course they were protective of her – but Lord, when would they realise that she *wasn't* a child any longer? She'd turned thirty-two a few weeks ago, and hadn't needed their protection for years.

She remembered telling them that she'd decided to do a yoga teacher training course after Leaving Cert. Granted, she'd been about fifteen at the time, with another three years of secondary school ahead of her, so they could still play the adult card – but honestly, the way they'd gone on, the raft of objections they'd raised, you'd think she'd announced that she was planning to embark on a life of crime.

And even when she'd stuck to her guns and got her certification, and landed a permanent job in a prestigious Dublin yoga studio not long after, she'd sensed their faint but enduring disappointment that she hadn't opted to study medicine like them. Having two doctors as parents was a pretty hard act to follow.

And here they were again, banging the familiar are-you-sure-you-know-what-you're-doing drum into their child's thirty-two-year-old ears. In the year and a half since Lydia had told them she was going to marry Damien, and all through everything that had followed – the big house bought, both Lydia and Damien's properties sold – they'd missed no opportunity to impress on her that she could still change course.

Why couldn't Damien come to Dublin and move in with Lydia while they looked around for something bigger? they'd asked. The city was full of restaurants, he'd have a job before he'd unpacked, and he could work towards opening his own place in time. She'd heard it all – and so had he, whenever he was around. He'd done his best to change their minds, telling them what a special property he and Lydia had found in Chance House, and how after seventeen years of working for someone else he was more than ready to go his own way, something that would take him another seventeen years to afford in Dublin.

*We'll visit often,* he'd promised them, *and there'll always be a room for you in Chance House,* but Lydia could see that they were just as set on their course as she and Damien were on theirs. When they saw the finished house, she told herself, when it was all done up and looking splendid, they'd be forced to love it, and to be happy for Lydia.

Her mother gathered her coat more tightly around her. It was the last day of the coldest November in years, a month of sleety showers and biting wind, and frozen fingers and toes. 'We're just concerned for you, Lydia. We can't help it.'

'I'm following my heart, Mum. You can't object to that.'

'You're taking a huge risk.'

'And it's a risk Damien and I are happy to take.' How many more times would she have to say it?

Her mother's mouth tightened at the mention of his name. They'd always been fond of him, but now he was the cause of their daughter selling her home and moving so far away from them. The irony wasn't lost on her. Kathleen had been afraid Lydia would steal Damien from her, but now the reverse was happening, and her parents were the resentful ones. At least they'd remained on good terms with their future son-in-law, for which she was grateful.

People passed by, gloved and scarved and wheeling suitcases. 'I'd better get on,' Lydia said. 'Thanks for putting me up for the last few weeks.'

Happily, her apartment had sold for considerably more than she'd envisaged, so after repaying her mortgage there was still plenty left. She'd tried to return the deposit her parents had given her but they'd told her to hang on to it, which was decent of them (although she couldn't help feeling that it was more babying). In any event, she had funds in the bank to cover Brendan's bill for the renovations, with a bit extra to add to her own savings, so that was all good.

Giving up work, her last class just two days ago, had been a wrench. *There'll always be a job here for you*, her boss had promised – was he worried too that everything would go wrong, and she'd come crawling back?

Her mother reached out to hug her. 'Mind yourself, love. We'll see you at Christmas.'

'Bye, Mum.'

In truth, Lydia was regretting her promise to return to them for Christmas Day: she'd far rather be spending it with Damien. Then again, it would be her last Christmas as a single woman, and her last spent without him. In the summer they'd finally marry – and this time next year they'd be looking forward to their first Christmas together in Chance House.

They might even start a tradition of hosting both families – no point in marrying a chef if you couldn't make use of him now and again, and the big house would provide the perfect location for a large family gathering. In another year, with the destination restaurant hopefully well underway, and her yoga studio up and running, Lydia's parents would see that it had all worked out, and Kathleen might finally have warmed to her second daughter-in-law.

As the train left the station and began to gather speed, she watched the familiar Dublin suburbs flash past the window, and took stock.

Excited as she was to be embarking on what still felt like a wonderful adventure, she did have some qualms. Even though she'd travelled to the village lots of times, she still knew virtually nobody outside Damien's family. Her interactions with his friends had been limited to the occasional drink in a noisy pub, or a chance meeting on one of the local beaches, and she couldn't now recall a single name she'd heard.

She wondered how it would be, with Damien working right up to Christmas Eve – they'd agreed that he was going to take all the shifts he was offered between now and when the house was finished in May or June – and Lydia left to her own devices.

*You could look for part-time shop work*, he'd said. *Not in the village – they couldn't really give you a job over a local person, not until you've been here a while and got to know everyone. I mean in the town – there's a bus from the village every morning.*

She wasn't sure what she thought about that. She'd never worked in a shop, never had a summer job as a teen – she and her friends had been more interested in going into the city centre, or hanging around the tennis club – but she would have time to fill, and earning a bit couldn't hurt. Some day next week she'd take a walk around the town, see what businesses were there. A bakery might be nice, or a boutique, or maybe a bookshop.

And the good thing about getting a job was that she'd be meeting people, and the more people she got to know, the more opportunities she'd have to sound them out about the yoga classes at Chance House – although she wasn't sure she'd pick up many students from the town. Marian had told her there was no yoga studio there, but would they drive half an hour for an hour-long class?

Damien still maintained she had nothing to worry about. *There'll be lots of interest,* he'd said, *even in the village alone. You'll be turning them away.* Time would tell if he was right about that.

But she was looking forward to seeing Chance House again. She hadn't travelled west since Damien's house sale had closed just before last Christmas, and he'd moved back in with his parents. She couldn't imagine Kathleen being too impressed if Lydia had landed on her doorstep with her weekend bag, so Damien had done all the travelling, and she'd seen none of the work so far.

*Don't send me photos,* she'd said. *I don't want to look at it on a screen. I want to wait till I can see the real thing.*

*What about our apartment?*

*Not even that.*

The architect Brendan found had drawn up a plan for the renovations that had set aside roughly a third of the ground floor to make a two-bedroom apartment for them. The yoga studio would be close by, just off the main entrance hall, and the rest of the downstairs space would be taken up with the restaurant.

She'd seen the plans, but you couldn't get a proper sense of it from drawings on a page, however detailed. In her head, Chance House was still the ruin they'd viewed with Deborah the estate agent, picking their way around gaps in the floorboards, seeing – or trying not to see – enormous black patches on the walls, and a fossilised bird in one of the huge fireplaces.

They'd been denied access to the upper floor due to the uncertain condition of the staircase. *I couldn't have it on my conscience,* Deborah had said, *if one of you fell and broke your neck. I chanced going up myself when I came to assess it, so I can tell you it's got eight sizeable bedrooms and one bathroom, and they're in the same condition as this level. On the plus side, you'd definitely qualify for a grant to do it up.*

That viewing had brought home to them just how much work was involved, but it hadn't scared them off. They'd taken Brendan to view it, and a light had appeared in his eyes that Lydia hadn't seen before. *I can bring it back,* he'd said. *Take a good while, mind you,* and they'd told him he was hired if they got it.

They'd put in a bid that was slightly under the asking price, and Damien had put his own house on the market. They'd held their breath for three weeks, four weeks, five weeks – and finally Deborah had rung with the news that their bid had been accepted.

And now, at last, their adventure was beginning properly. What was that expression? Today was the first day of the rest of her life, and she was going to share it with Damien, and she couldn't have been happier.

The apartment finished, their wedding in the summer, as soon as the rest of the house was done. They were on the home stretch.

All would be well.

It was almost three by the time her train pulled into the station, the sky as leaden as it had been in Dublin. She gathered her things and searched the faces on the platform, like she always did when she landed – and there he was, holding up a small sign reading *Welcome home* above a line drawing of a house that made her laugh.

'The yoga teacher has arrived,' he said, wrapping arms around her, pressing cold lips briefly on hers. 'Are you ready for this?'

'Ready as I'll ever be.'

'Right then – let's go.' He handed her the sign, gathered up her luggage and led the way to his car.

'How's everyone?' she asked.

'Grand. Mam's making the Christmas cakes today, so the house smells like a distillery.'

'Cakes? More than one?'

'Two – one for themselves and one for Tom's house. Marian makes the puddings. Shame you won't be here on Christmas Day.'

'I know.' She told him of her idea to host future Christmas dinners at Chance House. 'You think your mother would like to have the day off?'

'We could certainly run it by her,' but she saw the doubt in his face, and understood it. Kathleen wouldn't relinquish the reins easily, particularly to Lydia. If she refused to travel for her turkey dinner, Lydia would just have to grin and bear her way through the meal at the senior Cotters' house – or maybe she and Damien could start a different tradition, and take themselves off to the sun every Christmas instead. Definitely worth considering.

They got to the car and climbed in. 'I'm dying to see the apartment,' she said, turning up the heat as he reversed from his space, 'and the rest of the house. Are we allowed upstairs yet?'

'We are. I'll show you around tomorrow. The outside is still a mess: don't expect it to look good. They're leaving that till last.'

The roads were quiet, most people still at work. By the time they reached the village the light was beginning to fade from the sky. She saw coloured lights strung along the main street, and a tall fir tree already erected in the church grounds. They probably had a switching-on ceremony like in Dublin: she and her friends used to go every year, not so much to see the ceremony as to soak up the Christmas spirit in their favourite pub afterwards.

The hedgerows on the cusp of December were twiggy and bare. When they took the coast road at the fork she felt a dart of déjà vu. *I've got something to show you*, he'd said. The novelty of owning the house and all that went with it was still fresh, probably because they hadn't lived in it yet, but she suspected she'd never stop delighting in the fact that Chance House was their home.

'Nearly forgot,' he said. 'I have someone taming the jungle out the back. He started a few days ago, so we're on the way to a proper garden. You'll meet him tomorrow if the day is dry. Get ready,' he said, turning down the lane, and she felt a sudden rush of excitement at what might await her.

The rusted gates were gone, allowing Damien to drive straight in. The car lurched and bumped over the short curve of driveway. 'The vans and lorries have churned it up,' he said. 'They'll level it off before they leave, but in the meantime you'll have to watch your step coming and going.'

He cut the engine and they sat in the quiet half-light. No other vehicles, workmen obviously having downed tools for the day and gone home. It must be freezing for them, working in an unheated house. Thank goodness the apartment had heat.

The place looked bigger than she remembered. The ivy was gone from the walls, leaving them patchy and bare.

'Great that they've got that ivy off,' Damien remarked. 'Can't wait to see the walls painted.'

With Marian's help they'd chosen a beautiful soft grey-green shade for the outside. 'It'll be fab,' Lydia agreed.

'And the new windows have started going in at the back. They'll make a big difference too.'

She smiled. It was obvious he was looking forward to showing her the apartment: he was giving off the same anticipation she'd seen on the day he'd proposed. They got out and made their way around to the side, where she saw a brand new door between two sash windows in what had been a solid wall last time she'd looked. Door and window frames were black, to match what was planned for the rest of the house.

'This is us,' he said. 'Our apartment.'

She gave the brass knocker a tap. 'Anyone home?' she called.

'Better not be. Hang on.' He dropped her bags and opened the door, then turned and scooped her without warning into his arms. 'Over the threshold with you, missus,' he said.

She laughed. 'I think that's for newlyweds, darling.'

'Shush. I need the practice.'

He set her down in a space that was pleasantly warm, and smelt of fresh paint. While he retrieved her bags she took in the little entrance hall – yes, she remembered it from the plans – with its row of hooks on one wall, a black umbrella and Damien's raincoat the only things hanging there right now.

She spotted a light switch and flicked it on – and nothing happened. Her heart sank. 'Don't we have electricity?'

'We do – they must have forgotten the bulb in that one.' He dropped her bags and closed the door and took her hand. 'Come on, I'll show you around.'

The kitchen – with a light that worked – was a decent size, with black and white floor tiles, and white units that wrapped around two of the pale grey walls, and big windows for lots of daylight. At one end of the room his round table was set for dinner, along with an opened bottle of their favourite Malbec. His slow cooker sat on the worktop, the savoury aroma of its contents wafting in the air.

He led her into the sitting room, slightly smaller but delightfully cosy, with an open fireplace, again in keeping with the style of the big house, and a lovely floor of wide wooden boards. She'd forgotten about the floorboards Brendan had offered them, salvaged from old houses.

*Easy to clean them up*, he'd said, and he had. Their beautiful mellow glow lent character and warmth to the room, and Lydia's big orange rug was the perfect finishing touch. Damien took away the fireguard and poked the reddened coals back to life, and added more. 'We can have our coffees in here,' he said, replacing the guard, and again she was touched by his eagerness to please her, his delight at showing off their first home.

The rest of the apartment comprised two bedrooms, one double, one single, and a bathroom with the bath and separate shower

Lydia had insisted on. Wall colours throughout were pale, and furniture was a mix of his and hers: his kitchen appliances, her crockery and glassware, his chef's knives, his couch, her bookshelves, her bed, dressing table and wardrobe. His television in the sitting room, her smaller one in their bedroom.

'So,' he said, 'what do you think of our home sweet home?'

'I love it. It's wonderful.' It was compact, but for now it had everything they needed. 'And that must lead to the rest of the house,' she said, indicating the door at the end of the short corridor.

'That's right.'

'Could I see it?'

'Now? It's not hooked up with electricity or heat yet. You'd see nothing in the dark.' By now the sky had lost the last of its light, winter daylight hours firmly established.

'We could bring a torch, and wrap up.' After waiting for so long she was suddenly impatient to see what lay beyond the door. 'Just a quick look.'

'Go on then.' They got back into jackets they'd shrugged off and he found a torch, and they opened the connecting door. Immediately she felt a blast of frigid air. The floor was bare concrete, the walls unpainted. The ceiling here was considerably higher than in the apartment, giving her the sense that they were entering a bigger world.

The hall as she remembered it had been reduced in size, but was still plenty big enough to accommodate the reception desk it would need. Set into its back wall were two doors.

She pointed to one. 'The office?'

'Correct.'

'And . . .' she approached the other, the one closer to the apartment '. . . what could be behind here, I wonder?'

He shrugged. 'Can't remember.'

She turned the handle and pushed in the door – and there it was.

It had the same high ceiling as the hall. She swept the torch beam around and saw three tall windows on one side, and another at the end that took up nearly the entire wall. There was no flooring, no paint, no fittings or furnishings. The air was so bitingly cold they might as well have been outdoors, but in her mind's eye she saw the sprung floor of pale wood, the creamy yellow walls that would make the room sunshiny even on a cloudy day, and the built-in storage unit to hold mats and blocks and the rest of her paraphernalia.

She saw the ceiling spotlights in place – dimmable so she could offer a restorative class with subdued lighting – the slimline radiators that were going in vertically between the tall windows, the framed mantras she'd chosen for the walls, duplicates of the ones in her old workplace, and the mirror that would run the length of the room, across from the three windows.

Her very own studio, something she'd never in a million years have afforded in Dublin. She'd use it every single day when it was finished, even if hers was the only mat in the room. She'd teach their children, if nobody else came.

'You like it?'

His voice startled her. She'd forgotten he was there. 'I love it. It's going to be amazing.'

'It is. Now come and check out the dining room before we freeze to death.'

From the hall she followed him through a newly created arch that led directly into a large room that used to be four smaller ones.

They'd decided on seating for forty, so they could feed the general public as well as the number the house would sleep. With nothing apart from chipper fare and pub sandwiches on offer in the village, the locals would surely be glad of a restaurant closer than the town.

It was a splendidly proportioned room, expansive and elegant, with the large fireplace they'd retained, and no fewer than three bay windows, two to the front and a third to the side. Right now it looked a little less than magnificent, with a huddle of wheelbarrows in a corner, a stepladder propped against one of the unpainted walls, the fireplace empty and the floor not yet put down. Lydia was glad to see a pair of gas heaters there – at least the workers had some comfort.

'Imagine it,' Damien said softly, encircling her with his arms from behind. 'Tables spread out, white cloths, silver place settings, sparkling glasses.'

'Candles,' she said. 'The fire blazing. Maybe we could put a little piano in, have live music at the weekends.'

'Great idea. And a small but perfectly formed menu.'

'Vegetarian option.'

'Naturally – and vegan if we must.'

She searched for his hand in the near-darkness, trying to stop her teeth chattering. 'I wish we didn't have to wait so long.'

'For what?'

'For our wedding. It feels like a million years since you proposed.'

'You're shivering. Let's go and eat. You can see the rest tomorrow' – and when they were back in the warmth and light of the apartment, after she'd poured wine and he'd ladled sweet potato and coconut curry into bowls, he said, 'Maybe we don't have to wait.'

'For what?'

'To get married.'

She shook her head. 'We said we'd have the reception here.' Somewhere along the way they'd settled on that. With the seating limitations it would mean a smaller event than Lydia had envisaged, but they could have a big party later for everyone else.

He tore bread from a loaf. 'We could still have it here, just bring it forward.'

She laughed. 'What – you mean as it is now? In the freezing cold?'

'Why not?'

'Damien Cotter, I know you're joking. Stop it.'

'We could light a fire – the chimney could be cleaned, if it hasn't been already. And you saw the gas heaters?'

'I did.' She imagined a wedding reception taking place in what was to all intents and purposes a building site. People would certainly remember that one. 'What would we do for lighting?' she asked, still sure he was joking. Wanting to catch him out.

'That's easy – battery-powered fairy lights around the walls, hurricane lamps with candles in the windows, and a few of those rechargeable lamps on the tables.'

'What tables?'

'We'd borrow them from Susan.'

'Who's Susan?'

'The school principal. She has trestle tables she lends out for street parties and fairs and things, and folding chairs too.'

Lydia laughed again, shaking her head. 'Folding chairs. You're hilarious.'

'Think about it,' he insisted. 'People start planning their weddings months ahead, sometimes years, because that's when they have to book their venue, but we have the venue right here. We could get married before the end of this year if we put our minds to it.'

'Damien, the end of this year is in four weeks – now I know you're crazy. And it's not just the venue – we'd need food, for a start. Don't tell me we could feed forty from this apartment.'

'Not at all – I could get a few lads from work to bring a buffet.'

'It would need to be piping hot.'

'Food warmers. Simple. Hot for three hours.'

'OK – what about a wedding cake?'

He didn't miss a beat. 'Greta in the café makes all the occasion cakes around here.'

Lydia had never laid eyes on Greta, never even seen the café open, although allegedly it did open. Tom's wife Marian had told her it served very good coffee.

'What about flowers?'

'Marian's best friend is a florist in the town.'

He had an answer for everything. Was nothing beyond possibility for him? 'Music?'

'Music would be the least of our worries. People would bring instruments.'

'What people?'

'The locals. They'd be coming to the afters. It's a thing here, a general invitation to the whole community to turn up after the wedding meal for cake and a singsong.'

She pictured the entire village population crowding into the dining room with fiddles and bodhráns and whatever else. Pure bedlam, it sounded like – but one way to get to know them.

'And before that we could ask a few of the pub buskers to come. They're very good, very versatile.'

Buskers. She was beginning to wonder if he could actually be serious – and more to the point, if she wanted him to be.

Married before the end of the year, when she'd assumed they'd have to wait till summer. They could sweep the bare floors, or throw down some rugs – and maybe the new windows would be in by then.

Firelight, candlelight: readymade romance right there. God, it might just work.

'Look at me,' she commanded, even though he already was. 'Are you serious? Tell the truth.'

'I am,' he said. 'I want to marry you, Lydia Foley. I'm tired of waiting.'

So was she. She thought of something else. 'What about a photographer?'

'Denny O'Neill,' he said promptly. 'He's a taxi driver, photography's just a hobby – but he's very good. Everyone gets him to do their weddings.'

Buskers for their band. A taxi driver taking photos. Catered food. An elusive café owner baking the cake.

'We could do it,' he said, watching her face.

'You think we could?'

'I know we could.'

There were other considerations. Her parents, and doubtless his too, would prefer a church wedding. Exactly how much notice did a priest need? And her parents would definitely have been planning a lavish reception – if she and Damien went ahead with this crazy idea, it was not going to go down well with them. It was a terrible time of year to be asking friends and family to drive across the country. And she didn't even have a wedding dress, for goodness' sake.

On the other hand, she was the one who'd said she didn't want to wait, and here he was, making it happen. Here he was, finding a solution so she didn't have to wait. And by the sound of it, this wedding would cost a fraction of any other one. She didn't imagine taxi-driving photographers were very expensive.

She'd have to put her job-hunting plans on hold till January. Not a big problem.

She looked at him. She saw the smile that had attracted her the night they'd met. She saw the man she loved deeply, the man she'd follow to the other side of the moon if he asked her. She took a breath. They could do this. Together, they could do anything. 'Let's go for it,' she said.

'Honest?'

'Honest.'

He raised his glass. 'To our wedding,' he said.

'To our wedding,' she echoed.

# 2

IN THE MORNING, THEY WERE WOKEN EARLY WITH the arrival of the workmen. *They start at eight,* Damien had warned, and there they were at eight sharp, slamming vehicle doors, calling to one another. Was one of them whistling?

'They're making it beautiful for us,' Damien murmured, his lips finding her neck, and she forgave them.

After breakfast he rang the local priest, who had space in his diary on the twenty-eighth of December, which was twenty-seven days away. When Damien told him they'd done a pre-marriage course in Dublin, he booked them in for a three o'clock ceremony, and suggested they drop around to see him at noon for a chat.

They had a wedding date. It was getting real. Lydia thought she'd better phone her mother, who didn't take the news well.

'The end of this *month*? Lydia, that's completely out of the question. Far too soon.'

'Mum, we've been engaged for more than eighteen months.'

'You know I don't mean that, Lydia. I mean there's no chance we can get anything organised in that time.'

'You and Dad won't have to organise a thing, Mum – it's going to be a very simple affair.' She crossed her fingers. 'We're getting married right here in the village church, and we'll have the reception in the house.'

'Which house?' By now her mother sounded totally bewildered.

'Our house, Mum. The one we bought. The one we're living in.'

'The big house? But you said it wouldn't be finished until the summer.'

'That's right. We've decided to go ahead anyway.'

'Oh Lydia, this is just nonsense. Apart from anything else, how on earth could it hold all your guests?'

'Well, that's the other thing.' She tightened her crossed fingers. 'The capacity of the dining room is forty, so it's going to be a small wedding, just close family and friends. And I know it's not finished, but we'll make it as pretty as we can. We'll manage.'

'Well, I don't know what to say. And I know your father is not going to be best pleased.'

'Mum, I know it's vastly different to the wedding you'd imagined for me, but this is about what *we* want. Can't you be happy for us? Who cares about a fancy wedding? We just want to be married.'

But her parents cared, she knew that. A fancy wedding was exactly what they wanted – or at least her mother did. She wanted to help with the preparations, and go shopping with Lydia for a dress, like mothers of the bride generally did. She also didn't want their friends looking down their noses, which some of them undoubtedly would. Was it cruel to subject her to all that?

'We'll have a big party down the line,' Lydia promised. 'Once the businesses are up and running we'll celebrate in style, but we have our hearts set on having our reception in Chance House, and we're more than ready to be married. It'll be different, but I think just as memorable.'

Her mother's sigh floated down the line. 'So your minds are made up on this?'

'They are.'

'In that case, we have no choice but to go along with it.'

'And hopefully you'll both enjoy it.' Silence. 'Bye, Mum. Talk soon.' No point in saying more, not at this stage. Let the news sink in.

'Well?' Damien asked, when Lydia returned to the kitchen.

'She wasn't thrilled, but she'll come round.'

'We'll make it up to her,' he said. 'We'll have them down for a weekend when the work is done. We'll give them the best room in the house, and wine and dine them, and they'll have to forgive us.'

They would. Wouldn't they?

At half past ten, the sound of power tools stopped.

'They're on a break,' Damien said. 'Now's our chance.'

They found Brendan talking with one of his team in the hall. He shook hands with Lydia. 'Welcome,' he said. 'I hope you'll be very happy here.'

'Thank you. The apartment is beautiful.'

They told him of their wedding plans. He received the news more calmly than Lydia's mother had.

'The twenty-eighth,' he said. 'The twenty-eighth of this month.' Doubt evident in every word, but no sign of any real concern. He'd stay calm in an emergency, Lydia thought.

'We're not expecting it to be finished,' they assured him. 'We'll take it as it is – as long as you're happy for people to be in and out.'

He nodded slowly. 'We can tidy it up, make sure it's safe for a bit of traffic. How many were you thinking?'

'Forty,' Damien said, 'including ourselves – but we'd have more coming after the meal, the usual cake-and-dancing crowd.'

Brendan gave a small laugh. 'You'll have plenty of body heat so. You think you can sort everything out in a few weeks?'

'No bother,' Damien said.

'Does your mother know about this?' his father asked.

'Not yet. I'll call over to her later.'

Lydia tried to imagine Kathleen's reaction, and failed. Maybe she'd be happy with a smaller celebration, and maybe the humble surroundings wouldn't bother her – who could tell? Not Lydia, who felt she didn't know the woman at all.

'You'll want to have a look around,' Brendan said to her.

'I'd love it.' Better not mention their visit last night, without his permission.

'Hang on,' he said, and returned with two yellow hard hats for them. 'Watch your step, especially on the stairs, no banister yet. And mind yourselves up there – it's still very rough.'

Lydia peeked again into the yoga studio, which now had a few big bags of something – sand? cement? – propped against one of the walls, and which was every bit as bright as she'd anticipated, even on this dull day. She couldn't wait for it to be functional.

The workmen were sitting on stools in the dining room around one of their heaters, a huddle of flasks at their feet. Damien introduced Lydia, and she shook hands with each of them.

'I can make teas and coffees for your breaks,' she said, but they assured her they were fine with the flasks. She saw an opened packet of Hobnobs on a stool and made a mental note to add biscuits to her shopping list. She could do that at least for them.

Behind the dining room was a large kitchen, with a larder and a cold room off it. Still a shell, bare of appliances and sinks, no shelving yet in the larder, the cold room waiting for a power supply, but Lydia saw the look on Damien's face as he scanned the room, and knew he was seeing it all kitted out and full of bustle, with him in the centre of it. Her in the studio, him in the kitchen.

The curved staircase, even without its banister, was graceful and lovely. 'Navy,' she said, looking up. 'A navy runner is what it needs.'

He shook his head. 'Dark red. Much more classy. Here,' he said, drawing a coin from his pocket. 'Toss you for it.'

'Heads,' she said, and tails came up.

'I won't gloat,' he said.

'Not half.'

What would happen, of course, was that Marian would be consulted and they'd abide by her decision, but let him enjoy his moment of triumph.

Making her way up, Lydia thought again of past residents, saw them sweeping down nightly in gowns and dinner jackets. Would they approve of her and Damien's changes now? Notwithstanding all the alterations, they were doing their best to remain faithful to the design of the old house, retaining and restoring where possible, availing themselves of reclaimed materials whenever they could, hanging on to the character and stately beauty of the building.

Upstairs, as Brendan had warned, was still very much a work in progress. The eight bedrooms had all been large enough to introduce ensuites, and the original bathroom was now a guest lounge, so everywhere was jutting pipework, and wheelbarrows piled with blocks, and barely-begun dividing walls – but when they negotiated their way past the jumble to one of the rear-facing windows, the view was everything Lydia had hoped for.

The wide splendour of the Atlantic was laid out before them, light playing on the water to make it dance and dazzle. 'Clare Island,' Damien said, indicating a landmass straight ahead. 'We can get a ferry out in the summer – and there's Achill to the north. I'll take you there too.'

It was an ever-shifting, mesmerising panorama. As Lydia feasted on it, the ambient sounds – a transistor radio playing tinny music somewhere, the men's voices below – fell away, and the same sense of peace descended that she remembered from the first day they'd seen it.

The garden was still pretty much as overgrown as she remembered, and there was no sign from where they stood of the little strip of sand that was their private beach. Even when everything was cleared it mightn't be visible from the house with the small drop down to it, but it was there, waiting for them.

'There's Gareth,' Damien said, and below them she saw a figure in navy overalls and a grey woolly cap that she'd missed. He was slashing at the weeds, next to a piled-up mountain of them.

They had a big house and a gardener – and you could say Damien was the cook. All they needed were a butler and a few maids, and maybe a footman or two, to make Lydia the lady of the manor.

'Hello there,' Gareth said, setting down his scythe and pulling off a glove to shake her hand. 'I was wondering when I'd get to meet the woman who'd put this mad idea into Damien's head.'

Lydia laughed. 'Is that what he told you?'

'It was.' He cocked his head at Damien. 'I hope you weren't lying to me now.'

His easy manner was instantly likeable. He was good-looking, broad-shouldered, tall and green-eyed, hair hidden under the hat, dark stubble on his jaw, a mole to the left of his nose. She asked how long he thought it would take to clear the garden, and he said it depended on the weather, and his day job.

'Web designer,' he said, when she asked. 'Couldn't be more different.'

'A nice combination. Indoor and outdoor work.'

'Give me the outdoor any day, but there isn't enough demand for a gardener around here to make a living from it, so I have to give priority to the other. All going well though, I should have this place ready for planting in the spring. Think about what you want in terms of beds and lawns and paths and whatever. You have a good acre and a half to play around with, so dream big.'

They were already dreaming big, she thought, about as big as they could go. 'Would you help us to plan a garden?' Neither she nor Damien had a clue.

'Sure, if you want me to – but do have a look online, plenty of ideas there.'

Her first house, her first garden – and presumably her last house and garden. Whatever happened here, however their fortunes went, she couldn't imagine them ever leaving Chance House.

And soon, her first and only wedding.

Just before noon they pulled up outside the priest's house.

'Phil,' he said, shaking Lydia's hand. 'Delighted to meet you, and looking forward to joining you in holy matrimony with this boyo.'

'You don't mind that I'm an outsider?'

'Well now,' he said, 'I thought you two were the new residents of Chance House. Did I get that wrong?'

'Only since yesterday.'

'Yesterday's good enough for me. I'm assuming you've been baptised into the one true faith?'

'Yes.'

'Ever been excommunicated?'

She laughed. 'No.'

'Any active marriages you've forgotten about?'

'None.'

'And you have your course done, so we're sorted.'

He didn't look like a priest. His hair was shaved too tightly for her to be sure of its colour, but she thought reddish brown. His skin was pale and lightly freckled, his eyes a deep blue. His jeans met a pair of hiking boots. A tattoo of ivy trailed from a sleeve on to the back of his hand.

He made coffee that smelt like toasted nuts. 'Try the ginger biscuits – home baked by a lovely parishioner. They're always trying to fatten me up.' He took one and dipped it into his cup. 'Lydia, I hear you're a yoga teacher.'

'I am.' She wondered how he felt about something that had originated in a different faith. 'I hope to run classes from the house when it's ready.'

'So I believe. You must let me know when you're advertising – I'll be happy to put a notice in the church porch.'

'That's very kind, thank you.' No objection then. She decided she liked him.

She might even start going to Mass again.

*

Bit by bit, their wedding plans took shape. Damien's brother Tom was to be best man. Tom and Marian's son Jack, recently turned five, would act as page boy, carrying the rings Lydia and Damien had bought in the town.

Brona, of course, would be bridesmaid. She professed herself charmed at the idea of this last-minute wedding, but Lydia wondered what her friend privately thought. Brona had married Shaun in a castle in the midlands, with around two hundred and fifty guests. The wedding had taken place over two days, and featured a household-name jazz band and a champagne brunch, and had to have cost a small, or not so small, fortune.

Kathleen had raised no objection to the unconventional wedding. Even though Lydia hadn't lured Damien to Dublin, she still felt the strain between herself and her almost-mother-in-law when they met, but on hearing their news Kathleen had simply said, *It's a bit different, but if that's what ye want, I suppose we'll go along with it*, and that had been that.

Damien didn't seem to have noticed his mother's coolness towards Lydia, and she felt to point it out would put him in the middle of the situation so she said nothing, and went on hoping that time would soften Kathleen's attitude.

As the days passed, having failed to find the café open anytime they tried, they drove out to the small farm owned by its proprietor. 'She keeps goats and ducks,' Damien told Lydia. 'She sells eggs and cheese in the café. Moved here from Germany years ago, been here as long as I can remember.'

The farmhouse kitchen was old and shabby and cluttered – yellowing newspapers piled on a wooden bench, a jumble of egg boxes on the table, threadbare towels draped on chair backs – but it was also warm, thanks to an enormous range that dominated the room.

Greta looked somewhere in her late fifties. Handsome, blue-eyed, high-cheekboned. Dark hair streaked with grey, its choppy cut making Lydia wonder if she'd done it herself. She wasn't exactly grim, but she wasn't given to smiling either.

'Yes,' she said. 'I will make a carrot cake for your wedding.' Taking reading glasses from her pocket, uncapping a fountain pen to write in a notebook she'd taken from a drawer. 'What date? How many people? One tier or more? Cream-cheese icing, or something else?'

All her questions were cake related. She didn't enquire about the venue, or ask whether they were having a church ceremony. She didn't offer congratulations. She told them to call for the cake the day before the wedding, and gave them a wedge of goat's cheese to take home, wrapped in greaseproof paper.

'If you like it, you can buy more in my café,' she said, meeting Lydia's gaze head on. It sounded like an order, and Lydia didn't dare ask what the café's opening hours actually were.

'She's very direct,' she said on the way home.

'Direct is the word. Does exactly what she pleases, but she's fair and honest. People have great time for her around here.'

'What about cake for the ones who come later?'

'That's being taken care of by our pastry chef.'

Denny the taxi driver agreed to act as photographer. 'He mightn't be able to come back to the house,' Damien reported. 'There may be an airport run – he's waiting for it to be confirmed. If it is, I'll have someone else lined up to take over.'

'Who?'

'Surprise.'

She suspected that meant he hadn't found a stand-in yet, but she let it go. Everyone would have phones. Plenty of photos would be taken, and some might even be worthy of an album. With every day that passed, she found herself more willing to go with the flow. As long as they were doing things differently, why not let everything be different?

The musicians were booked, a trio that played a regular Thursday night gig in the smaller of the village's two pubs. Marian sorted the flowers with her florist friend, and agreed to decorate the dining room on the morning of the wedding.

'Right up my alley,' she said. 'Susan will give me a hand – she's good at that kind of thing too.'

'Remind me who Susan is.' Lydia had heard the name, but couldn't remember who it belonged to.

'My boss. The school principal.'

Yes. Trestle tables and folding chairs.

Ten days before Christmas, Lydia went for a wash and blow dry at the village's tiny hair salon, feeling a stab of guilt. For the first time in years she wasn't using Caroline, her Dublin hairdresser. As she was paying – half the price of the salon where Caroline worked, and a nice blow dry – she asked the woman, who'd introduced herself as Marge, if she'd do her wedding day hair.

'I'm not wearing a veil, so I'll just need a nice updo, and my bridesmaid will want the same.' She hoped to God Brona would be happy with Marge.

'I'd be delighted,' Marge replied. 'Congratulations – we're all thrilled that Damien's getting married.'

'Thank you – and would you be able to come to us?'

'I would indeed. You'll be at Chance House?'

'That's right.'

She was getting used to how everyone around here knew who she was before she told them. They also knew where she came from, where she was living now, and the family she was marrying into. The woman behind the counter in the hardware shop knew, and so did the young girl in the chemist, and the man holding the lollipop stick outside the school.

Everywhere she went, she was introduced to herself: 'You're the yoga teacher from Dublin,' or 'You're Damien's fiancée from Dublin.' To all she was the newcomer from the big city, with different clothes and a different accent. She must stick out like a sore thumb.

She didn't mind. The friendliness she'd noticed from the start was everywhere. Everyone except Greta congratulated her on the upcoming wedding – it hadn't taken long for that news to spread – and all of them told her their names, and she promptly forgot them.

It was early days. It would take time to settle in. She did wonder if they'd be as welcoming if she wasn't marrying a local man. Damien seemed to know literally everyone, even the young kids. Would she ever feel as embedded in the community as he was, not having been born there? Again, time would tell.

Finally, all the wedding preparations were in place, apart from Lydia's dress. *I'll sort you out with something,* Marian had promised. *I've got lots of possibilities in my wardrobe.* Lydia had agreed, liking how it fit in with their unconventional theme, and how a borrowed dress would cut down further on the cost of the wedding – but the day before she was to be kitted out, she opened the apartment door to Marian and a woman she hadn't yet met.

'Hope you don't mind us showing up unannounced,' Marian said. 'This is Susan, the school principal.'

Marian's boss. She looked as likely a school principal as Father Phil did a priest. She was around Lydia's age, with a tangled mess of dark curly hair. Her lips were painted the same shade of orange as the stripes in the grey tunic Lydia could see through the gap of her opened coat. One nostril was pierced; a tiny blue stone winked there. She held a carrier bag.

'Come in,' Lydia told them. 'I was planning to drop into the school to thank you for the promise of tables and chairs.'

'You're very welcome. I love the sound of your wedding, so spontaneous. Mine took over a year to plan.'

They followed Lydia into the kitchen. 'Damien out?' Marian asked.

'Gone to work.'

'Just as well.' Susan set her bag on the table. 'I hear you're in need of a dress.'

'I told her I was dressing you,' Marian said, 'but she wanted to show you something.'

Susan slid the bag across the table to Lydia. 'Just have a look. You mustn't feel under pressure.'

'Wow, that's . . . very kind of you.' Lydia stepped forward, terrified it wouldn't be to her taste, and she might offend by refusing it – or worse, feel she had to wear it.

She reached in and lifted it out and held it up.

'It's raw silk,' Susan said. 'I came across it in a boutique in Lanzarote over the summer. I didn't have any occasion in mind when I bought it, but I couldn't resist it. I haven't worn it yet, but I'm happy to let you be the first wearer, if you like it.'

'I told her you were about the same size,' Marian added.

It was lilac. Three-quarter sleeves, with a fitted top and a gently flared skirt. Its neck was scooped, with a small V in the centre.

'Side slit,' Susan said, 'and look.' She turned it around and Lydia saw the line of tiny covered buttons travelling all the way down the back. 'They're just decorative – there's a concealed zip.'

Lydia examined it silently. The fabric was nubby and soft. It was light as a feather. She held it against her and it fell to a few inches above her ankles. She'd be frozen solid in it.

She loved it. She loved everything about it. Lilac was one of her favourite shades.

'Could I try it on?'

'Sure.'

In the bedroom she hurriedly shed her clothes and stepped carefully into the dress. The zip went up easily. She stood before the full-length mirror on the wardrobe door and looked at her reflection, blinking back tears that were suddenly there. And when she returned to the kitchen, feet bare, both women smiled.

'Ah look. It's perfect on you,' Susan said.

'And I have a gorgeous cherry-red wrap to keep you warm,' Marian said. 'The colours would be wonderful together.'

And just like that, Lydia was ready to get married.

# 3

CUPPING THE MUG OF HOT WATER THAT SHE BEGAN every day with, she stood in her dressing gown at the kitchen window as morning crept slowly into the sky and thought, This is my wedding day.

She recalled her friends' big weddings, all along the same lines as Brona's. Every bride in a designer dress with all the trimmings, vintage cars ferrying them to the church, masses of guests, receptions in hotels with at least four stars, honeymoons somewhere exotic, like Antigua or Bali.

Lydia loved that she was being different. She was a trendsetter – not that any of her Dublin gang would have wanted to set this particular trend. *Exciting*, they'd said when she'd told them of her and Damien's plan. *Adventurous*, they'd said. *Daring*, they'd said – but she knew none of them would have dreamt of doing the same.

*I wish I could invite you all*, she'd told them, and they'd assured her they were happy to wait for the big summer party. Brona was here now of course, and three other friends, along with partners. They would be enough today.

As the light grew brighter she turned her attention to the view beyond the kitchen windows. Lots still to do out there, but thanks largely to Gareth the bulk of the vegetation was gone, leaving in its wake yellowed clumps of grass pockmarked with the stumpy remains of hacked-away briars, and many stones. Lydia and Damien were pitching in when they could, filling wheelbarrows and trundling them around to a trailer at the front, their wellingtons pressed into service again, gloves from Gareth protecting hands from blisters.

She imagined how it would look in another few months, when the earth would be smooth and free of debris, and the camomile lawn they'd decided on would be growing in, beyond the reclaimed slab patio that was also planned.

*Don't make your planting too tame,* Gareth had advised. *A bit of unruliness is good,* so after much online trawling for ideas they were going to sow lots of bee-friendly wildflowers in places where they could spread in years to come, and swathes of coastal grasses, and climbers for some unruly rambling: roses, sweet peas and honeysuckle. They were planting lupins and lavender and anemones, and a herb garden would be positioned outside the restaurant kitchen. A greenhouse or polytunnel would follow later, so Damien could grow his own vegetables and salads.

The rusted railing at the end of the garden would be replaced with a low hedge, and Brendan was going to install new wooden steps to the beach in place of the old rickety ones.

They already had a shed, sort of. Roughly a third of the way down the garden, Gareth had unearthed the remains of an old stone one, and they'd asked a local mason to restore it in the new year.

Starting at the patio, a slate walkway would wind its slow way down to the sea, branching off to access all the different areas, and widening out to form seating places here and there.

Lydia sighed happily, looking forward to seeing it all unfold in the months that followed. In the meantime, she had a wedding to prepare for, starting with morning yoga to centre her.

She slipped into leggings and T-shirt, unrolled her mat in the sitting room and went through her forty-minute routine. She hadn't missed a morning since moving here, couldn't imagine starting her day without it.

As she rolled up her mat afterwards she wondered how her various guests were faring in their accommodation. The family members – parents, two aunts and their husbands, one uncle and his wife, a grandmother from each side and one grandfather – were staying in a hotel in the town, and her Dublin friends had been booked into an Airbnb house on the edge of the village that Marian had recommended.

Last evening, the parents of the bride and groom had finally met, at a dinner Marian and Tom had hosted. Lydia had been a little apprehensive in advance of the meal, unsure of how the older couples would get along with so little in common, but to her relief the meal had passed off fairly smoothly – mainly, and surprisingly, thanks to Brendan.

At the start he'd been his usual quiet self, content to leave the conversation to others – but once the talk turned to the renovations he'd become almost animated, describing the challenges of marrying period features with modern conveniences, and the satisfaction of seeing the old house coming back to life. Lydia could see his genuine passion as he spoke, and she was glad the house was in the hands of someone who really cared about it.

*Did you know the previous owner?* Lydia's father had enquired, and Brendan had spoken of Lawrence Chance, the last direct descendant of the family who had inhabited the house for six generations.

*He was a walker, out every day, rain or shine, but never in the direction of the village. Had a little dog that was always with him, but then it disappeared. Must have died. Remember the little dog, Kathleen?*

*I do.*

*He had an arrangement with Paudie O'Connor in the supermarket – a grandfather of the man who owns it now – to have his groceries delivered every week. This would have been before the vans that deliver now. And a rector, or a vicar, I don't know which, would drop in on him every couple of weeks from the Church of Ireland in the town. That was about it, wasn't it, Kathleen? He wasn't one for visitors.*

*No, he was not.*

She hadn't spoken much throughout the evening. She'd been perfectly civil to Lydia's parents but she'd asked them no questions, none at all. When Lydia's mother had said brightly that tomorrow would be a big day – in fairness, both her parents were rising to the occasion – Kathleen had agreed, civilly, that it would, but her face had taken on an expression that was halfway between a smile and a grimace.

After dinner, Lydia had said goodnight to Damien. He was spending his last night as a single man at his parents' house, keeping with tradition, and Lydia was being ferried back to Chance House by her parents.

*Next time we meet,* he'd said, *I'll be at the altar trying not to have a heart attack, and you'll be walking up the aisle looking beautiful.*

He'd kissed the ends of her fingers in turn. *Thank you for choosing me. Love you for always, Lydia Foley.*

*Love you, Damien Cotter. Sleep tight.*

*How do you get on with Kathleen?* Lydia's mother had asked her in the car.

*We don't have much to do with one another*, Lydia had answered truthfully. *I think it's a case of her not wanting to let Damien go to any other woman.*

*Oh dear – but I'm sure she'll change her tune once children come along.*

Lydia wished she could be as sure.

The doorbell rang, startling her out of her reverie. She pulled on her dressing gown over her yoga clothes, and the cold air hit her as soon as she opened the door.

'Morning,' the man said. 'I'm Susan's brother. She asked me to drop in some furniture. Hope I didn't come too early.'

'No, you're fine, thank you.' His eyes were what she noticed, a black rim surrounding the blue irises. Striking. His dark hair had the same messy quality as his sister's. Maybe they were non-identical twins. He wore a warm-looking black jacket. 'I'm Lydia.'

'Andrew.' He put out a hand. 'Congratulations, by the way.'

'Thanks.' She was conscious of her appearance: tousled hair, morning face, tatty dressing gown, ancient slippers. Far cry from a bride. 'I'll open the main door for you.'

His white van had no lettering on it to give her a clue as to what he did. He slid back its side door, and she glimpsed the folded tables and stacked chairs within. 'Let me help,' she said, feeling obliged to offer, but to her relief he told her no need, he'd manage.

She brought him through and thanked him again. The workmen had cleared the hall of clutter and swept the floor. It made little difference: it was still a bare, unpainted space, but she was grateful they'd made the effort. Hopefully her guests wouldn't take too much notice as they made their way into the dining room, which should look halfway decent once Susan and Marian had dressed it up.

They arrived shortly after he'd left, carrying large boxes that Lydia was forbidden to look into. They refused the offer of coffee – 'We'll have something stronger later' – and vanished into the main house just as the door of the spare bedroom opened.

'I can't believe I slept through half your wedding morning,' Brona said, smothering a yawn. They'd picked her up at the Airbnb on the way back to Chance House the previous evening. 'You should have woken me. Who was that just now?'

Lydia told her. 'You'll meet them when they've finished.'

'Are you excited?'

'Of course I am, full of butterflies.'

'What time is the hairdresser coming?'

'Around one. We've piles of time.'

'Have you eaten?'

'Not yet. I waited for you.'

'Good. I'll fix us something. You go and get started.'

After a shower, Lydia placed the shoes she planned to wear on the floor by the bed. She opened the wardrobe and lifted out the lilac dress and hung it on the back of the door. She eased up the stockings she'd bought online, splashing out a little on them since she'd saved on the dress. She took the blue garter Brona had given her last night and slid it up her right leg. Shoes, stockings, dress, garter. Something old, something new, something borrowed, something blue.

'Breakfast!' Brona called, and Lydia got back into her dressing gown and slippers, and found a poached egg waiting on a toasted slice of Damien's sourdough.

'This is it,' Brona said. 'No more single life for you after today.'

'Single life's overrated.' Lydia poked at her egg with a fork, letting the yolk ooze onto the toast. 'I can't wait to be married.'

'Can I have a sneak peek at the mansion before the wedding?'

'I wasn't going to let anyone see it yet. It's still such a mess. I want to wait till it's all done before showing it off.'

'But I'm not just anyone, and I promise I won't tell.'

Lydia considered. 'I'll show you one thing,' she said. 'No, two things.'

When they'd finished eating she brought her into the yoga studio – floor down now, radiators installed but not connected, walls still unpainted – and Brona shook her head in wonderment. 'This is marvellous, Liddy. Your own studio. I'm so happy for you.'

'I know. I can hardly believe it.'

'What's the other thing I'm allowed to see?'

'It's outside. You'll need your coat.'

She brought her round the back and along the planks Gareth had put down to give access to the bottom of the garden. At the sight of the little cove, Brona gave a surprised cry.

'You told me about this – I'd forgotten. Is this the place Damien popped the question?'

'Yes, right there.'

'Ah, Liddy. Promise me we can drink wine down there when I visit.'

'Every night, winter or summer.'

They were on fresh coffees when Marian and Susan reappeared. Lydia made the introductions. 'My oldest friend,' she told them.

'Sorry you're losing her to the west,' Marian said to Brona.

Brona made a face. 'Me too. As if there weren't enough eligible Dubs, she has to fall for a culchie.'

'They're just better all round,' Susan said. 'Lydia, Damien rang Andrew last night to ask him to take the reception photos – turns out Denny's doing that airport run, so he'll have to leave after the church. Maybe Andrew told you when he brought the furniture.'

'No, he said nothing.'

'He's good,' Marian said, seeing the slight fall in her smile. 'He's done lots of other weddings.'

'Who are we talking about?' Brona asked.

'My brother,' Susan told her. 'He's the local butcher.'

Brona smiled. 'Wow. You certainly like to do things differently here.'

'Yes, we do. You're not in Dublin now.'

It was lightly said, but Lydia saw Brona's smile stiffen a little.

'Champagne,' she said, reaching swiftly into the fridge to pull out the bottle Damien had given her yesterday. 'I'm under orders from my future husband to open this.' Earlier than she'd planned, but so what? It was her wedding day.

The cork was popped, glasses filled. 'To the bride and groom,' Brona said, raising her glass.

'To a long and happy marriage,' Marian said.

'To Chance House, and all who sail in her,' Susan said.

The day moved on. Marge appeared with her bag of hairdressing supplies. Marian's florist friend brought the bridal bouquet – a gorgeous mix of deep red rosebuds, gypsophila, mistletoe, berried holly and trailing ivy. Denny arrived with two cameras – 'Colour and black and white, so you'll have a choice.'

After Marge had styled their hair, Lydia and Brona did each

other's faces – no make-up artist to be had in the village – and got into their finery. Brona had brought a dress in duck egg blue that she already owned, to tone in with Lydia's lilac.

'Lovely,' Susan said when they reappeared.

'Beautiful,' Marian said.

'Picture perfect,' Denny said, snapping with his cameras.

Lydia's parents were the last to arrive, bearing another bottle of champagne. Her mother was immaculately dressed, pale pink with navy piping. Very Chanel. Chances were it *was* Chanel.

Lydia felt her excitement mounting. In a couple of hours she would be Mrs Lydia Cotter. She'd toyed with keeping her maiden name, like some of her friends had done, but after thirty-two years she was tired of Lydia Foley.

Her phone pinged. Damien.

*Good morning. Hope you're feeling bridal. Just getting into the good suit here. x*

She smiled.

*We're drinking champagne. Not sure I'll make it to the church actually. Would you mind?*

Quick as a flash, he came back. *Don't make me come and get you. You've met your match, lady.*

She remembered him scooping her up and carrying her over the apartment threshold the day they'd moved in – had it really been only a month ago? *I need the practice*, he'd said. Today would be the real thing, no more practising.

*I'll be there. x*

She sipped champagne and thought of him.

*

At a few minutes past three, she climbed into her father's car with Brona, her mother having already left with Marian. Denny had also gone ahead, to capture their arrival at the church. Even though her father turned up the heat fully Lydia was very glad of Marian's red wool wrap. Beside her, Brona put an arm around her. 'Have a ball, Liddy,' she whispered. 'You look wonderful, and this is your day – enjoy it.'

'I intend to – and you too. Thanks for being here.'

'Where else would I be?'

Denny was waiting for them outside the church. She stepped from the car, trying not to hunch in the intense cold as he started snapping. Cars were parked around the grounds in the haphazard way she'd seen on Sunday at Mass times, but this was Thursday. Odd, she thought – until fiddles started up inside with their version of 'Here Comes the Bride', and she entered the church on her father's arm, and saw that the place was packed.

Some she knew – Gareth, Marge, Susan, Greta. Other faces she recognised – the woman from the hardware store, the girl from the chemist – but there were a lot she didn't. They were predominantly female, some in hats, all beaming at her as she made her way up the aisle – and there at the altar was Damien, his smile making her melt as it always did.

Her father kissed her cheek and moved away as she went to stand beside her groom. 'You look wonderful,' Damien murmured, taking her cold hand. How were his always warm?

Father Phil, resplendent in white and gold, smiled as they turned to face him. Before beginning the ceremony he welcomed Lydia to the village, and wished her and Damien success with their new venture and promised that everyone would support them.

'Just as they've turned out today,' he said, gesturing towards the congregation, 'to witness the start of your journey together as husband and wife, and to wish you both long life and happiness in Chance House. As I found out on my own arrival here eight years ago, this is a place where community is strong, where newcomers are welcomed, and connections forged are never broken.'

It felt surreal. Most of them were still strangers to her – and while she was touched by their presence, she couldn't help suspecting that they were here for Damien more than for her. Or maybe it was just another village tradition, everyone piling into the church, no matter who was getting married.

The ceremony began. When invited by Father Phil, her mother read from the Book of Genesis, and her friends lined up for Prayers of the Faithful. At the vows, Lydia's voice wobbled when she promised to love Damien for richer or poorer, in sickness and in health. 'Till death us do part,' she repeated after Father Phil.

She'd never liked that phrase, the depressing reminder of what must come one day, but they could hardly have left it out, being part of the familiar profession.

Their little page boy, about to become her nephew by marriage, thrust out his cushion with the rings when prompted, before scrambling back to the safety of his mother's arms. 'With this ring I thee wed,' bride and groom recited in turn. A beaming Father Phil declared them husband and wife, and informed them that they might now kiss, so they did, accompanied by an enthusiastic round of applause.

Directly afterwards, Kathleen and Brendan left their pew and brought the offertory gifts to the altar. *We'd prefer that*, Brendan had told Damien. *Neither of us would be comfortable doing a reading or that.* Not ones for the limelight, despite being among people they'd known all their lives. Lydia was happy they were participating, even in this small way.

As the older couple turned from the altar, Kathleen caught Lydia's eye and gave a small nod, accompanied by the ghost of a smile. She was in navy, with newly set hair. Lydia's mother-in-law, for better or worse.

After the ceremony they followed the priest into the sacristy to sign the register, and when they emerged the crowd had melted away, leaving just their guests.

Everyone embraced the new Mrs Cotter, even Kathleen. 'Congratulations,' she said, her hug brief, and Lydia tried to quash the thought that she'd had to do it, for form's sake. She'd done it, and that was what mattered.

'Anyone who's not working comes to the church for weddings,' Marian told her, as Denny organised photos on the steps. 'They love a good walk up the aisle. Jack, stop making faces – give Denny your best smile.'

'Snow,' Jack said, gazing at the sky, and everyone looked up to see a few tiny flakes drifting in the air.

Damien tightened his hold on Lydia. 'Are you frozen, Mrs Cotter?'

'I am completely frozen, Mr Cotter. I hope we're going back to a warm house.'

'We are, all sorted. The boys texted.' His fellow chefs, who were bringing the food, had been charged with lighting the fire and switching on the heaters on their arrival at the house.

'Thank God for that.'

Denny rounded them up again. 'Last time,' he promised, 'everyone in,' and they huddled together on the steps and smiled before scattering gratefully to cars and driving in convoy to the house, the newlyweds leading the way.

Someone, probably Marian, had dressed Damien's car in white ribbons. Drivers coming towards them on the way to Chance House beeped and flashed in celebration. When he pulled up on the lane, Lydia looked at him. 'You're not driving in?'

'I thought it would be more ceremonial if we walked.'

She laughed. 'You're crazy,' but she got out, tightening her wrap around her. The other cars parked behind them and everyone followed. As they turned into the driveway Lydia saw a strip of red carpet laid down, its end tucked into the gravel, running from where they stood all the way to the front door.

She looked at Damien.

'Dad came across it somewhere,' he said, 'probably some old hotel. He thought you might like it.'

Lydia turned and found Brendan and hugged him, and everyone paraded, laughing, to the door, where Damien lifted his bride into his arms and carried her over the threshold. He whisked her right through the hall, red carpet continuing, and didn't release her until they reached the dining room.

The heat welcomed them as they entered. The fire was blazing behind a guard, and several heaters were positioned around the room. The borrowed tables had been arranged in a T-shape and covered with thick white cloths that dropped to the floor, and decorated with swathes of ivy twined with gold tinsel.

In each of the three bay windows hurricane lamps, surrounded by more tinsel, held fat white candles. There were strings of lights draped along the walls, and crossing the ceiling. Tables at the side, manned by Damien's colleagues, held covered dishes sitting on food warmers. With the light almost gone outside, the room was transforming into something cosy and magical.

The chefs offered steaming glasses of mulled wine. The musicians were already playing in their corner, two men and a woman with a fiddle, a tin whistle and a concertina, and more instruments grouped beside them.

Greta's carrot cake sat on another table, its sides wrapped in a silver band and with a little bride and groom on top. Andrew the butcher photographer, poised with his camera, started moving around as soon as they arrived. Not putting anyone into groups, content to capture them as they were.

It was perfect. It was Lydia's day – their day – and so far it was completely perfect. She couldn't keep the smile off her face. 'Isn't this lovely?' her mother said. 'They've made it look really pretty,' and Lydia squeezed her arm in wordless gratitude.

They took their seats. The food was eaten, the wine drunk, the fire topped up by Andrew, who stayed in the background with his camera. Had he eaten anything? Lydia slipped from her chair.

'I'm fine,' he said, but she was having none of it. She asked one of the chefs to fill him a plate, and directed him to the table at the side where the musicians were eating.

'It's my wedding day,' she said. 'I'm in charge. Thank you for stepping in and doing the photos.' He lowered his camera and gave in.

The speeches – Tom, Damien, her father – were mercifully short, and laughter rang out in happy bursts. When her father resumed his seat she heard the introductory chords of their chosen first dance emerging from the wireless speakers Gareth had organised.

'We're on,' Damien said, and led her to the floor. They moved in perfect sync, drawing apart and coming together as if they'd been born knowing the steps, oblivious to the couples who joined them halfway through the song. As the music faded, their feet stilled but they remained pressed close, rocking gently.

'My love,' her new husband whispered.

Soon after the start of the dancing, the villagers began arriving. Lydia wondered if they'd been alerted by text that the time was right. They brought unexpected wrapped gifts that they presented to Damien and Lydia, and bottles they opened, and musical instruments they brought to the corner where the other musicians sat.

The music swelled in volume, the floor filled with dancers, and the room grew so warm that heaters were switched off and wheeled away.

Susan appeared. 'No getting away from me,' she said. 'The dress looks wonderful on you – I'm so happy its first outing was up the aisle. Marian says you're only doing a short honeymoon.'

'We're heading to Connemara, just for the weekend.'

'Oh, good – you'll be back in time for my birthday hooley: I'll hit thirty on January the third.'

'I'd love it, thanks a million.' December had been largely taken up with wedding preparations, but once they got back from honeymoon Lydia would be on a dual mission, to find a job and get to know people, and a party was the perfect way to start. 'Where are you holding it?'

'At home. I'm on the far side of the village, just half a mile out.'

'Great. Looking forward to it.'

'Tell Damien it's women only – I had to put some limit on the numbers – so he can come and collect you.'

'He'll probably be working, so he could stop in on his way home, if that's not too late. Around eleven?'

'Not too late at all.'

Gareth materialised from the crowd. 'Fair play,' he said. 'I can tell you now that I had my doubts about this venue, but you two pulled it off. If I ever get married, I'll know where to come.'

To Lydia's surprise, Greta also appeared. 'You liked my cake?' she asked, and Lydia told her that she had.

'It's all gone, that's how popular it was, but Damien's colleagues brought more – can I get you some?'

'You cannot. I shall do it myself.'

Lydia watched her making her way through the crowd. There was a woman who knew her mind.

Both sets of in-laws left around the same time, while the celebrations were still in full swing. Lydia walked her parents out to the hall, and they told her that for a wedding present they were giving her and Damien a proper honeymoon. 'We'll cover the cost, wherever you decide to go,' her father said, 'whenever the time is right.'

'Thank you,' she told them. 'Damien will be thrilled.' They were finally starting to believe in the future Lydia and Damien were mapping out, and it felt wonderful.

The celebrations continued. At some stage Tom sang a Christy Moore song, everyone joining in the chorus. A medley of traditional tunes from the musicians led to an impromptu Irish dancing session, nobody having much idea of steps but delivering the performances with great gusto. More singing, more dancing, until finally people ran out of energy and began to gather coats and instruments.

'Don't clean up,' Marian ordered, blowing out candles. 'We'll come tomorrow.'

'Brilliant night,' Susan said. 'You should get married more often.'

'Well,' Damien said, as they stood at the front door waving off the last departures, flakes of snow still drifting, not enough to cover the ground, 'were you happy with that?'

'Very. Come on,' she said, shivering. 'I need central heating – and more cake.'

The leftover food had already been packed neatly into foil containers. They stowed everything in the freezer before bringing tea and cake to bed.

She told him of her parents' gift of a honeymoon. 'Where will we go?'

He thought. 'I've always wanted to see the Giant's Causeway.'

She laughed. 'Seriously? We could go anywhere in the world – and you choose to stay in Ireland?'

'Why not? Why travel if what you want is right here?'

'Let's do both,' she said. 'Let's start at the Giant's Causeway and then fly off to somewhere exotic. I want to see the world with you.'

'Where you lead, I'll always follow,' he promised.

And on that note they set cups and plates on the bedside locker and turned off the lights, and set about consummating their marriage.

# 4

NEXT MORNING, AS THEY WERE PACKING FOR THEIR Connemara weekend, it started to snow in earnest, huge flakes whirling and tumbling to the ground. By lunchtime every surface was white, and radio reports were predicting several more inches before nightfall.

They had no option but to put off the trip, at least until they saw what the following day looked like. Lydia phoned all her wedding guests in turn, to find everyone had either landed home in Dublin or was well on the way, the snow having trailed them across the country.

'Hunker down,' Brona told them. 'This is not stopping anytime soon. Stay in your cosy apartment and wait for another long weekend. I'll talk to you before the new year.' It was two days away.

The following morning the entire country was blanketed, forcing businesses to close, making roads and pathways treacherous, leaving remote rural dwellers trapped at home and causing the cancellation of many social gatherings. Cut off from the rest of the world, Lydia thought. Marooned with her new husband. It was like the snow was falling especially for them.

At lunchtime on New Year's Eve, she rang Brona. 'It's a winter wonderland here,' she said. 'We're tempted to build a snowman, but it's too cosy inside. Damien has to pile on layers just to refill the fuel basket and top up the bird feeders.'

'You were lucky,' Brona said, 'getting the wedding in just before. I presume he's not working tonight.'

'He was supposed to be, but the restaurant is closed, not that he'd have been able to get into the town, even if it was open – the roads are completely blocked. We're going to have a nice dinner and champagne by the fire.'

'Same here. Happy New Year, Liddy.'

'Happy New Year, Bro. I'll think of you at midnight.'

'I doubt it – you'll be too busy canoodling.'

'I fear you may be right. Love to Shaun.'

And a few hours later, one year ended and another began, as snowflakes continued to drift dreamily earthwards.

The thaw finally set in on the third day of January, six days after the wedding. By lunchtime snow had turned to slush, causing everything outside to drip, bringing drivers cautiously back into their cars, amid warnings of icy conditions prevailing in sheltered areas and on minor roads.

In the afternoon Lydia rang Susan.

'Happy New Year,' Susan said. 'Did you survive your first week of wedded bliss? Presume your cute little honeymoon didn't happen.'

'No – but it was lovely to be marooned here. We lit the fire and watched black and white films, and ate too much. Happy New Year to you – and happy birthday. Is your party still on tonight?'

'It sure is – I hope you're still coming.'

'I am. Tom's going to drop myself and Marian over, and Damien will pick us up.'

'Lovely. See you then.'

Damien hugged her as he left for work. 'No chatting anyone up at Susan's.'

'We'll see. I need to keep you on your toes. Love you.'

'Love you.'

Later, waiting for Marian and Tom, she flicked on the news and caught the Lotto results. *We didn't win the Lotto again*, she texted Damien. A joke: they never bought tickets.

His response was a sad face emoji. Busy.

The roads were clear, but snow was still lodged in the hedgerows. Susan lived at the end of a short cul-de-sac of detached redbrick houses. *Happy 21st Birthday*, a banner above the front door proclaimed, next to a big bunch of balloons.

'All the hardware had to offer,' Susan told them cheerily when she answered their knock, glass in hand. 'A girl can dream. Come on in, warm up. Thanks for chauffeuring, Tom.'

The room was open plan, all the living spaces in one. People milled about, none of whom Lydia recognised apart from Andrew, in conversation by the kitchen island with the only other man. A Hosier song was playing. Without Damien by her side, she was glad to have Marian there.

'Happy birthday,' she told Susan. 'I brought you wine – all I had at my disposal with the snow, I'm afraid.'

'No need at all, and thank you. Get a drink from Owen – he and Andrew are bartending.'

Owen turned out to be Susan's husband. Crew-cut blond hair, outdoorsy complexion, shorter than his brother-in-law.

'Good to meet you,' he told Lydia. 'We were a bit worried when we heard you were from Dublin – we have to be careful who we let in.'

She laughed. He sounded as gregarious as Susan. 'I'll try not to disappoint.'

'You're already disappointing us,' he said. 'We hear you're vegetarian. That didn't go down well with the butcher, let me tell you.' Shooting Andrew a glance.

'Who did you hear it from?'

'Susan. She tells me everything I need to know. Is it true?'

'I'm afraid so.'

'Pay that man no heed,' Andrew said. 'My sister is a bad influence on him. What are you drinking?'

'Red wine, thanks, and the same for Marian.' Again she noticed the dark rim around the irises. 'You're not twins, are you?' she asked him. 'You and Susan?' That would make it his birthday too.

He shook his head as he filled two glasses. 'I'm older and wiser. Your wedding snaps are ready, by the way. I was thinking of calling by Chance House tomorrow to collect the school furniture, if it suited. I could bring the snaps. It would be evening, after work.'

The furniture had sat in the dining room since the wedding. Over the snow days that had followed, she and Damien had taken down the lights, stripped the tables and boxed everything up again. They'd folded the furniture and stacked it by the wall, ready for collection. She'd been hoping Andrew would show up before the workmen returned.

'That would be great, thanks. I'm sorry Damien doesn't have the wherewithal to return it to the school.'

'It's no bother with the van.'

'About this vegetarianism,' Owen put in. 'We'll have to arrange an intervention. I'd say Damien will help – and you'll come along, Andrew.'

'Wouldn't miss it,' he said, deadpan.

'I didn't know,' she said, 'that only meat-eaters are allowed to live here. Damien never mentioned it.'

Owen looked shocked. 'We'll have to have a word with him too so. He's forgetting the rules.'

'Come away from this nonsense,' Marian said, drawing Lydia across to a group and introducing her – and right away she became the centre of attention. She was the unknown quantity, and everyone wanted to find out more.

'Tell us how you planned a wedding in a few weeks.'

'It's so great you're doing up Chance House. When will it be ready?'

'Is it true you'll be teaching yoga there?'

'Do you miss Dublin?'

'How did you get into yoga?'

'Where did you and Damien meet?'

Every so often her wine glass was topped up, either by Andrew or Owen. Slices of pizza appeared, and she avoided the pepperoni and ham and stuck to the margherita. When the pizzas were gone, a giant chocolate cake was produced. Lydia joined in the 'Happy Birthday' chorus, Susan blew out the candles, and slices were passed around.

She'd forgotten the fun of a house party, couldn't remember the last time she'd been at one. She felt buoyed up, optimistic about the future. It looked like it would be easy after all to create a new band of friends here – not that any of them would ever replace

Brona, or the rest of her Dublin crew, but it would be good to feel a sense of belonging in her new neighbourhood.

When there was a break in the music she crossed to the kitchen sink and filled her empty wine glass with water. She didn't want a fuzzy head next day, not when she and Damien had planned to celebrate their one-week anniversary with a drive up the coast for lunch at a remote but very popular restaurant.

As she set down her glass she smothered a yawn and checked her watch – and was amazed to see that it was past half eleven, a lot later than she'd expected him to show up.

She rummaged in her bag for her phone – should have checked it sooner. He'd probably left a message telling her he was delayed – but there was no message. Strange.

He was taking his time on the roads, watching out for icy patches, being careful – but all the same she felt uneasy. It wasn't like him not to let her know.

She stepped from the room to the hall where it was quieter. She tried his number and listened to his phone ringing out. Where was he?

Just then she heard a toilet flushing and Marian emerged from the bathroom, pink-faced and happy. 'He's fine, I'm sure,' she said, when Lydia told her. 'He might have been delayed at work. He'll have an explanation when he arrives' – but the knot of dread was tightening inside Lydia.

The doorbell rang, startling them. Marian reached across and opened it – and they saw Tom standing there, a figure in a high-vis jacket a little way behind him.

Something was wrong with Tom's face. The colour was gone from it, and he was blinking too quickly, his mouth slack.

'Tom?' Marian said quickly. 'Is Jack OK?'

He seemed not to hear her. He looked instead at Lydia. He moved his mouth but nothing came out.

'Damien?' she asked, her voice sounding too high, sounding like someone else's, her insides dissolving. 'It's not Damien, is it?'

He didn't answer. He didn't need to. She felt her heart give a painful leap, and another. She began to shake, her hands suddenly icy. 'No,' she said, in the same unfamiliar voice. 'No, no, no, no, no,' reaching blindly for Marian as her legs threatened to give way, as the blood rushed from her head, as the guard behind Tom hurried past him to grab her before she hit the floor.

# 5

IT WAS EARLY WHEN SHE ENTERED THE ROOM, NIGHT not quite folded up and put away. She closed the door with a soft click and leant against it, waiting for her eyes to adjust, the studio lit only by the dawn sky that was casting a pale luminescence through the big end window, lending the place a ghostly quality.

At length she slipped her feet out of her slippers and padded past the large mirrors to the far end of the room, bare toes curling against the chill of the floor. The air was frigid too, her breath coming out like fog as she unrolled her mat in front of the big window.

She planted her feet hip width apart on the rubber, arms resting by her sides. For a scatter of seconds she just stood, her gaze directed outwards as she began to deepen her breathing, skin prickling with goosebumps.

She welcomed the cold. It made her feel something.

The trees that bordered the garden were jagged and black against the first grey fingers of light in the sky. Through a cracked-open side window came the familiar chirrups and cheeps of the robins and blue tits and thrushes and sparrows, the early risers that populated the trees.

The sky continued to lighten. Still standing at the top of her mat, she dropped her shoulders, lifted her ribcage, tightened her abdomen, tucked in her pelvis. Her adjustments automatic, born of long practice and many hours spent on the same mat she stood on now.

When the cold began to take feeling from her toes she swept her arms above her head on an inhale. Her palms came together as she curved into a gentle back bend. On an exhale she folded forward, feeling the familiar sweet release in her lower back as her hands found the mat. She inhaled and rose to a halfway lift, neck long, back straight. She exhaled and folded again. She continued with the rest of the sun salutation, taking three long breaths in downward-facing dog, feeling the peace beginning to settle over her.

She pulled off a sweatshirt and cycled through several more salutations before moving on to the warrior poses, following them with a series of hip-openers, inhaling, exhaling, her heart pumping now, the cold forgotten as she gathered momentum.

More poses followed, chair, bridge, cat and cow, fish, bow, camel, plank, locust, dancer, plough, flowing from one to the next, not allowing herself to stop until finally, spent, she came to a panting halt. She pulled on the outer layer she'd removed earlier. She rolled on to her back and surrendered into her final relaxation, while beyond the window the sky shuffled off the last of the night. Only here, on this mat, could she calm her mind now. Only yoga was keeping her from shattering into a million pieces.

Not ice that had caused his car to swerve across the road and ram into the tree at the other side, halfway between the village and Susan's house. No ice there, not that evening. Possibly an animal, she was told, a fox or a badger appearing suddenly in front of him, causing him to veer away in an effort to avoid it.

Speed may have been a factor, they said, going too fast to correct the manoeuvre before hitting the tree. Tyres probably not helping either, treads worn, no grip when it was needed. *I should replace those tyres*, she remembered him remarking a few days before Christmas, but he hadn't replaced them.

Died instantly, they said. As if that was supposed to comfort her. Three weeks without him.

She got to her feet and rolled up her mat and left the studio. Back in the apartment she filled a bath. She undressed and climbed in, welcoming the warmth that began to spread through her body as she stretched out. She closed her eyes and returned to the night of the accident and its aftermath, to the series of disconnected images that were all she could remember, called back by some masochistic impulse, compelled to relive the horror of it again and again.

The plastic seats in the morgue, too-bright strip lighting overhead, someone draping a heavy jacket over her party dress. Sweet tea, her mouth horribly dry. Everything too loud: Marian's sobs, the scrape of a chair, the click of heels, someone clearing a throat. Damien on a slab under a sheet, his face hidden from her, a hand all they would reveal. Cold and stiff, the hand that had never been cold. His new wedding ring still in place. *With this ring I thee wed.*

His parents' house later in the night. Kathleen's face raw and ugly with grief, Brendan rocking on his chair, the light gone from his eyes, his builder's hands useless in his lap.

Her parents showing up at some stage. Her mother pale and weeping, her father grim-faced, embracing her wordlessly. A glass of something golden in her hand, setting her throat on fire, making her cough, sending heat to her frozen fingers and toes.

A woman with auburn hair offering Lydia two white tablets. *For sleep*, she said. Warm milk, Lydia's head woozy, no memory of falling asleep or returning to Chance House, but waking in her bed, their bed. Her wild anguished cries as the night came back, as the huge, crushing realisation that he was gone almost drowned her.

Her mother appearing, holding her, *Shush, shush, dear*. Rubbing her back, *Shh*.

Three weeks without him.

The evening before the funeral, the horrendous wake in his parents' house. The closed coffin inside the sitting room window, also closed. The air too hot, heavy with sweat and alcohol and perfumes that collided. The hideous patterned carpet, green and red on brown. Strangers' hands reaching for hers, again and again and again. The feeling of wanting to be anywhere but where she was. Wanting to walk out of her life and into someone else's.

Father Phil reciting a decade of the rosary at the end that Lydia didn't join in with. Nothing to say to God ever again.

The funeral. Walking up the aisle of the church with her parents, a cruel stab of memory – lilac dress, flowers, happiness – prompting a wail of unconscionable grief, causing her father's arm to tighten around her waist.

Father Phil pressing her hands between his own, his face as full of sadness as all the others, preparing to bury the man whose marriage he'd celebrated a little over a week earlier. *My heart goes out to you*, he had whispered, his mouth close to her ear.

Her family and friends from Dublin, hugging her in turn. Aunts, uncles, cousins. Old neighbours, some of whom she hadn't seen for years.

Mourners from the village and its surrounds. Greta from the café pressing her hand, Gareth pulling her into a brief hug, Susan on the verge of tears, shaking her head wordlessly, Susan's brother Andrew. *Hold on,* he had murmured, *just hold on,* but she didn't want to hold on.

Everyone had known Damien. That was it. Everyone had grown up with him, had watched him go from a boy to a man, had seen the lovely man he had become. Everyone had adored him, because it was impossible not to. He left a gulf in his wake, a chasm so wide it threatened to swallow them all.

She would be nothing to them now. Without Damien, what did she mean to them? She didn't care. Nothing but his absence mattered.

When the bath water began to cool she rose from it and patted herself dry. She brushed her teeth and swirled mouthwash. In the bedroom she dressed in the uniform of tracksuit bottoms and sweatshirt she wore now. Who cared?

Three weeks without him.

After the funeral, her parents had brought her back to Dublin. She'd stayed with them for a week, eating little and sleeping less, spending much of the time in bed or slumped in an armchair, wrapped in a throw and staring at a wall, not seeing the courtyard outside the window, impervious to the little pond at its centre, the border of artificial lawn, the canopy over built-in seating.

All the time her heart had bled as she'd struggled to endure the unendurable. *Where are you?* she had cried silently. *Where did you go? How could you leave me?*

Her friends had dropped around, nobody knowing what to say. Brona had brought the roasted salted almonds they both loved, and had cried with her as the almonds had sat untouched. *I'll come,* she'd promised, when Lydia told her she was going back.

Her parents had wanted her to stay longer in Dublin. *What are you going back for?* her mother had asked, the words slicing like a sharpened blade through Lydia. Nothing left for her in the west now, apart from a big half-finished house by the sea that called to her each night as she lay sleepless in her childhood bedroom and wept for Damien.

She'd yearned for it, the place where he'd been, where they'd been. The place where she'd become engaged to him, the place where they'd got married. The place she'd been happiest. She'd been desperate to go back, to be among all the things he'd left behind, even as she knew the absence of him there would break her heart all over again.

*My apartment is sold,* she'd reminded her parents. *The only place I have to live in is Chance House.* It was solely in her name now, hers to do with as she chose – but what could she do with it? No more destination restaurant, not without Damien.

*Sell it,* her father had said, as if reading her mind. *It's far too big for you on your own; it makes no sense to keep it. Stay with us until you find another apartment here.*

*I can't sell it until it's fully renovated.*

*Of course you can. A developer won't have a problem with an incomplete renovation.*

No, she wouldn't do that. She hated the thought of leaving the house in its unfinished state. Brendan had begun the renovation, and Brendan would finish it – if he still wanted to. Lydia would stay there for as long as it took for the work to be done, and then she would think about what next to do.

She didn't want to live there without Damien, for any length of time. The idea was beyond sad – but she thought it was what he would want her to do now, to stay until she could close the chapter properly.

*I have to go back*, she'd told her father. *I have to finish what we started. I need to be there. I can't explain it.* She could have explained, or tried to, but she didn't have the energy – and anyway, they wouldn't understand.

*I'll come with you*, her mother had offered. *I can take a few days' leave. We'll go for walks by the sea, just the two of us* – but Lydia had said no to that too.

*I need to be alone now. I appreciate all you've done, but I need you to give me some space. I will move back to Dublin, but I don't know when that will be.* Finally they'd given in and brought her to the station, and she'd taken the train west as she'd done so often in the past.

Three weeks without him.

She pulled her hair into a ponytail and went to the kitchen. She switched on the radio, and classical music wafted out. She needed background noise, the silence unnerving her, but music without words was all she could countenance. No lyrics were possible, no playlist of her favourites, for fear of the memories they'd stir.

In between the music she listened to news bulletins that meant little to her. Reports of crashed planes or erupting volcanoes or wars left her unmoved. What happened in the rest of the world was not her concern.

For breakfast she hard-boiled one of Greta's duck eggs and

chopped it into a mug. Food was the last thing she wanted. She had to force it into her, pushing past a sickish feeling in her gut – and sometimes it refused to stay down for long – but her fridge was full, and Damien had hated to waste food, so she ate for him.

Three weeks without him.

The sight of Marian waiting at the station instead of Damien had caused more tears, and they'd clung weeping to each other on the platform as travellers had walked around them, looking elsewhere.

*Would you not stay with us for a while?* Marian had asked on their way to the village. *I don't like to think of you in that big house all on your own,* but Lydia was mindful of Tom who was grieving too, and Jack, who would have to be shielded from the worst of her pain, and she'd said no, she wanted Chance House.

As they'd approached the village, Marian had enquired whether Lydia wanted to visit the grave, and Lydia had said she didn't. On the day of his funeral she'd closed her eyes as they lowered him into the hole they'd dug for him, and she hadn't been back there since. She couldn't face the thought of standing by a mound of earth, funeral flowers maybe still piled on it, brown and withering.

He wasn't there. The Damien she knew, the smiling, positive Damien she'd loved, she still loved, was not lying there.

Three weeks without him.

Glancing through the kitchen window as she ate her egg, she saw that Gareth had arrived and was working in the garden, turning earth over with a fork, stooping every so often to lift something – a rock, a stump – and aim it into his nearby wheelbarrow.

She'd spotted him there several times since her return from Dublin. He hadn't rung the bell, had made no attempt to interact with her. Giving her space, content to potter until she told him what she wanted next. Maybe he thought the sight of him might help her, might make her feel less alone, and maybe it did a bit, but she didn't go out to him, not yet.

Further down the garden, Noel the stonemason was working too. *Sorry for your trouble*, he'd said, woolly hat in hand, ringing her doorbell a day after she'd got back. *I said I'd do up the shed*, cocking his head in its direction, *if you still want me to*. His cheeks ruddy from outdoor work, his eyes with no clue what to fix on.

She'd recalled their meeting with him before Christmas, a lifetime ago when she'd been happy. She couldn't care less now about the shed, but she hadn't wanted to turn him away so she'd said yes, he could go ahead, and he'd shown up every day since, recreating the small building stone by stone, and she couldn't remember if they'd agreed on a price, and it didn't matter.

Brendan and his team hadn't returned to the house. Work had stalled while everyone took a breath, and it waited now in a state of limbo. Brendan hadn't been in touch since Lydia's return, although he would have known from Marian that she was back, and Lydia hadn't sought him out. Nobody seemed to know what to do, now that plans had been dashed in the cruellest way.

She would never get used to the absence of Damien, the not-thereness of him. Not in bed beside her when she woke from fitful bouts of sleep, not uncorking a bottle of wine on the evenings he was at home, not humming in the kitchen as he beat eggs for her favourite French toast on Sunday mornings.

His was the name that would never again come up on her phone when it rang. He was the owner of clothes that still shared wardrobe space with hers, still smelt of him. Reminders of him were all around – the book he'd been reading on the bedside table, the top corner of page thirty-six turned down; the sad-face emoji that had been his last text to her; his welcome-home sign with its line drawing of a house – but he was truly, shockingly, agonisingly *gone*.

She called his number now and again, just to hear his voice: *Damien here, sorry to miss you. Do leave a message and I'll get right back.* She wished it was longer. She ached to hear him say her name.

Three weeks without him.

She poured tea and sat, the music washing over her, the harmony of it bringing some tiny comfort. In a corner of the worktop there was a growing pile of the Sunday newspapers whose delivery Damien had organised when they'd moved in. Still coming, still being pushed through the letterbox on the three Sunday mornings since he'd died, the newsagent obviously thinking Lydia might still want them. She should cancel them, but she couldn't bring herself to cut this tie with her old life.

Brona came, as she'd promised, the weekend after Lydia's return. She'd arrived in her shiny black Beetle around lunchtime on Saturday. They'd done a beach walk, all wrapped up, arms linked, not saying much. They'd reheated something from the fridge for Saturday dinner and opened the wine Brona had brought, and she had mostly talked about the goings-on in Dublin, and Lydia had mostly listened, and then they'd sat by the fire and watched old comedies on Netflix, neither of them laughing.

And when Brona had got back into her car on Sunday afternoon, promising to come back soon before driving off, Lydia had been pierced with fresh loneliness, and the apartment had felt even more hollow, more empty.

Three weeks without him.

An unfilled prescription sat on the kitchen table. A few days earlier a woman had rung the doorbell. *Avril is my name*, she'd said. *I'm the local doctor, I met you at Kathleen and Brendan's house*, seeing that Lydia had forgotten her. She was somewhere in her sixties, empathy in the grey eyes, blue jacket missing a button, the auburn hair probably helped along by Marge in the salon. She'd brought a brown paper bag of mandarin oranges, and a jar of honey.

*Are you eating?* she'd asked, and Lydia had said yes, and hadn't said how little, or the trouble she had in keeping down very much. She hadn't told her parents about that either, not wanting them to fuss.

*Are you sleeping?*

*Not a lot* – so Avril had written a prescription, and Lydia had thanked her and left it on the table. There were yoga poses she could do to encourage sleep – legs up the wall, child's pose, supine twist, seated forward fold – but she did none of them, and no meditation either.

The benefit of no sleep was that she didn't have to face reality crashing in on waking, bringing with it a fresh avalanche of loss. Lying awake was ongoing torment, but ultimately less painful – and meditation was simply out of the question, with its power to dig down and stir everything about.

Father Phil dropped by every day, usually in the middle of the afternoon, before darkness fell. He didn't sugar-coat anything, didn't tell her that everything would be alright, that she'd get over this.

*You won't get over it*, he'd told her. *It will always be there, but you'll learn to live with it, because you have to.*

*Why do I have to?*

*For your parents. For your friends. For Damien's memory.*

*I can't imagine ever being happy again.* This in a whisper, with tears streaming.

*Time is kind, Lydia. Time is your friend. It moves slowly, but it will help you if you allow it,* he'd replied.

He never talked about God, or His mysterious ways. He didn't urge her to pray. Instead he asked, every dry day, if they could walk to the end of the garden, and together they negotiated the path of boards and stood huddled in their winter coats as the sea moved before them, shimmering and cold, and she breathed it in, and it felt . . . medicinal.

On one of those days, out of nowhere, came the image of a little table on the strip of sand with a wine bottle and two glasses on it, another plan that had never happened, and more tears came, and he gathered her in and she pressed her face to his coat that smelt of gooseberries, and he let her sob into it until she was emptied out.

Father Phil wasn't her only caller. Marian turned up every other day, making tea that Lydia felt obliged to sip, issuing dinner invitations that were still declined. If there were ashes to be taken in the sitting room she would take them, and set a new fire. If the tumble dryer needed emptying she would do it, and fold its contents. Tom was coping, she said, when Lydia asked. Kathleen wasn't spoken of.

Susan was another frequent visitor, bringing a box of teabags, or a pair of still-warm scones, or a trio of bananas. Every time she appeared Lydia would think of the lilac dress, still hanging in the wardrobe. The sight of it prompted fresh daily torment, but bringing it to a dry cleaner in the town was completely beyond her, and she kept forgetting to ask Marian to take care of it. Susan never brought it up, but she must be wondering if she'd ever see it again.

Greta came, with duck eggs or goat's cheese. She would stow them in Lydia's fridge and sit silently for a while, never more than ten minutes. If Lydia happened to be close enough, Greta would reach for one of her hands and hold it wordlessly, a thumb absently stroking. She was a surprise, more humanity in the blue eyes than Lydia had initially given her credit for.

Had they paid her for the wedding cake?

Others came in twos and threes, their faces vaguely familiar, but Lydia couldn't recall from where. They murmured their names on arrival, and Lydia promptly forgot them. They brought food in tinfoil containers, casseroles, pasta bakes and apple crumbles. She got other things too: a wedge of Christmas cake, a candle, a bar of soap, a book. Whoever brought the book must have thought Lydia was still capable of reading.

None of her callers stayed long. She was glad they demanded nothing of her. It was good of them to come. She recognised the kindness in a detached way.

Three weeks without him.

Two people had called, but hadn't come in. Denny was one. It had taken Lydia a moment to place him as the taxi driver and photographer. He'd looked deeply uncomfortable, no trace of his previous cheeriness.

*I just came to give you this*, he'd said, thrusting a small white card at her. *In case you need to go anywhere. I know you don't drive. Give me a shout, anytime at all, no charge – I mean that now.*

Denny O'Neill, she'd read. Taxi service, reasonable rates, and his phone number. She'd thanked him and he'd gone away, and it had come to her later that he hadn't mentioned the wedding photos, the ones he'd taken with two cameras. She couldn't imagine ever being able to look at them, ever wanting to put them into an album, or choose a frame for her favourite.

The other person who hadn't come inside was Andrew. He wasn't there to collect the school furniture – all of that had been taken care of while Lydia was in Dublin. The dining room had been cleared and the decorations carted away, every trace of her wedding reception removed. It must have been organised by Marian, who'd had a key since the wedding.

Like Denny, Andrew had made no mention of wedding photos. *Chicken soup*, he'd said, offering her a plastic lidded beaker. *You mightn't feel like*— He'd broken off, his face changing. *Jesus, I forgot you're vegetarian, I'm sorry*, and Lydia's eyes had filled, she cried at the drop of a hat now, and seeing the change in her face the colour had risen in his own, and he'd repeated his apology, and she had shaken her head to ward off his words, not able to speak, not able to tell him that it wasn't the chicken soup that was making her cry, all her energy taken up in trying to stem the tears, and then he'd said, *I'll get out of your way*, and he'd made off with his beaker, and she'd closed the door slowly and leant against it, still weeping, as his van had started up in the driveway.

*About this vegetarianism*, Owen had said, the night of the party. *We'll have to arrange an intervention. I'd say Damien will help* – and maybe Damien had already been dead as they'd laughed about it.

Three weeks without him.

When she looked through the kitchen window again Gareth had gone. Noel was still at the shed, but now he was perched on one of the half-built walls, a plastic cup in his hand, a flask balanced on the wall next to him. Lydia had seen him do this before, and had thought she should bring him out tea. Maybe next week.

The rest of the day passed with its usual visitors – fewer now than at the start, the tapering-off inevitable. In between callers Lydia swept and mopped floors that didn't need it, emptied the fridge and washed the shelves, reorganised the contents of the freezer, ran a cleaning tablet through the washing machine, hunted for cobwebs she'd already found. The apartment had never been so clean.

*Time is your friend.* She wondered how true it was.

Three weeks without him. Three endless, agonising weeks.

# 6

FINALLY, FOUR WEEKS TO THE DAY AFTER THE accident, Brendan came. He looked a decade older, in a blue jumper she didn't recognise, and his usual denim jeans that were baggier than before. 'Lydia,' he said quietly, just that. No hug, no handshake. He sat at the kitchen table and didn't touch the tea she'd made for him. For ten minutes or so the symphony on the radio was the only sound in the room, until finally he spoke.

'I'm wondering will you be heading back to live in Dublin,' he said, a world of pain in his eyes.

'I will, Brendan. I'll have to sell this house. It's all wrong for me now. My father says I should sell it as it is, and let whoever buys it finish the renovations.'

He shook his head. 'You'd make a big loss trying to sell it now – nobody would be keen on working from someone else's plans. I'm not telling you what to do, but in my opinion you'd be better off letting us finish the job. There's only a few more months in it, and you'll get a better price then.'

She was glad to hear him make the offer himself. 'That's what I'd prefer too. Start again whenever you're ready, and let me know when the next payment is due.'

'I will, I will.' He got to his feet and shrugged into the jacket he'd draped on the back of his chair. 'Are you managing alright yourself?' he asked, fumbling with the zipper.

She took the ends from him and slotted them together and pulled up the zip. 'I am, Brendan.' She felt a communion with him, both lost in their grief. 'How's Kathleen?' she asked, knowing she couldn't leave it unsaid.

'Only middling,' he said, which didn't tell her much, but she didn't enquire further. She knew the older woman's grief must be as all-encompassing as her own: maybe it was best they had no contact. What possible good could they be to one another now?

After Brendan left she rang her father and told him that the work was resuming. 'I'll stay here until it's done, and then I'll put it on the market.'

'Whatever you feel is best,' he said, making it plain that it wasn't what he felt was best. 'Come and see us again soon.'

'I will.'

She'd been back once, just four days ago. She'd stayed a night. Her mother had told her she was too thin, and had cooked Lydia's favourite sweetcorn fritters, and her father had said she was too pale, and had given her a month's supply of iron tablets. *Take them with food*, he'd said, and Lydia had suspected his main reason for suggesting them was to get her to eat. But he meant well, and she was taking a tablet each morning with breakfast.

Next day the renovations resumed, and she became accustomed again to the sounds of the workmen drilling, hammering, calling. She didn't feel able to go out to meet them, and sensed anyway that it would only embarrass them, but the noise they made had a reassuring quality to it, and Brendan took to dropping into the apartment for a few minutes each day, just to sit with her, and that provided its own small comfort too.

February moved along, the weeks without Damien growing in number. Time didn't matter to her. She rose when she woke from the half-sleep of her nights, and went to bed when she grew weary of trying to fill the hours.

She rarely felt hungry, even if she ate nothing from breakfast to evening, which happened unless Marian or Greta or Susan came by around lunchtime and urged food on her. Dinners were meagre, eaten purely from habit.

The crosswords she'd loved made no sense now, the clues meaningless. Reading remained beyond her: the words on the page might as well have been hieroglyphs. Once she took out a pack of playing cards – they'd loved gin rummy and twenty-five – but solitaire was too sad; even the name brought tears.

Another day she tore the plastic film from a jigsaw box that had been sitting on the kitchen table for a while. Who had brought it? She couldn't recall. She'd never made a jigsaw, had never felt the urge to fit little pieces of card together, but she'd thought it might help to use up time.

The picture was of a rowing boat moored at a pier, with mountains behind it. The boat was blue and the water a different blue; the mountains were dark blue and purple, and the sky was pale blue threaded with white. It took a while to turn the five hundred pieces right side up, but then the idea of trying to recreate the picture was too much, and she swept them back into the box and found space in a drawer for it.

In the evening she would turn on the television – something

undemanding, a game show – and her mind would wander, and as the credits rolled she would have no idea how the game had gone.

Once, she took clothes from the washing machine and bundled them into the dryer but forgot to switch it on, and they sat there for three days before Marian discovered them, and they had to be put through the wash again.

And the Sunday newspapers continued to arrive, and she never opened them.

A few weeks after the work resumed she saw Gareth again out the back. He appeared every few days. Without stopping to think she took her jacket from its hook and pulled on one of Damien's woolly hats and went out.

He was stringing yellow twine around short canes he'd stuck into the ground, creating a rectangle that ran the length of the recently completed patio. He glanced up and gave her a smile, but said nothing.

She sat on the studio windowsill and watched him work. She presumed he was marking out the flowerbed they'd wanted there. He must have taken a decision to make a start, probably needing to get going with the planting. She remembered how chatty he normally was; she supposed he didn't feel he should talk now, or not until she did.

Should she let him go ahead with the development of the garden? What was the point now? Then again, why not? She knew he enjoyed working out of doors, and a garden, however unfinished, should help with the sale of the house. He might as well keep going.

She let her gaze roam beyond him to the stone shed. No Noel today: he worked Monday to Friday, and it was Saturday. The shed walls were more than halfway up now, too high for him to perch on them for his breaks. A space had been left for the door, another for a single window in the wall that faced the sea.

She looked past the shed to the ocean that stretched all the way to the next continent, and the faint yellow ribbons at the horizon as a pale sun made its descent. Still the days came and went, bringing sunshine and rain as they always had. Still the nights threw stars into the sky. Still the sea washed to the shore and pulled away from it. Still the wind rose and fell.

The world carried on as if nothing was wrong. How was that possible?

'How is what possible?' Gareth asked, and she realised she'd said it aloud, and she shook her head and got up and went back inside.

She felt bad. He was so nice.

A few mornings later, her phone rang. She saw her father's name and sighed. Every other day he phoned, or her mother did. She knew she should be grateful that they were checking in but the calls, full of their careful questions, invariably left her unsettled.

'Dad.'

'Hello, love. You OK?'

No, she was not OK. She was tired and she had no appetite and her stomach was queasy and her heart was in pieces. 'Yes.'

'Just wondering,' he said, 'how the work is coming along.'

'They're here every weekday,' she told him, like she'd said the last time he called. 'They're working away. I don't bother them.'

'And they're still on track to finish in the summer?'

'Yes. Brendan says late May or early June.'

Brendan had said no such thing because Lydia hadn't asked. The last thing she wanted was to put him under pressure.

'And you're still resolved,' her father said, 'not to put the house up for sale till then?'

'I am.' Every time they had the same conversation, just different words. Different approaches.

'Your mother and I have been thinking,' he said.

She closed her eyes.

'We could give you a deposit now for a new place in Dublin, and you could take out a short-term loan to buy, just till the other was sold.'

'No, Dad.'

'Hang on. We've actually found a lovely apartment, close to your old—'

'*No!*' It came out too sharply. 'Sorry, Dad, and thank you for the offer, but you must let me do things my way, in my own time. I'm trying to get through the days here. I'm trying to keep from falling apart, and you and Mum need to back off right now. I'm staying in Chance House till it's finished, and that's that.'

Before he could respond, she hung up. Before he could ring back she left her phone on the kitchen table and yanked her jacket off its hook in the hall and let herself out. She skirted the cluster of workmen's vans and cars in the driveway and walked rapidly up the lane.

At the top she swung left, away from the village, away from everyone. She marched along the road, half running, half walking, no thought in her head but to keep moving.

When she grew tired she slowed her pace, pressing a hand to

her stomach in an effort to combat the familiar sickish feeling. Just an orange she'd had for breakfast, and still it was complaining. Maybe an orange hadn't been enough to absorb the iron tablet, or maybe all the stress and grief had given her an ulcer.

Within a short while she became aware of the cold. She'd come out without hat or scarf or gloves, and it was a day for all three. She turned back, shivering. She dug her hands into her pockets, still unsettled by the phone call.

Why was he pushing her so much? She was going back to Dublin, that was a given – but she couldn't think about viewing apartments now. She was nowhere near ready for all that. She couldn't decide on a new toothbrush, let alone a new place to live. Why couldn't they let her be?

She should be grateful to them. She knew that. They were doing what they thought was best for her, and they worried about her now, living alone here – but as always, it felt like she was being managed, not allowed to live her own life, make her own decisions.

She wasn't happy here. She couldn't be happy anywhere right now, but she had a connection with Chance House that she wasn't ready to break. Leaving it would feel like leaving Damien. He would always inhabit her heart, that would never change, but moving back to Dublin would mean travelling miles from everything he'd loved, miles from all the people who'd loved him, and who'd shown her such kindness after his death.

It wasn't even that she didn't want to return to Dublin. There was so much she loved about the city. There was Caroline, who knew exactly how she liked her hair cut, and the Slow Brew, just two blocks away from her old apartment, best coffee and eggs Benedict in Dublin, and Wordsmith, the bookshop down the road, the perfect spot to while away a rainy afternoon, curled up in one of its many alcoves with a novel.

In Dublin there were shops for everything, and spas to relax in, and parks to walk or run in, and pubs to suit whatever night you wanted. There was Friel's bar in Donnybrook, with Chris who loved jam tarts on duty behind the counter, where the gang used to meet on the last Friday of every month for cocktails, and where the only rule was no work talk. She used to look forward so much to Cocktail Fridays.

And, of course, in Dublin she had Brona.

So she would follow the plan. She would return to the city once Brendan had finished and Chance House was back on the market. In time it would become a bittersweet memory, a place where she'd briefly lived and loved. If she survived into old age, she knew the memory of the big house would always cause a soft pang.

She'd have to move back in with her parents until she found a new apartment. That could take a while. And depending on timings, she'd have to do as her father was suggesting and borrow to pay for a property if something came up before Chance House was sold.

But . . . A new thought occurred, halting her steps. Why not go on living here, rent free, mortgage free, until someone bought the house? Why borrow, either from her parents or from a financial institution, when she didn't have to?

It seemed the most obvious course of action. How had she not seen it until now? Even as the question occurred, the answer came: because it was taking everything she had to keep from giving in to the despair that threatened to crush her, and because she was listening to one or other of her parents repeatedly trying to persuade her to move back east.

No. Her mind was made up. She would stay here until she had to hand over the keys to Chance House, however long that took. Her head felt clearer than it had in weeks. Now all she had to do was break the news to them.

She phoned her father as soon as she got home, wanting to get it over with. 'I'm sorry,' she said. 'I didn't mean to snap.'

'That's OK, love. We understand.'

She took a breath. She told him of her decision – and got precisely the response she'd expected.

'Lydia, love, I'm not sure you're thinking straight right now.'

'I'm sure I am.'

Silence.

'I'm sorry,' she said. 'I know you and Mum are looking out for me, and I'm very lucky to have you both, but Dad, I have to put myself first here. Please try to understand. Please just let me do what I feel is best.'

'It could take ages to sell,' he said. 'How will you support yourself? What do you propose to live on?'

'I have money, I'm OK . . . and if I need more, I'm sure I can get a part-time job here.' She wasn't a bit sure. 'I'll be OK, Dad.' She searched for something more to say, but it was all said. 'Thanks,' she added, knowing how inadequate it was. 'I'll come to see you soon, I promise.'

After hanging up, wanting to run her idea by someone who might be more sympathetic, she went out to find Gareth forking seaweed from his barrow into the earth of the yellow rectangle.

'I'm putting on the kettle,' she told him. 'Will you come in?'

He stabbed the fork into the ground and peeled off his gardening gloves. 'Thought you'd never ask.'

He stepped out of his boots at the door. His socks were thick, the colour of sand. He washed his hands and opened presses till he found mugs, and took milk from the fridge while she scalded the teapot. She remembered he preferred it to coffee. He didn't ask how she was doing, and she was glad of it. People meant well when they asked, but she wished they wouldn't. Nobody wanted to hear how broken she was.

'I'd like your opinion,' she said, and told him of her resolve – and like her father, he made the point that Chance House mightn't sell all that quickly, even fully restored.

'I can wait,' she said. 'I'll probably have to look for work at some stage, but that's OK. I can try the shops in the town.' She remembered Damien saying she wouldn't get a job over a local in the village, and she was still enough of an outsider for that to apply. 'I don't want to leave,' she said. 'Not until . . . everything's done.'

'I get that,' he said. 'And you don't mind being here on your own?'

She did mind. She minded very much. 'I don't have a choice, if I want to stay.'

He nodded, giving it some thought. 'I'd say you should do what makes you happy,' he said slowly, and then he heard the words and his face changed, and she told him quickly that she knew what he meant. So careful everyone was, tiptoeing around her. She was reminded of Andrew with his chicken soup, and his face when he'd realised his mistake.

They drank tea, and the talk changed to inconsequential things. He spoke of the snowdrops on the lane; she said she'd seen them. He commented on what was playing on the radio, and confessed his ignorance of classical music. She asked what he preferred, and he said American country and told her of an older couple from Milwaukee who spent summers in their house up the coast and brought their guitars to the village pubs now and again.

He offered to light the fire, asked if she had enough fuel. Asked if she wanted him to take away the stack of newspapers.

'How about a hug?' he said, when he was leaving. They'd never hugged, apart from at the funeral. She wasn't sure what to say so she said nothing, just nodded, and he wrapped her in his arms and she smelt the sea and the earth from him, and her eyes filled but she felt safe.

Her mother rang, of course. 'Sweetheart, we know it's hard for you now, and we want to do everything we can to help, but we really think you're making a mistake, wanting to stay long term in that big house all on your own.' Lydia had to repeat everything she'd already said, and bat away the same arguments she'd already countered, and her mother was no happier than her father had been, but there was nothing she could do about that.

Next day, the sky holding no threat of rain, she walked into the village after breakfast, her first time to go near it since the accident, and rang the bell of the parochial house.

'I hope you don't mind my dropping in,' she said. 'I felt I should make the effort, since everyone's been coming to me.'

'I'm delighted to see you, and your timing is impeccable. I've just brewed up.'

She remembered the nutty aroma of his coffee from the day she'd first met him, when she'd called with Damien to fix on a wedding date. She'd loved it then, asked him for the name of it, but today the taste and scent were too much for her. Grief seemed to have altered her tolerances. She sipped it out of politeness.

'It's good to get out,' Father Phil said. 'You need roses in those cheeks again. I'm driving to the town this afternoon – want to sit in?'

'I don't, thanks.' That level of social interaction was still beyond her. She was too fragile, too damaged.

'Want me to pick anything up for you then?'

'I have everything I need,' she told him. It was true, with occasional food donations continuing, and everything else – groceries, toiletries – supplied by Marian, and anonymous bags of fuel left regularly at her door. 'People are very kind.'

'Kindness is built into the folk around here,' he agreed. 'How are you finding the time?'

'Long,' she admitted.

He nodded. 'Hard to believe it's March already. Is Gareth working on the garden?'

'He is, whenever he can spare the time, and when the weather's OK.'

'He might be glad of some help, if you're of a mind to.'

With a pang, she recalled herself and Damien helping out with the initial clearing, carting barrow loads of weeds and emptying them into a trailer. Yes, working in the garden would be something she could manage.

'Look after yourself,' he told her as she was leaving. 'See you soon. My door is always open – even when I'm not here. Come in and make yourself a cuppa.' He hugged her without asking. He was good at hugs, and gave them freely.

At the gate she turned back in the direction of Chance House, not wishing to meet anyone else, unable yet for the casual encounter, the bright small talk – or worse, the pitying enquiries – but she'd hardly left the village before a car pulled up beside her. She would refuse the offer of a lift, pleading a need of fresh air, but when the window slid down, Susan was behind it.

'I was coming to see you' – so Lydia had little choice but to get in.

'Nice that you're out and about,' Susan remarked, as they covered the short distance.

'I called to Father Phil for a chat.'

'Good for you.'

Back in the house Lydia took the lilac dress from its hanger and folded it into a paper bag. 'Not cleaned,' she said. 'I was waiting to ask Marian to get it done, but I kept forgetting. Sorry it's taken so long.'

'No problem at all.'

'Will I make tea?'

'Don't, I'm not staying. I just wanted to run something by you.'

The house was quiet, no workmen on a weekend, no Gareth in the garden. Through the window Lydia could see a tiny patch of blue in the sky. Spring weather on the way, for all the difference it would make.

'You must find the time long,' Susan went on. 'I was thinking you might be glad of a diversion.'

'. . . Oh?'

'I wondered if you've ever taught yoga to young children.'

'I have. There was a mother and toddler class in the studio where I worked.'

'In that case, would you consider giving a class to Marian's junior and senior infants? There's a hall you could use. For payment, naturally – and it could be a one-off, if you didn't want to commit to any more. I like bringing outsiders in, giving the kids new experiences, and the poor infants don't get much.'

'Well . . .' She *was* looking for something to fill her time, and yoga was what she loved, but a class of lively five- and six-year-olds?

'You don't have to decide right now, just think about it. There are only fourteen children between the two classes, and they're a sweet group. Jack is in there, don't forget, and Marian would stay with you all the time, and twenty minutes or so would be plenty. Just think about it,' she repeated, and Lydia promised she would.

'Also,' Susan said, 'I wondered if you'd like a bike.'

'. . . A bike?'

'Owen got me a new one for my birthday, and my old one is sitting in the garage, and I feel bad that I'm not trying to find a home for it. It's working fine, just a bit ancient. And it's not a bribe – it's yours if you want it, whether you say yes to the yoga or not. I thought it might be handy for getting you in and out of the village. Would you be interested?'

She would. She would be interested. She'd had one in Dublin and she'd loved it. So satisfying to be able to whizz past a line of cars – but the apartment five floors up, and with a temperamental lift, had been the end of it. She wasn't comfortable leaving it in the communal storage space out the back, so she'd sold it, and had missed it right away. A bike here would be most useful. It would bring her a lot further than the village, in any direction.

'If you're sure,' she said, 'I would like it.'

'It's yours. I'll get Owen to drop it over. And have a little think about the yoga – no pressure, honestly.'

After she left, Lydia went into her studio. Fully functioning since last weekend, Brendan had told her on Monday. *Just*, he'd said, *if you had a use for it*, unaware that she'd been using it all along for her own sessions. Lights and heat connected now, storage unit installed. Plenty of room in it for all the equipment her old workplace had let her have at a special price – mats, blocks, belts, blankets – but everything was still piled up in her spare bedroom. What was the point of moving it into a studio that was never going to host a class?

She wondered what would happen to it after the house was sold. It was a space that would lend itself to all manner of classes or workshops – or maybe the new owner would do something entirely different with it. A little bar maybe, if the restaurant idea went ahead.

Perfect for yoga, though. She missed teaching it, missed the energy a class always brought into being. She missed seeing beginners discover the difference yoga could make, or taking improvers on to the next level. She remembered all the questions she'd been asked about yoga on the night of Susan's party.

The night her world had ended.

She shut off the thought. She considered the very different kind of yoga class Susan was proposing. She couldn't deny the enjoyment she'd got from the mother and toddler one in Dublin. That they were young children wouldn't make it any easier – they could be a lot more challenging than adults. But maybe a challenge would be good for her.

And Susan had helped with the wedding, and lent her the dress, and was giving her a bike for nothing. And Marian would be with her in the hall.

One class wouldn't kill her. One class wouldn't commit her to anything more. And it would be a kind of a start, wouldn't it? It would be the beginning of being able to plan a little beyond the day she was in.

She would definitely think about it.

# 7

HE OFFERED HER WHAT LOOKED LIKE THE SAME beaker as before. 'Vegetable soup,' he said. 'Left out the chicken this time.' A minuscule lift of an eyebrow.

'Thank you.'

'I have something else . . .'

While he was gone she took the lid off the beaker and smelt herbs and garlic. She wondered if he'd made it from scratch, or cheated with a can.

The bicycle he returned with was the pale yellow of the little flowers she remembered growing in clumps along the roadside, the spring before last. Wild primroses, Damien had told her. No sign of them yet this year. 'I thought Owen was bringing it.'

'I was over at their house yesterday, and Susan happened to mention it. Only three gears, so it won't be much good to you on the hills, but it'll get you in and out of the village until you find yourself a car.'

'I don't drive,' she said. 'This will be fine for me.'

'It's tricky around here without a car.'

'I'll manage,' she said. 'I'm not staying permanently.'

He nodded. 'You'll go back to Dublin.'

'I will, but not for another while.'

Until now, Gareth was the only one she'd said it to. Nobody else had asked, not even Marian, but people probably assumed that was what she would do.

'Right so.' He pushed a hand through his unruly hair. 'Sorry the way things worked out for you. You got it very tough.'

The sympathy, as always, made her eyes sting. She blinked the tears back, not wanting to cry in front of him again. 'Thanks for the soup.'

'About the only thing I can make without burning it. Mind yourself on the bike.'

It wasn't in bad shape. Its yellow paint was chipped in spots, easily touched up. The chain was a little rusty but someone had oiled it, and a small rip in the saddle had been glued. The brakes worked. Best of all, it had a carrier, a wicker basket, lights front and rear and a bell that tinkled. All she needed was a lock and a helmet.

She could keep it in the shed, which was finished. Gareth was already storing his garden tools in it. Good that it was being put to some use.

She decided to take it out for a quick run. Despite its lights, she wouldn't fancy cycling on dark country roads, but it looked like there was enough daylight left in the sky if she didn't go too far. She pulled on her outdoor things and wheeled the bicycle to the lane. She put a foot on a pedal and swung herself up into the saddle. She negotiated her wobbly way along the pitted surface until she reached the road, where she turned in the opposite direction to the village.

She pedalled hard then to gather speed, feeling the remembered rush of air on her face, the pleasant ache that developed in her calves as the hedgerows flashed by. She loved it, loved how the physical act of cycling left little room for the quiet despair that still so often threatened to swamp her.

She pumped the pedals for a mile or two, then turned around, blood racing, face warm despite the cold air. She guessed she had the roses in her cheeks that Father Phil had said she needed.

By the time she got home, twilight was setting in. She wheeled the bike around to the shed, leg muscles singing, and pushed open the thick weatherbeaten wooden door that Brendan had salvaged from a derelict house.

It was only her second time to enter it. When she pulled the door closed behind her to take in the space the air felt different, scented with earth and old stone, marginally warmer than outside. The floor was plywood, solid and plain. The light was soft, the small window not allowing a whole lot of it through.

She saw Gareth's fork and spade leaning against a wall, and his battered wheelbarrow standing on its end next to them. A pair of well-worn gardening gloves was draped across one of its handles, and hanging from the other was the watering can he filled from the rain butt he'd installed at one of the drainpipes. She stood the bicycle behind the door and looked through the window at the sea. Its sound was more muffled in here.

Back in the house she rang Susan. 'I just took the bike out for a spin. Thank you so much. It's great.'

'Oh good, I'm delighted it's found a home. It's a bit of a workhorse, but it'll be handy for short hops. Sorry I didn't have a helmet to go with it, but you'll get one in the hardware store.'

'Yes – and about the yoga . . .'

'No pressure – I told you the bike wasn't a bribe.'

'No, I know. Let's give one class a go,' so they settled on Tuesday, right after the morning break.

'Come in time for a cuppa beforehand, if you feel like it,' Susan said. 'Ours is just a four-teacher school, me being one of them, and someone is always on yard duty during the breaks, so you'll only have three of us to cope with in the staffroom,' and Lydia said yes to that too. She had to start saying yes to things again.

A few minutes later, Marian rang. 'Susan tells me you're going to do yoga with my crew on Tuesday.'

She sounded elated. Lydia imagined the two of them cooking up this plan, trying to help her find a way back into the world. Did it matter if they had, if Susan hadn't really needed something for the infants? Lydia wasn't sure how she felt about being a charity case, but their motive, if she was right about that, was good.

'I'm delighted you're doing this, Lydia. They're a lively bunch, but very lovable. I'll pop over to you tomorrow after school for a quick hello.'

After hanging up, she rang her parents. They'd both been a little quiet since Lydia had told them of her intention to delay her return to Dublin, so here at least was her opportunity to pass on some positives.

'That's good,' her mother said, of the infant yoga, 'as long as they're not too rowdy. I don't think you should have to deal with that at the moment.'

'Marian is the teacher, and she'll stay in the room. And I'll get paid a bit.' A sum hadn't been mentioned, but she didn't imagine it would run to much, schools not exactly rolling in money. 'And there's more good news.' She told her of Susan's gift.

'That's kind of her. Is it just a loan, while you're there?'

'No, it's mine to keep.'

Pause. 'But you are still coming back?'

'Mum, I've told you I'm coming back. I'll be bringing the bike to Dublin, whenever I return.'

'That's good, dear. Make sure you wear a helmet, and take care on those country roads. They can be lethal.'

Lydia said nothing to that. People didn't mean to hurt: they just didn't think before they spoke.

The following morning she cycled into the village. She dropped into the hardware shop and picked up a helmet, and then she kept going, pushing through the stiffness in her legs as she sped past cottages and haysheds and fields full of silent cows. Again she loved it, even when she had to puff her way up the rises.

On her return to Chance House, when she wheeled the bicycle around the back she saw Gareth kneeling at the edge of the patio, trowel in hand, a green plastic tub and his watering can next to him.

He sat back on his hunkers when she came into view. 'You've found yourself a bike.'

'Susan gave it to me. She got a new one.'

'Very good. Mind yourself on the road.'

'I will. What are you doing?'

'Wild primroses,' he said, lifting a clump from the container, parting the bright green wrinkly leaves to show her buds. 'You have to have some bit of colour till I get everything else down. They should open in a week or so. Don't tell anyone – I lifted them from up the road, but the cultivated ones are an abomination, and I spaced out what I took, so they won't be missed. They spread, so you'll have more every year.'

She could picture him, covertly digging up the wild flowers to give her something cheery to look at. Funny that they'd crossed her mind when she'd seen the bicycle's colour.

'I'll probably be gone before next spring,' she said.

'Maybe you will, but they'll still come back.'

She wondered if she could dig up some and bring them to Dublin. If she didn't have a garden, maybe she could plant them in a window box or on a balcony. She liked the idea of bringing something from this garden to the middle of the city. 'Could I help you out here?' she asked. 'I know nothing about gardening, but maybe there's easy stuff I could do.'

'Absolutely, lots of easy stuff. You can give a hand with the next round of planting. Root out those wellies again.'

'I will.'

Damien's pair still sat next to hers at the back of the wardrobe. She couldn't imagine the day would come when she would be able to part with anything of his. She watched Gareth digging in the rest of the primroses, and then he got to his feet, brushing earth from his palms. He crossed to the rain butt and refilled the watering can and handed it to her. 'Your first job. If it doesn't rain, throw a bit of water on them every day, to help them settle in.'

When she went back inside she became aware of hunger pangs, the cycling maybe, so she heated Andrew's soup till it sent up soft wisps of steam. She poured it into a bowl and dipped chunks of Greta's rye bread into it, and relished every mouthful.

And didn't throw it up.

On Tuesday she cycled to the school, her rolled-up yoga mat sitting in the basket. She was apprehensive. She hadn't thought to ask about mats. Would the floor be suitable, if there were none? What if she couldn't control the children? Had she taken on too much, too soon?

Why was she so nervous? It was a group of infants. It was only twenty minutes, and Marian would be there.

But still it was worrisome. It was her trying to inch forward, trying to move past the nightmare, and she wasn't at all sure she was strong enough.

She arrived to find the yard full of flying-about children, and a woman she didn't recognise patrolling among them. As long as they're not rowdy, her mother had said. They looked pretty rowdy as they barrelled about, yelling loudly at one another. She wheeled her bicycle carefully towards the supervisor, eyes peeled for Jack – the sight of him might settle her – but she didn't see him.

'You're Lydia,' the woman said. 'I'm Cara, third and fourth class teacher. The others are in the staffroom, first left when you go in.'

'Where should I leave the bike?'

'By the door there is fine.'

'I don't have a lock.' She'd forgotten to look for one when she'd bought the helmet.

Cara smiled. 'You're not in Dublin now.'

Wasn't that what Susan had said to Brona, the morning of the wedding? It was tossed away lightly, then and now, but still it made Lydia feel like the girl from the big city with a lot to learn. Maybe it had sounded offensive, the assumption that she'd have to lock a bike. 'Sorry.'

'Oh, don't apologise. I can imagine an unlocked bike wouldn't survive two minutes in Dublin, but it'll be grand here.' Her voice changed then. 'You're coping OK?'

'I am.'

'I'm glad to hear it. Head on in, or you'll miss your cuppa.'

Susan and Marian were in the staffroom, with another teacher they introduced as Josephine. Lydia was given a mug of tea that was stronger than she liked, and they talked of the weather, and Easter holiday plans, and Father Phil's upcoming annual coach trip to Knock – before the sound of the bell summoned them.

'The hall's just down there,' Marian said, indicating double doors at the end of the corridor. 'You go ahead, and I'll get them out of their jackets and follow you in.'

The hall was warm, and smelt faintly of socks and cough medicine. Four large PE mats, the kind Lydia remembered from her own schooldays, had been spread out on a floor that didn't look entirely clean. She cracked open windows and was unrolling her own mat when she heard the slaps of small feet in the corridor, and high-pitched voices cannoning into one another like in the yard, and Marian's call for quiet ringing above.

The doors opened and they descended on the mats in a rush, ignoring Lydia, their chatter starting up again. It felt like there were more than fourteen of them. She got an impression of navy tracksuits, and ponytails and hair slides, and shoes with lights that flashed as they jumped and bounced and tumbled.

Jack materialised on a mat close to her, hopping on one leg with another boy and appearing not to see her. She stood uncertainly as Marian scurried about, allocating places and managing complaints.

'Peter is looking at me!'

'No, I'm not!'

'This mat is tore!'

'I want to be beside Helen!'

'I have a pain in my tummy!'

'This is Lydia,' Marian said firmly, when order of a sort had been restored. 'She's Jack's auntie, and she's the lady I told you about who's come to teach you yoga, so I want you to show her how good you are at listening. Robbie, please sit up,' aimed at a boy who lay on his back, legs in the air, and ignored her.

The rest stood on their mats and regarded Lydia without much interest. From her experience of small children she knew she had about five seconds before she lost them for good.

'I've got something to show you,' she said. 'Watch this.' She dropped into a headstand and held it, letting the silence stretch as long as she dared before righting herself.

'Who knows what that's called?' she asked.

'Standing on your head,' Jack ventured.

She smiled at him. 'That's right, Jack – and in yoga it's called a headstand. Now look at this one, and see if you can guess what it's called in yoga.'

She went straight into a handstand, and walked off her mat to the nearest wall, and came back. 'What's that?' she asked, right way up again.

'A handstand,' came back in a ragged chorus.

'Exactly right, excellent. And watch this.'

For the next few minutes she chose the most impressive balance poses – crow, tree, wheel, half-moon – and challenged them to guess the names of each. By the end of it, they were with her. She could feel it.

'That's yoga,' she told them. 'All that cool stuff is yoga. They're called poses, and there are lots more, hundreds more. Who'd like to learn how to do some?'

Most hands shot in the air. Robbie, she was pleased to see, was now sitting up. Progress.

'You won't be able to learn them all in one day, nobody could do that, but today I'm going to teach you how to do the first part of tree. It's not too hard, so let's see how we get on.' She steered them slowly through the beginner version, and when they stood in the pose, arms raised and outstretched, she walked among them, praising softly.

From tree she guided them into a few other simple poses, getting them to stretch and bend, twist and fold and curl, encouraging, praising and assisting, and it felt good. It felt like she remembered.

When Marian signalled that the twenty minutes were almost up, Lydia put them lying down and told them to close their eyes and instructed them in belly breathing.

Not a pin dropped. She caught Marian's eye, and got a silent thumbs up. At the end she guided the children back to standing and taught them how to say *Namaste*, palms pressed together.

'It means thank you,' she told them. 'I love to teach yoga, so *namaste* for letting me teach you.'

'I love yoga,' a child declared, and others echoed it.

'Can we do some more another day?' a boy asked.

Lydia looked at him. 'I think that's a very good idea,' she said.

# 8

WHEELING HER BICYCLE ACROSS THE YARD afterwards, she felt satisfied. She'd done it, and they'd enjoyed it. *I love yoga*, from the mouth of a child who didn't yet know how to pretend, and from other little mouths too. Marian would relay that to Susan, and Susan would ring at some stage and ask if Lydia felt like making it a regular thing, and Lydia would say yes. It would be a nice landmark in the week.

She reached the school gates, and had just placed a foot on her pedal when she noticed that Greta's café across the way was open. She'd never been inside: anytime she'd passed it, with or without Damien, the blind had been pulled down in the single window, but today it was up.

With her taste for coffee having abandoned her, it was the last place she'd choose to visit – but Greta had been kind, and Lydia wanted to support her, and maybe she could get something harmless, like peppermint tea.

She leant her bicycle against the nearby presbytery wall, smothering the small qualm that rose up at the thought of leaving it unlocked. *You're not in Dublin now.*

She pushed open the café door and stepped inside. Her first

impression was of a small room – no more than half a dozen tables, two occupied. A counter at the top and Greta behind it, in the act of placing something on a plate – but before Lydia could advance, the heady, coffee-laden atmosphere caused her insides to rise in sudden protest, and she was forced to withdraw.

Outside, her face prickling with sweat, she moved out of sight of the window and bent over, hands on thighs, praying she wouldn't throw up, and hoping she was unobserved – but she heard the café door open, and felt a palm coming to rest on her back.

'Breathe,' Greta ordered, and Lydia obeyed until the sick sensation receded, and she was able to raise her head.

'Sorry. It was the smell of the coffee.'

'Don't apologise. Come.' Greta led her down by the side of the café and through a gate that led into a little walled-in courtyard with a garden seat, its wood silvered with age. 'Sit,' Greta commanded, and vanished through a door that must have led back into the café. Lydia remained where she was, feeling foolish, until Greta returned with a steaming mug, a rug and a cushion.

'Ginger tea,' she said, handing it over before tucking the rug around Lydia and settling the cushion at her back. 'Good for the stomach.'

'Thank you. I used to love coffee, but lately I can't tolerate it.'

Greta studied her. 'You are too thin.'

Like Lydia's mother. 'I'm not eating much,' Lydia admitted. 'I'm a bit wary of food: I've been throwing up.' She wasn't sure why she was saying all this. She hadn't even told the doctor, when she'd asked.

'Drink the tea. How long has this been going on?'

'. . . Since the accident.' Wasn't it obvious? Damien's death had thrown everything out of kilter.

'When was your last period?'

The question came out of nowhere. Lydia, in the act of raising the mug, frowned. 'What?'

'Weeks? Months?'

'... I don't know.' She couldn't think. In her mind's eye she saw the box of tampons she kept in the bathroom cabinet. When had she opened it last?

Greta looked directly at her, as she always did. 'Perhaps,' she said, 'you are pregnant.'

The word echoed in the brief silence it left in its wake. It drifted about the little yard until Lydia found her voice. 'Pregnant? No, I'm not. Definitely not.'

'You are quite sure?'

Another silence. Lydia opened her mouth and closed it again. Pregnant? No. Absurd. Impossible. Ridiculous.

Greta sat next to her. 'You are not eating. You feel sick after food, and the smell of coffee makes you want to throw up. And it sounds that maybe you have not had a period in some time.'

Her voice was calm, her words slow and clear, as if Lydia was a child who needed to be taught. 'Is it possible,' she asked, 'that you are pregnant?'

Lydia stared dumbly at her. It wasn't impossible. They'd taken a few chances during the snow-bound days following the wedding, just for the hell of it. *In for a penny*, he'd said. *New businesses, new baby*, and it had felt like another part of the big adventure.

No. She couldn't be pregnant. She couldn't do that without him. Out of the question. She didn't want to do it alone, didn't want a child who had a mother but no father.

She reined in her galloping thoughts, conscious of Greta's gaze still fixed on her. 'It's possible,' she said slowly, 'but it's also possible that I'm not pregnant. Everything's been so . . . awful. It might just be that, mightn't it?'

'You need to see Doctor Avril – or take a test,' Greta said in the same composed tone.

She was right, but the thought of doing either filled Lydia with dread. 'Please don't tell anyone.'

Greta frowned. 'Of course not.' She rose. 'Finish your tea. You must find out, Lydia.'

Pregnant. The possibility hadn't once occurred to her, but it would explain a lot. She sat cradling her mug in the quiet space, inhaling the steam that was flavoured with ginger.

Pregnant.

In the end, after two sleepless nights, she took the bus to the town and bought two pregnancy tests in a chemist where nobody knew her.

The following morning she took both tests, one after the other, and sat on the side of the bath in shock after they gave her the same result, after they'd told her that sometime during their six blissful days of marriage, she had conceived.

She should have known. She should at least have considered pregnancy as a reason for her problems, but she'd been too deep in grief, too stunned by loss – and now the proof was there, two tests giving the same result, and she had no choice but to see it.

It felt like someone's sick joke, a cruel, triumphant *ta-dah!* from some evil cosmic magician. She couldn't cope with it, not when the wound was still so raw, when she could still close her eyes and see his face, hear his voice and his laugh, smell his skin.

But this would be his baby, part of him. It would have his DNA

– it might look like him, laugh like him. It would carry him on, like a legacy he'd left in her care. His final surprise, even if he hadn't planned it. Even if she didn't want it – did she? Oh, she didn't know what she wanted. She hadn't a clue what she wanted, except for him. She wanted him, every second of every day.

She blotted her eyes with a towel, overwhelmed by sadness at the thought that he would never know, never meet his child. She bagged and binned the tests, and washed her hands. She paced the apartment, her morning yoga for once forgotten as she tried to think straight.

Her last period, as far as she could recall, had occurred in the middle of December, when she'd been rushing about making wedding preparations, and now it was March. Did that make this her third month? When should she count from?

She went back to bed, burrowing beneath the duvet, wanting to shut everything out. She tried to push away this new catastrophe and think of nothing at all, to enter a state of mental blankness, but her mind circled back stubbornly, refusing to let it go.

It wasn't that she didn't want a baby. They'd talked about children lots of times during their engagement. Having been an only child and envying her friends with siblings, she'd wanted four, two of each. He'd said he'd be happy to take whatever came.

They'd played with names. Sophie, Aisling, John, Adam. They'd planned to wait until they'd got Chance House up and running – but after the wedding, giddy with happiness, they'd broken all the rules.

And now, barely a wife, she was a pregnant widow – and soon, within months, she would become a single parent. What had she done to deserve any of it?

Lying in bed with no distraction was worse than being up. She threw back the duvet and got into yoga gear. She went through the motions in the studio, but for the first time it didn't pull her out of her thoughts. It gave her no peace, her racing mind refusing to calm.

Afterwards, showered and dressed again, she made ginger tea from one of the sachets Greta had given her. She tried to eat a slice of toast but it defeated her, and she threw most of it into the compost caddy by the sink. She took her jacket from the hall and jammed on a woolly hat. She wrapped a scarf around her neck and went out to the shed for her bicycle and helmet.

She didn't question what she was doing. She moved instinctively, drawn to a place she'd been avoiding since January. She cycled into the village and down the main street. She passed the always open gates of the presbytery, and Marge the hairdresser in her salon. She saw the closed door and pulled-down blind of Greta's café, and the schoolyard, quiet between breaks on a Friday morning, and Andrew in a white coat behind the counter in his shop.

Pregnant. It felt like the word was written in neon letters on her forehead. It felt like everyone she met would know instantly. She left the village and passed the creamery on her right, and a farm beyond that. She slowed then, not wanting to arrive, her feet heavy on the pedals.

At her destination she dismounted. She leant the bicycle against the old stone wall and rubbed eyes that burned with tiredness and willed herself to be strong.

The graveyard was built on a gentle slope, around the ruins of a small church. That morning, it appeared to be empty of people. She pushed open the stiff iron gate and made her way up the incline until she located the grave, where Damien's paternal grandparents and Brendan's infant sister had earlier been buried.

The earth they'd dug up in January and then replaced was still mounded. A small bunch of flowers, not withered, leant against the headstone, next to a red jar with a lit candle in it. Brendan or Kathleen or Tom. Did Kathleen visit her son's grave?

The candle reminded her of the dining room in Chance House the day they'd promised to love one another till death parted them, not realising that death didn't kill love, and she cried her way through giving him the news that they'd made a child together.

'I should be happy. I know I should. I wanted your child more than anything, and I know I'll love it because it's yours, but I wish so much I wasn't doing this alone. I wish . . .'

She trailed off miserably. Look at her, talking to a headstone. She'd come in desperation to the last place they'd put him, but she'd been right in thinking he wasn't there. She couldn't feel him there. He wasn't anywhere she could find him.

She swiped a sleeve across her face and looked down at the road. She saw a red car parked now at the gate, and hoped it wasn't anyone she knew. She turned her head to follow the road away from the village, imagining Damien travelling along it on the night of Susan's party, unaware that his life was nearly over. The accident had happened just a quarter of a mile beyond the graveyard.

She plodded back down disconsolately, getting all the way to the gate before a figure emerged from the car.

'I spotted the bike,' Susan said. 'I'm on the way back to the school. I had to run home to get my phone, left it behind.'

She'd rung Lydia on the evening of the infant yoga class, and they'd agreed to make it a weekly thing. Now, with everything up in a new heap, Lydia couldn't plan beyond the next half hour, let alone the next few weeks.

She looked dumbly at Susan, who frowned. 'Are you OK? It must be tough, coming here.'

'It's my first time, since—' She broke off, fresh tears blurring everything. 'Susan, I'm pregnant.' Out it blurted, unplanned, along with the fresh tears that she made no effort to stem. Would she ever run out of tears?

'Oh God.' Susan put arms around her. 'Oh, you poor thing, as if you didn't have enough to deal with. Oh, Lydia. Here, leave the bike – I'll get it sorted later. Sit in.'

'But you have to get back to school.'

'Another few minutes won't make a difference. Go on, sit in.'

'Don't say it to anyone,' Lydia begged. 'You're the first person I've told.'

'My lips are sealed,' Susan promised. On the way to Chance House she asked Lydia no questions. Instead, probably in an attempt to distract, she spoke of her aunt Lorraine, who was getting married for the second time, and who had a problem.

'She's Dad's sister, lives an hour away. She rang him last night in a tizzy – the hotel where they were to have their reception has gone into liquidation, and the wedding's scheduled for Easter Saturday, only a couple of weeks away. They've probably lost their deposit – well, they might get it back eventually, but they're not holding their breath.

'The thing is, they aren't planning a big do, just family and close friends – it's second time round for both of them – but they'll have a job finding another venue. Everything's booked up so far in advance.'

'That's too bad,' Lydia said. Not really listening, someone else's wedding plans holding no interest for her. She saw the sun sliding out from behind a cloud, washing the countryside in pale light. The days were getting longer now, the air beginning finally to soften.

The car was warm: Lydia felt her eyelids growing heavy. She tipped her head back and dozed until a bump on the lane jerked her awake.

'Sorry,' Susan said, 'I was trying not to disturb you. You're shattered. You should go back to bed.'

'I will.'

She didn't, fearing a daytime nap would only worsen her already broken nights. She busied herself around the apartment, emptying wastepaper baskets, cleaning windows, stowing glass bottles and jars in a box for recycling.

As she tipped ashes from the previous night's fire into the metal bin around the back, she saw a ginger cat padding up the garden. She stopped, and so did he, fixing her with an unblinking yellow gaze. His fur was bald in spots.

She fancied his eyes held sadness – had someone he loved died too? They stood regarding one another silently. She'd always had a soft spot for cats, but had never owned one.

'Hello,' she ventured quietly. At the sound of her voice he sat, still a safe distance away, and continued to stare fixedly at her.

Maybe he was hungry. She returned to the house and took a bowl from a press and spooned in cold tuna casserole. When she went out again he'd come as far as the patio, but he darted away when she approached. She set the bowl down and returned inside, and when she looked through the window he was already eating, wolfing the food into him. He ate everything, apart from a scatter of peas and carrot chunks, and she watched him cleaning his face before padding away.

She'd fed a hungry cat. It made her feel a tiny bit better.

Her bicycle was returned later. She came on Andrew by chance, propping it by the apartment door as she was coming up from a walk to the end of the garden to smell the sea. Well after six o'clock, and still full daylight.

'I was going to leave it here,' he said. 'Susan thought you might be asleep.'

'No.' Her helmet still hung on the handlebars. She wondered what reason his sister had given for Lydia having left the bicycle at the graveyard. 'Sorry – you're having to do a lot of running around on my behalf.'

'It's no bother,' he said. 'I live out this way, about a mile further on.'

'I didn't know that.' She'd presumed a flat above his shop, although he could be a family man for all she knew. She wondered if Susan had told him of the pregnancy. She'd promised not to say it to anyone, but Susan might not be the best secret keeper.

'Would you like tea?' It would pass another while, force her out of her thoughts. 'Unless you're rushing home.'

'No, I'm not in any rush,' so he came in and sat at the table, and she returned the beaker that had been sitting on the worktop since she'd washed it.

'Sorry – I meant to give it back sooner. The soup was lovely.'

He gave the same small eyebrow lift she'd noticed another time. 'Handy way to eat vegetables – for those of us who prefer our meat.'

She told him of the ginger cat she'd encountered earlier who'd left his vegetables behind when she'd fed him.

'That's cats for you,' he said, 'pure carnivores. I get two strays that show up at the back door of the shop most days.'

'Do you feed them?'

'I throw them out a few scraps. I hate to see an animal hungry.'

'Me too.'

The radio was on, like it always was. 'I like a bit of classical,' he remarked. 'I like all music really. How about you?'

'At the moment, just classical,' she said, and didn't elaborate. 'Do you play any instrument?'

'Well,' he said, 'play might be a bit of an exaggeration, but Susan gave me a ukulele for my birthday a few years ago, and I tried to teach myself some tunes from YouTube videos. I'm very bad.'

'I bet you're better than you say.'

He smiled, shook his head. 'Ask Susan. She'll back me up.'

He told her of the teenage assistant he'd taken on part-time in the shop a few months ago. 'Left school early, broke Susan's heart when he was in primary. His mother asked could I find a use for him, so I gave him a three-month trial, and he's turned out to be a decent lad, quick learner and great with the customers. He just wasn't one for the schoolbooks.'

He was surprisingly talkative. She suspected he was making an effort for her. 'I wasn't one for the schoolbooks either. My parents weren't impressed when I told them I wanted to be a yoga teacher.'

'How did you get into it? The yoga.'

'I was thirteen, on holidays in Madeira with my parents. The hotel we stayed in offered free classes. Right from the start, I loved it.'

'Is that why you're vegetarian?'

She shook her head. 'They weren't connected. Giving up meat was a gradual thing, a few years later. The idea of eating animals just became more and more off-putting... No offence,' she added, and he assured her none had been taken.

He didn't put milk or sugar in his tea. He ate three of the custard creams she put out. The eyebrow thing, she decided, was a sign that he wasn't serious. She liked his smile. It wasn't like Damien's, which had lit up his entire face. Andrew's was gentler, with a warm, quiet feel to it.

'The photos you took,' she said, as he was getting up to leave, feeling that she should make some mention, conscious of the passage of time, and knowing he'd been paid nothing. 'I'm not sure...'

'No rush,' he said. 'They'll keep.'

She was glad she'd asked him in. He was easy to talk to.

In bed that night she found herself swinging again between disbelief and sorrow, her mind and heart still struggling to come to terms with the pregnancy. She didn't think she'd fully processed it, couldn't yet take in how it would change her future.

She remembered with a lurch of dismay the drinks she'd had at Susan's party, and the wine she'd unknowingly drunk since then, with Brona and alone. Too late for regrets: all she could do now was hope no harm had been done.

She was glad she hadn't filled the doctor's sleeping tablet prescription – they couldn't be good in pregnancy – but the iron tablets she was still taking that her father had prescribed should be OK, shouldn't they? She knew so little.

She had to tell people. Tomorrow morning she would visit Brendan and Kathleen, and afterwards she would call in to Marian and Tom, and in the afternoon she would take the train to Dublin to break the news to her parents, and spend the night.

It would be good if this development brought herself and Kathleen closer together. She doubted that they'd ever be close, like Kathleen and Marian seemed to be, but she was fond of Brendan, and for his sake she wanted to be on cordial terms with his wife. Maybe a second grandchild would soften her heartbreak a little, particularly when it was Damien's child.

And after telling everyone, what then? But even as she asked the question, she knew what the answer must be.

She would go back to her original plan of returning to Dublin as soon as the work on the house was finished. She would need help with the baby, so she would move in with her parents until Chance House was sold and she could get her own place.

She knew they'd be delighted with the news of her pregnancy, and thrilled to be giving their grandchild a home for as long as it was needed. And Lydia would remind herself every day how lucky she was to have them.

She would have to find an apartment on the ground floor, or at least one with a reliable lift, so she didn't have to climb stairs with a baby and a buggy. And what about the bike? Would she ever get to use it again, once the baby arrived?

Her friends who were already mothers would be a big help. They could recommend crèches and babysitters, and child-friendly places to go for coffee, if she ever felt like drinking coffee again.

She'd talk it all over with her parents tomorrow, see what they had to say. She planned to take the three o'clock train to Dublin, so she'd have to get the two o'clock bus from the village. She'd cycle in from Chance House and leave her bike overnight behind Father Phil's house. She hadn't asked him if she could, but she knew he wouldn't mind.

Andrew was right: it was awkward without a car here. If she'd been staying long enough to sell Chance House she might have looked for driving lessons. Susan or Marian would be bound to know someone. It wouldn't surprise her if the lollipop man at the school was a driving instructor in his spare time.

Outside the window she heard, for the first time in a while, the quiet hoot of the long-eared owl that lived somewhere in the trees. Damien had told her what species it was. She'd never once heard an owl in Dublin, which had amused him no end. He'd called her a city slicker: she'd told him it was better than being a country bumpkin.

She closed her eyes and roamed back into her memories, hands resting lightly on her abdomen.

# 9

IN THE MORNING THE GINGER CAT WAS BACK IN THE garden, sitting close to the patio. Was he waiting to be fed? Lydia put more food into the bowl and brought it out. Again he ran away at her approach.

Back inside, she called her mother. 'Just for one night,' she said, 'to catch up.'

'That's wonderful, love. We'll have your room ready. Text when you're on the train and Dad will meet you – he's on a half day today.'

As she was returning it to her pocket, her phone rang. When she saw a number with no name attached, she hit the red button – but less than a minute later, it rang again.

'Greta is trying to call you,' Marian said. 'I gave her your number – I hope that's OK. She wants to talk to you about something.'

She was wondering about the outcome of their conversation in the little yard behind the café. Lydia should have let her know. She went to retrieve the call she'd cut off, but Greta beat her to it.

She received Lydia's news with the same equanimity she'd shown when she'd taken the wedding cake order. 'How do you feel about it?'

'Shocked. Sad. Frightened. Not sure I'll be able to do it alone.'

'But you won't be alone here.'

'I can't stay, Greta. I'm going to Dublin this afternoon to tell my parents, and I'll be moving back there before the baby is born. I was leaving anyway – I'll just be going sooner than planned.'

'How are you travelling to Dublin?'

'Train.'

'I will drive you to the station. Tell me the time of your train.'

'There's no need. I can get a bus from the village.'

'You will not get a bus. I will drive you.'

Having learnt that argument was futile with Greta, Lydia gave in, and arrangements were made.

Cycling through the village an hour or so later she passed the Saturday market stalls with their organic offerings, their home-baked goods and barn fresh eggs and honey from local bees and just-picked vegetables. She nodded at familiar faces – there was Greta with her eggs and cheese – but kept going, not wanting to be diverted from a task she wasn't exactly looking forward to. Better get it over with.

The Cotter family home was located down the road from Damien's old house, and around the corner from Tom and Marian's. All the Cotters close together, until Damien had made the break. It must have been hard, she thought now, for Kathleen to see Damien selling the house his father had built for him. It might have seemed to her that he was splitting up the family, even though he was only moving a mile away.

She had to pass his old house to get to theirs. It had a new red front door, and curtains had replaced his blinds. An older couple had bought it, downsizing after their family had moved out. They'd planted flowers in the front garden where only grass and dandelions had grown. She was glad it looked different. It made it easier to pretend she'd never been inside it, never spent happy times there.

When she reached Brendan and Kathleen's house she saw his van in the driveway. She propped her bicycle inside the garden wall, careful to keep it well away from Kathleen's rose bushes, and walked around to the back of the house, like she and Damien had always done.

It felt strange, coming here without him. Strange and sad. She rapped on the kitchen door, avoiding the window, not wanting to be seen looking in. She hoped Brendan would answer, and he did. In shirtsleeves and unshaven, looking concerned at the sight of her.

'Is anything wrong?'

'Nothing's wrong, Brendan. I just wanted to give you and Kathleen some news.'

'Come in, sit down. Kathleen's upstairs – I'll get her.'

Lydia didn't sit, not yet. The kitchen was as she remembered it, dated and cluttered and warm. A smell of toast hung in the air. A newspaper lay open on the round table, a half-filled mug and Brendan's reading glasses next to it. A familiar brown teapot sat on a trivet. Plates were stacked on the draining board: no dishwasher for Kathleen. Two eggcups in the sink, still holding their empty half-shells.

When had she been in this room last? A day or two before Christmas, wasn't it? Brendan had been working at Chance House, so it had been just the three of them. They'd sat at the table and been given cups of tea, with whatever Kathleen had baked – mince pies? – and Lydia had let mother and son speak, keeping a determined smile on her face. She remembered that Kathleen hadn't brought up the wedding, less than a week away.

She heard voices, steps descending. She felt suddenly uncertain of her reception, of Kathleen's reaction to the news. She stood by the table, feeling a rising heat in her face. Her hands curled around the back of a chair as the door opened.

'Kathleen – there you are.' A small fluttering in her gut. 'I'm sorry, I should have called in to check how you were before this.'

Kathleen didn't respond. Like Brendan, she'd aged. The furrows around her mouth had deepened; new lines were scored in the skin between her eyes. She'd stopped colouring her hair, an inch of greying roots visible. Her top, green with a lacy collar, one that Lydia didn't remember, had a small dark stain near the neckline. As ever, she looked slightly past Lydia.

'I have something I need to tell you both. Do you want to . . . will you sit down?'

Again, there was no reaction from Kathleen. It was as if Lydia hadn't spoken. Brendan pulled out a chair and put a hand on his wife's arm to steer her in its direction. 'Here,' he said. 'Here, Kathleen, have a seat. Would I make tea?' he asked, the question directed at Lydia, and she shook her head. Poor man, trying to manage his wife's grief as well as his own.

She waited until they were both seated before taking a chair. Brendan, she saw, had pulled his closer to Kathleen's. Was he nervous too of what was to come?

Now that she must tell them, Lydia found herself tongue-tied. She decided to be direct, get it over with – but it didn't come out very direct. Instead, it stuttered out in little jumps. 'I discovered yesterday – that I'm . . . pregnant.' Looking from one of them to the other. 'I did a test – actually I did two, just to be . . .'

She let it trail away. There was a dead silence. She saw how her words changed their faces, the astonishment in Brendan's, the hardening in Kathleen's. Outside, a bird began a sudden loud chirruping.

Brendan was the first to speak. 'Well,' he said slowly, 'that's . . . it's . . . a surprise.'

The calmness in his voice encouraged her. 'It is. I – I must admit I got a shock. I'd been feeling – a bit off, a bit sick, but I just put it down to . . . everything.'

'It's a good thing,' he said, doing his best to look happy. Making an effort for her sake, and she loved him for it. 'And how are you feeling now? Are you still sick?'

'Not too bad,' she said. She looked at her mother-in-law and gathered her courage. 'What do you think, Kathleen?'

There was another silence, a longer one. Brendan dropped his gaze to the table, looking weary.

'Will it bring him back?'

The words were uttered in a hoarse half-whisper. Lydia couldn't speak, couldn't think how to answer.

'Kathleen,' Brendan began, and she rounded on him.

'Don't!' she cried suddenly, making Lydia's heart jump. She pushed her chair back roughly, rising to her feet and turning to glare at Lydia, face splotched with angry red. 'Thanks to you, he's gone! I wish he'd never met you!'

Lydia stood too, and found her voice. 'Thanks to me?'

'He was going to collect *you* that night. It's *your* fault!' Jabbing a finger at Lydia, her face contorted. Looking right at her, maybe for the first time.

Lydia stared back, dumbfounded. Brendan, on his feet now too, placed a hand on his wife's arm – 'Kathleen,' he began again – but she shook it off angrily.

'Don't!' she repeated sharply, before returning to Lydia. 'And now you come to tell us of a baby, as if that will help! Where will you raise it, let me ask?'

'I'll be moving back to Dublin,' Lydia admitted, 'but I'll bring—'

'Dublin!' Kathleen spat. 'That's right, run away, now that you've done all the damage! Run away, and don't bother coming back – I don't ever want to set eyes on that child!'

She turned and swept from the room, and they listened to the angry thump of her feet on the stairs, echoing the thumps of Lydia's heart, and the slam of a door.

'Sorry,' Brendan said. 'She's not herself. Sorry, Lydia. She doesn't know what she's saying.'

He looked utterly woebegone, and Lydia wanted to weep for him. She wanted to speak some words of comfort, but was too dazed by Kathleen's outburst. *It's your fault.* How could she say such a cruel thing? Was it possible that she believed it?

'She'll come round,' Brendan said. 'It'll be good to have another grandchild. Don't pay any heed to what Kathleen said.'

Lydia crossed to the back door, her legs trembling.

'You'll be back to see us,' Brendan said, 'when the baby comes?'

She nodded. She'd bring the baby as far as Tom and Marian's house, and he could meet them there. She would probably never set foot in this house again. Her child would grow up without one of its grandmothers. How would Damien have felt about that?

'Does Tom know?' Brendan asked. 'Have you told them?'

'I'll give them a ring when I get home.' She was in no state to call to them now.

All the way back to Chance House, the harsh words followed her. *She's not herself*, Brendan had said – or maybe this was exactly who she was. Maybe this was Kathleen laid bare by grief, saying what she normally kept hidden, not caring any more.

She'd resented Lydia before the accident, but this was something far bigger. Now it felt as if she truly hated her. How could she think it was Lydia's fault? How could she be so monstrous as to throw an accusation like that at her?

Back at the house she rang Marian.

'Oh, Lydia, I don't know what to say. In a way I'm really happy for you, but it must be tough.'

'I'm still trying to take it in, to be honest.'

'You must be. How are you feeling – I mean physically?'

'Still a bit iffy, but I think it's easing.'

'Hopefully. Have you told Kathleen and Brendan?'

'I was there earlier. Kathleen—' She broke off, unable to speak of the horrible scene.

'She took it hard,' Marian said.

'She did.'

'Lydia, it's not you. You mustn't think it's you. It's just how she is now,' but Lydia knew it *was* her. It had been her from the very start.

'Will you come to us for dinner tonight? Tom will collect you and drop you back, and you can eat as little or as much as you want.'

Lydia told her about her trip to Dublin. 'I'd love it next week.' She needed friendly faces around her.

'I'll hold you to that.'

*

'You're quiet,' Greta remarked in the car on the way to the station, and Lydia gave a brief account of Kathleen's outburst.

'Not nice,' Greta said. 'Not kind.'

'She's heartbroken.'

'Yes, she is. For a mother to lose a child, that is the worst kind of loss. But still, it was not good to be cruel to you.'

'No . . .' Lydia watched a silver car overtake them, going too fast. *Slow down*, she wanted to say. *Be careful.*

'So you will return to Dublin.'

'Yes, when the house is finished.'

'Another few months.'

'Yes.'

'And what will you do to pass the time here until you go?'

'Well, I've been helping Gareth in the garden a bit – I enjoy that. And I told you about the yoga in the school.'

'You did.' Greta pulled out to overtake a cyclist. 'What about teaching yoga to adults in your own studio?'

Lydia looked at her.

Greta kept her eyes on the road. 'It is not such a crazy idea, I think. The studio is there, and you are staying for the next few months. You have told me it has light and heat now so why not use it?'

Yes, on the face of it, it was a no-brainer. 'I'm – I don't think I can face the organisation it would need.'

'Just some leaflets around the village, I think,' Greta said.

Lydia sat back wearily and looked at the sky. Greta took the hint and they covered the rest of the journey in silence, until the station approached.

'Susan has told me,' Greta remarked, pulling into a parking space, 'of her aunt who needs a venue for her wedding reception.'

Lydia was only half listening as she watched the first patter of drops on the windscreen. 'Sorry?'

'Susan's aunt, getting married with no hotel.' She said 'aunt' to rhyme with 'gaunt'.

'Oh . . . yes, she mentioned it.'

'The wedding is in two weeks.' Greta turned off the engine and rested her hands in her lap. 'What time is your train?'

Lydia checked her watch. 'Not for twenty minutes.'

'So wait until the shower passes.'

'OK.'

Lydia watched a trio of teenage girls emerging from the station. Short skirts, furry jackets, biker boots. Piercings in their faces, dark colours on their lips and around their eyes, long hair whipping about in the breeze that had sprung up. She watched as they pulled jackets over their heads.

Lydia had always loved the sound of rain hammering on a roof or lashing against a window. In a car it sounded different, all around, and so close, and hitting metal. Water ran down the windscreen, blurring the features of the teenagers.

'Maybe I know of a venue,' Greta said.

'Hmm?' One of the girls took a phone from her pocket. The other two clustered around her.

'For the wedding. I thought you might consider letting them use Chance House.'

Lydia turned to stare at her. She couldn't have heard right. 'Sorry?'

'I thought,' Greta said, 'you might wish to accommodate her, since she is Susan's aunt.'

'You thought,' Lydia repeated faintly, 'that I might wish to *accommodate* her?'

Greta gave no response, just went on looking enquiringly at Lydia.

'Are you seriously suggesting that I let another couple have a wedding reception in Chance House?'

'Yes, I am thinking it would be—'

'No,' Lydia said quickly, and again, more forcefully: '*No*. How can you even suggest such a thing? Have you any idea what you're asking of me? It's where Damien and I . . . It's not even three months since he died! I can't believe—' She broke off, struggling to stay in control, fighting against tears, her face hot.

'Lydia, please do not be upset,' Greta said. 'I am simply throwing out the possibility. She needs a place, and you have a place, that's all. You need only give a key, and not get involved.'

'And *you* needn't get involved,' Lydia shot back, 'because it's none of your business – and what I do with my remaining time in Chance House is not your business either, so kindly stop telling me what I should and shouldn't do! Chance House is *not* a wedding venue – but even if it was, I'm *appalled* that you would be so insensitive at this time!'

She wrenched at the door handle, but nothing happened. She gave another tug, again to no avail. 'How do I open this blasted door?'

'Hold on,' Greta said calmly, getting out. She walked around and opened the door, and Lydia scrambled out, pulling her bag after her.

'Lydia, please don't be angry. It was just an idea that came to me, but I can see I upset you, and I am sorry. That was not my intention.'

'How could I not be upset?' she snapped, hardly aware of people rushing past, of the rain still falling, of one of the teenage girls looking up from the phone to stare at her.

'I was trying to help,' Greta said. 'That is all. I'm sorry,' she repeated. 'What time are you coming back tomorrow?'

Ignoring the question, Lydia stalked into the station, and nobody followed her. On the platform she tried to shake off her anger, to breathe herself calm again, but she was still fuming when her train arrived.

How could Greta be so heartless? How could she think that Lydia would be OK with letting another wedding reception take place in Chance House? Couldn't she see how it would churn everything up again? Lydia had been wrong about her: only a cold, unfeeling person would suggest such a thing.

And what a busybody, telling Lydia that she should use the studio. Of *course* she should use the studio, all ready and lying idle – but it wasn't up to Greta to point that out.

She found a seat and turned her face to the window. She dropped her bag onto the adjoining seat, hoping nobody would ask her to move it. She was tired, so tired of trying to push against despair, to cope with her loss. Kathleen had seriously upset her, and Greta had only made things worse. She wished she could see even a glimmer of light ahead.

The train started up and began gathering speed. Lydia tried to shake away Greta's thoughtless suggestion, but it persisted. She did feel sorry, in a detached way, that Susan's aunt and her fiancé had been left high and dry – but they would just have to find another venue. There might be heat in the dining room now, and maybe light too – she wasn't asking Brendan for updates on the work, and he wasn't offering them – but the kitchen was still bare and useless.

Having a wedding reception there hadn't been a problem for her and Damien, but that was because it was their place, and because they'd been able to get around the lack of proper cooking facilities, with Damien's connections. She supposed any caterer would be able to supply food but really, would another couple want to go to all that bother, no matter how desperate they were?

Their wedding was in less than two weeks. They were probably pretty desperate.

The train stopped at Tullamore station. She watched people disembarking, others climbing on. It wasn't that she didn't want to help them – of course she'd like to help, and yes, maybe they could get around all the limitations – but the bottom line was that she couldn't bear the thought of another wedding celebration in the house.

Maybe if she was miles away she might be able to countenance it, but she wasn't. Greta had said she wouldn't need to be involved, but she'd have to have some involvement. At the very least, as the owner, she'd have to meet the couple in advance and show them around, or they'd think her very odd.

But she could bow out after that, couldn't she? She could absent herself from the house on the day, have nothing at all to do with the event. She could get the bus to town and pass the day there, or make an arrangement to go somewhere with Marian.

She could do it, if she had to.

She thought of the beautiful dress Susan had lent her for her wedding, and the yellow bicycle that could easily have been sold. She thought of the tables and chairs that had been provided for their reception, and the infant yoga classes Susan had more than likely conjured up, just to give Lydia something to do, something to get her out of the house.

And Andrew, nephew of the bride, was so helpful too. It could be Lydia's thank you to them, to help their family now.

She should offer Chance House. Could she do it?

She could. She would. She would do it.

Before she could change her mind she rang Susan. 'Has your aunt found a wedding venue yet?'

'No, she's still looking. Why?'

'Well . . .' Lydia watched a pair of birds circling in the sky. Wheeling and swooping, coming together and parting. Playing, it looked like. 'I was wondering if they'd like to use Chance House. I'm not sure what stage the room is at – I don't go in there. And you know there's no overnight accommodation, and no working kitchen, but if they were really stuck, I thought . . .'

'Oh wow,' Susan said softly. 'Lydia, that's an incredibly kind offer – but are you sure you'd be OK doing that?'

Was she? She honestly didn't know. 'I'd like to help them. But they'd have to come and see it – they may not want a place that's so . . . inadequate.'

'I think they'd be thrilled, to be honest. They're not looking for luxury, not in the least, just somewhere that could accommodate them. I'll call her right now, and get back to you. Whatever they say, I'm bowled over, Lydia. This is so generous of you.'

Within ten minutes she was back. 'They'd love to come and see it – when would suit you?'

They settled on the next day at six, when Lydia would be back from Dublin and the workmen gone home, and when it would still be bright enough to see it properly. So Lydia was committed, at least to giving them the option of the space.

She turned her thoughts back to the studio. This would be her only chance to make use of it, before she left for good. Would she regret it if she didn't at least put the offer of classes out there? Would she think of it when she was back in Dublin, and kick herself that all she'd used it for were her own solitary sessions?

Maybe setting up a few classes wouldn't need much organisation. Maybe it would just be a case of putting a leaflet out there, like Greta had said, and taking names when they phoned. She'd seen how fast word travelled in the village. She'd think about it. She'd talk it over with Marian and Tom.

Tomorrow she would ring Greta and apologise for her outburst. Maybe she needed a Greta right now to prod her onwards. She spent the rest of the journey gazing through the window as the world flashed by outside.

# 10

HER PARENTS RECEIVED THE NEWS OF HER pregnancy with muted pleasure. Not wanting to appear too happy, given the circumstances, but she could sense their delight. She knew they'd been dying for a grandchild, envious of friends who'd already become grandparents.

'How do you feel about it?' her mother enquired.

'Ask me in another few months.'

'Oh, sweetheart,' squeezing her hand. 'You haven't seen a doctor yet?'

'No – just the two tests.'

'Do you know roughly how far along you are?'

'It happened after the wedding,' she said, 'so . . .'

So she could be accurate about conception to within six days.

Her mother consulted a calendar on her phone. 'You're around thirteen weeks along, starting your second trimester.'

'What about the iron tablets, Dad? I've been taking them every day.'

'Carry on with them,' he said, 'and I'll write you a prescription for folic acid.'

They gave Lydia one of the leaflets they'd put together for their pregnant patients. *Negotiating pregnancy* had lists of recommended foods and those to avoid, and suggested supplements, and a sleep hygiene plan, and an exercise regime, and a timetable for scans.

'You need to eat properly now, Lydia – that's very important. How's your appetite?'

'Improving.'

'That's good. Have you told Damien's parents?'

Lydia nodded. 'I called to them this morning.' She left it at that.

'This might cheer them up, the poor things.'

'So how do you see your plans now?' her father asked.

She saw their hopeful faces. 'I'll come back sooner,' she said, 'if you'll have me.'

'Oh, thank goodness!' her mother exclaimed. 'I'll organise your first scan – and one of us can drive down and get your luggage. What about next weekend?'

'No, Mum – I'm not moving back right away.' She watched them deflate again. 'I just want to stay another few months. I'll be back in plenty of time to have the baby here. Will you both be OK with two of us in the house until I find another apartment?'

'Of course we will,' her mother said, 'but it's not ideal to be changing doctors halfway through your pregnancy, particularly your first. Would you not come sooner?'

'Mum, when I leave Chance House, it will be for good. It was our first home, and I'm attached to it. I just want to spend a bit more time in it while I can. I'll visit the GP as soon as I go back. I'll do everything right, I promise – and I have lots of people to help me if I need it, lots of drivers to bring me to appointments and that.'

A sigh. 'Well, please don't wait too long. I'll ask Robert Nestor to take you on: he's always busy, but he'll oblige us.'

Robert Nestor, obstetrician and gynaecologist, had been to college with her mother. Lydia had met him and his wife Charlene, at least ten years his junior, at a few of her parents' dinner parties. She liked Charlene, a blow-in from Meath as she said herself, but she didn't care for Robert, loud and self-important with a guffaw that showed all his fillings. Still, she didn't have to like him.

'Terence can handle the conveyancing for Chance House,' her father said. Terence Mannion, who'd done the conveyancing for Lydia's apartment sale, and who'd taken care of all the family's legal requirements for as long as she could remember.

'And you'll need a nanny for when you go back to work,' her mother said. 'I'll ask around, see if I can get a recommendation.'

'You should probably think about learning to drive as well,' her father said. 'Travelling with a baby on public transport is not ideal. I remember all the luggage we had to bring anytime we went anywhere with you. It was difficult enough with a car.'

'Good idea,' her mother said. 'We could find you one of those cute little Fiats.'

'Hold on,' Lydia told them. It hadn't taken them long to take over, or try to. 'I've only just discovered I'm pregnant. Can we slow things down please?'

'Sorry, love,' her mother said. 'We're just looking forward to our new grandchild, and to having you home again.'

*Home is where the heart is.* The phrase flashed into her head. The trouble was, since Damien had died her heart had lost its moorings. She was adrift, not knowing any more where she truly belonged – but for now, Chance House was still where she wanted to be.

After dinner she rang a few friends to give them the news, all of whom offered the same guarded congratulations that her parents had, but no one was free to meet her the following morning for brunch. Babies, husbands, jobs. Life was going on without her, which of course she understood but still it hurt. She would have to work at fitting in again, she thought.

'We'll see you when you're back,' she heard, in the soft, sympathetic tone they all used with her now. 'We'll make a plan, as soon as you're landed.'

She texted Brona, on holidays in the Seychelles. Two minutes later, her phone rang.

'Oh my God, so many congratulations!' Brona said excitedly. 'I know it's probably a bit weird and sad, but it's wonderful too. We fly home on Tuesday so I'll come to you next weekend, and I'll bring zero-alcohol wine, and a book of names – and we can plan a big baby shower when you're back in Dublin. Can't believe you're going to be a mum! Sorry, I've had a couple of cocktails, it's nearly midnight here, but I'm so happy for you!'

Whether it was the cocktails or not, she did sound delighted. She and Shaun were planning to start a family next year, when he turned thirty-five – *Two is all we want*, Brona had told her. When Lydia had got engaged to Damien, she'd assumed that she and her friend would be pregnant together, or around the same time, but here she was.

In a few months she'd join the ranks of parenthood, and the old gang would gather her back into the fold. She'd bring her child to their children's birthday parties, and host her own. Life would take on a new rhythm. *You'll learn to live with it*, Father Phil had said, and she knew now that she would, because she had to.

But she'd miss him when she left. She'd miss them all.

# 11

'IT COULDN'T BE BETTER,' LORRAINE SAID.

Lorraine was the bride-to-be. She was short and curvaceous, with a head of salt and pepper curls and an olive green jersey dress that flowed almost to her ankles. Around her neck she wore a delicate gold chain on which hung a heart studded with a pair of stones that looked like diamonds.

*Arthritis*, she'd said, displaying a left hand to show Lydia her swollen finger joints. *This is my ring,* catching hold of the heart. *I love it.*

She was possessed of a warm gap-toothed smile and a deep, rich laugh, and on being introduced to Lydia she had taken her into her arms and pressed her close. *Susan told us,* she'd said quietly. *You poor, poor pet.* Lydia had been enveloped in a spicy scent, and when they'd drawn back Lorraine's eyes were wet.

'This is such a kindness,' she said now. 'Ian and I are both deeply grateful, especially considering your terrible tragedy. Aren't we, Ian?'

'Deeply grateful,' Ian echoed. 'You're our saving grace, to be quite honest.'

They repeatedly declared themselves more than happy with the offered room – which had, it turned out, electricity and heat now, along with a proper wooden floor. 'It's beautiful,' Lorraine said. 'Just perfect – isn't it, Ian?'

'Perfect,' he agreed. 'Beautiful altogether. That high ceiling is magnificent.'

He was about a foot taller than Lorraine, with the shoulders of a rugby player and a mouthful of large white teeth. They held hands as unselfconsciously as teenagers, and every time Lorraine looked at him he beamed back at her.

Over tea in the apartment afterwards, they told Lydia that they'd known each other for years, due to their separate friendships with the other's previous partner.

'Myself and Anne were in the same book club,' Lorraine said, 'and Ian and Rory sang in a choir together. Ian is a tenor, Rory was baritone. Ian and Anne had two children and so had we, but they had boys and we had girls. We'll be like the Irish Brady Bunch when we all get together.' A big laugh followed.

'The two families used to go on holidays together,' Ian added. 'Lanzarote.'

'And Tenerife.'

'And the Lake District. We all liked walking.'

'And Portugal. That was lovely. Remember the sardines?'

'I do indeed remember the sardines.'

Both spouses, they told Lydia, had died of cancer within eleven months of each other. 'We stayed friends,' Lorraine said, 'Ian and I. We supported each other. Neither of us liked being alone, did we?'

'We did not, no.'

'I popped the question,' Lorraine said. 'Remember, Ian?'

'I do, of course.'

'Mind you, I didn't go down on one knee – my hips wouldn't let me!' Another rich laugh – and then she seemed to collect herself, maybe remembering Lydia's situation, and her laughter died, and she grew quiet.

'I'll sort everything,' Susan put in. She'd accompanied them to the house. 'You won't have to do a thing, Lydia. I'll organise the furniture like before, and Marian's going to give a hand to get the room ready.'

Also like before. 'What about food?' Lydia asked.

'Our school secretary's sister is a caterer: she'll handle it. She does all the school functions – she's great.'

'And our children will provide the music,' Lorraine said. 'The girls will bring keyboards, and the boys have fiddles. Ian's choir will sing in the church.'

It was surreal, like the present superimposing itself on the past. Lydia remembered Andrew arriving on the morning of the wedding with a van full of furniture, and Susan and Marian turning up later with their boxes.

Remembering brought pain with it – how could it not? – but having met Lorraine and Ian, having seen how happy they were to be marrying each other, and how delighted with the venue, Lydia knew she was doing the right thing.

'We were wondering,' Lorraine said, 'if you would come too, Lydia. We'd really love you to be part of it, if you felt able.'

Lydia shook her head. 'Thank you, I appreciate that, but . . . I think it would be too difficult. I'm planning to be out of the way on the day.'

Lorraine's smile dimmed. 'Of course you are – sorry, I can see it's still so raw.' She reached across to give Lydia's arm a squeeze. 'I really hope you can be happy again.'

'Me too.'

Ian gripped her hand on leaving. 'We can't thank you enough,' he said, 'honest to God. We'll never forget it.'

Lorraine gave her another hug, and so did Susan. 'You're the best,' Susan whispered.

Lydia stood at the main door until the car turned on to the lane and disappeared. On her way back to the apartment she paused in the hall, whose floor was tiled now, and regarded the lovely curve of the stairs, complete with banister. Little by little, Brendan and his team were transforming it.

She took a step towards the stairs – and stopped. Going up alone was too sad. She'd wait until the work was finished, and then walk through every room with Brendan.

She turned to regard the door of the yoga studio. She crossed to open it, and stood for a minute on the threshold, lost in thought. Seeing in her mind's eye what was not yet there, but what might be possible.

Yes.

Back in the apartment, she drafted a leaflet.

*8-week yoga course with Lydia at Chance House studio*
*Tuesdays or Thursdays 7.00–8.00 p.m.*
*All levels catered for*
*Wear loose, comfortable clothing, mats provided*

She added a price she thought was reasonable for the eight weeks – roughly two-thirds what her Dublin studio would have charged

– and her phone number for booking, and set the start dates for the following week. If she passed out the leaflets tomorrow, people would have six days to sign up for one class or another.

Time would tell.

Next morning she cycled into the village for her second infant yoga class, with an envelope of leaflets and a heart full of trepidation. No fear about the children's yoga this time: now it was all about the adults.

She met the same three in the staffroom, Cara on duty in the yard again. 'Yes please,' she said, when Lydia showed her a leaflet on her way in. 'Thursday would suit me.'

'I'll take two leaflets for the windows,' Susan said, 'and put me down for Tuesday.'

'Tuesday for me too,' Josephine said.

'Thursday's better for me,' Marian said, 'and I know two more who'll definitely be interested. This is so great, Lydia.'

Despite the success of her first infant yoga class, the second began just as chaotically, and again Lydia had to work hard at gaining her little students' attention – but once she had them, they stayed with her. It looked like they would always keep her on her toes, which was no bad thing.

After the class, she brought the remainder of her leaflets around the village.

'I'll take one for the window,' Marge said in the hair salon. 'And can I sign up for Tuesday? I've always wanted to try yoga.'

'I'll put one in the church porch,' Father Phil promised, 'and I'll say it off the pulpit on Sunday too.'

Lydia made a silent vow to show up more often for Mass. She

was still angry with God, but Father Phil was innocent. 'I hope I won't get you into trouble. You know Hinduism and Buddhism both claim yoga, don't you?'

He laughed. 'I'd say the pope has better things to worry about – and I doubt I'll upset anyone around here. I suspect you'll be inundated. I'm happy you're doing this, Lydia.'

'No bother,' Andrew said in his shop a few minutes later, reaching into a drawer for a roll of Sellotape and sticking up the leaflet there and then, next to a sign that read *4 lamb chops €7*. 'Best of luck. And Susan tells me you're letting Lorraine and Ian have their reception at Chance House. That's very good of you.'

In the supermarket she pinned one to the noticeboard. She gave another to the girl behind the counter in the chemist, whose name she kept forgetting, and another to a man in the hardware shop she didn't remember meeting before.

'Ah, yes,' he said, 'Chance House,' and looked up from the leaflet to regard Lydia over the top of his glasses. 'Very sorry for your trouble. I had great time for Damien. He was at school with my lads. My wife and I were away for the funeral – we spend our winters in the Canaries – but the boys went. Jerry McCormack is my name, happy to make your acquaintance.'

Her phone began to ring before she got home. By six o'clock both courses were fully subscribed, along with two more she created to meet the demand, one on Monday, another on Wednesday. Four classes a week for eight weeks, a dozen signed up for each class. Forty-eight people in total, and five more who'd asked her to let them know if she had any cancellations.

Were they doing it out of pity, wanting to support the grieving widow? Maybe some were. Did it matter, as long as they came?

She told herself to call it kindness, rather than pity. She'd wait and see how many lasted the course.

The day was cold and bright. She pulled on a fleece and went out to the garden, where Gareth's stolen primroses were all blooming prettily, and the camomile lawn he'd sown was just beginning to send tiny green needles up.

The bee- and butterfly-friendly patch – buddleia, sedum, salvia, catmint, verbena – was coming along. She'd been concerned that they were planting everything too far apart: he'd assured her they'd spread.

The wildflowers – poppies, ox-eye daisies, cornflowers, foxgloves, sea asters – that he'd started from seed in his greenhouse were all going into the earth tomorrow, in the area they'd prepared. The sea grasses he'd got in pots from the garden centre in town were already long enough to wave in the breeze.

The slate pathway now curved its way down the length of the garden, branching off to access the shed, which had a rambling rose bush beginning to inch its way up one side, and a seating area further along, within the shelter of a hazel.

Lydia followed the path down to the end. The rusted railing was gone, the new hedging not yet planted, but the old steps had been replaced with a set of sturdy ones.

She sat on the top step. She hugged her knees and closed her eyes – and there was the blue sky and the sunshine, and Damien on one knee, offering her a box with a ring in it, and the rest of his life. She remembered the joy of that day, their happiness as they'd splashed in the water and danced to their own music on the sand.

'You were right,' she told him softly. 'You said they'd come to yoga, and you were right.' She opened her eyes and watched the sparks of light hitting the sea. 'I miss you so much, my darling,' she whispered, feeling her throat clog, her eyes burn. An ocean of tears cried since she'd lost him.

On her way back up the garden she felt a presence behind her. She turned to see the ginger cat padding along in her wake. She hadn't given him a name. He no longer streaked away when she appeared but he still didn't allow her to get close enough to touch him. She'd never heard him mew, or make a sound of any kind. The only time she saw him was when he wanted food.

Not old, she thought. Not much out of kittenhood, to judge by the balletic way she'd seen him leap at anything that moved – a leaf caught by the breeze, a stray feather, a small flying creature. The bald patches on his coat were filling in, and she figured she could take the credit for that.

Maybe she could ask Gareth to drop by now and again with food after she'd left, just until the house was sold. And maybe the new owners would continue to nourish him.

Back in the kitchen she found an empty cardboard box, destined for recycling but not yet broken up. She lined it with newspaper and brought it out with his food, and while he was eating she deposited it in a corner of the shed and pushed the window open wide enough for him to leap in and out. She must ask Gareth not to close it. He'd probably think her foolish to be indulging a wild cat.

He might be wild, but he needed her, like the growing life in her womb needed her. It was good to feel needed.

# 12

'ALL LOOKS GREAT,' THE MIDWIFE SAID BRIGHTLY. 'Baby is the right size, and that heartbeat is fine and strong. Now, do you want me to keep referring to it as Baby, or would you like to know if you're having a he or a she?'

Lydia saw her – young, blonde, pretty – through a blur of tears. The screen that had been turned towards her she couldn't see at all. She hadn't been prepared for how tough this was, how a wave of emotion would hit her as soon as she'd lain down. It was all she could do to stop herself bursting into loud sobs. She tightened her grip on Greta's hand, unable to speak.

'Tell you what,' the midwife went on, in the same cheery voice, 'I'll write it down for you, and you can decide later, after you've had a cuppa. You can open it or tear it up. Is that OK?'

She made it sound like a game, no doubt assuming Lydia's emotion was the usual mix of trepidation and excitement that most mothers-to-be, especially first-timers, went through. The truth, if she only knew, was that Lydia would have happily swapped her pregnancy for another hour with Damien.

Although she was doing everything she could to protect their baby – eating right, exercising, getting as much sleep as she could manage – she still felt no emotional bond with it. She took the little envelope when it was offered. 'Thank you,' she said, and wiped the gel from her abdomen with paper towels.

Greta had driven Lydia to the medical centre in the town, Marian and Susan both at work. Lydia had phoned her from Dublin as she'd planned, and told Greta she was sorry for getting angry at the station.

*Do not apologise*, Greta had replied. *You were upset – it was understandable. And of course you were right: it was none of my business.*

*Actually, I've decided to let the couple see the room.*

*Ah.* A short silence had followed, and then: *If you tell me the time, I will meet your train when you return.* And no more had been said on the subject.

They left the medical centre now and found a café, where Greta ordered two bowls of vegetable soup without consulting Lydia. 'No more goat's cheese for you,' she said, 'but I have eggs in the van. Make sure you cook them well.'

For someone who wasn't a mother, she seemed familiar with what pregnant women could and couldn't eat. As if she was reading Lydia's mind, Greta said, quite matter-of-factly, 'I had a son, a long time ago.'

Lydia regarded her in astonishment. 'Greta, I had no idea.'

'I do not speak often of him. It was in another life. I was married. I married young, my husband was older. We were happy – or I thought we were. I was twenty-one when I got pregnant. The prospect of a child felt like a gift from the universe.'

The café was warm, and full of diners. The clatter of cutlery and the buzz of conversation faded as Lydia listened to the story unfold.

'My labour was long and difficult, in the middle of a harsh winter – but as soon as I saw him, I forgot the pain. He was perfect. I know every mother must think the same, but . . .' One shoulder lifted, just a fraction.

Lydia sensed the ending wasn't happy – *I had a son, it was in another life* – but maybe she was wrong. Maybe he was still in the world, a scientist in a lab in Germany, or a diplomat somewhere else. Maybe he taught German to foreign students, or baked bread for a living.

'We called him Gerhardt. He lived for six months, and then he died.' The devastation, wrapped up in a handful of simple words. Her face gave nothing away. 'He left us the way some babies leave, without warning and without explanation.'

She paused, reaching to touch the salt cellar, stroking the side of it with her thumb. It reminded Lydia of the gentle, absent way she'd stroked the back of her hand when she'd called to sit with her in those first nightmarish weeks.

'We didn't deal with it, which is to say we never spoke of him. We remained married, but it wasn't the same. Because of my traumatic labour I was advised that another pregnancy would not be sensible, so we never tried again. We stayed together for six more years, until he found a substitute for me. Another younger woman.'

'Oh, Greta.'

She came across as so capable, so strong. Lydia was reminded again of Father Phil's words: *You'll learn to live with it, because you have to.* She imagined all the people who'd learnt to live with their grief, holding down jobs and raising families and meeting friends and going on holidays, the sadness tucked carefully inside, its sharpness blunting, becoming a little more bearable with each day that passed, but never leaving them.

'I came alone to Ireland,' Greta continued, 'a few years after my marriage ended. I knew nobody here, not one single person. I was thirty-one, and I wanted to go where I could begin again, and I had heard that Ireland was a good place for that. In the village I was welcomed, so I stayed.'

'You'll never move back to Germany?'

'No.' Without hesitation. 'I will never live there again. Here is my home now.' She studied Lydia. 'I think,' she said, 'that you would like to stay longer.'

'You mean at Chance House?'

'Of course.'

'I need to be back in Dublin before the baby's born. I don't fancy moving house with a baby in tow.'

'And kindly remind me why you are moving back to Dublin.'

So direct. Despite the sad story that had just been told, Lydia felt a faint stir of exasperation. 'Greta, the house is far too big for me. It was perfect for what we'd planned, but it's not right any more. There are ten bedrooms, two in the apartment and eight more in the main house, and the dining room and kitchen are designed to function as a business. It would make no sense to live in it as a private home.'

'There is always more than one way to do something,' Greta observed. 'We do not always have to choose what makes sense. But I see you do not wish to speak of it, so I shall stop.'

Their lunch arrived just then, and Lydia picked up her spoon, relieved. The soup had been lightly blitzed, leaving some chunks of carrot and turnip, and curves of red onion, and shredded greens.

Lydia thought of Andrew's vegetable soup, and how it had tasted better.

'I shall tell you of my goats,' Greta said.

That afternoon she went for a cycle, keeping it shorter than she would have liked because of the darkening clouds – heavy rain on the way, according to the weather forecasters, and she didn't relish the thought of getting caught in a downpour.

Back home, she coaxed the cat to the shed with its bowl of food, the rain just beginning, and lit the fire and prepared a lentil curry as the London Philharmonic Orchestra played a Schubert symphony. And while she chopped onions and made stock, she imagined living here with her child.

She saw them on the little beach at the bottom of the garden on a sunny afternoon, the baby lying contentedly on a soft blanket under a big umbrella.

She saw them again on the beach, this time at the water's edge, a toddler holding fast to Lydia's hand, shrieking as a wavelet rushed towards them.

She saw herself wheeling a buggy into the village, stopping to chat with everyone she met.

She saw herself dropping her child to the school every morning. She saw her child playing in the garden with friends. A swing, a seesaw, a sandpit. Plenty of room for everything.

Ridiculous – but not the first time she'd envisaged staying here, not the first time she'd imagined a different possibility. Greta hadn't put the idea into her head: she'd simply prodded it awake again.

It was crazy. A big old house, even a fully renovated one, needed a big income to run it, to pay its utility bills and keep it in good repair. Unless Lydia planned to open a small hotel – she didn't – there was no earthly way she could live in it.

She ate her dinner watching an episode of *Frasier* that she'd seen countless times, and then she watched another because it was too early to go to bed.

And it wasn't until later, after getting into pyjamas and brushing her teeth and cleaning her face, that she sat on the edge of the bed and found the midwife's envelope and pulled out the page inside, and read the five words written there.

*You're having a girl – congratulations!*

A girl. A daughter.

She reached into her bag again and retrieved the printout of the scan, but the image was frustratingly unclear, full of dark smudges she couldn't identify. Was that the head? Could that be one of the legs? She had no idea. She took a photo of it with her phone and sent it to both her parents. *Your granddaughter*, she wrote – and in less than a minute her phone rang.

'Lydia!' her mother exclaimed. 'A little girl! We're just thrilled!'

'Does everything look alright?'

'It looks perfect, exactly as it should.'

'I can't make sense of it.'

Her mother explained, and it became a little clearer, but not much.

'What did the midwife say?' her mother wanted to know, and Lydia reported all she could remember.

After the call she climbed into bed, still digesting the news that she was to be mother to a daughter. What was that rhyme about a girl with a curl in the middle of her forehead?

Two of her Dublin friends had daughters; Lydia had bought

sweet little dresses when they were born. Such pretty clothes for baby girls.

A girl. Sophie Cotter. Aisling Cotter. Or maybe a different name, one she had yet to think of.

*There was a little girl, and she had a little curl.* She smiled sleepily and closed her eyes.

# 13

SHORTLY BEFORE SEVEN THEY BEGAN TO TRICKLE IN, alone or in pairs, depositing jackets on the rail borrowed from Marian that Lydia had left outside the studio doors, chatting while they took off footwear. They gave Lydia their names as she ticked her list. All shapes, all ages, the youngest still in her teens by the look of her, the oldest somewhere in her seventies. All female.

Because it was Monday, one of the extra nights she'd added, none of the people she'd come to know best were there. Most of the names meant little to her, but the faces were becoming more familiar. She'd remember the names better, now that she was looking at them on a list and encountering the people who owned them every week.

'Complete beginner,' a few told her.

'Done a little,' a couple of others said.

'Dicky hip,' one admitted.

'Bad knees.'

'Weak back.'

'Awful balance.'

'Can't tell my right from my left.'

To all, she said what she'd said before every class in Dublin: 'Just do what you can. Listen to your body and don't compare yourself to anyone else.'

When everyone had arrived she regarded them seated on their mats, looking expectantly at her, just as she'd imagined them. She took a deep breath, aware of the inner trembling that had been with her since she'd got up that morning. The children were one thing: this was quite another.

'Thank you all for coming. I really appreciate it. I'm not sure how this will go, but I'm grateful to you for giving me the chance to find out. I've taught yoga for years – I'm just slightly nervous this evening, because this is my first adult class . . . in a while, so please bear with me.'

Looking from one face to another, she saw their encouraging smiles, their silent support, their wish for her to succeed. Sisterhood came to mind. She closed her eyes and summoned her old workplace in Dublin. *You can do this*, her boss said. *It's like breathing for you.* She opened her eyes.

'Yoga,' she began, 'is a way of waking up your body, of letting it know you love and respect it. Yoga is never about pain or punishment – it's about enjoyment, and release, and satisfaction. It's about giving your body exactly what it needs.'

With every word she spoke, her confidence returned. As with the infant class, she felt herself slipping on her yoga-teacher persona as easily as a beloved dress. It was going to be OK.

'I know I have mixed abilities here, so I'll be gauging everyone's level and keeping a good eye out as we go through the class – and sometimes I'll offer a more advanced version of what we're doing, for those who feel able. Give every movement your full attention. Let your day go, whatever kind of a day it's been, and forget about the person on the next mat. This is your hour, your gift to yourself. So let's start by taking a deep, loving breath in through your nose.'

The hour passed, not without its mishaps. A few stumbles, a few nervous giggles, a few frustrated hisses. 'Don't be hard on yourself,' Lydia told them. 'If you don't quite get there, try again.'

During the final relaxation she remained silent, letting them digest what they'd experienced, allowing them to let everything go, undisturbed. Afterwards, as they got back into shoes and jackets, they told her what they thought.

'I didn't know what to expect – I absolutely loved it!'

'I had no idea how tightly wound up I was – I feel so much looser now. That spinal twist you did was beautiful.'

'I loved that too.'

'I could do the forward fold every night.'

'Do the ones you like as often as you can,' Lydia told them. 'Anywhere you can, anytime you think of them. Make yoga part of your day and your body will thank you.'

'See you next Monday,' they said as they filed out, and as she worked her way through the rest of the week she made many more new acquaintances, and everyone seemed happy with what she was offering.

They all loved the studio, with its view of the sea. Nobody asked what she was going to do with the rest of the house once it was finished. Maybe they thought it would upset her to be asked about future plans, reminding her of the ones that would never come to pass.

'They're going down well,' she told her parents midway through the week. 'People seem to like them.'

'How's the sleep?' they asked. 'Are you eating enough? Are you taking your supplements? Has your GP booked your next scan?'

'I mentioned Chance House to Terence,' her father said. 'He'll be happy to take care of the legal stuff for you when you put it on the market. He sends his best wishes.'

She didn't tell them about the wedding reception that was taking place on Saturday. She wasn't sure they'd approve, so she played safe and said nothing.

On Friday night, Susan rang. 'Just checking in.'

'All set for tomorrow?'

'We are. How about you?'

'I'm going to Marian's.'

'Good. I wish you were staying here,' Susan said. 'I mean, not moving away. I get why you're going, and I know it makes sense, but it's still a shame, isn't it? We'll all miss you.'

A lump in her throat. 'I'll bring the baby back,' she said, 'for a visit.'

'Make sure you do. By the way, Andrew has a key to drop the furniture in tomorrow – Marian gave it to him so he wouldn't disturb you.'

Lydia felt a bolt of déjà vu – her tatty dressing gown, her ancient slippers. After the call she was unsettled.

This might be more difficult than she'd anticipated.

She was still in bed when she heard him. She'd intended not to go out, but now it seemed mean to ignore him. She showered and dressed and went to the hall to find him emerging from the dining room.

'All done?'

'All done. I hope I didn't wake you.'

'No. They have a lovely day for it.' Clear blue sky and April sunshine, no sign at all of clouds. Not that warm, but nothing like the bitter cold of her own wedding day. She remembered hunching in the church porch as Denny had taken snaps. 'Are you the photographer today?'

'I am.' He gave the eyebrow lift. 'I could hardly say no.'

'You should bring everyone around to the back if the weather holds, get the sea view into a few of the photos.'

'Good idea, thanks.'

She was glad Gareth had taken off with a couple of friends for a city break in London. She could imagine his reaction if he heard her inviting a small crowd into the garden. He was endearingly protective of it, nursing the lawn along, keeping the weeds at bay in the various beds, charging her with equal vigilance in his absence.

After Andrew left she went online, and whiled away the rest of the morning scrolling through nursery furniture websites, shocked at the price of cots and changing tables, feeding chairs and nappy bins. Small babies evidently cost big money: just as well she had a big house to sell.

As one o'clock approached – the reception was set for three – she packed a bag with towel and togs, just in case, and got the bicycle out. As she rounded the corner of the house she came face to face with a woman – fortyish, athletic build – getting out of a small blue van. Already?

'Lydia.' Her brown hair was pulled into a tight bunch. She was dressed for work in black trousers and white shirt. 'I'm Cathy, good to meet you. I'm doing the catering today. This is my first trip of two – I just want to see the lie of the land, and drop in desserts. I'll bring the hot food closer to the time.'

Lydia shook the offered hand. 'Welcome to Chance House.'

'Thank you. It's something else, isn't it? You wouldn't have a clue it was here from the road.'

'No . . . I hope Susan warned you about the limited resources.'

'She did indeed, and I'm not worried – I'm self-sufficient when I have to be. By the way, I have a daughter, Clodagh, in junior infants. She loves your yoga.'

'I'm glad to hear that. They're a great little group.'

'I'm raging I didn't sign up myself for your classes here – I suppose you're full?'

'I am, but I've had a few more enquiries, so I'm thinking of offering a Friday class.' Why not? Her evenings were free, and it was only an hour. Two more names had joined her waiting list, so Cathy would make it eight. Nearly enough.

'Oh, please put me down if you do.' Cathy took a white card from her wallet and passed it to Lydia. 'You might let me know if it goes ahead.'

'I will.'

'Are things getting easier for you?' she asked then, her voice softening.

'. . . They are.' Were they? Maybe. Sometimes.

'I'm glad to hear it. Have a good day.'

'And you.'

She pedalled into the village, bound for Marian and Tom's house. *Come to us,* Marian had said. *We'll have lunch and then we'll head off for a swim somewhere if the day is nice. We'll have to bring Jack – Tom's meeting a client in Galway.*

Turning on to the road where they lived, she was reminded of the last time she'd cycled this way, the day she'd told Kathleen and Brendan of the pregnancy, and Kathleen's furious reaction. Soon she must let Brendan know that she was carrying a girl, not wanting them to hear it from anyone else.

She found Marian slicing a quiche into wedges on the patio while Jack kicked a ball around the garden.

'There you are – I thought we'd grab the chance to eat al fresco. I can give you a fleece if you need it. Jack, mind the flowers. Anything happening yet at your place, Lydia?'

'Just the caterer. She arrived as I was leaving.'

'Cathy. I have her Clodagh in my class – she's the little redhead with the glasses. They're lucky with the weather anyway.' She put a plate in front of Lydia. 'Help yourself to salad.'

After lunch they headed to the beach, although by now the sun was dipping behind clouds, more hidden than visible. A few others were there ahead of them, and even some hardy souls in the water. As they sat in fleeces on a big orange towel, watching Jack digging up sand at the water's edge, Marian told her she was worried about Kathleen.

'She's not good. She's really low. Brendan has his hands full. I go up sometimes to give him a break, just to sit with her, but I may as well not be there. All she does is stare into space.'

'What does the doctor say?'

'She's given her medication, but Kathleen won't take it. And she refuses point blank to try counselling.'

*Will it bring him back?* she'd asked, when Lydia had told them of the pregnancy. And then her sudden, shocking outburst – *Don't!* – when Brendan had attempted to intervene, and to Lydia: *I wish he'd never met you! It's your fault!* The sting of her words persisted – but Lydia did feel sympathy. Sounded like Kathleen was a long way from learning to live with it.

After pulling off socks and shoes and paddling in water that hadn't yet lost its winter chill they decided against a full swim. They built sandcastles and collected shells with Jack, and then got ice-cream cones from a van that appeared at the top of the beach. 'He'd show up in a tornado,' Marian said.

It was the perfect distraction. Whenever her thoughts drifted to Chance House, she pulled them back. On the way home they stopped in the village and Lydia bought bags of chips from the takeaway, and they sat on the school wall to eat them.

By the time they got back to the house, Tom had returned from Galway and was uncorking wine. He greeted Lydia with a hug, something he'd never done before they'd lost Damien. 'You had a good day?' he asked her.

'We did, lovely.'

He was pining for his younger brother. She could see it in his eyes, sense the sadness behind his smile. Damien's death had changed them all.

'Would you stay the night?' Marian asked Lydia. 'I can give you pyjamas' – but Lydia said no, weary from an afternoon of having to put on a cheerier front than she felt because of Jack, and craving the peace of her own company.

'I'll head off,' she said – but her sister-in-law wouldn't hear of her cycling.

'I'll run you home. Tom, will you put her bike in my boot, and I'll bring you back chips? Jack, say goodnight to Auntie Lydia.'

It was just gone seven when they turned into the lane. They saw the straggling line of cars.

'Still here,' Marian said, cutting the engine. 'I was hoping they'd be gone. We should have kept you a bit longer.'

'I don't mind. I'll stay out of their way.'

When they opened the car doors they heard music. Together they manoeuvred Lydia's bike from the boot. 'Want me to come in with you?'

'Not at all. Go home and enjoy your evening. Thanks a million for taking me in.'

'Never a problem, my dear. Night, night, hope you sleep.'

The music was louder at the entrance, a buzz of conversation and laughter audible beneath it. Sounded like it was going well. Lydia skirted the driveway, giving the house as wide a berth as she could, hoping she wouldn't be spotted.

But then, just before she rounded the corner, something made her stop and glance back. From this angle she could see only a small section of the dining room through the bay window closest to her – but there they were, the newlyweds, just inside. The bride was in royal blue, her groom in navy or black. Arms entwined, talking with a few others, a sudden loud laugh erupting from Lorraine, their companions joining in.

Happy again, after losing their partners. Here was their second chance, in Chance House. She remembered Damien saying something about the name, the day he'd brought her to see it for the first time.

An omen, he'd called it. *Our chance to make something wonderful*, he'd said, or words to that effect. And then he'd died, and Lydia had wanted to die too. No more chances for her, nothing wonderful any more.

But now there was a baby on the way. Maybe this was *her* second chance. Maybe, rather than being cruelly treated by fate, she was in fact being offered a different kind of love.

She brought the bike around to the back of the house, where the sounds of the celebration were muted enough for her to make out the softer music of the sea. As she crossed the patio she saw that the bowl of food she'd left out before leaving for Marian's was still full.

Odd. He'd never missed a feed, not once. She cast about, straining to see any sign of him, but nothing stirred, nothing emerged from the border of trees. 'Puss,' she called, 'puss,' but he didn't come. She told herself he was a wild cat, used to roaming, and no doubt well able to look after himself, but still she felt a small uneasiness.

She left the bicycle on the patio, too tired to go down to the shed. She tucked his bowl of food behind it, where it would get some protection if rain arrived. She might be running the risk of feeding less desirable creatures, but she hated the idea of him going hungry.

She went inside to shower off the sand from her afternoon on the beach, and it wasn't until the following day that she found him.

# 14

ALL THROUGH HER MORNING YOGA, RAIN LASHED against the studio's picture window. The sky was a uniform sludge-grey, no chink of blue to be seen. She didn't mind: she had no plans to go anywhere today. After finishing her session she ventured into the dining room, wanting to see how they'd left it. She didn't imagine much cleaning would have taken place at the end of what had sounded like a lively evening.

She was wrong. Tables had been cleared and folded and propped with the chairs by the door, along with a pair of black bin bags, neatly tied. Crockery, glasses, cutlery – all unwashed, no way to wash them without water – were stacked in boxes, along with salt and pepper cellars, candlesticks, placemats, trivets and the like.

Tablecloths were folded, the stack left on a windowsill. The floor needed cleaning, but other than that they'd done pretty well.

For breakfast she hard-boiled one of Greta's duck eggs and ate it with toasted granary bread, still enjoying the novelty of being able to eat normally again. She was brushing her teeth afterwards when she suddenly remembered the missing cat. She put on her raincoat and went out.

The food bowl was empty – but was he the one who'd emptied

it? She'd have to wait and see if he turned up. She wheeled her bicycle down to the shed and opened the door – and there he was, in the box.

No, not he. She'd been wrong to assume the cat was male.

She was lying on her side, with – Lydia counted, or attempted to count, the tiny, squirming, wriggling creatures – four, no, five kittens, three with their mother's ginger markings and two patched with black and tan. They clambered and wobbled blindly over each other as they snuffled into the fur of their mother's underbelly in search of a teat to latch on to.

She'd been pregnant too. She regarded Lydia now as her babies fed, watchful but not showing signs of fear. Lydia propped the bicycle against the wall and inched closer, the cat's gaze never leaving her.

'Clever girl,' she whispered. The cat remained unblinking, and still calm. Deciding, finally, to trust her feeder – and emitting, Lydia could hear now, a low, steady purr. Contentment. Achievement. Knowing instinctively what to do as a mother, as all animals did.

She'd never seen newborn kittens in the flesh. She dropped quietly to her hunkers, fascinated by the minuscule tails and ears, the pudgy little bodies, the tiny paws kneading the mother's belly as they fed. So fiercely focused on the food, instinct again telling them where to find it.

Not a stray, like their mother. These kittens had been born in a shed, to a cat that had come to expect regular meals – and now that she was feeding five babies, those meals were more important than ever.

How would she cope when her food source disappeared?

Lydia was deserting her. Before the kittens, it had been easier to tell herself that the cat would manage without her – but now, leaving her seemed much more heartless.

Then again, Lydia would still be here by the time the kittens were weaned, and rehoming them should be simple enough. Susan would find takers among the school's parent body, or maybe some of Lydia's yoga students would be interested – but who would want to give a home to an adult cat? Bringing her to Dublin wasn't an option – her parents weren't cat people. Even if they were, how could Lydia subject an animal accustomed to the freedom of the countryside to the constraints and dangers of the city?

She watched as one by one the sated kittens drifted off and fell asleep, so heaped together that it was difficult to say where one stopped and another began. Relieved of her duties, the mother cat sat up and began washing herself.

Lydia left the shed and hurried through the rain back to the house. She texted Gareth: *The shed is a maternity ward now. The cat had five kittens. You'll have to tiptoe in.*

*I take it this is the male cat you were feeding,* he replied. *A modern miracle. Should I bring flowers when I visit, or would he prefer a few grapes?*

Later, as she was changing the sheets on her bed, she heard a van pulling up outside.

'Morning,' Andrew said. 'They chose the right day for the wedding.' By now the rain had lightened to a drizzle.

'They did. It went well?'

'Very well. Hope we didn't disturb you.'

'Not at all – and you left it very clean.'

'All apart from the floor. Susan's bringing some fancy mop from the school to clean it later. She'll take away Cathy's stuff too.'

'Fine.' On impulse, she said, 'Have you a minute to spare? There's something I want to show you.' He fed stray cats too. He might enjoy the kittens.

She brought him through the apartment and out to the back. 'Shaping up well,' he said of the garden. 'It must have been pretty bad.'

'Like a jungle. Did you get any outdoor photos yesterday?'

'No – they decided it was a bit on the chilly side.'

They approached the shed. 'Looks freshly built,' he remarked.

'The ruin of it was here. We got Noel to restore it.'

We. It hurt.

She wondered if the mother cat would take fright at the sight of Andrew – but the kittens were alone in the box, still all tumbled up drowsily together. He hunkered down beside them.

'These are from the cat you were feeding?'

'Yes. I thought she was a tom. I discovered them this morning.'

'Gingers and tortoiseshells,' he said. 'Beauts. What colour's the mother?'

'Ginger.'

'Unusual,' he said. 'They're normally toms.'

'I didn't know that. I just assumed she was male.'

He reached in and eased one of the kittens away from the rest. It gave a surprisingly loud protesting squeak, and another. In his hand it looked even tinier. He stroked the furry little head with a finger, and the squeaking stopped. 'We always had cats growing up,' he said. 'Lots of kittens.'

'Is it OK to handle them when they're this young?'

'It's fine, good to get them used to it' – so Lydia squatted to lift out her own, and cradled it to her chest. It weighed nothing at all.

She ran her thumb along its back, and to her delight, it set up a tiny purring. She felt the rapid beating of a pulse against her palm, and something quickened in her.

'If you're looking for homes,' he said, 'I'd take a couple when they're good to go.'

'Really? That would be great – I was hoping people would want them.'

'I had a dog, but he died last year. I always felt bad leaving him on his own for the day while I was at work so I didn't replace him. Cats would be more independent, especially if there were two of them.'

'Well, you can take your pick – you're the first offer I've had.'

'Maybe one of each then.'

'I'll earmark them for you.' She replaced her kitten and watched it push its way back into the huddle. 'I'm not sure I want to move back to Dublin,' she said, all in a rush – and was immediately shocked. What was she saying – and why was she saying it to him? They hardly knew each other.

She turned from the kittens to find him regarding her. Their faces were on a level.

'You want to stay here, in Chance House?'

'I think so. Yes.'

He gave one of his slow smiles. 'So stay then.'

'It's not that simple.'

'Why not?'

'Because . . . this house was meant for a different life. It doesn't fit into the life I have now. You know I'm pregnant,' she added. He had to know. Everyone knew by now.

'I do . . . I'm not sure,' he said hesitantly, 'if congratulations are in order.'

'Neither am I,' she told him. It felt like she could say anything at all to him. 'It's partly why I have to go back to Dublin.'

The eyebrow lifted a fraction. 'People have babies here too. They're not confined to Dublin, you know.'

She had to smile. 'I'd need help from my parents. I have no experience with babies.'

'You'd have plenty of help here. You've seen how people are.'

'I have . . .'

'And you're giving classes in the studio now, and you're living in your bit of the house. You're making use of it.'

'That's just it though. I'm only using a small part of it. The rest will be lying idle when Brendan and the other men have finished.'

He considered this, still absently stroking his kitten. 'If you think it doesn't fit into your life,' he said, 'maybe you need to find a different life.'

'I don't know what that means.'

'Me neither,' he admitted. 'But if you really want to stay, maybe you should try to find a way to make it happen. What about selling this house and buying a smaller one in the area?'

'No,' she said quickly. 'If I stayed, it would have to be here. This is the only house I want to live in. This is the one we chose.' We. Her heart squeezed again.

He set down his kitten. 'When do you go?'

'July.' Brendan had said early to mid June for everything to be done. She was giving herself a few weeks with no sounds of workmen. She could pretend, just for a little while, that she was staying for good.

He rose to his feet, and she did too. The shed felt small with both of them in it. One of the kittens gave a squeak that sounded indignant: Lydia looked in to see one of the tortoiseshells clambering over the others.

'Think about it anyway,' he said. 'Explore your options. Just make sure you end up in the right place. That's important.'

This was the right place. This was where she wanted to be. Suddenly, having voiced it, she was sure of it – but how on earth could she make it work? With the last few months being so fraught, so rocky, she still didn't fully feel part of the community, even if the classes were helping her to get to know more people. And while the income from them covered her day-to-day expenses, it wouldn't be enough to run the house long term, particularly over the winter, when it would need lots of heat.

She could offer daytime classes, but how many more people would want to sign up? In such a rural area, her customer base was limited. It was nothing like Dublin, where you could offer classes all day long, and they'd come. And even with full-time yoga classes, she would still be using only a fraction of the house.

They walked back up the garden, the rain having stopped, and she left him to pack up his van. After she thought he'd left, he reappeared with an envelope. 'I was told to give you this,' he said. 'From Lorraine and Ian.'

She looked at it. 'I hope they're not paying me.'

'Honestly, I don't know what's in it, but I hope they are. You helped them out of a bind, and I'm sure they saved a packet on the balance of their hotel bill.'

The thought of payment had never crossed her mind. She'd done them a favour, that was all – but when she opened the envelope after he'd gone, she found ten fifty-euro notes, and a letter.

*Dear Lydia*

*A small token of our gratitude. You came to our rescue; we'll never forget it, and I'm certain we'll have a wonderful time in your beautiful home.*

*Wishing you lots of happier days, you so deserve them. And Susan tells us you're expecting! Warmest congratulations, and hope the baby helps to heal your heart.*

*Please keep in touch if you want to – I'll put my phone number on the end of this.*

*Yours in friendship and thanks*

*Lorraine (and Ian) xx*

And below, as promised, a mobile phone number.

She set the letter and money on the table. Five hundred euro, just for lending them the dining room for a few hours. No work on her part, no expense bar minimal electricity and heat.

She sent a text: *Lorraine, I certainly wasn't expecting your generous gift, sincere thanks to you and Ian. Andrew tells me you had a good day and I was glad to hear it. Wishing you every happiness – Lydia*

And the reply came almost immediately: *You're more than welcome, Lydia. It was the least we could do. We had the best time, and everyone had a ball! Mind yourself – L and I xxx*

When Susan turned up later in the afternoon she was charmed by the kittens, and tickled at the thought of a pregnant Lydia unknowingly feeding a pregnant cat.

'I'll find homes no problem when the time comes,' she promised. 'I'll put the word out in the school. Might even take one myself, if I can talk Owen around.'

'I only need three homes,' Lydia told her. 'Andrew's already offered to take two.'

'Has he really? I'm delighted. His dog died last year, and he was gutted.'

Lydia told her of the money Ian and Lorraine had given her. 'Did you know about it?'

'Not a clue, honestly, but it was only right. Have you any idea what hotels charge?'

'But the bare venue was all they got here – and they had to pay Cathy too.'

'Doesn't matter. They still saved a packet.'

Later that evening, Lydia thought about the conversation in the shed, the one she hadn't planned to have. Andrew saying she needed to find a different life, needed to make it happen. And what had Greta said in the café, the day of the scan? Something about there being more than one way of doing things, and not always having to do what made sense.

It was all very vague and unrealistic.

Dreamers, the two of them. Just like Damien.

# 15

TIME PASSED. LYDIA SPENT ANOTHER NIGHT IN Dublin, and Brona came west again twice. Lydia said nothing to any of them about her wish to stay put in Chance House. She felt bad at not confiding in Brona, the first time she'd kept anything from her, but there was a reason she didn't.

Brona, like her parents, wanted her back in Dublin, and she'd know exactly what to say to convince Lydia that it was the best course of action, and Lydia didn't want to be convinced – although finding a way to stay on in Chance House continued to elude her.

She'd considered Airbnb – with so many bedrooms, she should easily make enough to live on – but then she thought about a procession of strangers up and down the stairs, wandering into the kitchen at all hours, and bound to disturb the yoga classes she would want to continue. Without reconfiguring the space, she couldn't think of a workable solution, and she couldn't face more alterations.

She'd turned the idea around and thought of letting the apartment instead, and living in the big house with the baby – but she liked this idea even less. The apartment held special memories;

the thought of strangers in it was awful – and anyway, the main part of the house was far too big for just two.

She could let it long term, hand it over to another chef to run a regular restaurant from it while she and the baby remained in the apartment, but she really didn't like the idea of living in such close proximity to a business she wasn't involved in. Her yoga classes would suffer too, with diners in and out in the evenings.

No different life came to mind, or not one she wanted to live. Unless something unexpected happened and the perfect solution presented itself, she had to accept that she would be packing her bags in July.

In the meantime, her sadness remained a thing she carried around. Time had softened the ache of Damien's loss a little – it was proving to be her friend, like Father Phil had said – making it possible for her to function, to smile, occasionally even to laugh, but she could also be ambushed without warning.

A snatch of an overheard song drifting from an open car window, one that had meant something to them; a whiff of the aftershave he'd worn; a laugh that summoned the memory of his; all of these and more could bring the shock of her loss crashing back, strong as it ever was. Sometimes a gorgeous evening sky would be enough to reduce her to a sobbing mess, reminding her of all the sunsets they'd never share.

But along with the sadness there were times of contentment too. Whiling away a dreamy hour on the garden seat that Marian had picked up in a charity shop and donated to the Chance House patio; sitting in the shed with the kittens, captivated by their cuteness; digging weeds from one of the flowerbeds, with Gareth testing her on plant names; lying on her mat in the studio, watching the day begin beyond the window; pedalling to a quiet beach on dry mornings to walk barefoot along the sand and wonder about the future.

She told Brendan she was having a girl, and then she told everyone else, and they were all happy for her, and she told herself she was happy too.

Father Phil still dropped by about once a week. 'I wanted to see how this splendid garden is getting on,' he'd say, or 'I need help with Greta's rhubarb tart – there's only so much of it one person can eat.' Sometimes he came with no excuse, and she was always glad to see him. He was a dear man, and she'd grown very fond of him.

'You'll miss it,' he said one day. 'This place.'

She wasn't sure whether he meant Chance House or the area. She nearly told him what she'd told Andrew, but then thought, What's the point?

'It's for the best,' she replied, and he looked like he was going to say something else, but didn't.

Work continued in the house. The days became longer, the air softer. Lydia had a few brief solitary dips in the sea from the little beach, wishing she could do more than just dip, and remembering Damien's promise to teach her to swim.

In the garden, bright green leaves fluttered on trees, plants spread out, the climbing rose made its slow, steady way up the shed, new blooms appeared in flowerbeds, and the camomile lawn grew thick and lush.

Gareth was teaching Lydia how to snip tiny shoots of bindweed at soil level from the flowerbeds – 'Try to catch it coming up, or it'll wind around everything it meets' – and why to leave dandelions alone in the wildflower patch, and what and how and when to deadhead for better flowering.

'Coming on nicely,' he remarked one day towards the end of May. 'Taking proper shape now.'

'It's a credit to you,' she told him. 'You've worked a miracle here. But please let me pay you, like I'd pay any gardener.' All he'd taken from her so far was the cost of supplies, and that only after she'd pushed.

He shook his head. 'No payment required.'

'Why not? You've done so much work here. I can't let it go unpaid.'

He shook his head. 'This isn't a job for me though. Not this garden.' He swept a gaze around. 'I'd be lost without it. I love seeing it coming on every bit as much as you do, and I'd like to feel that I can come and potter in it and pull up a few weeds or do a bit of pinching out whenever I want.'

'You can do all that,' she said, 'and still take payment.'

He gave her a sad smile then. 'Damien was my friend,' he said quietly, and she understood. It was his tribute, his gift. No money needed, or wanted.

'Thank you,' she said. 'You're creating something wonderful here. I wish . . .' She didn't finish it.

'I know. I know you do. How're the kitties today?' he asked, and they set the topic aside and went down to inspect the goings-on. Since Lydia had discovered two of the kittens out of their box and racing around the shed one morning, changes had been made. She'd got one of Brendan's carpenters to fence off an inner section for them by the window, and to construct a little outside enclosure that they could access to play in the fresh air.

They stood and watched the rough and tumble. 'We'll be sorry to lose you,' Gareth said, 'when you head back to the big smoke.'

At least he didn't tell her to find a different life. She hadn't seen Andrew for a while, no reason for him to call by. They weren't friends exactly, although she enjoyed his company too. She hoped he remembered his offer to take two kittens off her hands.

And then, one evening as she was rolling up her mat after a class, when everyone had left and she was alone in the studio, she felt the oddest little flutter inside her. Like a confined butterfly, or popping bubbles.

She straightened up. She stood stock still for several seconds but nothing else happened, and she put it down to trapped wind until the following morning – and again she experienced the same light little whirring sensation as she reached into the fridge for milk.

She placed a palm on her abdomen, and within a few seconds she felt a tiny nudge, just the smallest movement against the wall of her womb – and it came to her with a little shock.

Her baby was saying hello.

Her daughter was making her presence felt.

Her mother had said, about a week ago, that she should start to feel some movement soon, and here it was.

Wow.

She was growing a baby. She would bring a new human into the world. It was such a huge thing to get her head around. She would be someone's mother. Up to this, the reality of it hadn't really sunk in. In just a few months she would give birth. *I have a daughter*, she would say, if anyone new asked about children after that.

She wondered what kind of person her child would grow into, what tastes she would have, what talents, what dreams.

She wondered how in the world she would keep her safe.

'Hello,' she whispered. 'I'm Lydia. I'm your mother.'

She would not bring her up as a vegetarian: she would allow her to make her own decision about that – although she wasn't sure she'd manage to cook meat for her. She'd have to figure that out.

She would introduce her to yoga, right from the start. She would do baby massage, and stretch and bend the tiny limbs. Imagine if she turned out to want to teach yoga too, like her mother.

She would read her stories, all the ones she'd loved in her childhood, and all the new ones that had come out since.

She would cook with her. She would introduce her to dishes that Damien had introduced *her* to.

She would make sure she looked after her teeth, and drank enough water.

She would teach her to be kind and thoughtful.

She hoped she would find true friends. She hoped she would love music, like Damien had. She hoped love wouldn't break her heart – but of course it would, at least once.

Later in the day she rang her mother to tell her about the stirrings.

'That's wonderful, sweetheart – always great to get that reassurance. You should feel regular movement from now on, and it'll become stronger as the baby develops. I wish you were here, so we could share this.'

'I'll see you soon, Mum.'

Now that they knew she was moving back in July, they'd stopped trying to manage her. She was grateful. They would be a big help in Dublin.

She rang Marian and got her voicemail because it was a school day, and left a message. 'The baby kicked,' she said. 'I thought you'd like to know.'

She rang Brona, who always took calls at work. 'Hey, that's fantastic! I'm thrilled, very exciting. Can't wait for you to be living here again, and I can babysit.'

'What do you mean, babysit? You'll be out with me. Mum and Dad will be babysitting.'

'That's true.'

It would be great when they lived in the same city again, and could meet up as often as they liked. One of the big positives about moving back.

She must focus on the positives, like Damien always had.

# 16

SIX DAYS INTO JUNE, SHORTLY BEFORE FOUR O'CLOCK in the afternoon, there was a tap on the door that connected the apartment to the main house.

'All done,' Brendan said.

'Finished?'

'Finished.'

It wasn't unexpected. The painters had been working on the outside for the past few days, their final task, and Lydia had heard the metallic clatters and bangs earlier that had signalled the dismantling of their scaffolding. Still, to have the work completed was quite momentous, and it brought with it a pang that was not unexpected either. Her and Damien's dream finally realised – except that only she was here to witness it. No celebrating, no new beginnings, just a sad closure.

But Brendan must have his moment. 'Will you show me around?'

'I will.'

The workmen were waiting in the hall to say goodbye. She gave them each an envelope into which she'd slipped a fifty-euro note a few days ago, and thanked them for all their labour.

Her overriding sense, as she walked with Brendan through the downstairs areas, was that it wasn't finished, not in the real sense. The floors were down, the walls and ceilings painted throughout, sockets in place, power and water connected. Brendan and his team had taken things as far as they could, but with no appliances chosen for them to install, not even a sink in the kitchen, it felt horribly ... abandoned, before it had even been lived in.

'Lovely,' she said, and it would be, once whoever bought it filled in all the gaps.

Climbing the stairs to the first floor, she remembered Damien tossing a coin to decide the colour of the runner. She wondered what the new owners would choose. Maybe they'd opt to leave the stairs bare.

At the top she recalled their plan to hang mistletoe from the ceiling there every December, where guests couldn't avoid it on the way to their rooms. *Ambushed by mistletoe*, Damien had said. *By God, we'll force them to kiss.*

'You OK?' Brendan enquired, and she summoned a bright smile and told him yes, she was fine, and they walked through the bedrooms and looked into the ensuites – more pipes with nothing to attach to – and she said it was all great, and he'd done a wonderful job.

'You don't want to choose the toilets and showers and that?' he asked. 'And sinks for the kitchen? I could get Joseph to come back and install them. You'd have a better finish for when you sell it.'

Lydia shook her head. 'I have no appetite for it, Brendan.' She couldn't bring herself to buy things for a house she was leaving in a few weeks, even if it meant the selling price would be lower without them. A few sinks and toilets couldn't make that much difference, could they?

They stood at the window of what was to have been the guest lounge, its shelved alcove never to be filled now with their selection of books – they'd planned to hunt down old volumes in second-hand shops and house auctions – and looked out at the view Lydia had last seen with Damien by her side. The sea blurred into the sky, and she blinked hard.

'Toughest job I've ever done,' Brendan said, so quietly she hardly made it out, even though he was right there. Without turning her head she found his arm and tucked her hand around it, and they stood close together in front of the magnificent view, lost in their joint sadness.

Afterwards they walked out to the gateway and turned back to take in the façade without the scaffolding, and she saw that the soft shade Marian had suggested for the walls, between grey and green, had been the perfect choice. Tasteful, she thought. Classy. He would have loved it.

'Send me your last bill,' she told Brendan, but he shook his head.

'Hang on to it for the moment,' he said. 'You can pay me when you sell the house. You might need it between this and then. Just . . . with the baby and everything.'

He really was the kindest man. He would make the best grandfather for her daughter.

Her yoga classes had been due to finish at the end of the week, but in response to the demands of her students – *You're going to be here anyway*, they'd said – she'd agreed to continue on a week-by-week basis. She'd pushed her departure date as far as she dared, to the last day of July.

Not a single one of her students had dropped out during the eight weeks of classes. They'd all keep coming if she stayed. Her studio could be in use all year round. She tried not to think about that.

The kittens had all been rehomed, with Andrew taking two as promised, and Marian, Susan and Greta claiming the others. The four new owners had come on different days, and Lydia had found it hard to see the little family diminish, her head knowing she was doing the right thing, but her heart wanting to keep them all.

Andrew had been the last to collect his. *One of each*, Lydia had said, *just like you ordered*, and he'd tucked them into the new carrier he'd brought along.

*You're sorry to see them go*, he'd said.

*I'll miss them*, she'd admitted, and he'd told her she'd be welcome to visit them anytime, which was nice of him. He hadn't spoken again of her admission that she wished to stay here. He'd probably forgotten about it.

The mother cat, newly spayed thanks to Greta, who'd done the vet drop-off and pick-up, had roamed the garden afterwards, mewing mournfully, hunting for her babies in the bushes and behind the trees, making Lydia feel like a monster. Bad enough that she was about to abandon the animal after gaining her trust; now she had the added guilt of giving away her entire family.

*She'll be fine*, Gareth told her. *They forget their kittens very quickly – and she'll have her fill of shrews and field mice here after you've gone.* But Lydia had known the remorse would follow her all the way to Dublin, and she'd lined the box with fresh newspaper and left it in the shed.

Her pregnancy was advancing. Her due date, the eighteenth of September, was just over fourteen weeks away now, a month to the day before what would have been Damien's thirty-fifth birthday.

If she could, Lydia planned to bring her daughter back to the village on that day.

*First babies are always late,* Marian had told her. *Jack was ten days over – I was the size of an elephant, and as cross as a weasel. Tom was on the point of divorcing me.*

When her changing shape began to make her clothes feel uncomfortably snug, Lydia took to wearing Damien's shirts over her stretchy yoga pants, until a box of maternity clothes arrived unexpectedly, donated by a few of her friends. *Your turn!* the accompanying note read, signed by everyone.

She lifted out the tunics, the cleverly draped dresses and elasticated-waist trousers and skirts. There was a time when every item in her wardrobe would have been the latest fashion: now keeping up with the trends meant nothing to her. She hadn't been in a clothes shop in months, and didn't miss them.

She still went to bed every night in one of Damien's T-shirts. They'd long since lost his scent, but wearing something that had also touched his skin offered bittersweet comfort. She'd tried to imagine his arms around her at night, but that had hurt too much, so she'd stopped.

Even after her morning sickness had ebbed, her aversion to coffee hadn't: in its place she drank ginger tea, and had grown fond of it. Oddly, she'd also developed a taste for liquorice, something that had never interested her before, and she now preferred dark chocolate to milk, which was just plain weird.

She'd reported crampy twinges at the sides of her abdomen to Doctor Avril, who had reassured her. *They're perfectly normal, just your ligaments complaining a bit as they stretch. You're very fit,* she'd added, *with all your yoga and cycling. You're sailing through this pregnancy.*

It didn't always feel like sailing to Lydia. Her head swam if she stood up too quickly. Her back ached when she was tired, which was a lot of the time. She demonstrated less in the yoga classes, finding volunteers instead among the students, and her own sessions were decidedly less spirited than they had been.

She needed the loo more frequently, especially at night. Her ankles had swollen and she'd gone up two bra sizes, which she didn't exactly welcome. She'd always been perfectly happy with her small breasts, and Damien had never complained.

The baby movements had increased, as everyone had told her they would. She imagined her daughter tumbling about the womb like the kittens had in their enclosure, only not quite so energetically. They had frequent one-way conversations.

*Let me tell you about your father*, Lydia would say, or *I fancy a cheese omelette tonight – what about you?* or *Will we try that jigsaw again, you and me?*

She'd had a second scan in May. Now it was easy to pick out the limbs, tiny feet tucked up, a thumb going towards a mouth, the overall curled shape of her child. All was well, she was told. Everything fine.

Marian had passed on a pregnancy pillow. *I found it a godsend in the last few weeks*, she'd said, *when no position was comfortable. You mightn't need it yet, but you will.*

'I'm coming down again,' Brona said, when Lydia rang to report that the renovations were finished. 'I want to see the house all shiny. Is it fabulous?'

'It is – or it will be, when it's furnished.'

'Will you find it hard to part with it?'

Lydia could at least be honest about this. 'I'm dreading it,' she admitted. 'I'm sure it'll be easier once I'm back in Dublin, but right now I hate the thought of leaving.'

'Oh, poor Liddy. I didn't realise you felt that strongly about it.'

'It's grown on me.'

Her reluctance to let go was tied up with Damien, of course – but it was also because of the people she'd met here, who'd held her up when she'd been unable to see the way forward, and who'd supported her every step of the way since then.

'I'll organise a coffee morning when you're back,' Brona promised, 'or a welcome home dinner, if I can get a date when everyone's free, and of course we'll be doing a baby shower. How's that bump coming along?'

And then, a week or so after the work had finished on Chance House, while Lydia was still enjoying the novelty of no more power tools, the postman arrived with a letter.

# 17

*Dear Mrs Cotter*

*You don't know me, but my husband and I attended the wedding in April of Ian and Lorraine Butler, who had their reception in your beautiful home. Ian was married to my late sister Anne, and I had met Lorraine too on a few occasions, and they kindly invited me and my husband to their wedding.*

*May I offer my condolences to you at this stage? Lorraine told us of your bereavement, and I thought it terribly good of you to help them out under the circumstances – but because you did, it's given me the courage to write to you now with a very cheeky request.*

*Our daughter Ursula is engaged to a lovely man, Paul. They met in Dubai, where they both work, and they'd like to get married in Ireland. They were hoping around the end of this month, or early July, but they've had no luck finding a venue, probably because they left it a bit too late to go looking. They don't want a big fuss, just something low-key. When Ursula said they'd probably end up just booking a restaurant for a meal instead, I thought immediately of your lovely house, which I felt would make it a bit more special for them. I offered to ask you, so here I am.*

*They're not having a crowd, just eighteen guests in total, twenty including themselves. They would, of course, be very happy to pay whatever you charge, and they'd be fine with the way the house is too. We could organise the reception in much the same way that Ian and Lorraine did – Lorraine said her niece would be happy to help – and you would have absolutely nothing to do.*

*Would you be open to that at all? Their situation is delicate, and I'm trying to help them out. It's hard to explain in a letter, but if you were willing to consider my request I'd be very happy to meet you wherever suited, and give you the full story. I live about an hour from Chance House, on the other side of the town.*

*I'll put my phone number at the end, and if you could let me know yes or no, that would be great. Thanks a million for reading this, and every good wish for your future happiness, whether we meet or not.*

*Yours very sincerely*
*Tessa Blake*

Lydia skimmed it, then went back and read it properly. She copied the phone number on to the envelope before throwing the letter into the bin. She'd send a text later and tell the woman she was sorry she couldn't help.

She couldn't believe another couple were looking at Chance House for their wedding. What was it about the house that seemed to make it a magnet for engaged couples? Hadn't this woman seen how little it offered?

She wondered what the delicate situation could be.

But wasn't it weird that the couple had no date set at this stage? Around the end of the month or early July, the letter had said, and now it was halfway through June. Talk about last minute. What about the eighteen guests? Didn't they need a date for their diaries?

It wasn't that Lydia would have a problem letting another couple have their reception at Chance House: having done it once, and having found it not to be as traumatic as she'd envisaged, she didn't think she'd object to offering the dining room again, if the couple truly needed help.

But this was different. This pair hadn't been let down at short notice by a venue they'd booked; they just seemed incredibly disorganised. If they couldn't be bothered, why should Lydia? Let them go to a restaurant.

And yet . . . this woman, this Tessa, came across as a nice person. Polite, sincere, wishing Lydia well whether she helped them or not. She supposed it wouldn't hurt to meet her, see what she had to say for herself, decide if there was a genuine case of need.

She sent a text: *Tessa, it's Lydia Cotter here. I just got your letter. I'm not sure I'll be in a position to help you, but if you want to drop by the house we could have a chat about it. Does tomorrow afternoon suit, around four?*

A few minutes later, her phone beeped. *Lydia, thank you so much for your prompt reply. I'd be delighted to come and meet you. I'll see you tomorrow – Tessa*

It was just a meeting. She wasn't committing to anything.

Next day Tessa arrived five minutes early, an old red Mini pulling up in the driveway as Lydia was polishing the brasses of the front door. She looked around the age of Lydia's mother, shoulder-length light brown hair shot with white, pinned back with little gold clips. She wore a flowery dress beneath a navy jacket, a string of pearls around her neck. She approached Lydia with a tremulous smile.

'Hello. Lydia, I presume.'

'Yes,' Lydia replied, peeling off rubber gloves to offer her hand, 'and you must be Tessa.'

'I am. I'm delighted to meet you. The house looks wonderful – the painting hadn't been done when we were here.'

'No, it's just finished. Please come inside – I'll put the kettle on.'

In the apartment she took Tessa's jacket and hung it in the hall. The sleeves of the dress stopped at her elbows. It was the kind of dress you could wear to a wedding.

Tea was made, biscuits produced. Tessa admired the granite worktop, the floor tiles, the colour of the walls. She commented on the fine day, and asked if the cat on the windowsill was Lydia's – and finally, she got around to the wedding.

'It's Ursula's first, but not Paul's – he was married before, and his wife died.' She hesitated, her gaze fixed on the biscuits. 'He's from Uganda. He and Ursula work in the same hospital in Dubai. He's a doctor, she's a receptionist.' She glanced at Lydia. 'He's a really nice man.'

'So you said in your letter.'

'Sorry,' she said, blinking rapidly. 'I just – it's . . .' She lapsed into silence, lips pressed together. Anxious. Wrapping hands around her cup.

'You mentioned,' Lydia prompted, 'that there was a delicate situation.'

'I did.' Pause. 'It's my husband, you see. He's . . . well, he's difficult.' She darted another look at Lydia. 'Domineering.'

Yes. Living with a man who told her what to do would explain the jittery manner.

'And Ursula doesn't really see eye to eye with him. Neither of the children do really.'

'I see.' Might he have been the cause of Ursula going to live abroad? Lydia told herself to stop jumping to conclusions.

'He's great friends with our parish priest,' Tessa went on, 'and he wanted Ursula and Paul to get married in our church – Paul's Catholic too – and have a big reception in the local hotel, but Ursula doesn't particularly like the priest, he's a bit old school, and to be honest, she wasn't that keen on her father telling her what to do. Besides, neither of them wants a big flashy wedding – my husband was going to invite half the parish – so the whole thing has been . . . tricky.'

She trailed off. Her voice was too brittle. She hadn't touched her tea, hadn't gone near the biscuits.

'They've been searching for a venue for the last few months. They thought it would be easy to find somewhere – they'd originally planned to have fifty guests. They wanted a group of friends to come from Dubai, but they didn't realise how far in advance you need to book here, and I'm afraid neither did I. I hadn't been to a wedding in years before Ian and Lorraine's. So now they've decided to do a family-only thing here, and have a party back in Dubai for the others.

'I know this is very last minute, I should have contacted you sooner – it did occur to me on the day I was here that it might suit Ursula and Paul, but I didn't know if you'd consider letting another couple into your home. I know you were just helping out Ian and Lorraine.'

She looked on the verge of tears. 'Have some tea,' Lydia said.

Tessa picked up her cup obediently. She sipped and put it down again. 'Sorry,' she said. 'I shouldn't have involved you, Lydia. You have enough to cope with – you don't need our problems too.' She made to stand up. 'I'll leave you alone, if you'll just get me my jacket. Thanks for listening. We'll sort something out.'

'Hang on. Wait.'

She was doing this, wasn't she? She was getting into this awkward family situation, and she was going to involve Father Phil too. She was doing it to help Tessa, who'd fixed her hair and dressed up to meet Lydia, and who looked completely wrung out. Caught between a husband who sounded horrible – toadying up to the local priest, regarded as a pillar of the community, no doubt – and a presumably beloved daughter, doing what she could to make the day a happy one. Lydia could help, so she would.

'I'll talk to our priest here. He might agree to marry them, if he has a date free. I can't guarantee anything,' she said.

Tessa's face lit up all the same. 'Oh, that would be wonderful! And they could have the reception here?'

'They could.'

It would all depend, she thought, on whether Father Phil was happy to marry a couple he'd never met at terribly short notice. Then again, she and Damien hadn't given him a lot of notice – but he'd known Damien, so that was different.

'Try not to get your hopes up,' she said – but Tessa's hopes, she could see, were already sky high. Her eyes shone; a small flush had entered her cheeks.

'It would be marvellous if he said yes.'

'I'll talk to him today,' Lydia promised.

As soon as Tessa had left, she cycled into the village and found him at home.

'I'd like to run something by you,' she said, and filled him in.

'They're both Catholic?'

'They are.'

'And free to marry?'

'Yes.'

He nodded. 'All sounds in order then. Give them my number and we'll make arrangements. There'll be some paperwork to sort out.'

'Really? It's possible?'

Father Phil smiled. 'Everything's possible if you believe in it. If two people need my blessing to get married, and if there's nothing standing in their way, I'm happy to give it.'

'Thank you so much. They'll be thrilled. It sounded like they were losing hope.'

'Shame the bride's father isn't giving *his* blessing, though.'

Lydia had felt obliged to let him have all the facts. 'I know.' She couldn't imagine having to tiptoe around the man you were living with. Had it been going on for years? Were her children estranged from him, or all but? How horrible for Tessa if they were, because that surely had to impact on *her* contact with them.

Father Phil sat back and interlaced his fingers. 'So this is to be the third wedding celebration in Chance House.'

'It is.'

'Strange how things happen, isn't it?'

'Well, I have you to thank for making this one happen.'

'You've been kind enough to offer them your house, so let's call it a collaboration. Tell them to get in touch as soon as they can, so we can get the ball rolling and fix on a date.'

And Tessa, when Lydia rang her, was ecstatic. 'Oh Lydia, I can't thank you enough – I'll pass his number on this minute to Ursula.'

The third wedding reception at Chance House, when hers and Damien's had been the only one supposed to take place there – and if they hadn't brought their date forward, they'd never have got married.

As Father Phil had said, strange how things happened.

# 18

'BUT I DON'T UNDERSTAND,' HER MOTHER SAID. 'WHY do you feel obliged to accommodate these people? You don't even know them.'

Lydia was beginning to be sorry she'd mentioned it. 'I don't feel obliged exactly . . . It's complicated.'

'But how did they even know you own Chance House?'

She hadn't told them about Ian and Lorraine's reception, so she couldn't explain the connection. 'Word of mouth, I suppose. News travels fast in the country.'

'Well, it sounds to me like they're taking advantage, Lydia. Far cheaper for them to have their reception in your house than book a hotel.'

'Oh Mum, they'd have far more comfort in a hotel. They don't even have a cooker here – they'll have to provide everything themselves, like Damien and I had to.'

'You *are* charging them though?'

'Yes, I'll charge them . . . Look, it's not as if I'm going to be making a habit of this. I'll be gone in a few weeks.'

Her father was equally doubtful. 'Why would anyone choose a house with no facilities for a wedding reception? I could understand you and Damien – that was different – but complete strangers? Are you sure it's safe, Lydia, letting them into the house? You've just had the whole place renovated.'

'Dad, what harm can they do? There's nothing to take, no antiques for them to cart away, and it's just twenty of them. They're hardly going to run amok.'

The last Saturday in June they'd settled on, which was the end of next week. Father Phil would marry them at three o'clock, and Cathy the caterer would feed them afterwards – and if the weather obliged, they might use the garden for photographs, like Lydia had suggested to Andrew for Ian and Lorraine's celebration. It might be warm enough for this wedding party.

She mentioned it to Gareth, Saturday being one of his usual days. She'd expected a protest – his precious garden invaded – but instead he promised to give the lawn its first proper cut in honour of the occasion.

Tessa had told Lydia in a follow-up phone call that she probably wouldn't stay very long. *I imagine*, she'd said, *my husband will want to go home after the meal – but please don't worry about your house. Everyone will take great care of it and do as much cleaning up as possible before they leave. And I'll come back the day after with my sister Delia to make sure it's spotless.*

She would spend her daughter's wedding day, or as much of it as she was allowed to stay for, trying to keep the peace. Lydia didn't think the atmosphere would be very celebratory. Would anyone even make a speech, or would they decide the less said, the better?

Was her father right to be concerned about letting a group of strangers into her house? They *were* strangers, with Tessa the only one Lydia had met, but she didn't feel she had anything to fear.

This time she was having more of an involvement, because she'd set a price on it, following Tom's advice. *Charge them five hundred, like the others paid,* he'd said. *You're giving them the use of your home: don't undervalue what you're offering.* But it had seemed too much to charge for donating a room to just twenty people for a few hours, so Lydia had told Tessa the cost was three hundred euro – and two days later, twice that amount landed in her bank account. The sender was named as Paul Thembo. The accompanying message read *A sincere thank you from Paul and Ursula.*

In the meantime, she had another event to organise, one she'd kept from her parents. If her father was wary at the thought of twenty strangers in her dining room, what would he think of a few hundred wandering through every room in the house? *I'd like to have an open afternoon before I leave,* she'd said to Susan, *and let the locals see how the place has turned out. I thought Cathy might put on a buffet, and maybe I could get a few musicians as well. Will you spread the word?*

It was something she could offer them, after the way they'd all rallied around her. She'd thought to wait until closer to her departure, but Susan had advised her to have it sooner. *You'll be preoccupied with packing, and you'll be more tired too, since you'll be more pregnant* – so they'd settled on the coming Sunday, before Ursula and Paul's wedding.

Cathy arrived early and set out her offerings in the studio – cold cuts, savoury tarts, salads, cakes – and stayed to refill the dishes as people came and went. They wandered about, opening doors, climbing the stairs to check out the first floor, following the slate pathway down to the sea. Thankfully, the rain stayed away, even if the sun did too.

Instead of asking a few musicians to provide the entertainment,

Susan had invited everyone who played to bring an instrument – and there was music upstairs and down, and more on the patio and more by the sea.

Everyone knew Lydia was leaving. Many brought little tokens to say goodbye: chocolates, locally made soaps and candles, hand-knitted baby bootees, picture frames. Everyone told her they would be sorry to see her go.

It felt wrong, leaving Chance House. It felt like she was going against some dictate. It was terribly hard to hide her feelings. Her smile felt pasted on; she wondered if it fooled anyone.

Deborah, the estate agent who'd sold Lydia and Damien the house, was one of the people who dropped in. 'I couldn't resist,' she said. 'What a beautiful job Brendan did.'

'Yes – it's a far cry from when you showed it to us.' She paused. 'I was wondering if you'd handle the sale, actually. I was going to phone you.'

'Of course I will' – and they arranged to talk again during the week. Lydia's father might have Terence lined up to take care of the conveyancing, but Deborah had to be the one to sell it.

Seeing the house full of people, and despite the emotion the occasion was stirring – memories of them crowding in during her wedding reception – Lydia had to acknowledge that she was doing the right thing in letting it go. It deserved to belong to someone with the wherewithal to fill it. It should be used fully, with lots of life happening in it.

Halfway through the afternoon the music halted in the dining room, causing conversations to peter out. Father Phil, standing by the fireplace, cast about until he found Lydia. 'I've been chosen,' he told her, 'to say a few words. I'll keep them brief, I promise.'

Someone at the back of the gathering cheered, causing a ripple of laughter. Father Phil smiled, and waited again for silence. Lydia saw more people entering the room, wanting to be part of it.

'Lydia, you haven't been among us for long. You came here with great hope, but you met with great tragedy, and we grieved along with you. Damien is sadly missed here, and will be remembered with fondness for a long, long time. We wish you the grace of peace as the days move on – and of course you do have a lovely event to look forward to in the coming months. It's wonderful to see this beautiful house restored, such a gem in our community. Brendan and his team have worked miracles, and Gareth and Noel have done sterling work outside, but it would never have happened without you and Damien having the vision, so thank you for that, Lydia, and thank you too for the gift of your friendship. We'll all be sad to see you go, but we'll look out for you on your return visits. We wish you well. We wish you a safe delivery, and a happy life in Dublin with your child. To Lydia and the future,' he said, raising his teacup, and the toast was echoed, and she looked around at the faces she'd grown accustomed to, and it was all she could do not to burst into tears right there.

She belonged here. They'd made room for her, adopted her, gathered her in. She was part of this community now.

The music and chatter resumed. People sought out Lydia to praise the house and marvel at its views. Others exclaimed at their discovery of the little beach. A few offered her accommodation if ever she needed it on her return visits to the village.

Five weeks, she thought, her pretend smile still in place. Five weeks, and she'd be waving them all goodbye.

# 19

URSULA WAS OLDER THAN LYDIA HAD BEEN expecting. Older than Lydia herself, closer to forty if not already there, with lovely dark-fringed grey eyes, a pale freckled complexion and a pointed chin that gave her an elfin look. Her frame was small, her wedding outfit a pretty rose-pink dress and strappy matching shoes. Her curly hair, brown and shiny, had been gathered loosely into a cream satin ribbon, some wisps escaping to trail around her face. Her smile, like her mother's, was tentative.

'Thank you so much for accommodating us,' she said. 'We really appreciate it.'

Mother and daughter had arrived in Tessa's little red Mini, just the two of them. It had been Lydia's suggestion for them to freshen up at Chance House before the church ceremony, after Tessa had told her that she and Ursula planned to spend the night before the wedding in a hotel in the town. *My husband will meet us at the church*, she'd said – and it was this knowledge that had prompted Lydia's invitation. As long as it was just bride and mother, she was happy to have them.

She wondered how Ursula's father had taken the news that his wife had organised a wedding without consulting him – Lydia assumed he hadn't been informed of her decision to write the letter that had led to this arrangement – but of course it wasn't a question she could ask. She was dreading her encounter with him, although she knew that some people could put on a show for outsiders. He might be all charm today. He might rise to the occasion.

Tessa wore a powder blue dress that fell to her knees, and what looked like the same navy jacket and pearls she'd had on to meet Lydia. She was not at ease: it was evident in the set of her mouth, the crease between her eyes, her quick, nervous movements. Lydia found herself feeling anger towards a man she had yet to meet. However pleasant he might be later, it was clear that he was robbing them of the joy they should both be feeling today.

'Come in,' she said. 'I've made a little salad to keep you going until the meal.'

'You're too good,' Tessa told her.

In the apartment, prompted by her mother, Ursula called up a photo on her phone of the groom, and Lydia regarded the handsome features, the wide generous mouth and dark, dark eyes, the tight-curled hair sprinkled with just a little grey.

'Where did he stay last night?'

'With my brother Stephen. His parents stayed there too. They're all travelling together.'

And her father, presumably, would be travelling alone.

'Can I ask when your baby is due?' Ursula enquired timidly.

'September, second half.'

'Best of luck.'

No mention of the tragedy. Maybe Tessa had said nothing to her. Lydia still wore her wedding ring, so Ursula might assume there was a husband at work somewhere.

'I'd love to have a baby,' she said then, a light flush entering her cheeks. 'Paul has a grown-up daughter but she's studying medicine in Canada and couldn't be here with exams coming up. We're going to travel there in the autumn, and I'll meet her then.'

Despite her initial shyness, Lydia began to sense an innate hopefulness, an air of fresh innocence about Ursula that belied her age. Might this have been what had attracted Paul, widowed like Lydia and possibly looking for someone to bring new optimism and sparkle into his life?

But there was spirit in Ursula too. There was courage in going against her father's wishes, rejecting the big wedding he'd planned for her. Beneath that quiet exterior, she wasn't prepared for him to push her about.

What she *had* been prepared for was to wait for the right man to come along. Although she was older, she hadn't settled for someone to have babies with. Maybe her parents' marriage had taught her the wisdom of holding out for someone who would truly make her happy. On her phone screen Lydia had seen in Paul's face the open look of a good man, and the affection in Ursula's voice when she spoke of him was lovely to hear.

'Come with me,' she said to them after they'd eaten. 'I'd like you to see the garden.' The day was dry, and there was time, and she enjoyed showing it off to anyone new.

'Beautiful,' Tessa said, as Lydia walked them around. 'Are you the gardener?'

'I'm the assistant gardener – I just follow orders. He's a local man: he created it from scratch.'

'Amazing.'

'Sorry,' Ursula put in, 'but I have to run in to the loo – I think it's a combination of tea and wedding nerves.' Lydia directed her to the apartment's bathroom and she disappeared. The other two continued their stroll towards the sea.

Tessa was charmed by the little beach. 'I used to love to swim, years ago, before I got married. There was a pier near the house where everyone swam – we even went out on Christmas Day.' The words were full of wistfulness. 'If I lived here I'd definitely take it up again.'

Lydia wondered why she'd stopped. She was only an hour away from the sea – surely not too far, even once or twice a week.

'I told you Ursula's father is difficult,' Tessa said then.

'You did.'

'From early on in the marriage, he was hard to live with. When the children moved out I started to look after babies while their mothers were working. It was something I could do, something I loved to do, and it gave me a bit of pocket money, but he hated the idea that people thought he couldn't support us, so for peace I gave it up after a couple of years.'

She sighed. 'He's an angry man, so easy to make him cross – and now that Ursula is doing her own thing with this wedding, he's become impossible.'

'I'm sorry.'

Was he going to walk his daughter up the aisle today? Surely he couldn't refuse, even if she'd gone against him, even if neither of them really wanted it to happen. 'What does Paul think about it all?'

Tessa's mouth twisted. 'Well, he's not happy, of course. He came to Ireland for Ursula, and for me, but I'm guessing he'd much rather have stayed in Dubai and got married there instead. They both would.'

'Could you have gone there?'

'I could, but my husband wouldn't – he hates flying – and it wouldn't have been worth it to go without him. I'd never have heard the end of it.'

'Can I ask if they've met, Paul and your husband?'

She nodded. 'Ursula brought him here after they got engaged, but it didn't go well. He resents the fact that Paul's an educated man with a profession – my husband's a farmer, and makes a good living from it, but he got it into his head that Paul was all high and mighty, and looking down on him, which wasn't true at all. It didn't make for a pleasant atmosphere.'

The man sounded thoroughly obnoxious. Why on earth did Tessa stay with him, especially now that their children were grown and gone?

'I know I should leave him,' Tessa said, no doubt guessing Lydia's thoughts. 'Ursula and Stephen both want me to – but I'm not sure I have the courage. I don't know if I could start again, at my stage in life. And,' bleakly, 'I did love him once.'

She turned back towards the house. 'Ursula will be wondering what's keeping us,' she said. She pulled a tissue from her jacket as they walked up, and dabbed her eyes. 'Look at me,' she said, giving a tearful laugh. 'I'm dreading this. I just wish it was over.' She drew in a shuddering breath. 'I mustn't let her see how nervous I am. You've been so very kind, Lydia. Thank you.'

'I wish I could do more.'

Not long after they'd left for the church Cathy appeared, and Lydia helped to set her up in the dining room. By four o'clock, an hour after the ceremony had been due to start, the wedding party hadn't arrived. They would be posing for photographs, chatting with Father Phil, taking their time, with a cold buffet requested from Cathy – but when there was still no sign of them by half past four, Lydia began to wonder.

She opened the main door just in time to see a beribboned car turning in from the lane, followed by two more. She arranged a smile on her face, bracing herself for her encounter with the father of the bride – but he wasn't there.

'He didn't come!' Ursula exclaimed, getting out of the wedding car. 'My father, he didn't show up!' Elation and relief in her voice, transformed from the subdued bride-to-be. 'Lydia,' she went on brightly, 'I'd like you to meet Paul, my new husband.' Smiling widely at the word. Yes, Lydia recalled the delightful novelty of having a husband.

Paul was big and affable, wearing an immaculately tailored navy suit and what looked like a permanent beam. Happier too, doubtless, at the non-appearance of his father-in-law.

'Delighted to meet you, generous lady,' he boomed, clasping Lydia's hand before sweeping an arm to indicate the house. 'Such a beautiful home indeed!'

His parents, climbing from another car, offered her quieter but equally glad greetings, the mother stooped and solid in yellow, the father portly, and in a navy suit like his son. 'Our first time in Ireland,' they told her. 'Beautiful! Beautiful!' Never having met Ursula's father, possibly unaware of the facts, what did they make of his absence from the wedding? It didn't seem to bother them particularly, so maybe after all they'd been forewarned.

He'd stayed away out of pettiness. That was clear. His childish protest at his wishes being ignored, on a day that belonged to the bride and groom. He'd thought nothing of sabotaging the ceremony, or trying to.

Tessa's sister Delia bore a startling resemblance to her sibling. 'We're twins,' she told Lydia. 'I'm the older one, and the bossier one.' She introduced her husband, bald and bearded and genial. 'If you're ever selling up,' he told Lydia, 'let me know. This house is something else,' and his wife laughed and told him not to be foolish.

Tessa had travelled from the church with them. Like Ursula, relief was written on her face. She looked calmer, but also less elated than her daughter. 'For the best,' she murmured to Lydia, and nothing else.

Ursula's brother Stephen, lean and long-jawed, in navy like the other men, sought out Lydia in the dining room. 'Thanks for doing this,' he said. 'Ursula's so grateful. We all are. Mum says she's filled you in a bit on the home front.'

'She has. I'm sorry things are . . .' what word had Tessa used in her letter? '. . . delicate.'

He grimaced. 'I'm no fan of his, but I didn't think he was capable of this. Mum kept trying to ring him, but couldn't get through – and finally he texted me to say he wasn't coming, no explanation, so we went ahead. I walked Ursula up the aisle.'

'I'm sorry,' Lydia repeated. What was there to say? 'Try to enjoy the reception.'

'Thank you, we will, but Mum is still going back to him. I'll bring her to my house tonight, and run her home in the morning.' He seemed to have given up trying to persuade her to leave the marriage.

The rest of the day unfolded. Before they sat down to eat, everyone was ushered to the lawn for photographs by a relative with a camera. From the window of the big kitchen Lydia watched Tessa, sandwiched between her daughter and her new son-in-law as she smiled for the camera. How humiliating it must feel for her, everyone witnessing her husband's shameful, childish behaviour.

What would await her on her return to the family home? Would he be remorseful? Would he regret his non-appearance, or would he simply carry on being the angry, domineering man that Tessa had spoken of?

It struck Lydia that loving someone who didn't love you back, who treated you badly, was a different kind of pain from bereavement, but maybe no less sharp. And Tessa had lived with that pain, day in, day out, for years. Could she still love him? Surely not – and wasn't the death of love another kind of loss? She wished again that she could help Tessa, but beyond facilitating today there was nothing she could do.

After the photographs everyone came in for dinner, including Father Phil who had been persuaded to join them. It was an informal, good-humoured affair that Lydia overheard from the kitchen, where she was helping to plate up the food. Cathy's surprise of a side dish of rolex, a Ugandan omelette rolled in chapati, caused Paul's mother to clap her hands in delight, and declare them delicious.

There were no speeches, and just one toast. 'Ursula and Paul,' Stephen said, pushing back his chair. 'Long life and happiness' – and Lydia heard the guests get to their feet to echo the sentiment. She recalled someone – who? – proposing a similar toast at her wedding. Her father, she thought, and maybe Father Phil had used the phrase on the altar too.

Long life. Little had they known.

Dessert was trifle, and platters of Greta's goat's cheese and fruit. No wedding cake. No fuss. Cathy poured teas and coffees and topped up glasses while Lydia listened to snatches of conversation and spatters of laughter.

The evident happiness of the bride and groom gave her a sense of pride. She'd helped to make this happen. She'd facilitated their joyful day, one they should remember with fondness. She considered the irony of the absence of the bride's father adding to the positivity of the occasion, rather than ruining it.

She was stacking plates, conscious of her aching back, when Father Phil materialised beside her.

'I'm heading off.'

'I'll see you out. Thanks again for doing this.'

'Always happy to help.' In the hall he gave her a searching look. 'Was it tough?'

'I'm fine, just tired. Things got stirred up a little bit, but I'm learning to live with it, like you said.'

He hugged her. 'I'm proud of you. You're my hero. Now go and say goodbye to everyone, and put those feet up.'

'I will.'

She returned to the kitchen. 'Can I leave you now?' she asked Cathy.

'Absolutely – I can take it from here. Thanks a million for your help.'

'Stay as long as you want,' she told the wedding party. 'Sorry I have no other space you can move to. I hope you enjoyed yourselves.'

'Thanks, Lydia,' Ursula said. 'We couldn't have asked for a better day.' She looked like what she was: a happily married woman. As she left the room Lydia caught Tessa's eye, and the older woman mouthed *Thank you.*

Back in the apartment she changed into pyjamas, although it was just gone eight o'clock. She was weary from being on her feet. She would treat herself to an early night – but first she would make a toasted cheese sandwich, not having eaten since the bowl of soup she'd had while the wedding party were at the church.

On impulse, she threw on her dressing gown and took her plate and a cup of tea to the patio, her favourite time to sit out there and watch the light soften. She had just finished eating when she heard footsteps, and her heart sank. Not more small talk.

'Oh!' Tessa halted when she saw Lydia. 'Sorry, I didn't think anyone would be here, I just wanted – I'll leave you alone.'

'Please don't go on my account.' Of all people, she didn't mind that it was Tessa. 'I'm not staying long, but join me for a few minutes.'

'Well, if you're sure . . . It's so lovely out here.' She sank down next to Lydia and let out a breath. 'What a day.'

'I felt it went well.' Best to stick to the good part of it.

'It was terrific, couldn't have gone better. Father Phil is such a nice man, isn't he?'

'He's great.'

'We were very late starting, and he didn't mind a bit.'

Lydia let that go. Silence fell between them. She watched the cat nosing into the shrubbery – on the lookout, probably, for unsuspecting field mice. She'd become accustomed to finding little gifts on the patio in the morning.

The shed window remained permanently open, the cat coming and going from it, but she'd also taken to sitting by the apartment door when it was time for her food. She hadn't yet crossed the threshold, even when Lydia called her from the kitchen, knowing she shouldn't encourage what couldn't be continued, but unable to stop herself.

'I'm leaving him,' Tessa said then, in a rush. 'I'm not going back. I haven't said anything yet to anyone. I didn't want to take from the day – but my mind is made up.'

She stopped. She sounded apprehensive, but hopefully there was enough resolve there too. Could she follow through? Would she be able to take this huge step?

'Sorry,' she repeated. 'You're probably wondering how on earth you got saddled with us.'

'Not at all.' Lydia shifted the plate from her lap to the seat, and placed her cup on top. 'Tessa, I've only just met you, and I probably shouldn't be offering an opinion, but I have to say I really feel you're doing the right thing now.'

Tessa nodded. 'I've known for a long time what the right thing was, only, like I said, I couldn't do it. I kept hoping he'd change, that *I* could change him, but today . . .' She shook her head slowly. 'You know what really brought it home to me, Lydia? When he texted Stephen to tell him he wasn't coming. I'd been trying to get him on the phone but he didn't answer – I must have tried about ten times, I was frantic – and when he finally decided to let us know, it was Stephen he chose to tell, not me. I didn't matter. I was nothing to him. I pictured him looking at his phone, seeing my name coming up and just . . . ignoring it. That was so hurtful.'

Lydia saw no sign of tears now. Her voice was steady, her decision made. She was ready for this, even if it terrified her.

'So what will you do?'

'I'll talk to my sister, ask her if I can stay with her and Robert for a while, until I figure out my next step. Stephen would take me in no problem, but he lives too near his father. I need to get further away.'

'What about your things?'

'I'll get Stephen to call to the house and pack up what he can in the next few days. There's no love lost between them,' she said sadly. 'Hasn't been for years.' She paused, twisting the ring on her wedding finger. 'I'm not going to answer the phone if he rings me. I don't think I can bring myself to block his number, not just yet, but I can ignore him.'

'Probably wise. I'm so sorry, Tessa.'

'Don't be.' She flashed Lydia a quick smile. 'Thank you for letting me say it out loud. And thanks so much for today. I'll leave you alone now.'

'Best of luck,' Lydia said. 'Do keep in touch. Let me know how you're doing.'

'I will,' she promised – but would she? Lydia watched her as she walked away, back to the wedding merriment. She'd found the determination she needed. Now, like Lydia, she would have to take a new path – one that would hopefully include lots of swimming.

A marriage had begun today, another ended. However you looked at it, two good outcomes.

# 20

SHE REGARDED THE CALENDAR ON THE KITCHEN wall. The first week of July already, the second half of the year underway. Part of Lydia couldn't wait for it to be over: another part of her didn't want it to end, but she needed to move on, if only for her daughter's sake.

She heard the shower cutting off. When Brona appeared, her hair was swaddled in a towel, and she wore the flowery kimono Lydia knew well. 'Hi – hope you slept.'

'I always have great sleeps here – must be the sea air.' Brona stretched like a cat. 'Can you bear the smell of my coffee?'

'Just about. I have sourdough rolls from Greta.'

'Remind me who she is.'

'The German woman who owns the café.'

'The one that's never open?'

'Only when she feels like it.'

'Love it.'

Brona had raved about the house when Lydia had shown her around the previous day. *The perfect small hotel,* she'd said, *in the perfect location. Plenty of room for an infinity pool in a corner of that garden – and the yoga studio would make a cosy little bar. You'll have no problem selling.*

*We'll see.*

The ad had gone online two days ago, with a price tag of roughly twice what Lydia and Damien had paid for it. Deborah had rung to let her know it was live. *I'd expect it to make considerably more than the asking price,* she'd said. *This is just to pull potential buyers in. It looks great,* she'd added, and maybe it did, but Lydia hadn't looked. Couldn't look.

Over breakfast she and Brona scrolled through apartments for sale in Dublin. Prices had continued to climb steadily since Lydia had sold hers. 'That won't be a worry for you,' Brona said. 'You'll make a packet on this house. Here's my favourite, Wellington Road – and it's ground floor. Look at those sash windows.'

'Lovely.' She tried to sound enthusiastic. It would be better when she saw places in reality, when she could walk through the rooms and see how the light fell. 'I'd like one with a garden,' she said. She couldn't imagine living without a green space now.

After breakfast Brona drove to their favourite beach, with a walk that began where the sand ended and followed a headland for a mile or so. They zipped up fleeces as the wind pushed in from the water, every so often pattering their faces with spray – or had a drizzle begun? So much for July weather.

'I forgot to tell you,' Lydia said. 'I've decided to learn to drive. I'm having my first lesson tomorrow morning.'

'Here? But aren't you coming back in a few weeks?'

'I thought I'd have a few here, to get me started. It might be easier on quieter roads.'

'I'm surprised the village has a driving instructor.'

'It doesn't – he's the butcher.'

Brona found this highly amusing. 'Not the one who took your wedding photos?'

'He's the only butcher around here.'

'This place is hilarious. Everyone seems to have at least two jobs. Careful he doesn't try to convert you – if he offers you shepherd's pie, resist.'

*An intervention* flashed through Lydia's head. She thought of the chicken soup, and how mortified he'd been. 'That won't happen. You have no idea how kind people are around here, Bro.'

'I know. I'm only kidding.'

*Andrew would teach you*, Susan had said, when Lydia had asked her to recommend someone. *He taught me. He's very patient. He has an old banger besides the van – it wouldn't matter if you put a dent in it.*

*I could do weekday mornings, eight o'clock for half an hour*, he'd said when Lydia had called into the shop.

*That would be great. You don't mind me asking?*

*I don't mind. See you Monday.*

He probably thought her daft, looking for driving lessons just before returning to Dublin, not to mention in her seventh month of pregnancy, but if he did, he kept it to himself.

'Mind yourself,' Brona said, as she was leaving. Earlier than she usually left, trying to get home before traffic built up for a Coldplay concert that Lydia would have dragged Damien along to, pregnant or not. 'I'm so looking forward to the flat-hunting – I love poking into other people's places.'

She smelt of the Tom Ford scent she'd worn for years. Lydia hadn't used perfume since Damien's death, her Jo Malone bottle gathering dust on the dressing table. She'd get into it again in Dublin.

As she filled a small vase with sweet peas, the doorbell of the main house rang. Odd: the only people who used that door were her yoga students.

'I'm sorry to disturb you,' the man said. American or Canadian, she could never tell. 'I hope I'm not interrupting anything.'

There was a silver car in the driveway. Was he selling something? Unlikely: he didn't have ID hung around his neck, wasn't holding a clipboard or toting a bag filled with his own paintings or books of poetry. Anyway, salespeople never called to Chance House. They probably didn't know it existed.

'Name's Tim O'Donoghue,' he went on. 'From California.'

He looked perfectly respectable, well dressed in beige trousers and tweed jacket. Her father's age. Pale brown hair, face tanned and creased, nose a little bulbous. Muscular. Worked out in a gym, or lifted weights in a basement.

'Fact is, my great-grandmother on my mother's side was one of the Chances from this house. I have an interest in genealogy, and I've researched the family tree. Since I happened to be in Ireland on vacation, I was curious to see where she came from.'

A tourist looking for his roots. Better than someone trying to convert her, or persuade her to change her service provider.

'I'd have called ahead,' he went on, 'if I'd had your number. I didn't really like turning up unannounced. I hope you don't think it too forward of me.'

What could she say? She could ask him for ID, but that would only prove his name was what he said it was. He'd still be a complete stranger.

'Full disclosure,' he said. 'I'm aware that it's up for sale, and I may be interested. I like the idea of closing the circle.'

Lydia thought of its hefty price tag. Even with the renovation cost factored in, it was a good return for their investment – and Deborah had said she expected it to make more than the asking. *This is just to pull potential buyers in*, she'd said, and here was a potential buyer. It wouldn't kill her to let him see it, especially if he really did have family connections. She'd have to take that part on faith.

'I could show you around, if you like.'

'That would be great, if you're sure I'm not imposing, Miss . . .'

'Cotter,' she said. 'Mrs Cotter.' She didn't offer a hand to shake. Keeping her distance, until he proved she didn't have to.

'Good to meet you, Mrs Cotter. I take it you're the owner.'

'I am.'

In the hall she told him it had just been renovated, but due to changing circumstances she was moving on. He asked no questions, just nodded. He spoke very little as she led him through the main house, apart from a murmured 'Excellent' as he stood looking out at the upstairs view. *The view alone will sell it*, Deborah had said.

'There's a small private beach at the end of the garden,' Lydia told him. She would have brought him down if he'd expressed a wish to see it but that just got a nod. Maybe he wasn't a swimmer, or a fan of beaches.

Back downstairs she indicated the door that led to the apartment, and told him about its two bedrooms, and the rest. She didn't offer to show it, and he didn't ask. Let Deborah bring him back, if he wanted to see more.

'It's great,' he said. 'I think it might be just what I'm looking for.'

Wait till Deborah heard. Lydia hoped she wouldn't mind that she'd shown it to him.

'I'd be happy,' he went on, 'to put an offer in right away.'

Lydia was astounded. He was prepared to bid on a house he'd barely seen, just like that? Was that the American way? 'You'd have to—'

'Name your price,' he said.

She stared at him.

He smiled. 'Sorry – that came out a little strong. Allow me to explain: I'm in the business of property acquisition, and when I see a place I like, I go for it.'

Property acquisition. She wasn't sure what that meant, but it seemed to imply that he went around buying up houses. 'You said you were interested in this house because of a family connection.'

'Well, sure, that's all part of it – but also I can appreciate a house of quality when I see one, and this is a real beauty.'

She wanted to ask what he planned to do with it. She wanted to know if he looked on it as a business opportunity or a possible home – but she had no right to ask. It was none of her affair what the next owner did with Chance House. Whoever bought it would have their own ideas, and they might well involve changes Lydia would prefer not to see. She would have to stop being so sentimental.

And wouldn't a quick sale be good? It would speed everything else up. She'd be able to buy as soon as she found the right property in Dublin. She and the baby could be installed by the end of the year, if not sooner.

'You'll need to contact the estate agent,' she said.

'I certainly will, thank you kindly.' He put out a hand; she took it wordlessly. 'Thanks so much, Mrs Cotter. A pleasure to meet you, and best of luck – I see you have a little one on the way. You have a good evening now.'

Before she could reply he was gone, walking smartly to his car. She closed the front door and leant against it, listening to the sound of his departure.

Name your price.

She hadn't taken to him. Property acquisition sounded soulless.

She fed the cat and assembled a salad for dinner. A text came in from Brona as she ate. *Got back before the concert rush, thankfully. Best of luck with the driving lessons. Keep your eyes on the road and your hands on the wheel – and remember, say no to any offers of meat!*

She debated telling her of the American's visit, but decided to say nothing. He might not follow through. He might decide, having slept on it, that he wasn't interested after all, family connection or not.

For the first time in a long time, she set an alarm to wake her in the morning. Chances were she'd be awake well before eight, but just in case. She found herself looking forward to the driving lesson. She felt Andrew would be a good teacher.

She got into bed and turned on to her side, and felt her baby bumping against the wall of her womb.

'Shh,' she said softly. 'We're going to sleep now.'

# 21

'LET'S GO AGAIN,' HE SAID. 'PRESS DOWN SLOWLY ON the clutch.'

She pressed down slowly on the clutch.

'Now move the gear stick into first.'

She jabbed at the gear stick. Why were first and third gears so close together?

'Remember,' he said, 'try not to look down. Watch the road, and your mirror.'

She looked up, lifting her foot without thinking. The engine cut out, causing the car to give a little hop forward. 'Blast!'

He smiled. 'It'll get easier. Let's go again.'

He was the soul of patience, and she was hopeless. Just as well they were still on the lane after twenty minutes. He had more sense than to let her loose on the open road. She couldn't imagine ever having the courage to go near it.

His car was old and grey and rusted in parts. The earthy smell inside reminded her of Noel's stone shed. Newspapers covered the back seat. He'd brought a cushion for her to sit on: 'I thought the seat might be a bit low, and I can't adjust it.'

This had been a mistake, a crazy, ill-judged idea – what had she been thinking? She should have waited until after the baby. Dublin driving instructors would keep her away from busy roads too, until she was ready for them.

'Don't worry,' he said at the end of the half hour. 'It's a lot to think about, but it will all come together. Few more sessions and you'll be flying it.'

'I'm a disaster.'

'Everyone is at the start. Susan was terrible until she got the hang of it. You needn't tell her I said that. You'll be fine, I promise.'

She doubted it. She might be his first failure.

'I'd better get off,' he said, and she thanked him and got out. He threw her cushion into the back and slid over to the driver's seat.

'Same time tomorrow?' he asked.

It was the last thing she wanted, but she couldn't very well give up after one lesson. 'Yes, if you don't mind.'

She'd said she wanted to pay, and of course he hadn't given her a price. *I like to help people out*, he'd said. *If you pay, it turns it into something else.* She'd have to get some gift ideas from Susan.

She'd meant to tell him about the American, see what he thought – but she'd been too focused on trying to manage the clutch and the accelerator and the brake, not to mention the blasted rear-view mirror, and it had slipped her mind.

She was finishing breakfast when her phone rang. She saw Deborah's name – already? He must have got his offer in first thing.

'Deborah.'

'Lydia – you'll know why I'm ringing.'

'I have a fair idea.'

'You should be sitting down for this.'

She sat down.

'You've had an offer on the house from the gentleman who called to you yesterday.' Deborah named a sum.

Not quite twice what they'd looked for, but not far off it. Despite his 'Name your price', Lydia hadn't expected that. She would have thought he'd start lower. Madness.

'Are you still there?'

'I am.'

'Needless to say, I'm recommending you accept it. I don't generally advise vendors to accept the first offer that comes in, but I'm pretty sure you won't do better.'

'Did he tell you why he wants it?' Lydia asked.

'He said he has family connections.'

'Just that?'

'Yes. Why?'

'He said something to me about . . .' What had he called it? 'Property acquisition, I think. What does that mean?'

'It means he's in the business of buying and selling. Maybe he's buying it on behalf of another party, for commission. It could be something like a hotel chain that has plenty of money.'

'Oh . . .' That made sense. *Name your price.*

'It's your decision, Lydia. I can only advise you. He's given you until the end of the month to decide, so you can have a think.'

Deborah was right. There was no chance of anyone topping that bid. If Lydia accepted it, she could afford a house in Dublin in a good area, one with three or four bedrooms, and a garden with room for the sandpit and the swing and the seesaw, and she would have enough left over to take her time about looking for work. Maybe she could be a stay-at-home mother for the first vital year of her child's life.

She still wished she knew his plans for it. A hotel that was part of a chain wouldn't be so bad. They could put a good finish on it, fill it with decent furniture. They could install pretty tables and chairs on the patio. They might even adopt the cat as a feature.

It could be a high-end boutique hotel, rooms pricey enough to attract only the wealthiest clientele. Gareth probably wouldn't like it – they'd surely put a pool somewhere – but it would be good for the village to have people with plenty of money staying in the area. Someone might open a little craft shop. The Saturday market might expand.

Her parents would tell her to take the offer. They'd think her crazy to be hesitating. Logic dictated that she accept it, common sense told her to jump at it – and still she couldn't bring herself to say yes. Couldn't let it go, not yet.

'I'll think about it,' she said.

# 22

BY THE MIDDLE OF THE MONTH SHE WAS TRYING TO psych herself up to begin packing – but before she did that, there was something else she had to do.

She wrote a letter, feeling like a coward. It took many drafts to get it right.

*Dear Kathleen*

*I hope you're finding things a little easier as time goes on. I'm wondering if there's anything of Damien's you'd like to have – an item of clothing maybe, or his watch. You or Brendan would be more than welcome to drop over and have a look through what's here, anytime between now and when I go on the thirtieth.*

*I'm sorry for the way things were between us. I think I wasn't the woman you wanted for Damien, but we truly loved one another. He was the love of my life, and I'll never forget him.*

*I hope we can meet in friendship when I come back to visit, and you can enjoy spending time with your granddaughter. I intend to bring her back often so she can get to know her dad's family. I'll send news and photos when she arrives, and you'll all be invited to the christening.*

*Take care, Kathleen.*

*Love, Lydia*

She didn't refer to their last ugly scene. Kathleen might well be regretting it by now. Lydia had caught sight of her a few times since then on the village street, but there had been no salute, no acknowledgement at all.

She was pretty sure her invitation wouldn't be accepted, but she thought Brendan might be sent in her stead to choose a keepsake, and she was right. Three days later, he rang the apartment doorbell.

'She'd like his watch,' he said, and Lydia took it from her bedside locker drawer, and then she brought him into the spare room and invited him to choose something for himself from the bundles she'd laid out on the bed of Damien's things.

'Maybe the wallet,' he said, after staring at them for a long time, and she found a bag and put both items into it – and then, without words, she and he came together in a hug, and it felt like they were closing some door that could never be opened again.

'You'll be back,' he said, 'when the baby comes?' and she remembered him asking the same question on the day of Kathleen's outburst.

'Of course I will, as often as I can.'

Next morning, she phoned Deborah and told her to accept the American's offer. Time to set that in motion. She hadn't told anyone of his visit to the house, or the offer he'd put in. By the end of the day, the holding deposit had been paid. The deal should go through quickly, with nothing to delay things at her end.

He wasn't the owner she wanted for Chance House, but his money would enable a lot.

She phoned her parents to tell them the house had gone sale agreed, and they were as delighted as she'd expected, particularly when she told them the selling price. She gave her father the contact details of Damien's solicitor who'd handled the house purchase for them. *Will you get in touch?* she'd asked. *He'll need to send the Chance House paperwork to Terence.* She didn't want to be involved.

The following week, she taught her last yoga classes in the studio. She bade goodbye to her groups in turn, and each one presented her with a collective gift, although most of them had already brought something to the open afternoon. She was given a beautiful christening shawl, a new-mother hamper of pampering products, a voucher for an online baby supply shop, a set of bedtime picture books and a pair of nursery nightlights in the shape of toadstools.

After her last group left she stood alone in the studio and cried for all she'd lost, and all that could never be. In four days she would be getting into her father's car, and leaving this life behind.

As she carried her gifts back to the apartment, still tearful, the doorbell rang. Must be one of her students who'd forgotten something. She blotted her eyes with a sleeve and went to answer it.

'Sorry,' he said. 'I hope it's not too late.'

'Is anything wrong?'

She'd seen him this morning for her last driving lesson, her tenth half-hour in his car, and she'd presented him with the air fryer that Susan had suggested: *He was asking me about mine lately – I was going to get him one for his birthday.*

At the sight of it – it wasn't wrapped – he'd given a laugh. *Are you serious?* he'd asked, but she could see he was pleased. He'd accepted it, and wished her well in Dublin. She hadn't thought they'd be meeting again.

'I wanted to run something by you,' he said now. 'Just an idea I had. I wasn't going to say anything, but then I thought maybe I should. It won't take long.'

'Come in,' she said, and the cat streaked from the kitchen as he entered.

'She's moved in,' he said.

'Not really. She comes and goes, just this far, and I put her out at night. Will I make tea?'

'Not unless you want it.' He looked more closely at her. 'Are you alright?'

'I'm fine.'

'Sure?'

'Sure.'

He leant against the worktop and folded his arms. 'When is your baby due?' he asked.

The abrupt change of topic threw her. 'September the eighteenth.'

'Roughly two months.'

She waited.

'Remember a while back,' he said, 'when you told me you thought you might want to stay here, but the house didn't suit you any more?'

He hadn't forgotten. She nodded.

'And I told you that you needed to find a different life.'

'Yes.'

The shed, the new kittens. Blurting it out to him. She should tell him it didn't matter now, not when she was leaving in a few days, and having agreed to sell the house to the first bidder.

She didn't tell him any of that. She remained silent.

'Do you still want to stay?'

She couldn't stay. She had to go.

'I want to stay,' she said.

'Well,' he said, 'it seems to me that the solution is right there in front of you, but maybe it's not the one you want.' He was watching her intently with those unusual eyes. 'Tell me to mind my own business at any stage, and I'll shut up.'

She said nothing. She waited for him to tell her how to stay.

'It struck me that three wedding receptions have taken place here since you moved in, even though there were no facilities to speak of. No furniture, no working kitchen.'

She knew all that. What was his point?

'Lydia,' he said, 'can you see what I'm getting at?'

'Not really.'

'I think, if this house was fully furnished, all the bedrooms good to go and the kitchen equipped, you could run it as a wedding venue, with overnight accommodation.'

A wedding venue. That was his solution? She felt a swoop of disappointment.

'You'd only have to do one a week, say on Saturday, for it to be financially viable. You could continue with your yoga classes during the week if you wanted.'

Silence fell. It wasn't an uncomfortable one. It was nice of him to have tried.

'It's an interesting idea,' she began, not wanting to shoot him down too abruptly, 'but the house is too small. The dining room's capacity is just forty, and there are only eight bedrooms.'

'So you cater for small weddings. Not everyone wants a big splashy affair, especially if it's their second time round. Ian and Lorraine didn't, or the other couple you had – and as far as accommodation goes, there are plenty of places within a mile of here for the overflow. You could put up immediate family, and the rest wouldn't be too far away.'

There had been no accommodation at all for her own wedding – she and Damien had been the only two to stay the night at Chance House. Nobody had seemed to mind – but it wasn't just a matter of finding beds.

'I know nothing about running a business,' she said.

'What about your yoga classes?'

'That's different. My students come, they spend an hour in the studio, and they go. All I had to do was take out insurance, and Tom helped me with that.'

'And Tom could help you with something on a bigger scale too. I run my own business, and so does Greta, and Susan has a fair bit of admin to do for the school. We could all help set you up.'

One wedding a week. Just one night a week she'd have to keep guests. Paying guests – but quite a lot of them, if she filled all eight rooms. 'I couldn't do it on my own.'

'You'd need an assistant,' he agreed. 'Someone to help prepare the bedrooms, and to be there on the day, and you'd want at least one chef too.'

Cathy. Cathy could be the chef, and she was reasonably sure she could find an assistant within the community. She felt something fire into being inside her – but then she reined herself in.

'The ensuites have no toilets or sinks or showers. The kitchen has nothing either, not even worktops.'

'Brendan would organise someone for all that,' he said. 'As long as the plumbing's in place, sinks and that could be installed in a couple of days. And you could ask the owner of the restaurant where Damien worked to advise you on kitchen appliances.'

'But even with all that done, it's still unfurnished. No cooking utensils, no crockery or cutlery or glassware. It hasn't so much as a fork. And there's no bedroom furniture, no linens or towels, no shower curtains, no bath mats.'

So much. It was overwhelming – but he had an answer for that too. 'Marian and Susan are on holidays till the end of August. I bet they'd love a project.'

Lydia bet they would too. Between them, they were a formidable team. She could just imagine them trawling through furniture shops and home stores, picking out beds, wardrobes, couches, and all the rest of it. And if she could work out a payment plan with Brendan for the final bill he'd postponed, she had a budget. Not enormous, but maybe enough if they were careful.

And he was right about Kieran, Damien's old boss. He'd tell her what to get for the kitchen. They could sit down together, all of them, and make a list. Make lists.

God, was it possible? Could she do it? Could she stay here?

'Gareth could organise a website for you, to get the word out. And then you'd be good to go, once everything was in place, and you'd had the baby.'

And at the mention of the baby, she came to her senses.

'I can't,' she said. 'A new business and a new baby – it's too much, Andrew. I couldn't possibly take all that on. Even with people to help me, I would be the one in charge, and it's just . . . too much.'

He let seconds pass, holding eye contact. 'OK,' he said then. 'I just thought I should mention it, in case there was a chance you went for it.'

A chance. A second chance.

'Thank you,' she said. 'I appreciate you trying to help.'

'One last thing,' he said. 'The wedding photos. Since you're leaving, I thought maybe you'd want to have them.'

'Oh . . .' She didn't think she was ready to face them yet, but she couldn't just walk away without claiming them. 'Yes, I would like them, thank you.' She was forever thanking him for something. 'And please let me know what I owe.'

'A food processor,' he said, 'would be nice,' and it was only by the eyebrow that she knew he was joking. 'I'll drop them in,' he said, 'before you go. I'll get Denny's too.'

She would tuck them away at the bottom of a suitcase. She would wait until they wouldn't break her heart all over again.

## 23

GARETH DROPPED BY THE FOLLOWING MORNING. 'Let me know,' he said, 'if you'll have any bit of garden at all in Dublin. Even if it's just a tub on a balcony or a couple of window boxes. I can harvest some seeds and send them on.'

'I'd love that. I won't buy a place without some kind of a garden.' She was planning a nice big one, with the funds she'd have at her disposal. 'I'd love the wild primroses.'

'I'll steal some more in the spring,' he promised, 'if the house is gone by then. What other favourites have you?'

'They're all my favourites. Once I get a place, we can see how much I can fit in. I can send you pics, or you might come up and have a look.'

'I could do that. OK if I still drop over here after you've gone? Just to keep it looking well until it's sold.'

'Actually' – she may as well go public – 'I've gone sale agreed. He's American.'

'That was quick. He must have put in a good bid.'

'He did.'

'That's great.' He swept an arm around the garden. 'This is your legacy, you know. This will go on when you're far away in Dublin, assuming the American doesn't want to dig it all up and put in a giant swimming pool – I might have to kill him if he does.'

He grinned, but her eyes filled with tears. What was she doing? How could she leave it?

'Hey, I'm sorry,' he said, and she forced a smile and told him to blame the baby hormones.

She walked him out. 'I won't say goodbye,' he said, 'because you'll be back in a few months showing off your baby. You'd better let me know when you're coming, or else.'

'I will.'

'Hug,' he said, and she walked into his opened arms.

On Sunday she went to second Mass, and accompanied Father Phil back to his house afterwards for the lunch he'd invited her to. 'So,' he said, tossing the salad he'd made to accompany the vegetarian lasagne he'd admitted to picking up in the supermarket, 'you won't feel it now till you're a city slicker again.'

'No.'

'Looking forward to it?'

'I . . . well . . .' She couldn't pretend with him. 'It'll be hard to leave.'

'I know.'

'I've made friends here. It feels like home. And' – she took a breath – 'Damien is here.'

'You're not leaving him behind,' he said. 'He'll always be with you.'

She knew that – and still it hurt.

His embrace as she left was warm. 'It's not goodbye, it's *au revoir*. Safe travels, Lydia. See you soon.'

\*

On Monday morning, her last full day in Chance House, Greta arrived empty-handed. Had she forgotten the elderflower cordial she'd promised to bring for Lydia to take back to Dublin? Maybe it was still in her car.

She stood on the doorstep, unsmiling, which in itself wasn't remarkable, but today there was an odd light in her eyes. They glittered with – what?

Anger? Was she angry?

'Greta,' Lydia said, 'come in. Is everything OK?'

Greta didn't move. 'I have heard,' she said, ice in her voice, 'of your plans.'

'My plans?' Lydia's back ached. It ached pretty much all the time now. 'Greta, I could really do with sitting down. Come into the kitchen.' Without waiting for a reply she went back inside, and Greta followed. What on earth was wrong with her?

She didn't sit. She stood glaring down at Lydia. 'How could you do this to us?' she demanded.

Lydia stared back at her. 'Do what? I have no idea what you're talking about. Won't you please sit down?'

Greta didn't move. 'He was in McMonagles last night,' she said.

McMonagles, the larger of the village's two pubs. The conversation was making no sense to Lydia. 'Who was?'

'Your *buyer*.' The word practically spat out. 'He was buying drinks for everyone.'

'What?'

'You thought,' Greta swept on, 'that we would not hear until you had left. You thought he would not tell.'

'Tell what? I haven't a clue—'

'The shopping mall,' Greta said loudly, 'that he is going to build here. The giant shopping mall that is going to replace Chance House. The one you were so happy to hear about.'

Lydia thought she might faint. She gripped the table edge. 'What? That's not true, he's not planning – he never told me—'

But Greta wasn't listening. 'He is giving jobs to everyone, he says. Good jobs in his shopping mall. We will all be employed there.'

'Greta, please sit down,' Lydia repeated. Her heart was pounding. She felt under attack. 'Look, this is the first I've heard of a shopping mall.'

Greta dropped into a chair. 'May I ask,' she said, cold and quiet now, her eyes boring into Lydia's, 'how much this American is willing to pay you?'

Lydia felt a drop in the pit of her stomach. 'Will you please let me explain? He didn't say anything about—'

'How much?' Greta demanded.

'A lot,' Lydia was forced to admit, 'but if I'd known for a—'

'A lot,' Greta repeated, nodding grimly. 'He is paying you so much that you cannot see the destruction he will bring to this community.'

'You're not even letting me—'

'So much money it allows you to shut your eyes to the disaster he wants to bring about. It allows you to pretend it's for the best, so you don't have to feel any guilt.'

Lydia became aware then of her own rising anger. Greta's confrontational tone amounted to nothing less than bullying, and she was not going to be bullied in her own home.

'Greta, hang on,' she said, her voice quavering with emotion. 'You have no right to speak to me like that. I'm trying to tell you

I didn't know what his plans were – but even if I did, this is *my* house, *my* decision.'

Greta sat back, her face still like thunder. 'So this is how you repay everyone,' she said. 'All those who welcomed you when you arrived, who came here to sit with you after Damien died, who brought you food, who left fuel at your door, who did everything they possibly could to help you. This is how you repay them, by destroying their village?'

'Of course not! I just told you I didn't *know*—'

'And Brendan, whose heart was broken too, but who came back to finish the work his son had asked him to do, to honour his son's wish – you think it's fine to allow all his work to be bulldozed, just because you were offered a lot of money? I cannot believe it.'

'For God's sake, would you ever—'

Greta rose to her feet. 'I was wrong about you,' she said. 'I thought you were a good person. I thought you knew what was important, and what was right, but I see now that I was wrong. It is better that you go back to Dublin.' She swept from the apartment, leaving Lydia badly shaken. No front door slammed: Greta hadn't bothered to close it after her.

Could it possibly be true, what she'd said about the shopping mall? Was that awful man really planning to demolish Chance House? She could just see him perched on a bar stool, ordering drinks for all while he played the big businessman, promising jobs for everyone, bragging about his plans.

A shopping mall. Concrete and bright lights, piped music that would smother the sound of the sea. Diggers ploughing up Gareth's flowers and shrubs, his labour of love for his lost friend. A wrecking ball toppling the stone shed that Noel had painstakingly restored

– she could still see him sitting on the half-built wall with his flask. Old trees chopped down to make way, nothing spared.

No wonder her buyer had shown scant interest in the beach. When he'd stood at the upstairs window he wasn't admiring the view, he was seeing how big he could make the car park, how many customers it would cater for.

Or maybe the cars would park in an adjoining field that he would buy too. Maybe the shopping mall would take up the entire grounds.

And could he actually have told people that Lydia was *happy* with this plan? Could he have uttered that barefaced lie? Of course he could. People like him didn't care about the truth. In all probability, his family connection with Chance House didn't exist. She guessed he'd never heard of the place till he'd seen it on the property website.

She dropped her head into her hands and thought of the friends she'd made here, Marian and Tom and Susan and Gareth and Father Phil, and Andrew who'd helped out so often, and who'd given her driving lessons for nothing, and who wouldn't take a cent either for the photos he was to deliver – and yes, Greta too. Greta was a friend – or had been.

She thought of Marge who'd done her hair on her wedding day, and Denny who'd come with his two cameras, and the support and kindness of Doctor Avril. She thought of all those who'd called to her in the wake of Damien's death, and all her yoga students, and all who'd come to see the finished house just a few weeks ago and brought her gifts, and told her they were sorry she was leaving. She couldn't bear the idea of them hearing of the shopping mall, and thinking that Lydia was perfectly happy with it going ahead.

She saw the main street behind her closed eyelids: Greta's café, Andrew's shop, the hardware store, the chipper, the chemist, Marge's salon, the church and the presbytery. She saw the wonderful farmers' market, with stalls full of fresh produce, and homemade bread and cakes, and local honey and eggs. How could they compete with the lower prices in a big supermarket?

Jobs for everyone – except that nobody would want them. Nobody, she was certain, would willingly leave the village street to move into an anonymous mall.

Her heart sank when she thought of Brendan, who had returned to finish the renovation of Chance House, even after Damien was gone. *Toughest job I've ever done*, he'd said, the day they'd finished – and now here was this despicable man prepared to smash it all into pieces, just to make money.

She yearned for Damien. She wanted him to be alive again, to fix this. She conjured up his laughing face, Damien who'd loved surprises, who'd always seen the bright side, who'd made her laugh every day, who would have been the best dad in the world.

Damien the dreamer, the fearless adventurer. What would he have made of Tim O'Donoghue and his offer? What would he have said to him?

She raised her head, the answer clear. Damien would have said nothing at all, because if he was still alive, Chance House would not be for sale. If his idea of the destination restaurant had failed, he would have tried again with something else. He wouldn't have let the house go without a fight.

Chance House. *It has to be an omen. The name, I mean. It's our chance to make something wonderful here.*

He was gone now, but she wasn't. She owed it to him, and to their shared dream, to take this chance.

She lumbered to her feet, still horribly upset, still battling with anger and shame and hurt, not noticing in her distress that the ginger cat had come padding silently in through the open door. She would phone Greta – no, she couldn't phone her yet: she'd still be driving. She'd phone Deborah, tell her she'd changed her mind. She saw her phone on the worktop, where she'd left it to charge – but as she crossed to get it she stumbled over the cat and crashed heavily on to the floor with a cry of fear.

She lay unmoving, heart hammering, cheek stinging from where it had slammed onto the tiles. An arm hurt when she tried to pull it from under her; a knee throbbed.

The baby – was the baby moving? She'd twisted in the act of falling, an instinctive attempt to protect her baby from the worst of the impact, so now she lay awkwardly on her side – but had damage been done?

She whimpered in terror, afraid to move, but she had to move. She had to get help. She had to get to her phone, which meant she had to stand up.

She planted the arm that didn't hurt on the floor. She pushed up with it, but the movement caused a stab of pain that made her cry out again. She waited, heart hammering, before making another attempt, and again the pain jabbed, pinning her to the floor. No. She *must* move – she had to.

Gritting her teeth, she gave another heave, shouting to get past the pain – and as she dragged herself to her knees she felt the release of a sudden hot gush between her legs, drenching the loose trousers she wore. 'No,' she moaned, 'no, no' – and then, and then, and then, she heard, or imagined she heard, the sound of a vehicle.

'Help,' she called, in a voice that came out like a whimper. 'Help, help,' straining, and footsteps, thank God, sounded outside, and someone materialised at the kitchen door.

'Jesus—' he said, rushing in, throwing something on the worktop before crouching beside her. 'Jesus, Lydia—'

'I fell,' she cried, conscious of the state of her, on hands and knees with wet trousers, 'I fell, I fell, I fell,' gasping in panic, able only to repeat it. 'I fell, I fell.'

'I need to get you up,' he said. 'I'll bring you to the hospital – quicker than waiting for an ambulance. Tell me if something hurts, and I'll stop. OK? Are you OK with that, Lydia?'

She nodded and he raised her slowly to standing, and it hurt but she clenched her teeth and bore it, and together – he holding her around the waist, she leaning into him and gripping his arm – they moved slowly out to his van, and he lowered the back of the passenger seat so she was almost lying, and her clothes were wet, and she was wetting his seat, and another sharp stab of pain sliced through her, making her forget her stinging cheek, her throbbing wrist. With her good hand she grabbed the side of the seat and gave a low, despairing moan.

'Hang on,' he said, and she heard him running back across the gravel, and she squeezed her eyes tight and concentrated on breathing in, two, three, four, out, two, three, four, and when he came back he had found a throw, and her bag. He covered her with the throw and they set off, and she heard him on the phone as he drove, but the words were lost to her, so half crazed she was with fear and pain.

Her daughter, her baby – and every so often a new agonising pain would knife through her, making her cry out, making her arch her back in an effort to find relief. She bit her lip, and tasted blood.

After an eternity he stopped. Her door was opened almost before he pulled up, and she was lifted gently on to something with wheels and ferried through doors and down a corridor and through more doors – and it wasn't until later, much later, until after she'd given birth, roaring and screaming, and crying for Damien, and the baby had been whisked off, and Lydia had been cleaned up, it wasn't until after all that had happened that she remembered she'd never thanked him.

'Well,' Susan said, 'that was an interesting few hours. Drink your tea. You must be exhausted.'

Susan was there. Susan had turned up sometime during Lydia's labour. *Andrew rang me from the van,* she'd told Lydia, when it was all over. *He would have rung Marian, only he didn't have a number for her, so I rang her on the way here. She said she'd tell Brendan and Kathleen.*

Lydia was still reeling. She felt both headachy and light-headed. She was fragile, and frightened. She felt close to hysteria, close to some edge. She wondered if she was still under the influence of whatever they'd given her during the labour. Had they given her something? She had no idea.

'My baby.' Her throat hurt when she spoke. Her eyes stung. Her cheek smarted. Every muscle ached. Her pelvis hurt when she moved. Someone had bandaged her wrist. She wanted to sleep for a week, for a month.

They'd shown her the baby before they'd taken her away, but

Lydia had been too stunned to take her in properly. Hair, she thought. Dark, she thought. She was afraid to be happy about becoming a mother. 'She was born too soon,' she whispered, tears rolling out sideways, into her ears. 'Too early.'

'Hey,' Susan said, 'you heard the nurse. She's fine, just a bit small, so they're putting her into an incubator for some extra help.'

'She's going to be OK?' She clutched at it. Grabbed at it.

'That's what they said. They're bringing you to see her later. She's tough, like her mama.'

'My parents.' Her father, due tomorrow – or was this tomorrow? 'What day is it?'

'Still Monday, around teatime.'

She tried to piece it together. She remembered Greta being so angry, and her tripping over the cat after Greta had left, and Andrew appearing. She remembered her terror, and snatches of the drive to the hospital, and the calamity of the labour. It felt like an eternity of a day, but it was only teatime.

'Where's my phone?' With a fall of her heart she remembered it charging on the worktop – but when Susan rummaged in Lydia's bag it was there. Andrew must have thrown it in when he'd run back for the bag. Susan went outside to update Marian on her own phone while Lydia called her mother and gave her the news.

'God almighty!' her mother exclaimed. 'Are you both OK?'

'I'm OK. The baby's in an incubator.'

'That's only because she's premature, Lydia. All early babies need a bit of help, and they'll know exactly what to do in the hospital. We'll come first thing in the morning. You need to sleep now. Try not to worry, darling.'

Try not to worry, when she was on the point of shattering into fragments from worry. Melting into the bed from worry. Bursting into flames from worry.

'You're getting a lovely shiner there, by the way,' Susan said on her return, 'and you look like you're about to fall asleep, so I'll head off and see you tomorrow. I know Marian has a key to Chance House. She said she'd drop by to check everything's OK, and to make up a bag for you.'

'Can someone feed the cat?' It wasn't the cat's fault. 'Her food is in the press by the fridge freezer.'

'I'll call Marian on the way home. If she's already been around, I'll sort it.'

'Thanks, Susan – and please thank Andrew.' She would never be done thanking him for this.

Susan had barely left when a woman in blue scrubs appeared with a wheelchair. 'You can come and see your baby now,' she said.

With the woman's help she edged gingerly from the bed. She was wheeled from the room and along a corridor to a lift that ferried her down to another floor and all the time she was afraid to speak, afraid of what she might find at the end of her journey.

So tiny, so tiny, in an incubator that dwarfed her further, a tube no wider than a fishing line disappearing up an impossibly minuscule nostril. Eyes closed, astonishing blue veins on the lids, lashes dark like the damp strands of hair on her head. Mouth pursed, skin pale, so pale. Fingers all there, toes too. Chest rising and falling with frightening rapidity: too fast, slow down. Wearing nothing but a tiny doll-sized nappy.

But she was moving, little arms batting the air, little feet kicking. She was alive. She was adorable. Lydia felt all the emotions in the world. Her and Damien's daughter, conceived in love.

'Her breathing was a little compromised when she was born,' the nurse told her, 'so the tube is just giving her a bit of help for the moment. Those tiny lungs are working hard.'

Lydia couldn't take her eyes from the miracle of her daughter. 'What's her weight?'

'Five pounds three ounces, not too bad at all. We've had full-term babies that size. We'll keep her here for a week or so, just to give every organ a chance to get stronger, and you can come and see her whenever you want. In the meantime, you'll need to express your milk – I can show you how right now – and we'll feed it to her until you can feed her yourself. It's the best nourishment she can have.'

'Can I . . . touch her first?'

'You can indeed – and all going well, you'll be able to hold her in a couple of days. Let's make sure your hands are perfectly clean.' She was wheeled to a sink and given soap and a nail brush to use, and at last she put her hand through an opening in the incubator and touched the soft, soft skin of her daughter's arm, and was reassured by the warmth of it. Never alone again: it was the two of them now.

Back in her bed, there was one more call she had to make before she could sleep. She found the contact and placed the call and waited to see if it would be answered.

It wasn't. After several rings there was a click, then Greta's voice said, *Please leave a message*. Just as well: she couldn't interrupt a voicemail.

'It's Lydia. I had no idea what that man was planning – of course I wouldn't have agreed to sell it to him if I'd known, no matter how much he'd offered. What do you take me for, Greta? How could you think I'd do such a thing? I'll phone the estate agent first thing in the morning and tell her I'm not selling to him. And by the way, I've had the baby, and I think she'll be OK.'

After hanging up she sank into sleep, waking only when the door opened. A nurse, she thought blearily, looking for her to give more milk.

It wasn't a nurse.

'I knocked,' Kathleen said, 'but you didn't hear.'

# 24

SHE TOOK THE CHAIR BY LYDIA'S BED, HER FACE expressionless. She wore a blue jacket and grey skirt. Her eyes were red and swollen, her hands tight around the handle of the bag she perched on her lap. Lydia said nothing, not knowing what to expect, or the right thing to say, or if there even *was* a right thing.

Eventually Kathleen spoke. 'You hurt your face,' she said. No smile, but no anger either. Her voice was quiet and calm.

'I fell. I'm OK.'

'And the baby?'

'She's in the neonatal ward. They're going to keep her for a while. She's very tiny, but I think she's OK too.'

Kathleen nodded, her gaze dropping to the handbag. More silence. Eventually she spoke again. 'I was hard on you,' she said, her voice little more than a whisper. 'I said things I shouldn't have.'

She opened the bag and took a tissue from it and pressed it to her eyes in turn. She looked up, and Lydia saw the raw grief. Still in so much pain.

'I miss him.' Kathleen wept. 'Every day, every minute. He's always in my head. I'm gone mad with missing him.' She gave a wet sniff. 'But I shouldn't have taken it out on you. I shouldn't.' Pressing her lips together. Another sniff. 'I want to say sorry, Lydia. I want to say how sorry I am for being so hard on you.'

'I'm sorry too, Kathleen. I miss him so much.' Both crying now, Lydia using the sheet to dab her eyes until Kathleen found another tissue and passed it over.

'I wanted a local girl for Damien,' she said, through her tears. 'I wanted him to get married and stay in his house, like Tom had. I was afraid he might move to Dublin – and then when he didn't, when he bought Chance House instead, I was afraid he'd lose everything.'

She pulled out fresh tissues, handed one to Lydia. 'Damien told me buying the house was all his idea, but I didn't believe him. I got it into my head that you were behind it, and I didn't want anyone telling me I was wrong. And then, when we lost him—' She broke off, interrupted by fresh tears, and Lydia waited.

'When we lost him, I told myself it wouldn't have happened if he'd never met you. I needed to make sense of it. I needed someone to blame, so I blamed you.

'When Marian rang us earlier to give us your news, it – I don't know, maybe it was the shock I needed. I thought if anything happened to the baby, to Damien's baby, then maybe it would be *my* fault, for treating you so badly.'

'No,' Lydia put in quickly. 'She'll be fine, Kathleen. None of this is your fault.'

'I was very unkind,' Kathleen said, 'and you didn't deserve it, and I'm sorry, Lydia. I'm very sorry. I am truly sorry.'

She put out a hand blindly, and Lydia caught it. The skin was rough and cold. 'Can we be friends?' she asked Lydia. 'Can we do that? I don't want to lose my grandchild too.'

'I'd love that, Kathleen.' Lydia found the bell to summon the nurse. 'We'll go to see her.'

'Brendan is waiting outside. Can he come too?' So the three of them travelled to the incubator, Brendan in his good suit waiting at the window for his turn while Kathleen saw her granddaughter for the first time.

'She has his chin. She has Damien's chin. It's my father's chin too.'

The nurse was a different one since Lydia's last visit. 'She's a strong little thing,' she told them. 'Whatever you did during your pregnancy,' she said to Lydia, 'she came on really well.'

'Yoga,' Kathleen said. 'Lydia is a yoga teacher. And she cycles too.' The nurse said that must be it, plenty of exercise, and Lydia understood that Kathleen was doing what she could to mend fences.

Brendan, when it was his turn to come in, gazed silently into the incubator for what felt like a long time to Lydia. He swallowed a few times. He blinked rapidly. 'Bless her,' he said eventually, his voice unsteady. 'Tiny little thing.'

Did he see his son in her face? Did he see Damien's chin? Maybe.

'You and Kathleen are alright now,' he said, his eyes still on his new granddaughter.

'We are, Brendan. We're fine now.'

She was sure when they left she'd collapse into sleep, but it didn't come, or not right away.

Instead she thought about Kathleen, and what it must have taken for her to come to the hospital and say all she'd said. She hoped it would give her some peace.

She thought about her daughter, spending her first night out of the womb under the same roof as her mother. In good shape, and soon, hopefully, allowed home to Chance House.

Home to Chance House.

She thought about Andrew, and the idea he'd mooted that she'd turned down, shying away from taking on that enormous project by herself. But now, after one of the most momentous days of her life, maybe *because* of the day's dramatic happenings, it was beginning to seem like something she could tackle – with lots of help.

Could it be the different life she needed?

Finally, she sifted through the people she'd come to know since relocating from Dublin, trying to find one who might help her with the baby, if it turned out that she was to stay living in Chance House. Someone reliable and available. Someone she could live with – because whoever she chose would need to move into the apartment, at least for a while.

And just before she drifted towards sleep, a name came to her.

# 25

IN THE MORNING SHE WOKE TO FIND HER PARENTS at her bedside.

'You have a black eye,' her mother said, horrified, and Lydia assured her it wasn't as bad as it looked. She brought them to see the baby, who seemed even tinier than she remembered.

Her size didn't seem to bother Lydia's mother. 'Darling little thing,' she said. 'She's got your pretty nose, Lydia,' and she went to quiz the nurse, and Lydia's father said he could never see family resemblances until babies were at least six months old, but agreed that this particular baby was very appealing. Lydia took comfort from the fact that neither of her doctor parents seemed worried.

'She's fine,' her mother reported. 'Vital signs strong, temperature and weight good. They're keeping her in just to be on the safe side – they'll be discharging her in no time.'

Lydia tried not to think about leaving the hospital without her daughter. Back in her room, she was brought a bowl of porridge that was too thick and not hot enough, and a slice of white bread that had been taken too soon from the toaster. She did her best with it, thinking of Damien's seeded sourdough, and Greta's dark rye.

Her parents stayed till noon. 'I'll come back when they're letting her out,' her father said as they were leaving. 'I'll pick you up first, and then we can collect her from here and bring her straight to Dublin.'

'No,' Lydia said quickly. 'Not straight to Dublin. I want to bring her to Chance House, just for a little while.' Or maybe a little longer. She couldn't reveal her plans, not when they were still so tentative. Not when she wasn't strong enough to push back against the opposition her parents were bound to put up.

Her mother frowned. 'Chance House? But you have no baby things there.'

'No, but I'll ask Marian – she'll have Jack's old stuff. I'll be fine, honestly. We'll be fine. Just for a bit, to show her off to everyone.'

'Oh Lydia,' her mother said impatiently, 'you have no idea how much work is involved in looking after a baby. And weren't you ready to move back to Dublin before all this? Your father was coming down today to collect you.'

Lydia thought of the things she'd boxed up that would have to be unpacked now. Not a big deal, not with her new resolve. 'I know – but things have changed now, Mum. I need to get my head around all this before I can think about moving.'

'You'll have to have help,' her mother insisted. 'It would be so much easier in Dublin, where both of us would be around to share the work. Now I'll have to look for more time off. It's really awkward, Lydia. We're already short-staffed at the centre, with Nora gone on maternity leave.'

'You won't have to come, Mum,' Lydia said. 'I've thought of the perfect person to help. She's older, and her children are grown up.'

'You've already asked her?'

'Not yet, but I'm pretty sure she'll say yes. I'm sorry,' she went on, 'I know this isn't what you want, but it's the perfect opportunity for all my friends in the village to meet the baby. Won't you let me do this?'

They agreed reluctantly. She'd given them no choice. 'I just wish you weren't so far away,' her mother said.

'I know, but honestly, we'll be fine. I'll keep you posted, I promise.'

After they left, she expressed more milk. 'You're getting good at this,' the nurse told her. 'You'll be feeding her yourself before you know it.'

Lydia couldn't wait. Still sore, still tender, still tired and weepy, but none of that mattered. Her priorities were so different now, all her focus narrowed to one little being in an incubator.

Father Phil came in the afternoon. 'Been in the wars, I see,' he remarked.

'Tripped over the cat, if you can believe it.'

'Oh dear.' He sat and claimed both of Lydia's hands and cradled them between his, and she was reminded of him doing the same at the funeral. 'So the world has a new little girl,' he said. 'Praise the Lord. How are you doing?'

'Up in a heap,' she said. 'Don't know if I'm coming or going. Don't know whether to laugh or cry. I'm terrified at how tiny she is, and how much she means to me already.'

He nodded. 'That all sounds about right. I have a feeling you'll make a heck of a mum.'

'Would you like to see her?'

'I would indeed – if they'll let me in. I know they're careful with the tiny babies.'

She brought him to the neonatal ward, and he told the nurse on duty he was a priest and a family friend, and he'd appreciate being allowed in. 'Just for a tick,' he said, and in they went.

He pronounced the baby a fine specimen. 'Want me to bless her?'

'Yes, please. I want her to get all the help she can, medical and divine.'

He murmured a short prayer, and made a sign of the cross over the baby, and another over Lydia. 'For good measure,' he said. 'Tell me, have you a name in mind?'

'A few, but I'm open to suggestion. Any ideas?'

He mused, his eyes on the baby. 'Some nice biblical ones, if you wanted to go in that direction. Ruth, Eve, Sarah, Elizabeth, Naomi, Rebekah – and of course, Mary.'

'Naomi,' Lydia repeated. 'Naomi Cotter.' She liked the sound of it.

'Naomi the Judean,' he said. 'The name means "pleasant" in Hebrew. She was mother-in-law to Ruth – they weren't always the best of friends, especially after Ruth's husband died. They were from different tribes, which Naomi didn't approve of for her son. She was a strong lady, not to be crossed.'

A mother-in-law on shaky terms with her son's widow, disapproving of his choice. A strong lady, not to be crossed. Lydia stared at him. 'Are you making this up?'

He laughed. 'No, it's all in the Bible. Why would you think I'm making it up?'

She told him about Kathleen, and the distance that had been

between them from the start, and how it had finally been bridged the previous evening.

'Ah, I see. Poor Kathleen. I'm glad she was able to reach out. This might be the start of her healing. Now I need to get going. I have a couple of sick calls to make.'

In the lift on the way back she told him she was thinking of staying on in Chance House.

He cocked a look at her. 'You mean not go back to Dublin at all?'

'Maybe. Andrew suggested a possible use for the house, and I'm trying to work out how to make it happen.'

He nodded. 'Your heart wants to stay here. I won't ask any more, just wish you the best and wait to see what occurs. Mind yourself, and trust that all will be well.'

'I will,' she promised. All will be well. Her new mantra.

'God almighty,' Gareth said, depositing a little tub of pineapple chunks on her tray, 'you gave us all a fright, Mammy. How's the new arrival?'

'She's doing fine. You didn't need to come – they're sending me home tomorrow.'

'I thought you were going to Dublin.'

'Not just yet. You'll have to put up with me for another while.'

'Well, that's good news, but you'll have to do without me for the next two weeks – I'm heading to Spain tomorrow to walk a bit of the Camino with Ultan Clancy. Wish me luck. Ultan's a lazy sod – I'll have to drag him along. Will you still be around when I get back?'

'Should be.'

'You and the baby?'
'Me and the baby.'
'Excellent.'

Susan and Marian arrived late in the afternoon. Susan brought a slab of chocolate, and ate half of it while they were there. Marian brought a tiny yellow hat, and a picture book about a ginger cat. They went to inspect the baby, only allowed as far as the window. 'Naomi,' Lydia told them. Both approved, and waggled their fingers at the baby, who ignored them.

They went to sit in the hospital canteen with paper cups of coffee. Suddenly Lydia could drink coffee again, and even the canteen variety tasted fine.

'I've been thinking,' she said. She opened her mouth and closed it again. They waited. When nothing else happened, Susan asked if she was OK.

'I'm OK. It's just . . .' Again she stopped. 'Do you think . . . I mean, would it be crazy . . . It's just— Look, I've been thinking, or rethinking, and it's probably daft – well, not daft exactly, just a bit . . . unexpected.'

She saw the look they exchanged. Putting her rambling down to hormones.

'You're tired,' Marian said. 'We should let you back to your bed.'

'No, I'm not tired, it's just . . .' Why couldn't she say it? What was stopping her? And then she realised why: she was afraid they'd dismiss it, tell her it couldn't be done – and suddenly that was the last thing she wanted to hear.

She wanted to try it. She wanted very much to try it.

'What do you mean, unexpected?' Susan asked.

'OK,' Lydia said. 'OK. Listen to this.' Deep breath. 'What if I stayed in Chance House? What if I didn't move back to Dublin?'

In the silence that followed, someone behind the counter dropped a cup, or a plate, something that broke when it hit the floor. Someone said, 'Damn it!'

Marian was the first to speak. 'What would you do if you stayed?'

'Well, that's the question.' She turned to Susan. 'You can blame your brother for this, because it's all his idea.'

*I wanted to run something by you. It seems to me that the solution is right there in front of you.*

'Nearly forgot, he says hello,' Susan said. 'Who wants more coffee? Say nothing till I get back.'

She got another round, and a plate of biscuits. 'Now, tell us my brother's brilliant idea,' she said, pulling in her chair.

'Weddings,' Lydia said, 'at Chance House.'

'Go on,' Marian said, eyes widening.

'Small weddings,' Lydia said.

'Second weddings,' Susan said. 'Like Lorraine and Ian. Family and close friends.'

'Exactly. With accommodation for some,' Lydia said, feeling a slowly rising excitement.

'Plenty of places around the village to put the rest into,' Susan said. 'I know them all. I could do up a list.'

Lydia looked from one to the other. 'I'd need help furnishing the rooms.'

'Me,' Marian said immediately.

'Us,' Susan said at the same time.

'And Cathy might come on board,' Lydia said. 'It would just be dinner on Saturday and breakfast on Sunday morning.'

'One wedding a week,' Marian said.

'One a week would be plenty,' Susan agreed. 'I'd say Cathy would jump at it.'

'Gareth could do a website,' Marian said. 'Spread the word.'

'Weddings at Chance House,' Susan said.

'Weddings by the sea,' Marian said. 'Tom would do the accounting.'

A short silence fell. They weren't dismissing it. They weren't telling her it couldn't be done.

'I think,' Marian said, 'this could really work.'

Susan nodded. 'I do too.'

It was a new dream, not totally unrelated to the old, but different. It was a half-formed plan with no guarantee of success, but something inside her was prodding at her to give it a go. It would be a huge challenge, and to embark on it without Damien would be beyond sad, but she wouldn't be doing it alone.

'When you get home,' Marian said, 'we'll get together and make a list of everything that needs to be done, and then Susan and I will go shopping. How's your budget?'

'I have money, but not loads.'

'OK, we can keep that in mind. We can get Tom on board for the numbers.'

'And while we're shopping, you can concentrate on being a mum for a while,' Susan said. 'How does that sound?'

It sounded good, really good. It sounded like the best thing she'd heard in a long time.

Greta turned up later, bringing a bunch of wildflowers in an old enamel jug, and a bottle of her elderflower cordial. She hadn't responded to the message Lydia had left the night before. She looked humbled.

'I have come to make up,' she said quietly. 'I apologise for the things I said to you. I should have known you were not such a person. I have told people that man was not telling the truth about you.'

'I'm glad to hear it.'

'Do you forgive me?'

'Of course I do. I've been in touch with Deborah. She's returned his deposit.'

'Very well. Let us say no more about it.' She paused. For once, she seemed uncertain. She was ill at ease, still clutching the bottle she'd brought. 'I must ask,' she said, 'if I was the cause of your baby coming early.'

Lydia looked at her in astonishment.

'I upset you. I said very hurtful things.'

She'd had a baby who had died – and now she thought she might have caused the premature birth of another. 'Greta, it wasn't you. I tripped in the kitchen, and my waters broke. You upset me for sure, but you had nothing to do with the baby coming early.'

She saw the relief that washed over her friend's face, the small drop in the shoulders. 'Thank you,' Greta said. 'May I please see her?' and at the window of the neonatal ward Lydia wondered if the sight of Naomi brought back memories of her own. Maybe every baby did. Maybe it was something she had learnt to live with.

When they got back to her room, Lydia outlined her new plan for Chance House, and Greta approved.

'You will have a lot of work to do, but you will also have a lot of help, and you will succeed, I think. I should be happy to help you prepare rooms and take care of guests on the day. Now I must go and feed my animals, but I will see you soon. Many congratulations on your beautiful new baby.'

Alone again, Lydia considered the wider implications of her change of heart. Breaking the news to her parents would certainly be difficult. It would be hard on them, living so far from their only grandchild. She fully expected that they would try to talk her out of it, but she was resolved to give this new idea every chance, and they'd just have to try and meet up whenever they could.

Brona would be disappointed – but Lydia would have more than enough bedrooms for all the Dublin gang. Cocktail Fridays could become Cocktail Wednesdays. She might have to rejig some of the yoga classes, but that was possible too. Suddenly everything was possible.

She'd offer Brona her pick of the rooms.

Brendan and Kathleen would be happy with the change, and the two cousins would get to know one another, once Naomi was old enough to be of interest to Jack.

All assuming she pulled it off, of course. She might go bankrupt while she was still trying to get set up. She might use what money she had on furnishings and appliances, then find there wasn't enough demand for small-scale weddings in a fairly remote location.

But the same gut feeling that had told her she was doing the right thing in letting Lorraine and Ian use the house was telling her now that this was also the right thing – and she knew, with a deep conviction, that Damien would approve and cheer her on.

She had one more thing to do before she slept. She reached for her phone.

'Lydia,' Tessa said, 'lovely to hear from you.'

'How are things?'

They hadn't spoken since the wedding. She'd crossed Lydia's mind more than once, but she'd felt she should give Tessa a chance to find her feet.

'I'm doing fine. I'm still living with Delia and Robert, and I'm on the lookout for work so I can get out of their hair, but so far I'm not having any luck.'

'What kind of work are you looking for?'

'Shop work, I thought, but I'd consider anything.'

That sounded hopeful. 'I've got something you might consider,' Lydia said.

It had come to her while she'd been casting about for a possible nanny, the memory of a conversation on the day of Ursula's wedding. *When the children moved out*, Tessa had said, *I started to look after babies while their mothers were working. It was something I could do, something I loved to do.*

Maybe she'd love to do it again.

# 26

AFTER THAT, LOTS OF THINGS HAPPENED.

The day before Lydia's discharge from hospital she took her daughter into her arms for the first time, and she felt the warm weight of her, and the surprisingly strong tug on her nipple when Naomi's mouth latched on.

Kittens, she thought. Babies looking for their mother's milk. She remembered their urgent clambering, their blind hunt for nourishment, and here it was again, the same urgency. She remembered the mother cat's purring, the deep contentment she'd shown, and she felt it too.

Marian brought her home the following day. On their arrival, Lydia discovered a baby buggy parked in the hall, and a baby sling hanging from a hook above it. In her bedroom a cot was installed, complete with overhead butterfly mobile. A stack of tiny clothes sat on her bed.

In the bathroom was a changing table, a giant box of nappies and a small plastic bath with a clutch of baby toiletries and a rubber duck in it. The sitting room couch had been moved to accommodate a rocking chair, a toy chest that already held an assortment of furry animals, and a play mat.

A baby monitor was plugged into a kitchen socket, another in Lydia's room.

'We didn't know where you wanted things,' Marian said, 'but it's easy to move them around. We have the promise of a high chair, and I'll drop over Jack's old car seat, and there's lots of other stuff ready for when it's needed. We didn't want to crowd you out.'

'Where did you get it all?' Lydia wondered.

'Oh, here and there. Susan put out a call. And just to warn you, you'll need a babysitter – everyone wants you back to your yoga classes.'

'Actually,' Lydia said, 'I have that sorted,' and told her.

'Excellent news,' Marian said. 'You're very organised.'

A large brown envelope Lydia hadn't seen before lay on the kitchen worktop. She didn't need to open it: she knew what was inside. She'd been wondering what had brought him to the house the day she'd fallen. She'd forgotten he was to hand over the photographs. She tucked the envelope under the cutlery tray and closed the drawer.

Not ready yet.

That evening she phoned Brendan. 'I'm staying,' she said. 'I'm not going back to Dublin.'

A beat passed. 'You're staying on at Chance House?'

'I am. I'm going to try to run it as a wedding venue.'

'Well . . .' he said. As the silence stretched, she wondered if that was all. He cleared his throat. 'That's great news,' he said. 'I'm really happy to hear it, and Kathleen will be too.'

He'd wanted her to keep the house because of Damien. How had she missed that? He'd wanted her to follow through with the adventure they'd started together. She told him she had Marian and Susan on the lookout for bathroom and kitchen fittings, and he promised the manpower as soon as she needed it.

Five minutes after she'd hung up, she saw a call coming through from his landline number, and she knew it had to be Kathleen, who didn't possess a mobile phone. She kicked herself that she hadn't thought to ring her with the news instead of Brendan. Force of habit.

'You're staying,' Kathleen said. 'You're not going back to Dublin.'

'I'm not going back, Kathleen. I really want to stay here.'

'I'm delighted to hear that. Tell me how the baby is getting on.'

It warmed her that they were friends now.

Next day, before her daily trip to the hospital, she called to the butcher's shop. As ever, she breathed through her mouth when the smell of meat hit her. She was glad the day was sunny enough for him to prop the door open.

'I just wanted to say thank you,' she said, 'for what you did that day.'

'Happy to help,' he said, wiping hands on a cloth. 'Glad you're home again. Susan tells me the baby is thriving.'

'She is . . . You know I'm staying on here.'

He gave his gentle smile. 'I do.'

'I have you to thank for that too.'

'Any help you need, you know where I am.'

'I suspect I'll have lots of help – people can't do enough around here. By the way, I saw you left the photos.' She paused. 'I might wait another while before I look at them.'

'Sure.'

'And I was thinking I might take a few more driving lessons soon, if you'd be happy to give them.'

'You don't need any more lessons,' he told her. 'You have the basics – now you just need practice, with a qualified driver sitting beside you.'

'In that case, maybe it's time to start looking for my own car.'

'I'll keep an eye out,' he promised.

'One more thing,' she said. 'I was wondering if you'd like to be Naomi's godfather. Don't feel you have to.' His had been the first name she'd thought of, after all he'd done, and because of the person he was.

For a moment he said nothing, just went on regarding her. Was he searching for a nice way to say no? 'You really don't have to,' she repeated. 'I won't be offended.'

'I'd like to. Thank you.' Up went the eyebrow. 'I'm not sure what class of godfather I'd make. I've never done it before.'

'I'd say you'll do just fine.'

'Have you chosen a godmother?'

'To be decided,' she told him. She *had* decided who she wanted, but she wasn't sure how the request would be received, so she kept it to herself till later that day, when she and Greta were sitting on the Chance House patio, and Greta was knitting a tiny yellow cardigan, needles flying.

'Yes,' Greta said placidly, when Lydia asked. 'I would like that, thank you.'

A few minutes later the clicking slowed, and stopped, and silence descended. From the corner of her eye Lydia took in her friend, hands stilled, looking down the garden to the sea.

She'd debated asking her, not knowing how Greta would feel about it, not wanting to put her in a position that might make her uncomfortable – but of all people, Greta would say no if she didn't fancy doing something, so she'd gone ahead, and it seemed that Greta had no objection.

She'd chosen well, in both cases.

She rang Cathy and outlined her plan. 'I have no idea whether anyone will want it for their wedding, but if they do, I'll need someone like you to feed them. Would you be interested, in theory even? It would mean giving up your Saturday nights if it took off.'

'I'd love it, Lydia, and not just in theory. Keep me posted.'

Another thing ticked off her list. She texted Gareth, walking in Spain. *Hope all's well. Just letting you know that I'll soon be in need of a website . . . big changes here. Give a shout when you get home and I'll fill you in.*

His response was swift. *Old news – my mother heard it from someone who heard it from someone. Delighted you're staying around, will put my web design hat on for the rest of the trip. I've managed to lose Ultan three times already but he keeps finding me.*

She went to dinner at Marian and Tom's. 'I need an accountant,' she said to Tom.

'So I hear. I'll sit you down some day that suits both of us, and go through everything.'

'Can you help me make a business plan, so my parents know I'm serious?'

'Sure thing. That's step one.'

It was coming together.

The day before Naomi was due home, Tessa moved into the apartment's second bedroom. From her suitcase she took a cloth doll, old and worn and faded, with yellow wool plaits and a blue knitted dress and tiny brown felt shoes that were sewn on. She had a painted smiling mouth and blue eyes and rosy cheeks, and a little pink triangle for a nose.

'I made her,' Tessa told Lydia, 'when I was pregnant with Ursula. When you asked me to come, I sent Stephen back to the family home to hunt for her in the attic. I've given her a wash to freshen her up. Don't feel you have to use her. I just said I'd bring her along to show you. You've probably got far nicer ones.'

Lydia took the little doll, noting the neat stitching that held her together, the pocket on the dress embroidered with a flower, the tiny dots of eyelashes. Faded or not, her soft smile made you want to smile back. She'd been put together with pure love.

'What's her name?'

'Sissy. I have no idea where that came from – I can't remember who picked it.'

Sissy. She was perfect.

While Tessa unpacked, Lydia phoned her parents, steeling herself for what she sensed would be a difficult conversation.

'Now, please hear me out,' she said, both of them listening. 'This will come as a surprise, but I'm not coming back to Dublin just yet.' She'd decided to pitch it to them as a year-long experiment – which it might well turn out to be. She told them of the preparations she'd already put in place, and the ones she was planning.

'So,' she said, 'what do you both think?'

A beat passed.

'You've just had a baby that came early,' her mother said. 'You're a first-time mother, and you've decided to start a new business? I can't believe what I'm hearing, Lydia.'

'Mum, can't you for once be supportive?'

Silence. 'Mum?'

But it was her father who answered. 'Lydia, I have to say this is a ridiculous idea.'

She felt as if she'd been slapped. 'Dad, this is my life. I'm an adult, I'm not your or Mum's responsibility any more. I'm free to make my own decisions, and you need to start respecting that. I'm following my heart.'

'You're following a dream!' her mother snapped. 'The same foolish dream that brought you to that wholly unsuitable house. Your head is in the clouds! You're going to spend all your money on this far-fetched notion of a wedding venue – God only knows who you're listening to there – and you're going to lose everything!'

Lydia's face felt hot with rage now. She was under attack from two fronts – but she was fighting back.

'So what if it doesn't succeed? It's my money, my decision! I'm not asking you for anything – it's got nothing to do with you!'

'Have you forgotten you have a child now, Lydia?' her father asked sharply. 'You're responsible for her, not just for yourself – how can you be so blasé about her future, for God's sake?'

'Of course I'm not blasé!' she shot back. 'Naomi is my top priority – I'd starve before I let her go hungry! But you're not even considering the possibility that my plan might actually work – you're shooting it down in flames before I even begin! Am I never allowed to take a chance?'

Her mother again. 'Lydia, you make it sound like you're trying out a new fashion. This is not taking a casual chance, this is investing everything you have in the idea that people will want to come and get married in the middle of nowhere! Can you not see how outlandish it is?'

'No!' Lydia retorted. 'I just see something that's worth trying – but don't worry, I won't bother either of you if I go broke! Thanks a lot for your faith in me!'

She jabbed the red button, knowing it was juvenile, like storming off in the middle of a row, but she couldn't listen to any more. Her cheeks were on fire, her blood racing. Typical of them, dictating what she should do. So negative, assuming she'd lose everything. If either of them called her back she'd ignore them, but when her phone rang twenty minutes later, it was Marian.

'I've found the perfect bathroom stuff. It's beautiful – and guess what? They're having a summer sale. I'm sending you photos as I speak.'

'Wonderful.'

She would put her parents from her mind, forget their hurtful words. Ironic, just when she and Kathleen had found a way to be friends, the people she'd considered her allies were suddenly on the other side.

It wouldn't last. It couldn't last. She didn't want it to last. She wanted them with her on this new path, not watching silently, disapprovingly, from the sidelines – but they would have to come with her on her terms. They would finally have to accept that she was in charge of her life, not them – and she would have to wait until they were ready to do that.

Next morning, she and Tessa drove to the hospital and brought Naomi home – and finally, life began to turn the right way up again.

# 27

OVER THE WEEK THAT FOLLOWED, DAYS BLURRED into one another, punctuated by feeds and changes and baths and more feeds, and precious little sleep for all three residents of the apartment. Nights became extensions of days, no designated rest time any more, everything dictated by one tiny, beautiful, irresistible human.

Thank goodness for Tessa, a replacement mother for Lydia in the absence of her own. Lifting the baby from Lydia's weary arms after a feed and transferring her gently to the cot. Filling the little bath before Lydia realised it was due, changing sheets, preparing food for Lydia to eat when she got a chance, laying out miniature clothing, emptying the nappy bin. Grabbing sleep, like Lydia, whenever she could.

People called to see the baby, people she now knew. There was a near-constant procession of visitors, none of whom stayed too long. Everyone had heard that Lydia wasn't moving away, and nobody at all mentioned the shopping mall, or the man who had been planning to bring it into being.

It was a chaotic and exhausting time – but it was also a time of deep happiness. The novelty of being a mother, of sitting in the borrowed rocking chair with Naomi at her breast made Lydia feel immeasurably content. Perhaps inevitably, with his child in the world, she fancied she felt Damien nearby during this time, watching them both. It was a comforting fancy, tinged as it was with the loneliness of knowing he would never be physically present again.

Ten days or so after Naomi came home, Tessa went to answer the doorbell. It was mid-morning, the day warm and dry. Lydia had just put Naomi down for a nap, and was filling a bowl with the fruit Tessa had chopped earlier. She was thinking she really must get back into the yoga studio – she hadn't gone near it since Naomi's arrival – when Tessa reappeared, followed by Lydia's parents.

There had been no word at all from them since the angry phone call almost two weeks ago. It was the longest time Lydia could remember without communication. She'd been on the point of calling them more than once, wanting to heal the rift, but she'd stopped herself. It had to come from them.

And here they were.

She lowered her bowl. 'Mum,' she said, 'Dad. You've met Tessa.'

She'd told Tessa they'd had a falling-out without going into detail, and now Tessa slipped away, murmuring something about letters to write.

They looked subdued, both of them. Neither attempted their usual embrace on meeting Lydia. Her father lowered a box on to the worktop. Lydia switched off the radio.

'Sit down,' she said. 'Will I make coffee?'

'Please,' her father replied, and nobody spoke while she did. The cat hopped on to the windowsill outside as Lydia arranged Tessa's almond biscuits on a plate.

'We've come,' her father said, as Lydia returned to her bowl of fruit, 'to make things right.'

He stopped. After a few seconds, Lydia gave a cautious 'OK.' She stabbed a half-strawberry with her fork and ate it.

'We've come to explain,' her mother put in, 'and to say sorry too.' She paused, stirring milk into her cup. 'We know we can be . . . over-protective.'

Lydia said nothing to this. She speared a chunk of pear.

'From the start,' her father said, 'we were dubious about you and Damien buying this house. You know that. We said it to you.'

They had. Lydia nodded.

'We hated to think you'd end up in trouble,' he said.

'It was my risk to take,' Lydia felt obliged to point out.

'Yes. Yes, it was, and we should have kept quiet, but there you are.' He reached for a biscuit, but then just set it by his cup.

'When the accident happened,' her mother said, 'we were – well, of course we were terribly sad, but also very concerned for you, especially when you decided to return here after just a week with us. We both assumed you'd move back to Dublin at that stage.'

'I know you did.'

'We hated to think of you alone here,' her mother went on. 'We couldn't imagine it was good for you, having no family or old friends around.'

'It was hard,' Lydia admitted. 'It was a terrible time – but this was where I needed to be. And everyone around here rallied.' Everyone except Kathleen. She kept that quiet.

'When you told us you were pregnant we were thrilled, naturally, and delighted when you said you'd move back to Dublin then – but . . .'

'I know I kept changing,' Lydia put in. 'I can see it must have been frustrating for you.'

Her mother sighed. 'It's difficult, having just one child. We wanted more, but it didn't happen. There was nothing wrong with either of us, it was just . . . one of those things.'

They'd never told her that before. She'd never asked.

'We can see now that it was hard on you, being the only one for us to worry about. I think we got so used to looking after you, of focusing all our parenting on you, that we didn't notice when you grew up and became your own person. Maybe we didn't want to see it.'

She turned to Lydia's father. 'Have you a hanky?' He pulled one from his trouser pocket and she blotted her eyes.

'Lydia, we're sorry,' he said. 'We should have been more supportive of your idea, even if we still worry about the outcome. I don't think we can stop worrying, to be honest.'

'That's fine,' Lydia said. 'I worry myself – but I still want to try it.'

He nodded. 'We'd like to lend our support. How about we finance the kitchen appliances you'll need?'

She was touched. She remembered their offer of a honeymoon, the day she and Damien had got married. *We'll cover the cost, wherever you decide to go, whenever the time is right.*

'Thank you,' she said. 'That would help a lot.' She regarded the box on the worktop. 'Is that for me?'

'Of course it is.'

They'd packed it with her favourites from the deli the three of them loved, located between Lydia's old apartment and their house. Oat crackers, truffle crisps, pink lemonade, smoked onion mayonnaise, blue cheese, black olive tapenade, Medjool dates.

They'd packed it with love that never wavered, just overwhelmed sometimes. She thanked them again. She brought them in to see Naomi, and from there she gave them a tour of the finished house, where they encountered Joseph the plumber installing a toilet in one of the ensuites.

She took them out to the patio, so she could show off the garden.

'It's really beautiful,' her mother said. 'You've done wonders here, darling.'

'I want to have the christening soon,' Lydia said. 'Will you come back for it?' and they promised they would – and three weeks later they did, and met everyone.

They'd stepped on to the new path with her. Cautiously, nervously, but they were there.

# 28

IN MID-SEPTEMBER, JUST A FEW DAYS BEFORE NAOMI had been scheduled to arrive, the sign went up at the entrance. *Chance House*, it declared, and below, *Weddings by the Sea*. Green lettering on a cream background, the same shade of green as the house, the same colour scheme as her beautiful new website.

The sign was the last step. After weeks of work the house was finally ready, the site going live later that day.

'Looks good,' Brendan said. 'You're all set now.'

She didn't feel set for anything. 'I'm very nervous, Brendan.'

'Don't be. You've done all you can. You have everything in place.'

'You mean *you* have everything in place.'

He'd been there throughout the preparations, along with many others, all happy to give their time and talents to make this happen.

Susan and Marian had spent their summer trawling the countryside, hunting down furniture at auctions and house sales and in charity shops, and occasionally through word of mouth. Nothing they brought back was new, but everything had history and character and charm. *You're not a chain hotel,* Marian had said. *You're a unique one-off, and people will remember staying here.*

The resulting feel was quirky rather than luxurious, with none of the bedrooms looking the same. Three of the eight rooms boasted magnificent four-poster beds, all different styles; three more had regular doubles, and the remaining two had three singles each, allowing for a capacity of eighteen overnight guests. In addition, a couple of cots and two fold-up beds sat waiting in the attic, just in case.

For the guest lounge they'd found a chaise longue in French navy, a large and battered but supremely comfortable black leather couch and a pair of rocking chairs. In addition there was a grandfather clock, a gramophone in perfect working order, and a growing collection of vinyl records.

The built-in shelves in the alcove were slowly filling with books, whose titles were written in gold leaf on their leather spines, and whose wafer-thin pages had yellowed and foxed with age. *Nobody will read them*, Marian had said, *but they look perfect in this setting, and they smell fabulous.*

For the walls of that room they'd found a clutch of black and white film posters – *The Birds, A Streetcar Named Desire, Twelve Angry Men* – rolled up in a tube in a charity shop, and had put them into thin black frames. *No television*, Marian had said firmly. *They won't play the gramophone if there's a television.*

They'd decided they should provide a tea and coffee station, which they'd agreed would be expected on this floor – but rather than install one in every room they'd opted for a communal one at the end of the corridor, since the guests would know each other, to some extent.

Greta had donated a bag of her most popular coffee – *You cannot offer them instant*, she'd declared – so Marian and Susan had added a coffee machine to their shopping list, along with a compact fridge.

If they were to have real coffee, they'd need real milk to accompany it.

Kathleen had asked among her friends and rounded up some mismatched china. Father Phil had offered a trio of silver teapots he'd found at the back of a press in the presbytery. Cathy promised to bring homemade biscuits each Saturday.

Downstairs the quirky feel continued, with four large tables installed in the dining room, each seating ten, and mismatched chairs gathered around them. The tables, they'd decided, needed to be of a uniform size, to allow for joining together if the occasion demanded, but in keeping with the eclectic theme they'd found two oak, one walnut and one pine.

For the walls, Marian had styled a series of food images – a sky-blue bowl of strawberries, an ice-cream cone with a chocolate Flake jutting from it (held by Jack), sausages on a yellow plate, a straw-lined basket of eggs, a string of onions hanging from an old wooden beam, a canvas sack with potatoes spilling from it – which Andrew had photographed before having them enlarged and framed.

Suspended from the three light fittings in the dining-room ceiling were not the classic crystal chandeliers Damien had envisaged, but simpler – and cheaper – pendant lights in the style of old brass ships' lanterns, a nod to the marine location of the house, and wall lamps in the same style were studded about. The hurricane lamps were still there, sitting on shelves in the larder, ready for whenever the electric lights weren't wanted.

Taking up most of the wall between the front-facing bay windows, impossible to miss, was a large print of the original illustration for the glorious mayhem that was the Mad Hatter's tea party in *Alice's*

*Adventures in Wonderland.* It struck exactly the right note in a house full of surprises and imagination.

Windows throughout were without curtains, the old shutters having been skilfully repaired or replaced. Bedroom floors featured generous mats in muted greens, lilacs and blues, and walls held watercolour landscapes by a local artist, a neighbour of Greta's. On her suggestion he had agreed to loan them to Lydia, in return for having his card displayed in the welcome folder she'd prepared for each room.

Outside, the patio was filled with a variety of pretty tables and chairs, and overhead a roll-out awning in wide blue and white stripes. It brought welcome shade on sunny days, and made a cosy evening haven of the space – *The perfect spot,* Marian had declared, *for a post-wedding nightcap.* Solar lighting on the tables echoed the lights Gareth had dotted around the other seating areas in the garden.

It wasn't in the least what Lydia had envisaged at the start, but she loved it. Secondhand or not, everything was top quality, and they'd sanded or painted or waxed where necessary. Thanks to Marian's sense of style, it had all come together beautifully.

In response to Lydia's appeal early on, Damien's old boss had dropped by, bearing a gift of chef's knives and advising her on kitchen appliances that Brendan had installed – and as promised, her parents had taken care of that substantial bill. At last, there was a working kitchen.

Tom had been a huge help, guiding Lydia through the steps to establish her business, making sure she understood them. He had also recommended a variety of price points for the weddings that she would never have dreamt of charging.

*Don't be afraid to set your rates high,* he'd said. *You've got a top-class facility here, and your prices should reflect that. You're offering a private arrangement, tailored to the wedding party, and with no other guests hanging around. And if you're bringing in decent money you can invest in good wines and quality ingredients, and still make your profit.*

He'd also advised her to set up an account with Andrew – *Handy to get a monthly bill instead of paying every time, and now that you're a business, you can shop at the wholesalers in town for most other things. I'll organise a card for you.*

She'd opened the account with Andrew as he'd suggested, and another with a florist in the town, and a third in a wine shop. Cathy had devised a choice of menus to put on the website, and the wine merchant had suggested some complementary wines, and had promised a good discount for repeat orders.

Lydia had called to Father Phil and asked if he'd be willing to come to the house to perform a marriage ceremony, if anyone looked for that as part of the package. *The yoga studio could hold forty*, she'd said.

*Sign me up*, he'd replied. *If Jesus was happy to be born in a stable, I can hardly object to a wedding in a yoga studio.*

She'd sought out Denny the taxi driver and asked him for more of his cards to issue to guests needing a lift to their village accommodation. She'd also given him the petrol voucher that Susan had suggested as payment for the wedding photos, in place of the money Susan said he wouldn't take.

He'd objected, of course – *There's no need for that at all. It's only a hobby to me* – but she'd pressed it on him. *I haven't looked at the snaps yet*, she'd told him, feeling he might wonder why she wasn't commenting on them, and he'd said no hurry at all. *You'll know when you're ready*, he'd told her.

New mattresses lay on the old beds. White bed linens, towels and tablecloths waited in neat bundles in the hot press. Crockery and cutlery, cookware and glassware filled the kitchen drawers and presses. Everything was in readiness.

And now she and Brendan were admiring the new sign, and she was trying to convince herself that she was in a state of readiness too.

'I was thinking,' Brendan said, 'you might like a little playhouse for Naomi when she's old enough. There's plenty of room between the shed and the patio. We could paint it the same colour as the big house.'

'She'd love it. You're the best granddad in the world. Don't tell my father I said that.' She was rewarded with a smile. He was learning to smile with his eyes again – and thanks to Naomi, so was Lydia.

# 29

'I MIGHT HAVE A CAR FOR YOU,' ANDREW SAID. 'A neighbour's mother has just gone into a nursing home. She has an old Golf that the son is selling. Want to check it out? I can pick you up on my way home from work any day.'

'That would be great. Maybe tomorrow?' She'd been out in the red Mini with Tessa a few times, still quite nervous but gaining a little confidence. The following evening she waited for him at the top of the lane, and sat into the van.

'He'll probably look for more than it's worth,' he said on the way. 'He knows you live in Chance House, so he might assume you're loaded. If you like it, I'd advise you to tell him you'll think about it. Ask what price is on it, but I wouldn't be inclined to make an offer on the spot.'

'OK.'

The Golf was dark blue, with no visible damage. 'Her mileage is low,' the son said. 'Mam was never a big driver, in and out to the village mostly.'

Andrew popped open the bonnet and inspected the engine, peering and frowning and pursing his mouth. 'Just the one owner?'

'Just the one.'

He folded his arms. 'She's old enough all the same.'

'Mam minded her though. Regular services, that kind of thing.'

Andrew nodded doubtfully, closing the bonnet.

'Sit in,' the son said to Lydia, and she opened the driver's door and got in. There was a little plastic bottle with *Holy water* written on it in the driver's seat pocket, and a very old road map of Ireland. She placed her hands on the steering wheel and tapped the horn.

'How much do you want for it?' she asked, and the son told her eight thousand.

She adopted a look of disappointment. 'Oh. Way above my budget, I'm afraid. I thought when the car was as old as it is, it wouldn't be so dear. Pity.'

'She's in good nick for her age.'

'Maybe, but still an old car.'

'I could go down to seven.'

She shook her head regretfully. 'I really can't offer more than five thousand five hundred. I'll have to leave it, I'm afraid.'

'Six thousand five hundred,' he said.

Another rueful head shake. 'Five thousand eight hundred would be my absolute maximum. Doing up Chance House was very expensive.'

She was conscious of Andrew standing nearby, affecting disinterest as he scratched at something on his sleeve.

'Thanks for showing it to me,' she said. 'I appreciate it.' She got out and made to walk away.

The son stuck out a hand. 'Six,' he said.

'Five thousand eight hundred,' she said. 'It really is as high as I can go. Higher than I want to go, really. Look, let's just forget it.' She turned again.

'Five thousand eight hundred,' the son said flatly. 'Cash.'

Lydia let a beat pass. 'OK,' she said. They shook, and she promised to return with the payment in the next few days, and left him the hundred she'd brought as a deposit, and took a photo of the log book so she could arrange insurance. Andrew took off smartly before the son could change his mind.

'Where did you learn how to do that?' he asked when they were well out of earshot.

'Melanie, one of my Dublin friends. We went to Lanzarote on holidays, and she was lethal at the markets.'

He changed gear. 'And there was me telling you what to do.'

'Is it worth five-eight though? What does the engine look like?'

'Haven't a clue – I know nothing about cars. But the body looks in good shape, and if Ber was the only owner I'd say you're safe enough. I'll bring you back when you're sorted with insurance and cash, and you can drive it home.'

Two days later the Golf, wearing the L plates Marian had picked up in town, sat in the driveway of Chance House. It had been transported there very slowly and carefully by Lydia, with Tessa sitting next to her and Andrew crawling along behind them in the van, while Kathleen and Brendan babysat their granddaughter.

'Don't forget,' Andrew said, 'to put your name down for the test. Drive safely. Take your time. Don't let anyone rush you.'

'Nice man,' Tessa said after he'd left. 'Considerate.'

In the weeks since Tessa's arrival, she and Lydia had been growing closer. Now that Naomi's routine was settling a little, they could eat together more often. Sometimes they brought the baby down to the little beach and dipped her tiny toes into the water, and occasionally they got Kathleen or Marian to come and babysit while Tessa led Lydia into the sea for a swimming lesson.

On warm afternoons they strolled to the village with Naomi in the sling, carried by one or other of them, and treated themselves to ice creams. They swapped books, both readers, and Lydia introduced Tessa to yoga, Naomi kicking on her playmat in the studio while the adults stretched and balanced and breathed.

On the evening of the new car, Tessa told Lydia that her husband had been in touch, a couple of weeks after she'd left the marital home. This was the first time she had mentioned him.

'He wrote to me,' she said, shaking her head. 'It may well have been the first letter of his life. He said he'd like me to come home, and he was willing to overlook my – what did he call it? – tomfoolery.'

'Oh dear. Did you respond?'

'I did. I was perfectly polite. I thanked him for his offer, but said I was very happy where I was, and I had no plans to move back home.'

'Did you hear any more?'

'No. Stephen calls in to him about once a week, just to make sure all is well. He says the house is in a mess, which doesn't surprise me.'

'You did the right thing,' Lydia said, and Tessa agreed, but for the rest of the evening she was quieter than normal.

Towards the end of September four of Lydia's Dublin friends, headed by Brona, arrived with a cocktail shaker and various bottles. They stayed for two nights, and marvelled at the house, and caused quite a stir when Lydia brought them to McMonagles pub on the second night. *We're making this an annual event,* they promised as they were leaving, and she really hoped it would happen.

A few days later, her parents came to view the fully furnished house. Although they'd spoken often on the phone since their reconciliation, Lydia felt nervous before their arrival, wanting them to approve. She prepared her favourite room for them, the one with the nicest four-poster bed.

The day they were due she dressed Naomi in her prettiest Babygro – too small still for any of the outfits she'd been gifted – and dressed herself in layers that hid the leftover pregnancy weight. She cooked the courgette lasagne they liked, and opened a bottle of wine.

'Relax,' Tessa said. 'They'll love everything' – and in fact, they did.

They exclaimed at how much Naomi had grown in the weeks since they'd seen her. They chatted with Tessa, who told them over dinner how Lydia had given her daughter a wedding to remember.

'This house is special,' she said. 'I feel so lucky to be living in it.' Lydia could have hugged her.

Her parents loved their room. 'Look at that bed,' her mother said. 'Magnificent.'

'Very nicely furnished,' her father said, as Lydia walked them through the rest of the upstairs. 'Different, not quite what you'd expect in this kind of house, but it works.'

'And it's so bright,' her mother added. 'What colour paint is that on the walls?'

'Calico.'

'Very nice.'

They gave the Golf in the driveway a cautious nod of approval. 'Just be careful,' her father told her. 'Eyes peeled at all times. Expect the unexpected,' and Lydia wondered if they thought of Damien then, as she did.

In the morning she took them on a tour of the area, wanting them to see what she saw: the gold and green patchwork of fields, the distant purple hills, the farmhouses and barns, the splendour of the ever-changing sea. 'It's a picturesque spot,' her father acknowledged. 'No doubt about it.'

'You might find a holiday home around here,' Lydia joked, and they laughed at that.

In the evening they dined at Kathleen and Brendan's with Marian and Tom. Kathleen served roast chicken, with a cheese omelette for Lydia. 'Getting there slowly now,' she said, when Lydia's parents asked how she was feeling, and Lydia's mother said she wished they lived closer to Naomi, like Kathleen and Brendan did, and again Lydia felt a pang for settling their only grandchild so far away from them.

'Good luck with everything,' they said, on their departure from Chance House the next day. 'We'll be hoping for some wedding enquiries. Let us know.'

It was generous of them. She knew they still had reservations. She would invite them to spend Christmas here. She would ask Andrew, closer to the time, if he had something ready stuffed that she could just pop into the oven for them.

It would be a different Christmas. Emptier and sadder without Damien, but also one to cherish, as Naomi's first. She would do what she could to make it happy.

Time passed. October brought a return of Lydia's yoga classes, and her students reappeared, and new enquiries trickled in until she introduced a Thursday morning class. 'Are you coming back to the infants?' Susan asked, and Lydia said she'd be happy to do that too.

On the day when Damien would have turned thirty-five, Lydia's parents returned, and a small party of Foleys and Cotters drove to the graveyard. Lydia walked up the hill with them, her daughter nestling in the sling.

It was over nine months since she'd lost him. She thought about all that had happened since then, all the changes to Chance House and its surrounds. The renovations complete, the house furnished, the garden an ongoing delight. The ginger cat and the birth of the kittens, the yoga classes for children and adults, and the second business she was hoping to coax into being. New friendships formed, and rifts healed; a car bought, and a driving test looming.

And of course, the arrival of their daughter.

She gazed into the beautiful sleepy face that she would never tire of looking at, the face of the child who had come to save her. She descended the slope with the others, and they drove in convoy back to Chance House, where Cathy waited with dinner in the big dining room.

As the month wore on, she tried not to check the website every day, then tried not to be disappointed when she did check and found nothing. Lots of views, Gareth reported, but no enquiries.

Until the last day of October, when the first email arrived.

# 30

Hello,

My name is Martina O'Neill, and my fiancé James Cassidy and I had planned to get married in Galway next February. We had our hotel booked, and a hundred and fifty guests invited – but sadly my sister was diagnosed last month with a very aggressive cancer. Her time is limited, so we want to bring the wedding forward and just have a small family wedding instead. Your venue sounds like it might be what we're looking for. Our guest list is now seventeen, including ourselves – I wonder if you could accommodate us, sooner rather than later, ideally within the next few weeks? I know it's a tall order, and you're probably busy, but I thought it was worth a try.

You might let me know as soon as you can,
Many thanks
Martina

Martina

First, let me say how sorry I am to hear your sad news: my heart goes out to all of you. On a more positive note, I can accommodate you and your guests as soon as you want – this is a new business venture, and you would be my very first guests. How about Saturday week, the ninth of November?

Let me know, and we can talk practicalities, like room allocations, dietary requirements, etc

My best,

Lydia

Lydia

That date would be ideal, thank you so much. We're very happy to be your first wedding party. I'll get back to you about bedrooms and food as soon as possible – I just need to check with everyone. I see you're offering an option of having the ceremony in the house as well as the meal, so we'd like to do that too, but one of my uncles is a priest – could he officiate?

A little more about my sister Karen. She's thirty-two, and she's my only sibling, and I can't imagine living without her. She's married, no children – they were planning to start a family next year. You never know, do you?

Love, Martina

Martina

Of course your uncle can marry you and James. It's your day, so you must have it as you would like it. Pass on my details and ask him to let me know if there's anything I can supply for him.

I lost someone very dear at the beginning of this year. Like *you, I didn't think I could go on without him. I thought I'd never get over it, and someone wise agreed that I wouldn't, but told me I'd learn to live with it, and I am. It's slow, and at times it's still very painful, but I'm learning. This might help you, later on.*

*You're in the diary for the tenth – talk soon.*
*Love, Lydia*

*Lydia*
*I'm so sorry. Thank you.*
*Martina xx*

And now everything was organised and the day was here – cold, dry – and Lydia awaited arrivals with inner flutterings, and was glad of Greta, in an unfamiliar grey dress, who'd helped with room preparations the day before and who was now on hand until she was no longer required.

*What about your animals?* Lydia had asked.

*They are not a problem – my neighbour looks after them when I am away, in return for all the eggs and cheese he can eat.*

*Is that Bob, your artist neighbour?*

*It is. He has painted my goats. I will show you some time.*

Cathy was in the kitchen with her teenage niece – *She wants to follow in my footsteps,* she'd told Lydia. *She's a great assistant.* Both had arrived in their black trousers and white shirt uniform, and Ann, the niece, had her long red hair secured in a plait.

When Lydia peeped into the kitchen later the two of them were scurrying about, taking things from the fridge, slipping trays into ovens.

Tessa had migrated to Marian and Tom's house with Naomi, armed with bottles of milk and the rest of the paraphernalia a travelling baby required. The apartment was needed, they'd decided, as a sort of holding pen for the bride before the ceremony began. Large as the house was, keeping the bride apart from the rest of the guests would be tricky otherwise. *Come around to the side,* Lydia had emailed Martina, *and tell everyone else to use the main entrance.*

The heating was on, the dining-room fire lit. The yoga studio had been transformed with bunting and flowers, the wooden floor polished, windows cleaned, chairs set out. The hall had more flowers, and a banner strung above the studio doors that featured a champagne bottle whose exploding bubbles formed the word *Congratulations!*

Lydia had debated hanging it – was it insensitive in this case? Marian, when consulted, hadn't thought so. *They'll probably be glad of all the cheer they can find,* she'd said, so up it had gone.

James the groom and his two brothers were first to arrive, forty minutes or so before the ceremony was due to start. All in suits, two pale grey, one darker. 'No buttonholes,' Greta observed, plucking three white carnations from one of the vases in the hall. 'Wait here,' she ordered, and vanished into the apartment, while Lydia, in a loose blue tunic that hid the elasticated waistband of her black trousers, pretended it was all part of the service, and hoped Greta wouldn't go in search of a veil, if the bride arrived without one.

When they'd been equipped with their flowers she showed the trio upstairs to the room where the brothers were to stay. 'I've been ordered not to let you into the bridal suite until later,' she told James apologetically. 'I have to do what I'm told.'

'No problem,' he said, dropping his bag against the wall. He struck her as having the look of a poet about him, pale of complexion, soft-spoken, dark-haired, dark-eyed, glasses. For a man about to be married, he seemed a little mournful.

She brought them across the corridor to the guest lounge and invited them to help themselves to tea or coffee from the station in the corridor, and told them about the drinks and nibbles that would be served shortly in the studio. 'All very informal,' she said. It sounded better than admitting she was making it up as she went along.

'Wow,' one of the brothers said. 'A gramophone. Does it work?'

'It works perfectly.' She showed him the record collection Marian was still adding to whenever she came across vinyl for sale. Somewhat to her surprise – all three looked to be in their twenties – he selected Louis Armstrong. 'Love jazz,' he said.

'Great view,' the third brother said at the window. 'So close to the sea. Can you actually go into the water from the end there?'

'You can – there's a little beach, not visible from here.'

'Amazing.'

The other came to join him, but James took a seat instead on the chaise longue, his expression still brooding. Maybe it was just normal pre-wedding jitters – or maybe it was something more, considering the sad circumstances.

'I hope it all goes well today,' she said quietly, and at that he gave her a grateful smile and murmured his thanks. Yes, she thought, conflicted about showing happiness, on a day that should be such a happy one for him.

The doorbell rang again, and Greta appeared shortly afterwards with more guests, and by a quarter to four, everyone but the bride and her immediate family was installed in the studio with a drink, and Ann from the kitchen was circulating with a tray of little bites, still warm from the oven.

Conversation within the group was easy, but under the smiles Lydia recognised a melancholy she knew well. Gaiety was a thing put on for form's sake, to mask the foreboding and get them through the day.

Just before four, the bride and her party arrived. 'Thank you,' Martina's mother said, in a burgundy dress and matching coat, 'for accommodating us at such short notice.'

'We're very grateful,' her husband said.

The strain showed on their faces, despite their efforts to hide it. Smiles didn't reach eyes. How did they cope, knowing what lay ahead for their daughter? Where did they get the strength? Again, Lydia wondered about the wisdom of the banner above the studio doors. Too late to do anything about it now.

Martina was in a white calf-length dress with a short veil, the first traditionally attired bride at Chance House. 'My sister Karen,' she said to Lydia, 'and her husband David.'

On the face of it, she looked no less healthy than Martina, wearing a dress the colour of Gareth's stolen primroses under a warm-looking shrug in the same shade. Perfectly made up, a soft cream beret perched on short blonde hair. Bird-shaped silver earrings, a silver stud in one nostril.

Lydia could see no obvious sign that she had received the diagnosis everyone dreaded – but then Karen reached out to grip the back of a kitchen chair, and lowered herself on to it. 'Sorry,' she murmured, 'bit tired,' and everyone turned to her. Her husband

– tall, auburn-haired – rested a hand on her shoulder, and silence descended.

Lydia opened the prosecco she'd set aside for them, and the conversation stuttered along until the bride's mother put down her glass.

'We'd better get going,' she said. 'They'll be waiting for us. Karen, love, are you able?'

'I am.' She rose and left the apartment on her husband's arm, her mother following, and Lydia showed them to the studio. She let the priest and the groom know that the bride was on the way, and watched them take their positions at the top of the room.

'You can start the music,' she murmured to Greta, who was poised by the sound system Gareth had donated, and as the opening chords of a Bach prelude sounded, father and daughter emerged from the apartment.

The ceremony was a muted affair. The vows, the ring exchange, the first kiss. The joy was quiet – but Lydia felt the love that was everywhere, drifting about, butting against the sadness.

When the ceremony ended the guests sat on in the studio, chatting while they waited to be summoned to dinner. Karen nursed but didn't drink the glass of wine someone had handed her, smiling when addressed, but not speaking much. David sat next to her, holding her hand, his smile as forced as those of his parents-in-law.

Was this a mistake? Lydia wondered. Did they regret booking Chance House? Maybe they wished they'd gone to a register office with immediate family, and left it at that. Should she tell Martina they didn't have to stay the night, they could eat and go if they preferred, and she would adjust the price she'd charged them?

Just then Cathy put her head around the door. 'Dinner is served,' she announced cheerily, and as they filed out, David approached Lydia and drew her aside.

'Karen's feeling tired,' he said. 'I'm going to bring her up for a nap' – and Greta, overhearing, offered to accompany them. Within minutes, as everyone was taking their seats at one of the two prepared tables, David reappeared.

'She's sleeping,' he told Lydia. 'Greta has offered to sit with her for a bit. I didn't want her to be alone.'

'Of course.' Lydia saw him murmur to his parents-in-law before taking his seat. As Ann emerged from the kitchen with starters, Lydia slipped in to help. Handing plates around, she thought of Greta sitting by the sick woman's bedside, in the same way that she'd sat silently with Lydia after Damien's death. Fearless and compassionate. It was a formidable combination.

When the cake had been cut and served, when the teas and coffees were finished, Cathy opened the champagne the bridal couple had requested for this part of the proceedings, and when glasses were filled, Martina and Karen's father rose to his feet and waited for silence.

From her vantage point just inside the kitchen door, Lydia saw him reach into a breast pocket and draw out a sheaf of cards – but after regarding them for a few seconds he put them back. He drew a long breath, his gaze roaming the tables, as everyone waited.

'Dolores and I,' he finally began, and stopped. He cleared his throat and started again. 'Our hearts are full today,' he said, 'as we welcome James to the family. We're delighted that—' He broke off for the second time and rubbed hard at his mouth, and Lydia could see how close to tears he was.

The groom pushed back his chair and stood. 'Patrick, let me,' he said quietly, and his new father-in-law resumed his seat without another word.

James didn't appear to have a speech waiting in a pocket. It looked like he hadn't planned on making one – or if he had, he'd decided, like Patrick, that it wasn't the one that was needed now.

'Thank you all for coming,' he began haltingly. 'Thank you for sharing this day with Martina and myself. We know the effort it's taking for you all to be happy for us, and we appreciate it, and will remember it. Thank you to Lydia for giving us this lovely venue at such short notice.'

Nobody stirred. Nobody lifted a cup, or a glass. His words were quietly spoken, but perfectly audible in the dead silence. Lydia observed the bride's mother, fighting tears like her husband.

Kathleen and Brendan flashed without warning into Lydia's head. Outliving one of their children, already travelling the hard road that was ahead of this couple. Something Greta had said came back to her, something about a mother losing a child being the hardest loss of all. Having gone through her own bereavement, Lydia wondered if grief could be quantified.

'I don't know,' James continued, 'what more I can say. I wish it wasn't so, I wish these things didn't happen. I'm part of the O'Neill family now, and I'll support them in every way I can, as I know all of you will too.'

David, destined like Lydia to lose his partner young. Would it have been easier, she wondered, if she'd known in advance that Damien was to leave her? Maybe it wouldn't have made that much of a difference. Either way, her heart would have been shattered.

James lifted his glass. 'The O'Neill family,' he said, and other glasses were raised, and the toast echoed around the room. As conversations resumed Lydia emerged to see if anyone wanted more drinks, more cake, more coffee, and while she was fulfilling requests David disappeared, and a few minutes later Greta was back.

'She's up,' she reported to Lydia. 'She wanted to get up. She's getting dressed. She'll be down shortly. I'll ask Cathy to get a plate ready for her.'

Karen's reappearance served to lift the mood a little as she picked at what was on her plate, and everyone took more cake to keep her company.

'I will go now,' Greta said to Lydia. 'I think you can manage without me.'

'Thank you so much, Greta. I'll organise an official assistant if I get more business.'

'I like being your assistant,' Greta said. 'I am happy to continue, if you are happy to keep me.'

'But would you let me pay you?'

'Certainly not,' Greta said, looking offended. 'I would do it because I enjoy it' – and accustomed as she was now to village ways, Lydia wondered why she'd even offered payment.

'I'd be delighted,' she said. 'Thanks, Greta.'


'I wonder,' Martina said, when the tables had been cleared of food, 'if we could have more lively music, for dancing.'

As requested, Lydia had put together a playlist of instrumental piano and guitar tunes as background music for the meal – 'Something relaxing,' Martina had said – but it wasn't music anyone could dance to.

'Hang on,' Lydia said, scrolling through her playlists, and when she found what she was looking for people got up and danced to Lady Gaga and Coldplay and Harry Styles and Taylor Swift, and even Karen and David took to the floor for some of the slower songs, and a stranger happening on the scene could have been forgiven for thinking it was just another regular wedding reception, with nothing more challenging ahead than catching the bouquet.

And watching it all, Lydia realised she could listen to love songs again without falling apart.

In due course, the guests began to gravitate to the upstairs lounge, their number reduced after a few – Karen and David, the parents of the bridal couple, the two grandparents in attendance – had opted for an early night. Lydia intercepted Martina's best friend, the only non-family guest, before she left the dining room, and brought her into the kitchen to show her the sandwiches Cathy had prepared before leaving.

'You want me to bring them up now?' she asked.

The woman shook her head. 'Not at all – I'll come down and get them in a while. You head off, we'll be fine.'

'How do you think it went?' Lydia asked. 'Did they enjoy it?'

'It was great – honestly. It was just what everyone needed, a few hours of distraction.'

'I was afraid they might have regretted it – you know, the strain of trying to be happy.'

'No. Martina wanted to do it for Karen, and you gave them a lovely occasion to remember – and it was good that we had the place to ourselves, under the circumstances. They'll have no regrets, believe me.'

It made her feel better as she switched off the main lights downstairs and made sure the dying embers of the fire were contained.

Later, lying in bed, with Naomi fed and sleeping in her cot, Lydia sent up a wish that her second enquiry, if she got a second enquiry, would lead to a happier occasion.

Two days later, her wish was granted.

# 31

*Hello,*

*We hope you're very well. We're Jason and Barney, and we've been together for over thirty years. We live in a dilapidated old mansion outside Roscommon, and we've decided to get married, just for the hell of it – we're due a nice day out – and we're wondering if you might fit us in. We'd be inviting twenty-four of our dearest friends, a very select gathering. If you think you could cope with us for a night, expect great style. We would also like one long table for the meal, if that can be organised – we want to be like a big Italian family out to lunch.*

*They're not on any of your lovely menus, but we're hoping you wouldn't mind serving cheeseburgers all round for our main course – not a vegetarian among us – because that was what we had on our first date, and we'd love a surprise for dessert. As to drinks, we would only require lots of sparkling water from yourself, as we'd like to bring our own champagne, which is all we ever drink, and which our guests would be very happy to share. We keep a good cellar.*

*In all seriousness, while we never really grew up, we're old enough to know right from wrong, and we always behave ourselves. The worst that would happen is you'd find one of us asleep under a table in the morning.*

*We were thinking the end of the month – or the end of any month, come to that. After thirty years, there's no great rush.*

*Yours in anticipation*

*J&B*


*Dear Jason and Barney*

*I would love to give you a nice day out – thirty years is more than long enough to wait! As you can see on the website, I have six lovely double rooms and two triples, so I could accommodate you and sixteen of your friends overnight (if two lots of three didn't mind sharing), and the other eight would be offered a choice of nearby self-catering accommodation. A taxi would take them there and ferry them back for breakfast.*

*Cheeseburgers for dinner will be no problem, and my chef would love to come up with some surprise desserts. Your own champagne will be fine, and I'll stock up on the sparkling water. Let me know about room preferences, and I'll send my quote.*

*How would the thirtieth of November suit you? And would you like any kind of ceremony in the house before the reception?*

*Best wishes,*

*Lydia*

'They sound fun,' she said, showing Gareth the email. He'd come to give her a lesson on how to update the website.

'Hmm,' he said. 'Sounds like they're going to bring truckloads of champagne. Hopefully they won't trash the place.'

'Ah no, they're too old for that – and I can cope with someone falling asleep under a table.'

'Great style. Bet they'll be in dickie-bows and top hats. By the way, I met someone.'

She looked at him. 'What do you mean? Who? When?'

'A woman. On the Camino.'

'Gareth McMahon, that was months ago – why are you only telling me now?'

'I wasn't sure it would last – she's been travelling since then, only got home last week. We were long-distancing.'

'Where's home?'

'Galway. Just outside Clifden.'

'Not too far at all. Have you met her since she came back?'

'I have.'

'And?'

He grinned. 'And mind your own business.'

'Hey, you started this – I'm only showing interest. So you're keen?'

He blushed. He actually blushed. 'I am a bit keen alright.'

'Well, I'm delighted for you. What's her name?'

'Celine.'

'Bring her around to meet me if she comes this way.'

'I will.'

He was happy. He'd never spoken of a girlfriend. She was glad for him, in the throes of new infatuation, on his way to love – or maybe already arrived there. She was reminded of her early butterflies when Damien was due in Dublin, or she was on her way to the west.

She remembered the thrill of seeing him again after a week apart. She recalled their first kiss (in his car, in the rain), their first night together (in her apartment, after dinner with Brona and Shaun), the first time they'd talked about love (the same night).

Magical.

*Lydia*

*You sound like our kind of hostess. That date is perfect – and we'd love to have our ceremony under your most interesting roof, thank you. We come fully equipped – one of our guests did a degree in something or other that he tells us qualifies him to marry us. What do we care? Nobody else would have either of us at this stage, so whether we get properly hitched or not, we're stuck with each other.*

*We'll take all your lovely beds. We're going to draw lots to see who gets the triple rooms, and you can book the eight leftovers into wherever will have them. They're happy to share rooms in pairs. They're all couples, of one sort or another.*

*This will be great fun. We're all about the fun. The world has more than enough of the other stuff going on, so we push back whenever we can.*

*We're so looking forward to meeting you. Is confetti allowed?*

*J&B xx*

*Jason and Barney*

*Yes, the world needs all the joy and happiness we can put into it.*

*Confetti is definitely allowed. In fact, I'm thinking of making it mandatory.*

*I'll sort out accommodation and let you know.*

*Lydia x*

She liked confetti. She decided she would pick up some herself, enter into the spirit of things. She sensed she was going to enjoy Jason and Barney.

Before their date arrived, she got another. 'My driving test,' she told Andrew, encountering him on the village street. 'Next Thursday.'

'How do you feel?'

'Very nervous.'

'I could take you out before it,' he said, 'revise a bit. Do a practice test.'

'Would you mind? That would be great.'

Early on Thursday morning he took her through the three-point turn, the reversing around a corner, the emergency stop. He directed her into the village and out as far as the graveyard, then they doubled back to Chance House.

'Am I ready?'

'You're ready. Just keep a cool head and take it handy. You won't fail for being careful. Best of luck.'

At the appointed time, she and Tessa dropped Naomi to her grandparents' house before Lydia drove carefully to the test centre in the town. Tessa waited with a magazine while Lydia was quizzed on the rules of the road before being led out to the waiting Golf.

The instructor sat silently throughout the test, speaking only to tell her where to go, or what to do, making occasional jottings on his clipboard. At one stage she took an eternity to turn right, terrified to move until the road was practically empty of traffic. That was a fail, she thought. An over-abundance of caution as bad, in its own way, as speeding. You won't fail for being careful, Andrew had said – what did he know?

She didn't fail. 'Well done,' the instructor said. 'Safe driving.' She took the form he gave her and thanked him, and left the centre with an N-plate on the car in place of the L. She was so happy to have moved from Learner to Novice. *I passed*, she texted Andrew when they were all home again. *Congrats*, he replied, and posted a car air freshener through her letterbox on his way home that evening. On her next trip to the village she called to his shop with one of Tessa's apple tarts.

The last Saturday in November arrived, and with it her two grooms. Jason was slightly taller than Barney and a little thinner, but otherwise their similarities were remarkable. They were in their fifties, bald and attractive, with skin that gleamed and tans that looked real, and wonderful teeth.

'My dear,' Jason said on meeting Lydia, 'we found you. You're so kind to take us in.' He dropped a kiss on both cheeks before handing her over to Barney for more of the same.

They didn't have dickie-bows or top hats. Despite the bitter cold of the day they wore identical pale blue, three-piece linen suits with crisp white shirts and shiny black shoes. From their right top pockets red handkerchiefs poked, perfectly matching their red carnation buttonholes. They both smelt wonderful. Next to them, Lydia felt dowdy.

'This is Greta,' she said, 'my second-in-command.'

'Enchanted,' Jason said, lifting her hand to his lips. 'What beautiful bone structure you have.' Greta gave him a surprised smile. Barney kissed her hand in turn, and Greta's smile widened. Lydia had never known her friend to beam like that.

'We'll get the booze,' they said, and only then Lydia saw the beautiful old car in the driveway, shining and immaculate in a shade of dark green. 'Our baby,' Jason said, as Barney opened the boot. 'Jaguar Mark II. We're as classy as Morse.'

They're rich, she thought, as they piled coolers onto a small trolley and wheeled it into the house. The mansion in Roscommon was hardly dilapidated, not with a good cellar and a pristine Jaguar in the driveway. In the kitchen she introduced them to Cathy and Ann – more hand-kissing – and stowed the champagne in the drinks fridge. For twenty-six people, they'd brought a whole lot.

'Would you like me to open a bottle now?' Cathy asked. It was three in the afternoon, the ceremony not scheduled for another hour.

'You read our minds,' Jason replied.

The first cork was popped, and Lydia, Cathy and Ann persuaded to have a small, delicious, ice-cold glass each.

'Here's to us,' Jason said.

'Got there in the end,' Barney said.

Lydia brought them to see the studio, all decked out for the ceremony.

'Delightful,' Jason said. 'Would you mind awfully if we rearranged the chairs a tiny bit? It'll take just a tick.'

'Not at all' – and the change was made, a circle rather than rows.

'Let me bring you up to your room,' Lydia said – but more cars were heard just then pulling up in the driveway. 'Aha,' Barney said. 'The hoi polloi have arrived.'

The guests piled in, everyone as beautifully dressed as the grooms. All were in great good humour, laughing and chattering as they greeted Lydia and kissed Jason and Barney, accepting glasses from the tray with which Greta had materialised. They climbed the stairs and trooped cheerily through the bedrooms, praising everything, exclaiming over the view, telling Lydia how lucky she was.

In the guest lounge, someone put Mario Lanza on the gramophone – and from every room, to Lydia's surprise, voices chimed in.

'Most of us are in a choir,' Jason explained. 'We're very highbrow, love our operas.'

Of course they did. *We're all about the fun.*

The ceremony in the studio was interesting. The grooms sat with everyone else, and the celebrant, dressed in what looked to Lydia like a version of Brona's kimono, positioned himself between them. After a short welcome, he invited people to share reminiscences, and round the room they went, each guest offering a memory that included Jason and Barney.

Some were amusing, others poignant, but what came across clearly to Lydia – hovering with Greta outside the studio, not wanting to intrude but reluctant to desert them – was everyone's affection for the couple. For all their light-heartedness, they were among genuine friends.

There were no vows – maybe they thought thirty years was

enough proof of their devotion – but there was something else. Together they sang, without any trace of self-consciousness that Lydia could discern, a song she didn't recognise. She thought the language was Italian.

They were in perfect harmony. It was beautiful. She closed her eyes and let it wash over her. Halfway through, the rest of the company joined in softly with more harmonies. Lydia opened her eyes to see Greta's reaction, and was amazed to catch her raising a tissue and dabbing. Greta, in tears. When they finished, there was a second of silence before a deafening cheer broke out in the studio.

When the grooms were finally pronounced married, confetti was flung amid more cheers and much laughter. Lydia entered and threw her own and embraced the newlyweds along with the others. A second glass of cold champagne was pressed into her hand. It tasted just as delicious as the first.

Greta hung back. Maybe an embrace, and champagne in the middle of the afternoon, was a little too much for her.

They assembled in the hall for photographs, the day too cold to venture outdoors. There seemed to be no official photographer, and not a single camera in evidence, but several phones were deployed as the group adopted a variety of dramatic poses, on and off the stairs, Barney and Jason taking centre stage in each one.

In the dining room, the cheeseburgers were produced – and judging by the looks of astonishment on the faces of the guests, it was evident to Lydia that the grooms hadn't shared the menu beforehand.

'We hope nobody minds,' Jason said. 'As the old romantics we are, we wanted to revisit our first date, so kindly indulge us.' This prompted more merriment, and nobody seemed at all disappointed not to be served something a little more gourmet.

'I've taken the liberty,' Cathy told them, 'of adding a few extras. We couldn't have you going hungry.' She and Ann went down the long table depositing baskets of chips and crispy onion rings and bowls of coleslaw, and prompting a round of applause that Lydia thought might have contained a little relief. Not gourmet either, but filling.

The platters of mini-desserts that followed went down well. Cubes of cheesecake, tiramisu and lemon meringue pie. Fingers of chocolate biscuit cake and little brownies, miniature cream horns and shot glasses of apple crumble. Lydia wondered how many hours had gone into their creation.

The evening wore on, with the champagne continuing to flow. After the remains of the food had been cleared away two of the guests produced a cello and a guitar, and a singsong ensued, with contributions from everyone. The offerings were varied, from country to jazz to more opera, and Lydia, giving a sweep to the kitchen floor after Cathy and Ann had left, found herself humming along to anything she recognised.

When there was a break in the singing she produced the supper sandwiches, and offered more teas or coffees – 'Or possibly champagne?'

'Always more champagne,' Barney replied, 'and you'll join us, dear Lydia. You must be dead on your feet.' When she demurred, telling them she had a baby who would need feeding in the small hours she was ordered to bed, with instructions to bring the baby out for inspection in the morning.

'We'll take it from here,' Jason said. 'You've been magnificent.'

Lydia was given a parting round of applause, and several of the guests leapt from their chairs to embrace her as she left. She was definitely the only sober one in the room, and she hoped they wouldn't set the house on fire. She also hoped Denny wouldn't mind being summoned at whatever hour, when they had finally had enough champagne.

The house survived. Everyone turned up for breakfast, looking remarkably well. 'Good champagne,' Jason told her, 'never causes a hangover. We're leaving the leftover bottles to say thank you. We had a ball – in fact, we're thinking of coming back next year to celebrate our anniversary.'

'You would be most welcome,' she told him. As promised, she brought Naomi to meet them after breakfast, and phones were whipped out for more photos, until the subject decided she'd had enough, and was returned, bawling, to Tessa's care.

They all departed together, in a flurry of hugs and kisses. Two of them told Lydia they'd be in touch when it was their turn to get married. After they were gone, the house felt too quiet without them. She wished they all lived closer.

Funny how she'd changed. She recalled her outrage when Greta had suggested she let Ian and Lorraine use the house, and how determined she'd been to have as little as possible to do with it. Now she could enter into the spirit of things, and enjoy it.

There were four bottles of champagne left in the fridge. Lydia took a picture of the label and showed it to her wine merchant.

'Wow,' he said. 'Big spenders.'

# 32

*Hi,*

*My fiancé and I are looking for a venue for our wedding reception, and we're wondering about yours. It's just family, but there are quite a few of us: between (adult) children, spouses, exes, siblings and half-siblings we are eighteen in total. We'd need all your rooms, and all your beds!*

*I should add that Ben, my fiancé, was married before and divorced, so we can't do the church marriage. We've booked a civil ceremony in Galway on the morning of December the twenty-ninth, and our plan would be to travel on to Chance House afterwards for the reception, if you're free. It's typical of us that we've left it till the last minute to get organised, so it'll serve us right if you're booked up, which you probably are!*

*Let me share our story anyway. We met in our early twenties and fell in love. Circumstances separated us for years, and when fate reunited us we were both a lot older, but the feelings were still there, so here we are.*

*Sorry, I'm rambling on. I'm a writer, so it's probably force of habit! Ben says my motto should be 'Why use one word when you can use twenty-one?' He thinks he's funny.*

*Many thanks*

*Ellen*

The twenty-ninth. The day after what should have been Lydia and Damien's first wedding anniversary. She was dreading it – but maybe it would be good to have a booking for the day after, something to look forward to after such a sad one.

Her parents were coming for Christmas, and staying for the anniversary. Susan and Father Phil had both issued lunch invitations for that day. Greta had suggested an afternoon trip to her farm. Marian had offered to do dinner for everyone.

All trying to distract, which was good of them – but she hated the thought of being away from Chance House on the anniversary of the day that she and Damien had celebrated their marriage there.

She made some calls and issued new invitations, and then she responded to the email.

*Ellen,*

*Many thanks for your enquiry. The twenty-ninth of this month is free, so I'll be happy to accommodate you and your family. What an interesting story you have. Let me know which of the Christmas menu options you'd like, and we can go from there. And just a thought – if you wanted a blessing from Father Phil, our lovely local priest, I'm sure he'd be happy to drop in on the day if he was free.*

*Best wishes,*

*Lydia*

*Lydia,*

*I'm thrilled you can take us! And what a lovely idea to get a blessing too – it would be like a seal of approval. Will you kindly pass on Father Phil's details?*

*It will be my first wedding – my ex and I didn't get married, just lived together and had two daughters. I would have married him, but he wasn't the marrying kind (or the faithful kind, as it turned out, but that's a whole other story).*

*Ben actually proposed five years ago, and we've been happily engaged since then. The irony is I always wanted to be married – I loved the idea of having a husband, and being someone's wife. I suppose the security of it appealed to me – but after Ben and I got engaged, I realised I didn't need to be married to him to feel secure. We're only doing it now because my daughters say that being engaged for so long at our ages – both in our sixties – is a bit ridiculous, which I suppose it is!*

*Anyway, I'm rambling again, so I'll consult the troops and come back to you about a menu. Can't wait to stay in your house – it looks truly beautiful.*

*Love Ellen x*

An hour later, before Lydia had a chance to respond to the first, there was a second email.

*Lydia,*

*Me again, with an odd request. Could we have pizzas all round for our wedding meal? Just a few we can all share, with a couple of vegetarian options. It's the only thing Ben* can cook, and it's a sort of running family joke. Would that be OK?

Also, I forgot to say I'm planning to bake the wedding cake myself – I was taught to bake years ago by an aunt – so we won't need desserts. We all like a nice glass of wine though – my ex fancies himself a bit of a connoisseur, and being half French he favours the Bordeaux – so I've taken the liberty of attaching a few suggestions for red and white, if you can find any of them. I hope I'm not being terribly awkward with these requests. We don't mind paying a bit more.

Love Ellen x


Ellen,

Not awkward at all. I've passed on your pizza order to my brilliant chef, and she'll be happy to prepare a variety – we could always serve some hors d'oeuvres in a separate space before the meal, along with a glass of wine, maybe when you get the blessing – and I'll show your wine list to the merchant I deal with, who I'm sure will find one of each colour.

It's your day, yours and Ben's. Your wish is my command – within reason!

Look forward to meeting you,

Love, Lydia x


Christmas came, and with it, her parents. They brought a fur-lined nest with carrying handles for Naomi, and earrings for Lydia, crafted by a designer she loved. On Christmas morning they all woke to a bright, crisp, blue-sky day. Having waved off Tessa to spend a couple of days with her sister, they bundled up and drove to a beach. They walked along the shore, Lydia's father carrying Naomi in the sling, she and her mother following, arms linked.

'So,' her mother said, 'a long, tough year is nearly over for you.'

'... Yes.' *You'll learn to live with it.*

The tide was receding, a line of seaweed strung out raggedly along the high-water mark, pieces of driftwood and shells scattered across the sand. Lydia crouched for a white one and slipped it into a pocket. She was making a collection for Naomi.

'We're so proud of you, sweetheart.' Her mother reclaimed her arm and pressed it. 'You've had so much to cope with, and look at all you've achieved.'

'Thanks, Mum. That means a lot.'

It did. Finally they were able to let their child go, and to embrace and accept the adult.

'We just wish we saw more of you.'

'I know. I'll come and see you more often when Naomi's a bit older – and you know you and Dad are welcome here anytime.'

For dinner that day Lydia served the spiced beef Andrew had given her. *Ready cooked*, he'd said. *I do it for my older customers who want something handy. Easy to reheat.*

'This is delicious,' her father said. 'You didn't have to do meat for us.'

'Andrew cooked it,' Lydia said. 'The butcher, Naomi's godfather. You met him at the christening.'

'I remember,' her mother said. 'He brought you to the hospital the day she was born.'

'That's right.'

He had also taken her wedding photos, taught her to drive and found her a car, adopted two of the kittens and come up with the idea for her small weddings business. If it wasn't for him, she might well have been back living in Dublin now, and Chance House gone to strangers.

But not to Tim O'Donoghue, not for any money.

On the morning of the twenty-eighth, Father Phil came to Chance House and celebrated Mass in the yoga studio, with everyone gathered. At the homily he recalled the wedding, and how it had been the first proper introduction of Lydia into the community. He spoke of the charm of the half-finished dining room, and how they'd managed to pull off a wonderful occasion with very few conveniences. He praised Lydia and Damien's family for their endurance, and wished them all an easier road going forward.

The rest of the day was gentle. A brief visit to the graveyard, lunch at Marian's house afterwards, the afternoon spent quietly with her parents and Naomi in the apartment. Tessa had made herself scarce, having arranged to spend the day with her son. Giving them space to remember privately, in her tactful way.

Dinner was omelettes, nobody hungry after Marian's lunch. They brought their coffees up to the guest lounge, carrying a sleeping Naomi in her new nest. Lydia's father put Bing Crosby on the gramophone, and listening to him sing about a white Christmas reminded Lydia of the snow that had kept her and Damien housebound for most of the six days of their marriage.

Her mother yawned as she set down her cup. 'I'm ready for my bed,' she said, so Lydia wished them goodnight and returned downstairs with Naomi, intending to go to bed herself – the rest of the rooms had already been prepared for the following day's guests, and the final one could be done in the morning – but she found Tessa in the kitchen, filling a hot water bottle.

'Would you care for a Baileys,' Lydia asked, 'for the day that's in it?' It was nice around Christmas, and her parents had brought a bottle.

'I wouldn't mind,' Tessa replied, so they put Naomi to bed and brought their drinks into the sitting room, and settled on the couch. The little room was warm, the heating set to stay on for another while.

'Was it tough today?' Tessa asked.

Lydia considered. 'Not as tough as I thought it might be.'

'Tell me about the wedding – if you want to.'

She did. They sipped their drinks as she recalled the poached egg breakfast Brona had cooked, and the champagne they'd opened with Marian and Susan afterwards, and Marge who'd come to do their hair, and Denny the taxi driver and Andrew the butcher, their two photographers.

She spoke of the bitter cold of that day, and the lilac dress she'd borrowed from Susan, and the unexpected crowd of locals in the church. She told of the red carpet Brendan had laid from the gateway to the house, and the gas heaters they'd used in the dining room along with the open fire, and the food Damien's colleagues had brought, and the musicians who'd played for them, and the carrot cake Greta had made, and the locals who'd poured into the dining room after the meal, bringing more drink and more food and more instruments, and who'd stayed till the small hours, singing and dancing.

'I hardly knew anyone,' she said. 'I know so many now – and you're getting to know them too.'

'I am, bit by bit. I wish I'd met Damien.'

'You would have loved him. Everyone did.'

Later, alone in the kitchen, she took the envelope of wedding photos from the cutlery drawer and went to open it – and stopped.

Not yet.

Ellen turned out to be Ellen Sheehan the writer. Lydia had read several of her books. She was in royal blue, a striking contrast with the dark red hair she'd pinned up with a tortoiseshell clip.

'Ben was a bookseller,' she told Lydia in the apartment, as they waited for the groom and guests to assemble in the studio for Father Phil's blessing. 'He's retired now. We met when I got a job in the Galway bookshop he was managing. I'd left home for the first time, and I was a huge reader, and a complete romantic. I was on a mission to find my soulmate, my Heathcliff or my Mr Darcy. I was determined to experience great passion, and I did.

'Ben was the first man I loved – and it was mutual, but it wasn't to be, long story, and it broke my heart. I couldn't believe it when we met again. The years just fell away.' She laughed. 'I could write a book.'

She was glowing. It was there in the shine of her eyes and the faint flush in her cheeks, and the frequent smile she accompanied with a little tilt of her chin. It was obvious to Lydia that she was deeply in love.

At length, Lydia went out to see if all the guests had arrived. Ben was hovering just inside the studio door, sandy-haired – what was left of it – and freckled. She'd liked him instantly when they'd met earlier.

'Will I do?' he asked now. 'Am I good enough for her?'

She adopted a rueful expression. 'Well, you did break her heart, so . . .'

He groaned. 'She's told you everything.'

'Just about – but I have a feeling you've been forgiven. Is everyone here?'

'Yes, all present and accounted for.'

'Are you ready for this?'

'I've been ready,' he replied, 'for over forty years,' so Lydia signalled to Ellen's son-in-law and brought him out to the apartment, and he walked Ellen through the hall to the studio, where her first and last love was waiting beside Father Phil.

Watching the look on his face as she approached, Lydia felt a softening inside. Yes, sadness for her own situation, but more. Gratitude, maybe, to be able to witness love close up like this, even if it wasn't hers. To be able to give couples of whatever age the space to declare and celebrate what was between them in the company of loved ones.

Photographs followed the blessing. One of Ellen's French relatives – no, her ex's half-brother, wasn't it? Hard to keep track of them all – produced a serious-looking camera and marshalled the guests into various groupings in the hall, and again the wonderful staircase featured.

In the dining room the pizzas were eaten, the wine drunk, and Ellen's cake cut. After that came the speeches: the best man and the new husband – and then, to Lydia's surprise, Ellen's ex Leo rose to his feet.

Good-looking in his day, she thought. Older than Ellen. She put him somewhere in his seventies now, his looks worn a little around the edges, a slight stoop in his bearing. His suit was immaculate.

His voice was beautifully modulated, his accent that of someone who'd had a moneyed English upbringing, and he spoke of his pride in Ellen's literary achievements, and his gratitude to her and Ben for inviting him.

It was polished; his words struck just the right balance. He had style. He was the father of Ellen's daughters, but he hadn't been the faithful type, and today she had married Ben, and Leo was alone. Yes, Lydia thought, there was a book there.

'This was wonderful,' Ellen said, as they were checking out in the morning. 'I may have left getting married a little late, but it was worth the wait. You're married too,' she said, indicating Lydia's ring.

'I was. He died.'

Her expression changed. 'Oh, oh, I'm so sorry. Oh, Lydia,' catching her hand and clutching it between both of hers. 'Oh, God, I'm sorry.'

'Don't be,' Lydia said. 'Please don't be sorry. I'm learning to live with it, and I'm glad we got a chance to marry, and I have a beautiful baby daughter who's helping me. And I realised yesterday that it's a privilege to see other couples take that step too, and I feel honoured when they choose to do it here.'

Ellen shook her head slowly. 'I'd love you to come and see us sometime,' she said, 'you and your daughter. I want to cook lunch for you. We're only an hour away, this side of Galway. Will you come, when you have the time?'

'I will,' Lydia promised.

# 33

THE THIRD OF JANUARY. ONE YEAR WITHOUT HIM.

At midday, Father Phil came to Chance House and said Mass again in the studio for the Cotter family, and Lydia's parents who'd arrived the day before. Afterwards he stayed for lunch in the dining room, with everyone gathered around one of the big tables, close to the fire.

Lydia served little bowls of leek and potato soup, and she set out wooden boards with cold meats and cheeses and chutneys and fruit. Greta had given her a big loaf of sourdough, and a coffee cake for dessert. It was simple food. It was all they wanted.

They were quiet, their voices soft. They spoke of Damien. They pulled up their memories and brought him into the room with them, and Tom sang a song about an elephant that packed her trunk and left the circus, because it had been Damien's party piece as a young child. They cried a little and laughed a little, and Lydia was glad to have them around her, the ones who'd loved him the most.

After they'd gone home, and her parents had started on the road back to Dublin, she and Tessa worked on the jigsaw that Susan had given Lydia for Christmas – Tessa, it turned out, was a big jigsaw fan – and later they ate potato cakes and sweetcorn fritters in dressing gowns as they watched an old Hitchcock film, with Naomi curled up and dreaming in her nest.

It had been a good day. It had been a sad, sweet, good day. After saying goodnight to Tessa, Lydia climbed into bed with the envelope Andrew had given her, and finally felt ready to open it.

She leafed slowly through the photos, wiping her eyes often as she gazed at all the happy faces, setting aside the ones of just her and Damien. When she'd seen them all she returned to that pile, and went through them again.

The moment when they met at the altar. Her lilac dress, his grey suit, their smiles in profile.

The rings being exchanged, Jack just captured as he scuttled back to his mother.

Their first kiss as husband and wife.

The two of them emerging hand in hand from the sacristy, their union made official.

Standing on the church steps, entwined because of the cold – and because they loved each other very much.

Walking on the red carpet to the front door of Chance House, Damien turning to laugh at someone behind him. Some smart comment, maybe.

Lydia being carried across the threshold, holding her bouquet high, Marian's red wrap slipping from that shoulder.

The two of them sitting side by side in the dining room, the place lit softly by tea lights and fairy lights and candles. Looking into one another's eyes, oblivious to anyone else.

In each other's arms for their first dance. *You've got all my love.*

And maybe her favourite, a view of them taken from behind as they stood beside the remains of Greta's carrot cake later in the night, her head resting on his shoulder as she leant into him, his head tipped towards hers, arm around her waist. Fitting together perfectly, like she and Naomi did now.

She returned them to their envelope and set it down on the bedside locker. She went to sleep with Coldplay running through her head, and the feel of his arms around her.

A week later, Brendan called to Chance House with a request – and on the last Sunday in February, Lydia granted it.

In the morning she covered two of the tables in the dining room with the usual white cloths, adding the ruby-red table runners that Marian had found. In the apartment she showered and dressed while her mother, back with her father for the occasion, got Naomi into the navy velvet dress that Kathleen had given her for Christmas. A little roomy, despite her slow and steady weight gain over the previous months. A little more formal, with its white lacy collar, than Lydia would have chosen, but Kathleen would be happy to see it on her.

Andrew stood waiting in the church porch with his camera. Lydia's father double-parked, like they all did on Sundays, and Lydia watched as Andrew approached the car. She liked him in a suit, all washed and scrubbed – but then, she liked him in everyday clothes too. She liked him, period.

He took photos like he always did as they emerged from the car, not waiting for them to pose, capturing them as they really were. 'Look at you,' he said to Naomi, as Lydia lifted her from her seat. 'Like a princess.'

'We're not late, are we?' Lydia's mother asked. 'They're not here yet?'

'Not yet. Go in out of the cold' – so they entered the church and made their way up the aisle to the two front pews reserved for family. The one on the left already contained Marian, Tom and Jack, and Marian's parents, so Lydia and her family took the opposite one.

Kathleen's book club friends, all hats and nodding feathers, smiled at Lydia from the pew just behind, and she hoped fervently that Naomi wouldn't make a grab for one of the feathers if the opportunity arose.

Within minutes, a stir ran through the church, and the organ struck up with 'Love Is The Sweetest Thing', Kathleen's surprise choice for their entrance. The congregation rose as Father Phil appeared on the altar, and everyone turned to watch Brendan and Kathleen processing slowly up the aisle, Kathleen in a tan skirt and jacket, a hand resting on her husband's arm, her hair newly cut and set into curls.

Brendan was in the grey suit he'd worn for Lydia and Damien's wedding, and for Damien's funeral, and when he'd come to the hospital for a first look at his granddaughter, and on the occasion of her christening. His all-purpose suit.

The couple reached the top and took seats in the chairs set out for them at the altar. The ceremony commenced, part Sunday Mass, part renewal of vows.

*We decided*, Brendan had said, when he'd come with his request to Lydia, *that it would be a good thing to do, after last year. We felt it would . . . turn a sort of corner.*

Forty years married today. So lucky, Lydia thought, as she heard them renewing their decades-old vows, to have had each other for so long. To have survived as a couple for that length of time, weathering the storms they'd met along the way. Weathering the biggest storm any parents could endure last year. They had gone through hell, and had survived together.

The family and their guests, twenty in total, adjourned afterwards to Chance House for lunch – but before they ate, everyone was ushered into the yoga studio, where Gareth was waiting with a projector screen.

'Tom gave me a bunch of photos,' he said, when everyone was seated, 'and asked me to put together a kind of slideshow to mark this occasion, so here we go.'

The lights were turned off. The room fell silent as the story of a marriage unfolded, from Brendan and Kathleen's wedding day through the births of the boys and their growing-up years.

Toddlers on the back of a donkey, with Brendan hanging on to them; Tom looking mutinous at the school gate, new bag on his back; Damien missing a small front tooth, grinning at a towering ice-cream cone Kathleen was handing to him.

The years moved on, through birthday parties and holidays and Christmas celebrations, through visits to Santa and school trips and graduations. And later, Tom and Marian emerging from a church, confetti flying around them; Marian with shorter hair holding a tiny swaddled Jack outside the church, Tom's arm around her waist; Jack standing by the school door, holding his mother's hand and looking happier than his father had on the same occasion.

And one photo, just one, of Lydia and Damien on the church steps after their wedding. One, they'd decided, was enough.

After the last slide, the projector was shut off and the lights came on – and just as Lydia was about to slip away to see if Cathy's lunch was ready, Brendan got to his feet and turned to face everyone, and thanked them for coming, and thanked Gareth for the slideshow.

'As you all know,' he went on, sliding hands into trouser pockets, 'our family suffered a great loss last year. But we have lovely memories, and we have each other, and a wonderful son and two great daughters-in-law, and two beautiful grandchildren. And without Kathleen, I would have none of those, so I want to thank her for the forty years we've spent together.'

That was it. That was as much as he wanted to say. As Kathleen got to her feet to join him everyone clapped, and for an instant, Lydia caught her mother-in-law's eye.

And both of them smiled.

# 34

AND NOW IT IS JULY, AND THE DINING ROOM, WHICH has hosted several more weddings since the ruby anniversary, is being prepared for a different celebration, with giant floating foil balloons, and a large corkboard filled with photos on a wall, and a banner saying *Happy Birthday Naomi!* in bright primary colours.

Jelly is setting in the kitchen larder, and ice-cream is in the freezer, and a cake made by Greta is sitting on the worktop under a dome, and Cathy is preparing cocktail sausages and homemade chicken nuggets for the younger guests, and grown-up finger food for the older ones, and the last two bottles of Jason and Barney's expensive champagne, saved for this day, are chilling in the fridge.

'Mama!' Naomi totters in, with Tessa following. The little girl's red raincoat is still on, and Sissy dangles from one hand as she generally does.

Lydia sets down her handful of cutlery and bends to sweep up her daughter. 'Hello, sweetheart. Did you have fun in the garden with Tessa?'

A nod. Naomi opens her free fist. 'Mama,' she says again, and Lydia inspects the daisy head.

'That's lovely, darling. Will we put it in your blue bowl?'

Pebbles, feathers, leaves and twigs she brings in, everything (including the odd dead insect and empty snail shell) added to the small plastic bowl on the sitting-room windowsill that Lydia or Tessa furtively culls every now and again. The ginger cat, named Fanta by Gareth, has been seen scrambling up trees at Naomi's excited approach, after some enthusiastic tail pulling and ear grabbing on their earlier encounters.

Every day, weather permitting and time allowing, they walk down to the sea, Naomi holding tightly to her mother's hand as they negotiate the steps. They take off shoes and socks and dip their toes into the water. Sometimes, if it's warm enough, they get into swimsuits, and Lydia carries her daughter in, and dunks her little by little in the water, and Tessa, who has turned Lydia into a swimmer, has promised lessons to Naomi as soon as she's ready.

Tessa swims nearly every day, regardless of the weather, often arriving back up to the house with blue lips and white fingertips, but always with a light in her eyes. Lydia is glad that Chance House helped put it there.

Watching her daughter grow is a constant delight, every milestone a little miracle, every new development a reason to rejoice. Her first smile, the first time she grabbed her toes, rolled over, sat up, crawled, clapped her hands, pulled herself to standing. Her first step, just over a month ago. The first time she wobbled across the kitchen floor without plopping down on her padded behind.

Wherever Lydia brings her, she's fussed over. Her cousin Jack kicks a sponge ball around the garden for her to chase. Her aunt Marian shows her how to turn her fingers into Incy Wincy Spider. Her uncle Tom scoops her up so she can touch the top of the garden wall.

Her granny Kathleen feeds her toasted cheese cut into fingers. Her granddad Brendan helps her to open the door of the playhouse he has built for her, where they make jigsaws and construct brick towers, over and over.

Her godmother Greta brings her to look at the ducks in her pond, and lets her slap the water with her hand to make a splash, and sings a little song in German to her.

Her godfather Andrew drops to hands and knees so she can clamber on his back, grabbing his collar and shrieking with glee as he trots around the lawn of Chance House, destroying the knees of just about every pair of trousers he owns.

Susan borrows giant picture books from the school, *Chicken Licken* and *The Pig in the Pond* and *Guess How Much I Love You*, and reads them to her with great gusto.

Gareth brings her fat sticks of coloured chalk so she can squat with him on the patio and scribble. When she tires of that they stretch out on the grass and he makes up stories about the clouds, and promises they'll plant sunflowers when it's the right time, and teaches her to love spiders and field mice and earthworms.

Sometimes Celine from Clifden comes with him, and Lydia is happy that a chance meeting on a pilgrim path is turning into something more. She suspects they may be booking a wedding with her in the not too distant future. She looks forward to exacting her revenge on him by refusing to take his money. Finally, she'll be able to reward all his hours of unpaid dedication.

Father Phil retrieved his old train set from the attic of his family home and set it up in a corner of his kitchen – and seeing him sprawl on the floor with Naomi while it runs around on its track, Lydia is well aware that her daughter was a convenient excuse.

She and Naomi take trips to Dublin when they get a chance, Lydia parking the Golf at the railway station in the town and making the rest of the journey on the train, not quite confident enough yet for city traffic.

Her father has opened a post office account for Naomi. He jiggles her on his knee as he sings endless verses of 'Old MacDonald', inventing animals when they run out of real ones. He lets her listen to his heart with his stethoscope, and she insists on listening to Sissy's heart too.

Her mother is happy for Naomi to wreak havoc in her kitchen when they make Rice Krispie buns, Naomi in a high chair, and an apron that matches her grandmother's, and Lydia has heard her mother sing 'You Are My Sunshine' very softly as Naomi falls asleep.

They're house hunting in the west. *A holiday cottage*, her mother said. *Just something small for when we can get away*, but Lydia suspects they're really planning for their retirement, gravitating towards their daughter and granddaughter. It would be very good to have them nearby.

Brona, who's expecting her own baby in the autumn, continues to visit Chance House every so often. She brings finger puppets and toy telephones and books and a xylophone. She and Naomi conduct marvellous garbled conversations on the telephones. 'Your daughter,' she's told Lydia, 'makes more sense than a lot of adults I know.'

Naomi, loved by so many. What a childhood she's having.

After the party, after they've all helped the birthday girl blow out her single candle, after the guests have left and Naomi has been put to bed, Lydia sends the Cotters and her parents up to the guest lounge, and tells them she'll follow with the champagne. On her way to the fridge, her phone beeps with a text.

*Hope you're not too tired after the day.*

*Not too tired – just about to open the bubbly.*

*Go handy now.*

She laughs. *Go handy yourself. I don't have to wield sharp knives in the morning.*

*Good point. Enjoy it, see you soon. A*

A. Andrew.

He's grown on her, so slowly it took ages for her to realise what was happening – and even when she did, she resisted, because he wasn't Damien. How could anyone but Damien make her happy?

And yet he does. He does make her happy. She looks forward to seeing him. She enjoys his company, loves seeing how gentle he is with Naomi, how dryly funny he can be. He slips into her head when he's not around.

Nothing has been said between them. He's confessed to no feelings, hasn't asked her out, hasn't said anything that might suggest romantic interest in her.

He doesn't have to.

She can see it in the look he sometimes gives her that squeezes her heart. She can hear it in his voice when he speaks to her of the most mundane things. She knows love when she encounters it, because it's not her first encounter. She has revelled in the wonder of love, and she hardly dares hope that it will visit her again.

He's waiting for her to be ready; she knows this. And soon, she thinks, she will be. It might take a few more months, till the second anniversary of Damien's death in January, or it might happen sooner. When the time feels right, she'll take a deep breath and suggest something small like a walk together, just the two of them. And he'll say yes, and they'll see where it takes them.

# Acknowledgements

Thanks to my invaluable editors, Joanna Smyth of Hachette Books Ireland and Molly Walker-Sharp of Sphere Books. Their hard work is much needed, and much appreciated.

Thanks to my agent Sallyanne Sweeney of ICA, always in my corner, always there when I look for her.

Thanks to my copy editor Hazel Orme and my proofreader Aonghus Meaney for catching all the bloopers.

Thanks to those who helped when I came to them with a query during the writing of this book: Michael and Annette Griffin, David Casey, Sheila O'Callaghan and Pat Murphy.

Thanks to my family for their unwavering support, in particular my sister Treasa and my mother Rose.

Thanks to you for being kind enough to choose this book: I really hope you enjoy it.

Roisin x
www.roisinmeaney.com
Bluesky: @roisinm.bsky.social

Dear Reader,

We'd love your attention for one more page to tell you about the crisis in children's reading, and what we can all do.

Studies have shown that reading for fun is the **single biggest predictor of a child's future life chances** – more than family circumstance, parents' educational background or income. It improves academic results, mental health, wealth, communication skills, ambition and happiness.[1]

The number of children reading for fun is in rapid decline. Young people have a lot of competition for their time. In 2024, 1 in 10 children and young people in the UK aged 5 to 18 did not own a single book at home.[2]

Hachette works extensively with schools, libraries and literacy charities, but here are some ways we can all raise more readers:

- Reading to children for just 10 minutes a day makes a difference
- Don't give up if children aren't regular readers – there will be books for them!
- Visit bookshops and libraries to get recommendations
- Encourage them to listen to audiobooks
- Support school libraries
- Give books as gifts

There's a lot more information about how to encourage children to read on our website: **www.RaisingReaders.co.uk**

Thank you for reading.

---

[1] OECD, '21st-Century Readers: Developing Literacy Skills in a Digital World', 2021, https://www.oecd.org/en/publications/21st-century-readers_a83d84cb-en.html

[2] National Literacy Trust, 'Book Ownership in 2024', November 2024, https://literacytrust.org.uk/research-services/research-reports/book-ownership-in-2024